MIKE EVANS

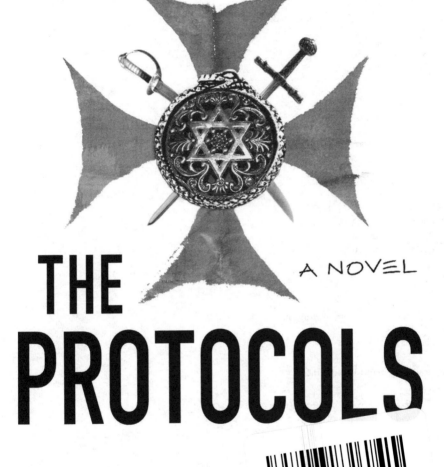

A NOVEL

THE
PROTOCOLS

D1066764

TimeWorthy
BOOKS

P.O. Box 30000, Phoenix, AZ 85046

Published by TimeWorthy Books
P. O. Box 30000
Phoenix, AZ 85046

The Protocols

Copyright 2011 by TimeWorthy Books
P. O. Box 30000
Phoenix, AZ 85046

Design: Lookout Design, Inc.

USA:	978-0-935199-52-9
Canada:	978-0-935199-61-1
Hardcover:	978-0-935199-62-8

This book is dedicated to

Tamar Raveh,

beloved daughter of Gideon Hausner,

Attorney General of the State of Israel

And the chief prosecutor of Adolf Eichmann.

He helped expose the brutality

of Nazism to the world.

CAST OF CHARACTERS

ESTHER ROSENBERG – a Jewish attorney in Washington, D.C. Her husband, Ephraim, worked for Mossad, Israel's primary intelligence agency. He was killed by a car bomb while on assignment in Jerusalem. Esther is now dating Paul Bryson whom she met at a fundraiser for the Ben Gurion Institute.

PAUL BRYSON – a former Congressman from Texas who now works as a consultant. His wife, Linda, was killed in the 9-11 attack on the Pentagon. While in Congress he became interested in issues affecting Israel. He is a Christian and deeply committed to his relationship with the Lord. His attraction to Esther has caused him to grapple with many of the things he knows and believes about Jesus and salvation.

ANTHONY WISEMAN – analyst with the Office of Naval Intelligence. An American Jew, he is accused of leaking classified information to Israel that allowed Israel to discover and destroy a nuclear reactor at Aleppo, Syria. Esther Rosenberg has been working to gain his release.

NEST – Nuclear Emergency Support Team – an obscure government agency charged with tracking and responding to nuclear emergencies and threats.

PETE RIOS – director of NEST.

RANDALL MORRIS – an assistant to Pete Rios.

ORIN COHEN – director of Mossad's operations center at Ashdod, Israel.

DEMETRIUS NILUS – Russian general and grandson of Sergei Nilus, author of *The Protocols of The Learned Elders of Zion,* a viciously anti-Semitic book that has fueled decades of anti-Semitic hatred. Through his nephew, Leonid Malenkov, Demetrius supplies arms from Russian stockpiles to the Middle East.

LEONID MALENKOV – nephew of Demetrius Nilus. He is an arms dealer who lives in Innsbruck, Austria. With Demetrius Nilus' help, he has been selling Russian arms to groups in the Middle East.

YURI IVANOVSKY – Russian mobster with extensive contacts in the United States and Canada.

THE ORDER OF MALTA – originally formed to protect crusaders traveling to the Holy Land during the Middle Ages. Later focused on eliminating a supposed worldwide Jewish conspiracy. Although many of its members are ordained clergymen, The Order is a landless sovereignty and is not directly accountable to any ecclesiastical organization other than itself.

DOYLE THOMPSON – former field officer for the CIA. Now works as a CIA analyst with the Middle East Analysis Group. He and Paul Bryson became friends when Bryson was a member of Congress. They worked together to fund and maintain covert operations in Afghanistan. He is secretly a lay member of the Order of Malta.

STEVE TAYLOR – works for the Defense Intelligence Agency. Previously worked with Paul Bryson's wife at the Pentagon. He is a lay member of the Order of Malta.

CARLO BUSCA – as the story begins, he is Grand Master of the Order of Malta.

ANGELO GIOVANNI – assistant to Carlo Busca.

IGNACIO SPOLETO – a member of the Order of Malta and head of the Military Vicariate, a group responsible for the Order's military operations and charged with maintaining the Order's viability at all costs.

CARMINE RUSSO – assistant to Spoleto.

NIKOLAI TREPOV – an assassin living in Moscow.

PHILIPPE JOBERT – an assassin living in Washington, D.C.

CHAPTER 1
RAMALLAH, ISRAEL

SWEAT DRIPPED FROM ABU FAYYAD'S BROW as he stood at the top of the darkened stairwell and listened. From the hallway below he heard the shuffling of footsteps. A door opened, then slammed shut. Somewhere a baby cried. There was the clank of a pot and the laughter of a child.

Crowded in the stairwell with Fayyad were Ahmed Haniya and Azzam Jubari. Easily half Fayyad's age, they had been recruited a year earlier from an Iranian-sponsored Madrasah in the Palestinian town of Jenin. Brought up on a diet of hate for America and the Jews since the day they were born, the nineteen-year-olds were easy prey for Hamas's recruiters. Since coming under the wing of Fayyad, they had been secluded at a house in the hills north of Ramallah near Bir Zeit, away from family and friends, where they underwent rigorous training in the latest techniques of urban warfare. Now they were ready to put that training to use.

Cradled in their arms, each of them carried a Russian-made Kornet missile loaded inside a self-contained launch tube. Designed as an anti-tank weapon, the Kornet had proven highly effective against a vast array of targets both on the ground and in the air. Its effectiveness and versatility made it the weapon of choice for Fayyad and his tight-knit group of Jihadists known as Jund Ansar Allah.

Fayyad blinked sweat from the corners of his eyes and looked down the steps at Haniya. "What time is it?"

Haniya took a cell phone from his pocket and pressed a key to light up its face. "Two o'clock," he replied. "We cannot wait here any longer. Someone will see us."

Fayyad eased open the door and listened, then quietly pulled it closed. "We must wait for them to arrive. That is the plan."

From outside came the heavy thump-thump-thump of a helicopter as it circled overhead. Jubari looked up, his eyes wide. "That helicopter is 667?"

"Yes. Israeli Security Service."

"They will see us when we step outside. They will be watching."

Haniya smirked. "Did you think they would not be here? It is the prime minister's motorcade. Of course they are here. Ehud Roham never travels without his security detail."

Jubari rested his head against the wall and closed his eyes. "Now I am worried."

Fayyad glanced over at Haniya. "Where is the motorcade?"

Haniya took the cell phone from his pocket and checked the screen for a text message. "They are leaving the airport. South of town."

Jubari looked back at Fayyad. "How long will it take from there?"

"Not long." Fayyad patted him on the shoulder. "Take heart. Allah is with us."

"I do not like waiting. They have helicopters in the air. They have informants everywhere." He looked down the stairway. "Even here."

"Stay calm," Fayyad replied. "This will all be over in just a few minutes. Half an hour from now, we will be far from this building."

"You sound so certain."

"We have studied this carefully," Fayyad nodded. "They are sched-uled to begin negotiations at the Mukata'a in thirty-five minutes. The Israelis have arrived precisely on time for every session—in Washington,

Jerusalem, and Cairo. There is no reason to think they will not be on time today."

Haniya checked a switch on his launcher, then glanced over at the one resting in the crook of Jubari's arm. "Turn your power to standby." He pointed. "You do not want to run down the battery."

Jubari flipped a switch and wiped his hands on his pants. "It is hot in here. Even my palms are sweating."

"That is your nerves," Haniya chuckled.

Jubari ignored him and looked back at Fayyad. "Will the plan work?"

"Trust in Allah," Fayyad replied. "When the missiles go off we will have plenty of time to get down the stairs and out of the building. The car will be waiting in the alley." Fayyad gave Jurabi a somber look. "Just remember your brother. Remember what they did to Saeb. That is the kind of peace the Israelis want. One where they can shoot anyone's brother, or mother, or sister, at any time, with no one to hold them accountable."

"They are close to obtaining it, too."

"That is why we must see that they never reach the negotiating table again."

Haniya took out his cell phone and checked the screen. "They are coming down Al-Shurafa Street now."

"Okay." Fayyad looked at them both. "This is it." He flipped a switch on the launcher. "Arm your missiles and follow my lead."

Fayyad pushed open the stairwell door and stepped out on the rooftop. Across the street he caught a glimpse of a soccer field. Farther to the west, down Al Nahdha Street, the buildings of Ramallah's old city glistened in the sunlight, but he paid them no attention as he hurried across to the parapet wall and crouched out of sight at the roof's edge. Haniya and Jubari followed close behind and took up positions beside him. Moments later, the squawk of a siren came from the street six floors below. Fayyad looked over at them. "Remember, they will slow as they cross Al Nahdha Square and turn onto Al Qasem. I get the lead

SUV." He pointed to Haniya. "You get the one in back." Then he looked Jubari in the eye. "And you get the prime minister. The one with the tiny flag in the corner of the window. Just like we practiced." Jubari nodded. Fayyad patted him on the shoulder. "Wait until we shoot, but do not hesitate."

Fayyad turned away and crouched on one knee, his muscles taut and ready. Then, as the motorcade of SUVs passed in front of their position, he raised himself up to see over the wall. In an instant, he sighted the lead car in the crosshairs of the missile launcher and squeezed the trigger. Fire and smoke billowed from the back of the launch tube as the Kornet missile shot through the air. A moment later, it struck the vehicle in the driver's door and exploded, sending a fireball rolling into the air.

As Fayyad's missile exploded, Haniya rose from a sitting position and sighted on the last car in line. He pressed the trigger and launched the second Kornet. A stream of smoke trailed behind as it hurtled through the air, struck the side of the car, and exploded.

Fayyad waited a moment, expecting to hear the third missile hit its mark. When he heard nothing, he glanced to the left to see Jubari in tears. "Shoot!" Fayyad shouted. "Shoot the missile."

"I cannot!" Jubari screamed. "It will not fire!"

Fayyad snatched the launcher from Jubari's hands, checked to make certain the switches were in the correct position, and raised himself above the wall. Down below he found the prime minister's black SUV trapped between the two burning vehicles. Through the car's tinted windows he saw the men inside, frantically pointing and shouting at the driver. Fayyad calmly sighted the crosshairs on the tiny Israeli flag at the corner of the passenger door, and squeezed the trigger.

He waited to see the missile gliding through the air toward its target, but nothing happened. He squeezed the trigger again, then again, but still nothing. Desperately, he lowered the launcher from his shoulder and flipped the power switch to off and back to on, then raised the launcher once more to his shoulder. This time, he squeezed the trigger and held it down. Thick, acrid smoke billowed from the launch tube and swirled around Fayyad's head. An instant later, a deafening roar pierced his ears. Pain shot through his head.

Suddenly, Fayyad was engulfed in the orange glow of a searing hot fireball as the missile, still in the launch tube, exploded. Through the flames he saw Jubari and Haniya, their clothes instantly consumed, leaving only raw, burning flesh. And then everything went black.

CHAPTER 2
THE PENTAGON

STEVE TAYLOR SAT AT HIS DESK with his chair cocked sideways. Legs crossed, coffee cup in hand, he stared out through the narrow window at the Potomac River shimmering in the morning sun. From his small office on the fifth floor of the Pentagon he had a commanding view of the parking lot on the north side and beyond it to the marina at Columbia Island. Every morning, his mind played over and over the same thought he'd had since that fateful day—he should have been there. He should have been seated there when terrorists crashed an airliner into the building, but an accident on the Beltway had made him late. When he arrived he went straight to a meeting on the opposite side of the building. Like many others, he heard the explosion and felt the building shake and, like them, ran toward the fire and smoke but it was too late. Later, while carrying the bodies of friends and colleagues from the rubble, he had decided to do everything in his power to make certain it never happened again. And every morning since then, he began his day just as he began this one—by reminding himself of that decision and of those who were ultimately responsible for the attack. Not the ones the political establishment blamed, and not those to whom the media pointed, but the true cause of the trouble—the Jews and their sympathizers.

On the desk beside him was a slender book entitled *The Protocols of the Learned Elders of Zion*. Bound in leather, its cover was worn smooth from years of handling. Inside, the pages were dog-eared and riddled with notes and smudges. He'd received it as a gift from a Russian friend, the great-grandson of the author, and since then it had been his guide, his help, his mentor. From it he became convinced the root of Islamic anger lay in what was in actuality a fallacy—a myth—but he, like many, believed it to be absolute truth. Taylor was certain it would guide free-thinking peoples to the conclusion Muslims reached long ago—the Jews were out to rule the world.

Already they controlled key elements of finance and media. With those, they dictated the terms of international trade and international opinion. Like twin rudders they guided sympathetic governments wherever and however they willed and all for one purpose—world domination. They had manipulated Germany's sound racial policy into the illusion of a Holocaust, and they were doing the same with Iran and the Palestinian Authority. But soon, very soon, that would come to an end.

The phone on Taylor's desk rang. He set the coffee cup aside and snatched the receiver from the cradle. The voice on the other end was terse and sharp. "We have a problem." Without waiting to learn more, Taylor slammed down the phone, bolted for the door, and raced down the hall toward the Pentagon situation room.

Located across the hall from the secretary of defense's office, the room was designed to keep civilian staff in constant contact with events occurring around the world. Filled with the latest in technology, the room was a clearinghouse for information, news, and live feeds gathered from around the globe—all of which were displayed on six large screens that lined the back wall of the room. Desks crammed with keyboards and monitors filled the space between the screens and the door.

As Taylor approached, a guard acknowledged him with a nod and opened the door. Taylor brushed past him and stepped inside to find the room already crowded. He stood shoulder to shoulder with a row of army officers along the back wall and watched as agents in the room went to work.

"We have video!" an operator shouted. Seated at his desk, he leaned forward and pressed a button on a control panel, then pointed toward the far end of the room. Instantly, video images appeared on one of the large screens. Everyone turned to watch.

Someone in back called out, "Is this happening now?"

"This is a live feed," the operator replied. "We're getting this from an Air Force drone loitering off the Gaza coast."

Taylor leaned close to an officer standing next to him. "What's happening?"

"Palestinian terrorists just fired two missiles at Prime Minister Roham's motorcade."

"Where?"

"Ramallah. Traveling with a team of negotiators on their way to round three of the peace talks."

Taylor struggled to suppress a grin. "Was he killed?"

"Nah." The man shook his head. "Rocket misfired."

An operator spoke up. "Okay. Officials on the ground are confirming an explosion on top of the building. Three bodies have been recovered. No identification on them yet."

A voice from the back of the room called out again, "Where's the prime minister?"

"He was evacuated by helicopter."

Taylor craned his head around to find Ray Fitzgerald, a Navy admiral, standing on the opposite side of the room. Fitzgerald spoke up. "He's back in Jerusalem now?"

"Yes, sir." The operator reached across the console and pressed a button. An image appeared on the large screen. "This is him arriving."

The room fell silent as everyone watched a line of black SUVs rolling slowly toward the prime minister's residence and came to a stop near the front entrance. Overhead a pair of Apache helicopters hovered just above the trees. All at once, the doors of the SUVs opened. Ehud

Roham emerged. Security agents immediately surrounded him and hustled him toward the building.

"Okay," the operator called out. "Anyone detect any unusual Israeli Defense Force activity?"

Someone at a workstation across the room responded, "They went on alert immediately. Sent a dozen helicopters up to Ramallah to cover Roham on the trip back to Jerusalem. Other than that there has been no movement of forces."

Then someone called from another desk, "Sir, I'm showing four IDF destroyers headed west seventy miles out of Haifa. Doesn't appear to be a routine patrol."

Fitzgerald stepped to the center of the room and stood near the operator's desk. "Anyone else got this? What are they doing?"

"There are two ships approaching the port of Gaza. Looks like the Israelis are trying to intercept them."

Fitzgerald took control. "How long until they meet?"

"At this rate, not long."

"Any radio traffic?"

"None, sir."

"What do we have in the area?"

"One Arleigh Burke destroyer and two Littoral Combat Ships."

"Where are they?"

"Two hundred miles away, sir."

Taylor stepped from the room to the hall and took out his Blackberry. He worked the keys with his fingers and typed a text message. "We need bodies." When the message was sent he returned to the room and found the images on the screen had changed.

On the monitor, an Israeli missile frigate plowed through the waves toward a cargo ship flying a Panamanian flag. Ocean spray from the frigate's bow shot through the air as it raced toward the ship. Moments later, the frigate slowed and came alongside the cargo ship.

A man to Taylor's left shook his head. "How could this possibly be a legitimate response to a missile attack in Ramallah? This is exactly why nobody likes the Jews."

An older colonel spoke up. "These are both relief ships, son. Israelis are convinced the Palestinians use them to smuggle arms."

"But this is Gaza. The attack was in Ramallah."

"Check your map. It's not that far and it's not that difficult to get them up there once you get them on land. We aren't talking about hauling them from Texas to Maine."

A general standing a few feet away nodded in agreement. "Last month they found rocket-propelled grenades in a crate labeled as medical supplies from the Red Crescent. Week before that they labeled it baby food."

"That's cold," someone groused. "Sending in weapons with the medical relief."

The colonel's eyes narrowed. "That's how much they hate the Jews."

Near the center of the room, Fitzgerald turned to the operator. "Can we get audio from the IDF?"

The operator pressed a button on the keyboard. Dialog appeared on a monitor, followed by a voice coming from a speaker near the large screen: "This is the Israeli Navy. You have entered a restricted zone. Steer a course for Ashdod."

"This isn't the live audio," someone complained.

The operator looked up, his forehead creased in an impatient frown. "They're repeating the same thing in English, Arabic, and Hebrew."

On the screen, the cargo ship steamed slowly forward, flanked by the frigate. The voice from the speaker continued. "Halt and prepare to be boarded."

Moments later, three inflatable speedboats were lowered from the frigate into the choppy seas. Soldiers armed and ready were seated inside. Tossed from side to side by the waves, the soldiers leaned forward and held tightly to the gunwales as the boats skimmed across the surface.

When they reached the ship, men aboard the speedboats shot lines up to the ship's deck, then scrambled up the side.

Those standing in the situation room watched as the ship's crew came from the superstructure, their hands raised high in the air, and knelt on the deck. A few minutes later, a voice came over the speaker. "Ship is secure. All engines stopped."

Around the situation room, Fitzgerald breathed a sigh of relief. "That went well enough."

Others smiled and nodded. "Better than expected."

"Let's hope they all turn out that way."

While they continued to talk, Taylor slipped from the room once more and stepped out to the corridor. A little way down the hall he came to a memorial display commemorating the soldiers who fought in the Spanish-American War. A guide was explaining the display to a tour group. Taylor stepped to the opposite side of the corridor and took out his cell phone. Working the keypad with his thumbs, he hurriedly entered a text message. "This will not work. Tell them to resist. We need an incident." He glanced over the message once, then pressed a button to send it. Almost immediately he received a reply. "Doing our best to follow up." Taylor returned the phone to his pocket and started toward the situation room.

As he came through the door, an operator spoke up. "We have a live feed of the second ship." The image on the screen switched to a cruise ship. "Ship is off the Gaza coast, a mile south of the one we saw earlier."

Admiral Fitzgerald leaned over the operator's shoulder. "Can we identify this ship?"

"Yes, sir. This is the *Rachael Moreno*. A cruise ship chartered from Crete. It flies a Turkish flag."

"Turkey? I thought they agreed to stay out of this."

"Looks like they changed their minds."

"Have the Israelis moved on this ship?"

"They have a second cruiser steaming in that direction."

A voice called out from a workstation near the video screens, "Sir, I'm showing three helicopters inbound on the cruise ship's position."

"Who are they?"

"IDF, sir."

Moments later, two helicopters moved over the cruise ship. While they hovered in place, doors opened on either side and ropes appeared as an Israeli Special Forces unit rappelled down from the helicopters toward the ship's deck. When the soldiers reached the deck, passengers emerged wielding poles and clubs. A pole sliced through the air, striking a soldier as he dangled a few feet above the deck. Seconds later, the air was filled with clubs and bottles as the passengers surged forward in an effort to prevent the soldiers from boarding the ship.

"This isn't good," someone murmured.

A cacophony of voices and screams poured from the speaker as passengers and soldiers collided, clubs and rifles swinging back and forth. Near the edge of the fantail, three passengers cornered a soldier. He struggled with them, then tumbled over the rail and plunged out of sight toward the sea. Voices shouted, "Knife, knife. He has a knife." Another voice, "Drop it now."

"Look out!"

Then, two loud, popping sounds, followed by two more.

Around the situation room, heads jerked up in disbelief. "Gunfire," someone shouted. "That was gunfire."

"Shhh. We can't hear."

Over the loudspeaker came a tense voice. "Passenger down."

"Behind you," another voice shouted.

"Soldier down. Soldier down. Bravo Six, we have a man down."

Then came the sound of an automatic weapon as it spit two quick bursts. *Brrrrrrrrrrd. Brrrrrrrrd.*

Someone spoke up. "Oh man! CNN will have this within the hour."

Another voice to the left chimed in. "Better start calling someone. We're going to need some help spinning this."

Images on the screen continued to move back and forth across the ship as the scene played out, but no one was watching. Instead, cell phones in hand, the group made its way through the doorway to the corridor outside.

As he wandered back to his office, Taylor took his phone from his pocket and typed in a text message. "That's what I'm talking about. That's what we needed."

CHAPTER 3
WASHINGTON, D.C.

ACROSS TOWN, ESTHER ROSENBERG lay in bed, warm beneath the covers in her Georgetown townhouse. From deep in a dreamless sleep, she was awakened by the phone on the nightstand. Only half awake, she rolled on her side and reached for the receiver. On her first attempt she missed and struck a water glass instead, sending it tumbling to the floor. When she finally succeeding in reaching the phone, all she heard was a dial tone. She pressed a button on the handset to end the call and flopped back on her pillow. A moment later, the phone rang again. This time she answered on the second ring. A voice on the other end spoke with a Middle Eastern accent. "We need to talk. Come outside."

Esther glanced at the clock on the nightstand and rubbed her eyes. "Can't this wait?"

"It's eight in the morning."

"I was up nearly all night at the office," she groaned. "I didn't get to bed until five."

"We need to talk."

Esther ended the call, climbed from bed, and stumbled across the room. The skirt and blouse she'd worn the day before were draped across a chair near the door. She pulled them over her petite frame, slid her feet into a pair of flats, and ran her fingers through her auburn hair. A jacket hung on the bedpost. She put it on and started down the hallway. "This better be important," she grumbled.

As she stepped from the townhouse, a car came to a stop at the curb out front. Reuben Brody sat behind the steering wheel. Esther made her way down the steps to the sidewalk and moved around to the far side of the car. "We shouldn't meet like this," she complained as she slid onto the front seat.

"Couldn't be avoided." Brody handed her a steaming cup of coffee, put the car in gear, and started forward.

"Thanks. I needed this. So, go ahead," she yawned. "What's so urgent that it couldn't wait until I got to the office?"

"There was an attempt on Ehud Roham's life."

Suddenly, Esther was wide awake. "What?!" Her hand jostled the cup. She had to move quickly to avoid spilling the coffee. "When?"

"Within the last hour in Ramallah."

"What happened?"

"A rocket attack ... Russian Kornets."

"So it was Hamas?"

"It's almost certainly Hamas. But they deny it."

"Of course they deny it." Esther gestured in frustration. "Where did they get the missiles?"

"We think they were smuggled in on one of the relief ships."

"Aren't they inspected?"

"Yes. But they can't look at every container and Hamas knows it. Some of the weapons get through. Last month they found six disassembled rockets in a shipment of flour."

"What has been our response to the attack?"

"Nothing yet."

Esther glanced across the seat at Brody. "We didn't do anything?"

"The Israeli Navy attempted to board two ships."

"Attempted?"

"They boarded one without incident. A cargo ship. They had no trouble."

"And the other?"

"It was a cruise ship. Chartered in Turkey. There were casualties."

Esther sighed. "How many?"

"No one knows for certain yet."

"Any Americans involved?"

"I don't know."

"And someone thought this was a good idea?"

"I do not make policy, Esther. I only carry out orders."

Esther sighed. She rubbed her eyes with her fingers. "So, what would they like for me to do?"

"You are meeting with Wiseman today?"

"Yes." Esther glanced at her watch. "In just a few hours."

"Good. The center at Beersheba wants you to talk to him about this. See if he has any ideas about who supplied the Kornets, and how they got to Ramallah."

"He's been incarcerated for a long time. Do they really think he knows anything?"

"They said for you to ask."

"He hasn't had access to raw intelligence or anything else in... years."

"He doesn't need access. The man is an expert. He's like a prophet. He can learn more from reading the newspaper than anyone alive. Just ask him about it."

CHAPTER 4
THE ISLAND OF RHODES, GREECE

CARLO BUSCA SAT AT THE HEAD of the conference table in the Hall of Saints and listened as Father Penalta prayed. His deep, rich voice reverberated off the stone walls of the Knights Castle in a melodic echo that sounded more like a chorus than the invocation of an elder statesman.

Located near the eastern tip of the island, the castle sat atop a hill that overlooked the sea on one side and the surrounding countryside on the other. It had been home to the Order of the Knights of Malta since they first occupied the island in 1309. Constructed of stone quarried in northern Greece, its walls were thicker than the length of a man's arm and had withstood the attacks of Arabs, pirates, Ottomans, and modern armies. And, though the island had been ceded from nation to nation, the Order retained ownership of Knights Castle as it maintained its independence, becoming the only landless sovereignty recognized by the United Nations.

A blend of political influence, military might, and ecclesiastical dogma, the Order had been formed in the Middle Ages to provide security for Christian pilgrims making their way to the Holy Land. They furnished armed escorts and established hospitals and lodging along the way. But even they could not stem the tide of history in the region. As the Middle East came under Islamic control, the Order changed. Slowly, the emphasis shifted from spiritual discipline to secular politics. Life, work, and purpose were viewed through a political prism and everything, even their view of Christianity, was tainted by it. Slowly, in an odd and perverted twist of purpose, the Order became the repository and embodiment of Christian anti-Semitism—the notion that the Jews as a race were responsible for killing Christ, an offense for which they must all pay. Though the Vatican later modified official church doctrine, acknowledging the fallacy of its previous anti-Semitic view, the Order by then had gained worldwide recognition of its sovereignty. As a result, the Pope held only advisory authority over its members. Unchecked, the Order redoubled its efforts to root out Jewish influence wherever it was found, even if it meant eliminating the Jews entirely.

As Father Penalta concluded his prayer, Busca looked around the room at the twenty-four men gathered before him. Known officially as the Legislative Council, they were the successors to a line of delegates that traced its lineage back to the time of the Crusades. For more than a thousand years they and their predecessors had been charged with the duty of setting policy for the Order. Each of the men gathered that day had risen through the ranks of the twenty-four provinces of Christendom, where they had proven themselves capable, decisive, and above all trustworthy with the darkest secrets of powerful men. Now they were assembled to make the hard, practical decisions necessary to preserve the way of life they held so dear.

Like them, Busca had risen through the ranks. Born on the island of Sicily, his father taught him from an early age to respect the truth of the Catholic Church. "The old Catholics," he said. "Not these new ones we have today." Then with a slow shake of his head, and in a voice laden with contempt, he would add, "It is a sacrilege to say the Mass in anything but Latin."

From his father, Busca learned that the Jews were responsible for the death of Christ, that they were the mortal enemies of Christendom, and that they must be made to pay for their sins. Yet, like all of Creation, grace and mercy had been extended to them, if only they would repent. Busca's father schooled him in the means by which that repentance should be effectuated. "Through scorn and ridicule many have already turned to Christ," he said with a smile. "It is our duty to subject the Jews to as much punishment in this life as one can attain, in order that they repent in this world and so that when they die their miserable souls may at least reach Purgatory." Busca adopted this as the mantra of his life.

After high school in Sicily, Busca attended seminary in Spain. Following graduation, he was assigned to the Cathedral in Lisbon. He labored there for three years, then turned to the Order of the Knights of Malta. The physical discipline and regimented life suited him perfectly.

Busca's first years in the Order were devoted to mundane service, much of it spent in the kitchen and garden. Then he was assigned as a messenger for the Grand Hospitaller at the Seventy-Fifth Assembly, a rare gathering of the order's entire membership. Very quickly after that he became Assistant Treasurer of the Elect, then Treasurer, Chancellor, and finally Prelate of the Grand Master—having supreme command of the entire order, a position he'd held for thirty years.

Busca scooted back his chair from the table and stood. "Gentlemen, we are gathered here today to consider our next course of action. As you are aware, in this liberal age, Christendom has grown slack in its treatment of the Jews. Tolerance reigns supreme. And as a consequence, the Jews have once again grown bold."

A little way down the table, Father Ignacio Spoleto nodded in agreement. As head of the Military Vicariate, Spoleto was charged with executing the Council's orders. Under his command were five thousand ordained monks, armed, trained, and ready to act at a moment's notice. They were supported in their effort by a vast network of laymen who held advantageous positions in businesses and governments around the world. With a single command from Spoleto, policy of the most powerful nations could be shaped and influenced and, if necessary, governments could be changed. Busca smiled in his direction. "Father Spoleto will brief you."

Spoleto stood. "Earlier today, the Israeli prime minister, Ehud Roham, traveled to Ramallah for the third round of peace negotiations. The Palestinians have made numerous concessions and because of their overwhelming cooperation, negotiations have moved rapidly forward. Only a few points remain unsettled between the parties and those could have easily been resolved at the Ramallah meeting. To prevent that from happening and to continue the heavy stream of military support from the Americans, elements within Mossad staged an attack on the prime minister's motorcade. Nine innocent Palestinians died in the attack. Once again our Palestinian brothers pay with their blood for Jewish crimes."

Those at the table began to murmur. Someone at the far end spoke up. "Do we have any report on the identity of those who launched the missiles?"

"Apparently there were three men involved. All three were killed."

Someone else spoke up. "How did they die?"

"A bomb exploded on the rooftop where they were stationed."

"Who planted the bomb?"

"One of the rocket launchers was sabotaged to make it appear as though it malfunctioned."

A voice came from the right. "We know this for a fact?"

Spoleto nodded. "Informants in Tel Aviv have assured me this is the work of Mossad."

"Killing Palestinians has become a preoccupation with them."

"What was the Israeli government's response?"

"Two ships lay harmlessly off the coast of Gaza. One a cargo ship flying a Panamanian flag. It was bringing relief supplies—food, medicine, and clothing. The other, a cruise ship from Turkey carrying doctors, dentists, and volunteers on a mission to aid schoolchildren. Immediately after the supposed attack on the prime minister, the Israeli Navy attacked those two relief ships. One was stopped and boarded without incident. The other was fired upon."

"And what was the result?"

"Israeli soldiers boarded the vessel from helicopters and attacked the passengers. Innocent civilians were needlessly murdered."

"Do we know how many?"

"Nothing has been confirmed yet. It is believed to be in excess of one hundred, but IDF has not released a statement yet and no one has been allowed onboard the ship."

An older man on the opposite side of the table spoke up. "Plus the Palestinians killed from the missiles and the three operatives."

"One hundred ten dead, to stop the negotiations."

"Will the negotiations go forward?"

"No," Spoleto shook his head. "The Israelis have canceled all further meetings and canceled all offers that were on the table from the previous rounds of discussions. I am told their forces are on highest alert."

"I saw this coming." A delegate seated to the left pushed back his chair and stood. "Last week, when the Israeli delegation met with the American president in Washington. You could see it in Roham's eyes and hear it in his voice. They knew then that this would happen and, I am certain, briefed the Americans in order to coordinate their response in advance. Jews are the scourge of humanity. This charade must be stopped."

The discussion proceeded as comments bounced around the table.

"It is all those rich Jews in America. They are the ones behind this. Without their support, none of this could happen."

"Why does their president not do something?"

"They own the president. A third of his campaign funds come from Jews."

"We know that?"

"Yes."

"We have discussed this before. The four cities—New York, Miami, Los Angeles, and Philadelphia—account for the majority of all campaign contributions. And those four cities are the four largest centers of Jewish population in America."

"Iran has been saying this for years."

"Muslims throughout the world have been saying it."

"And they are right. The Jews own the media, the entertainment industry, and finance. And now they are on the verge of controlling everything else."

"If we do not stop them, they will stage another Holocaust hoax.

Americans will fall for it again, and then the Jews will control the American military."

"They already do."

"Where is Hitler when we need him?"

Spoleto rapped his knuckles on the table. "Gentlemen, are we in agreement?"

"We cannot let this go unopposed. This is a golden opportunity to hit Israel. They are vulnerable now."

"We must end this charade. We have waited too long already."

"We have reached the tipping point."

Spoleto glanced down the table to Busca. "Your Excellency, the Twenty-Four are unanimous."

"Very well," Busca replied. "By previous order of the Council we committed to move against America to rein in its support of the Jews. Implementation of that prior decision was stayed pending a determination that specific circumstances warranted our action. The question before us now is whether that time has come. All in favor signify your vote by the usual manner."

In unison, the delegates pushed back their chairs from the table and stood.

"Any opposed?" The room fell silent. Busca let his gaze roam around the table, looking every man in the eye. When he had gone all the way around, he rapped the table with his fist. "So be it."

Then, as if on cue, the delegates responded, "In the name of the Father, and of the Son, and of the Holy Spirit. Amen." With that, the meeting adjourned.

As the Hall of Saints emptied, Busca took an iPhone from his pocket and typed in a text message. "Brilliant. Worked perfectly." He tapped the address box for Steve Taylor's number and pressed a button to send the message.

CHAPTER 5
WASHINGTON, D.C.

A FEW HOURS LATER, Esther Rosenberg was dressed and ready to meet the day. She stood at the front window of her home and peered out at the bright noonday sun. On the sidewalk, a woman wearing a green jogging suit moved quickly past. Esther watched as the woman pumped her arms in time with her legs in a brisk, rhythmic motion. Down the block, a sweeping machine cleaned the gutter. Even with the windows shut, she could hear the noise as it moved slowly along.

Esther glanced at her watch. By now she should have been at the office, seated at her desk, diligently working through a hundred details that awaited her, but after talking to Brody earlier she had returned to bed. She took a deep breath and forced herself to relax. She was a partner, she reminded herself, and she produced more than her share of the law firm's income. No one would say a word about how she spent her time.

After a moment, she turned away from the window. As she did, her eyes fell on a photograph that sat on a table beneath the window. Taken ten years earlier, it showed a slender, wiry man with deep-set eyes and a narrow face. He had a broad, cheesy grin that seemed to stretch from ear to ear and in the corner of his mouth his teeth gripped a cigar. Esther picked it up and held it gently in her right hand. With her left hand, she brushed a fleck of dust from the glass. A smile crept across her face as she stared at the picture.

"Ephraim," she whispered, "I have not forgotten you. I will always remember you. But I have to move on." Tears came to her eyes. "There will always be only one Ephraim Rosenberg," she sighed. "Only one Eph." Tears flowed down her cheeks as memories flooded her mind.

They had met while attending law school at Columbia University. She was the focused, disciplined student—top of the class, editor of the law review. He was the perennial PhD candidate, a free-spirited intellectual who spent most of his time sitting on a bench outside the library discussing politics with anyone who would stop to listen. They began dating their second year and, in spite of their temperamental differences, quickly became inseparable. Over late-night dinners and morning coffee she helped him finally take charge of his life and make progress on his dissertation. In return, he opened her eyes to the political realities of a world in constant turmoil. They were married at a synagogue on Long Island three weeks after graduation.

That fall, Esther took a job in Washington as law clerk for Justice Scalco on the Supreme Court. Ephraim went to work in the political affairs section at the Israeli Embassy. They rented a small apartment on Capitol Hill and settled into life as happy newlyweds. He was home by six each evening, she was there by seven. They enjoyed quiet dinners together and spent the evenings lying on the sofa, reading, talking, and indulging in the pleasure of each other's company. Then, gradually, work took more and more of their time. He was gone more than he was at home, and she spent long hours at the office researching opinions for Judge Scalco. Slowly, they drifted apart. By the end of their first year of marriage, she'd had enough. Over a rare Saturday morning breakfast together, Esther put their future to the test.

"I can't live like this, Eph."

He folded the newspaper to a new page. "What do you mean?"

"You know what I mean. You're never here and when you are you never talk anymore."

He frowned at her. "It's the nature of my work, Esther."

"Work?" Her voice grew louder. "Work keeps you out all night? Where do you really go when you don't come home?"

He took a sip of coffee. "I can't tell you."

"Well." She slapped the table with both hands. "That's it."

He lowered the paper and looked across the table at her. "What do you mean?"

"Stop asking me what I mean!" she yelled. "You know what I mean." She gestured with both hands to emphasize the point. "I married you because I wanted to be with you. Now I see you less than ever."

Ephraim laid aside the newspaper. "Esther, I work at the embassy."

"The embassy closes at five," she scoffed. "They aren't open all night."

He reached across the table and took her hand. "I work at the embassy, Esther." A smile spread across his face. "I don't work *for* the embassy."

"What are you saying?"

"I'm saying, I can't tell you what I do."

"How do I know you're telling the truth?"

"Renni Feinstein is in town." Ephraim leaned back in his chair. "Why don't you ask him?"

"He's in town?" Her voice softened. Her eyes were wide with interest. "You saw him?"

Ephraim nodded. "He asked about you."

"What did he say?"

"He wanted to know how long you intend to work for Justice Scalco."

"Why did he ask about that?"

"You still interested in practicing law?"

"Yes. Why? What's this about?"

"What would you think about consulting?"

A puzzled frown wrinkled her forehead. "What are you talking about?"

"There's a job opening later this year at the Ben-Gurion Institute."

"Why are you telling me this?" She had a questioning look. "Renni thinks I should apply for the job?"

"He wanted to know if you were ready to join the cause."

"What cause?"

He gave her a knowing look. "Israel's cause."

Esther stared at him a moment, then cackled with laughter. "You are such a putz."

Ephraim was startled. "Why are you laughing?"

"What's her name?"

He looked confused. "Whose name?"

"The woman you are seeing." Esther's voice took a strident tone. "The one with whom you spend all your time."

The color drained from Ephraim's face. His voice fell to a whisper. "I cannot believe you would say such a thing to me."

She grew even louder. "I cannot believe you would tell me such a tale."

"It is true," he insisted quietly.

"Prove it."

"Prove it?"

"Yes," she insisted. "Prove it." She tapped her finger on the table. "Prove to me you are who you say you are, and not some pitiful excuse of a husband."

"You remember—" He stopped short and gave a heavy sigh, then leaned across the table toward her. "Esther, I cannot prove it to you. You will have to trust me. Just as I must trust that you are actually at the office until late at night, and not out with one of your co-workers."

"Who would I possibly be seeing?"

"That cute guy. The one who likes to go to the gym."

She blushed. "How do you know he goes to the gym?"

Ephraim leaned back in his chair once more. "You think they would let me work where I work without knowing everything about you?"

Their eyes met. A smile broke across his face. "Call the Institute," he said softly. "They're expecting you."

That was a long time ago. Much had happened since then—five years at the Ben-Gurion Institute, many more than that practicing law, and the chaos of her life after the car bomb. Yet even now, after all that had happened, she could still feel the tingle from Ephraim's touch.

Just then, the glint of a reflection caught her eye. She glanced out the window and saw a blue SUV parked at the curb in front of the town-house. Through the front windshield she saw Paul Bryson seated behind the steering wheel. A smile turned up the corners of her mouth. She set the picture in its place on the table and started out the door.

CHAPTER 6
WASHINGTON, D.C.

PAUL BRYSON PUSHED OPEN the door of the SUV and stepped out to the curb. As he started toward the sidewalk, Esther's front door opened. Seeing her made him smile. "Everything okay?"

"Yes," she replied. "I'm fine."

"When you called I thought you were having car trouble."

"No." She pulled the door closed behind her. "We worked late last night. I had them bring me home rather than going downtown for the car. I hope it wasn't a bother to come by."

By then she was at the bottom step. Bryson slipped his arm around her waist and pulled her close. "You know better than that." He pressed his lips to hers. "Gives me more time to see you."

Like Esther, Bryson had enjoyed a long and full career. Born and reared in San Saba, Texas, he grew up on a ranch that had been owned by his family for six generations. After graduating from Texas A&M, he went to work as a sales representative for a chemical company. He married Linda McAdory, his college sweetheart, and settled near Longview.

At first the job was interesting and life was good. He enjoyed selling to the ranchers and farmers of East Texas and the work provided a decent income. Two years later, they had their first child, one of three who would eventually be born to the Brysons. But by the early 1980s, he and Linda were bored. In a quest for something new, he began dabbling in local politics. She went back to school, pursuing a graduate degree in history at LeTourneau University. Long conversations about immigration, taxes, and the oil industry led to broader political involvement. Not long after that the Congressional seat for their district came open. Bryson made a run for it and, to everyone's surprise, he won.

For seven terms he served the people of East Texas in the U.S. Congress. Linda remained in Longview until the children were out of high school, then joined him in Washington. While there, she attended Georgetown University, obtained a second master's degree, and landed a job at the Pentagon. She was at her office on September 11, when an Arab terrorist flew a 737 jet airliner through her window.

Linda's death left Bryson devastated. He spent the next few months in a daze, and was reelected largely on the basis of public sympathy for his personal tragedy. But he was no longer interested in electoral politics. The country was engaged in a war, but his heart wasn't in the fight. He had seen the raw intelligence and knew the threat of terrorism was real, but with Linda gone there seemed no reason to continue in office. "Let someone else do it," he told himself finally.

At the end of the term he left Congress and began to slowly pick up the pieces of his life. He took a year off, returned to Texas and reconnected with the life he'd known before politics. The following year he returned to Washington, opened a consultancy office in Georgetown, and began searching for clients. Several former campaign donors hired him immediately and business took off. Before long, he was busier than he'd expected to be. One of his clients was the David Ben-Gurion Institute.

While in Congress, Bryson had served on the Foreign Affairs Committee. Through that work, he became an avid supporter of Israel. He took seriously the challenges to Israel's security and understood that the threat was far greater than mere Arab opposition. He'd seen first-hand the vile, evil anti-Semitism that lay at the core of Arab, European, and sometimes even American politics—both conservative and liberal. And he'd become deeply committed to opposing it, an interest that continued after he was no longer in office.

A few months after he returned to Washington, Bryson attended a conference at the Institute, where he met Esther. By then, she was a partner with Litton, Lyle, and Levine, one of Washington's premier law firms. They were attracted to each other immediately.

* * *

With his arm around her waist, Bryson escorted Esther to the SUV. He held the door open for her as she slid inside, then he gently pushed it closed. As he came around the rear bumper, he noticed a gray Chevrolet sedan parked down the street. Two men sat inside. The driver stared at him. For an instant, Bryson was certain they were watching him on purpose, but he quickly brushed aside the notion. "Just two guys in a car," he said to himself. He pulled open the door and got in behind the steering wheel.

Esther smiled at him. "Everything okay?"

"Yeah," he nodded. "Everything's fine." He glanced in the mirror to check for traffic, then steered the SUV down the street.

At the corner, he turned left. As he made the turn, Bryson glanced in the mirror once more. The Chevrolet sedan was half a block behind them. He looked at Esther. "What are you doing this afternoon?"

"I'm seeing Wiseman."

"He's at Fort Meade?"

"Yes."

"Always struck me as odd to hold him there. That's not really the mission of that installation. They don't have a prison unit."

"He's not really a prisoner."

"They have him in an apartment?"

"Yes," she nodded. "A very small and very secure apartment."

"Still a prison if you can't leave on your own."

"Why do you ask?"

"Just curious." He checked the mirror once more. "Want me to drive you up there?"

"No." She shook her head. "I need to do a couple of things at the office first."

"You still coming to Texas with me for the party?"

"Wouldn't miss it," she replied. "I'm looking forward to meeting this Bert Driskell guy you keep talking about."

"He's a card," Bryson chuckled.

"Is that a Texas expression?"

"Yeah. I suppose so."

She reached across the seat and took his hand. "Think we'll have a few minutes alone while we're there?"

"I'm planning on it," he smiled. "Thought we'd fly down on Thursday night, spend Friday at the house, then go over for the party Saturday."

"Didn't you say Driskell lives near Austin?"

"Yeah. But they'll come get us."

"Isn't that a long drive?"

"Bert has a helicopter."

Esther frowned. "A helicopter?"

"When you ranch the way he does, a helicopter is a necessary piece of equipment."

Bryson glanced once more in the rearview mirror. "You see that car behind us?"

Esther looked over her shoulder, then turned quickly forward. "Yes."

"They've been behind us since we left your house. Have you seen them before?"

"I don't think so."

"Any idea why someone would be following you?"

"No." She looked away. "Not really." Then she flashed a smile in his direction. "Maybe they're following you."

"Maybe so," he shrugged.

Ten minutes later they reached the parking deck at Esther's office. Bryson turned the SUV into the entrance for the deck. The car behind them came to a stop at the curb on the opposite side of the street.

When they reached the third level of the garage, Bryson brought the SUV to a stop near the elevator. Esther leaned over and kissed him. "See you tonight?"

"Seven."

"Better make it eight," she suggested. "I'm getting a late start and I don't know how long it will take with Wiseman."

"Okay."

Esther stepped from the car and started toward the elevator. Bryson steered the SUV away and drove down to the street.

When he reached the exit he turned right. He made the block and came back around to the entrance to check for the Chevrolet sedan that had followed him earlier. As he turned the corner, the sedan moved away from the curb. Before Bryson could change lanes to follow, the car turned left at the next corner and disappeared in traffic.

CHAPTER 7

RHODES

CARLO BUSCA STOOD AT HIS DESK, arms across his chest, waiting. A moment later, there was a knock at the door. "Come," he replied in a loud voice.

The door opened and Angelo Giovanni entered. Tall, slender, and striking, he had been Busca's assistant for five years. Giovanni crossed the room and stood near the desk. "You called for me, sir?"

"Yes," Busca replied. He placed a hand on the back of his chair as if striking a pose and looked intently at Giovanni. "As you are aware, the Council met earlier today and reached a decision."

"Yes, sir," Giovanni nodded.

Busca clasped his hands behind his back and took a step to the left. "We shall liberate America from the Jews." He lowered his voice. "And the world from the Americans." He paused and took a long, slow breath, relishing the moment. "The Twenty-Four have met and we are of one mind." He focused his gaze intently on Giovanni. "You are to deliver the message that sets this mission in motion."

"Yes, sir," Giovanni nodded once more. "What shall I say?"

"Tell our brothers, 'Release the four angels who are bound at the great river Euphrates.'"

"Yes, sir." Giovanni nodded again. "That is the message? That is all?"

"It will be enough." Busca smiled. "More than enough." He came around the front of the desk and stood near Giovanni. "The message must be delivered exactly as I have given it to you. 'Release the four angels who are bound at the great river Euphrates.' Do you understand?"

"Release the four angels who are bound at the great river Euphrates," Giovanni repeated.

"That is it. Go without delay." Busca gave a dismissive gesture with his hand.

Giovanni bowed his head. "I shall deliver the message." He turned and started toward the door.

Busca called after him, "You have the numbers?"

"Yes, sir."

"Text or email only. No voice."

"Yes, sir."

Giovanni opened the door and stepped out to the hallway.

CHAPTER 8
FORT MEADE, MARYLAND

SHORTLY BEFORE TWO THAT AFTERNOON, Esther left her office and drove north on the Baltimore-Washington Parkway. Near Laurel, she turned onto Reece Road and made her way to the main gate at Fort Meade. After a security check at the gate, she drove toward the center of the base to a building off Cooper Road near Burba Lake. She parked and walked toward the front entrance.

Once inside the building, she was escorted to an elevator. A guard accompanied her from the lobby and rode with her down to the third basement level. When the elevator doors opened she stepped out. With the guard at her side, she walked down the hall to a set of large double doors that opened onto a transportation corridor. There, a tram picked them up.

The tram whisked them to a stop at a corridor marked only with the number 6. Esther followed the guard from the tram through the doorway to another elevator. From there, they rode six floors up and emerged in a carpeted hallway. A little way down the hall they came to a door with a coded entry. The guard punched in a series of numbers and opened the door.

Beyond the door was a small entryway. On the opposite side facing them was yet another door. As the first door closed behind them, the guard pressed his thumb against a square black pad mounted on the wall. A tiny green light blinked, then the guard leaned forward and said his name into a small microphone embedded in the corner of the thumb pad. Moments later, a lock on the door clicked. The guard twisted the knob and pushed it open.

Esther stepped through the doorway to an interview room sparsely furnished with a single stainless steel table that was bolted to the floor. Benches, affixed to either side of the table's frame, provided the only seating. Light from fluorescent tubes mounted on the ceiling bounced off the bare walls and filled the room with a stark glare. Esther stood near the table and waited. She'd done this before. She knew what to expect. Any minute now the door would open and Anthony Wiseman would appear.

Unlike most of the detainees Esther had represented, Wiseman was a U.S. citizen. He had been born in Philadelphia, where his father and mother, both Israeli, lectured as professors at Gratz College. During his senior year in high school, Wiseman's parents decided to return to Israel. He stayed behind and finished the school year in Philadelphia.

After high school he attended Cornell University and obtained a degree in history. While there, he caught the eye of Gordon White, a professor in the political science department who recommended him to a friend with connections in the intelligence community. When he graduated, Wiseman was offered a job as an analyst with the Office of Naval Intelligence in Newport, Rhode Island. He was smart, interested, and energetic—qualities that helped him excel academically and professionally.

While working with Naval Intelligence, Wiseman was assigned to a group of analysts that produced intelligence reports for dissemination to Israel and other U.S. allies in the Middle East. In the 1990s, intelligence provided by the group resulted in an Israeli raid on a West Bank refugee camp near the Jordanian border. Ten high-level Hamas leaders were captured, but in an ensuing gunfight a dozen civilians were killed. International protest forced the United States to curtail the type and amount of intelligence provided to the Israelis. As a result, a ship carrying North Korean missiles lay off the coast of Egypt, undetected by the Israelis, while Hamas operatives ferried the missiles into the Egyptian desert. A few weeks later those same missiles were smuggled across the border into Gaza and used in an attack on the Israeli city of Ashkelon. Forty-three Israeli civilians died.

In the aftermath of the Ashkelon attack, Wiseman conducted his own research and learned that the U.S. Navy had known about the freighter and its deadly cargo before the ship arrived in the Mediterranean. Satellite photographs captured images of the ferrying operation and pinpointed the precise location where the missiles were stored before being sent to Gaza. Even after the attack began, data from the Joint Surveillance and Target Attack Radar System (JSTARS) determined the spot from which the missiles had been launched. Had the information been provided to the Israelis in a timely manner, the attack could have been curtailed. Instead, the U.S. withheld the reports, in spite of numerous agreements between the two countries requiring the U.S. to immediately notify Israel of potential threats and in spite of repeated assurances that the U.S. would provide real-time information during ongoing attacks.

When Wiseman inquired further about the intelligence failure, he learned the State Department had blocked release of the information for fear that North Korea would react badly to the discovery, possibly taking military action against South Korea. Later, Wiseman raised the issue at a staff meeting and was met with unexpected opposition.

"You Jews complain about everything," he was told, "no matter what we provide. Every time the Israelis hear the words *gas* or *missile* they get paranoid. The Holocaust got them their nation. They should stop living in the past and be satisfied they even exist. They can't play that pity card just to manipulate us."

Wiseman was incensed, as much by the comments of his co-workers as by official U.S. policy, but rather than continue to fight openly he took the opposite approach. He worked diligently, kept a low profile, and did his best to follow accepted procedure. Then, with attention at the office no longer focused on him or events in Israel, he began sending copies of the latest intelligence reports to an Israeli naval officer he'd met at a conference in New York. He was careful not to disclose sources or methods by which the intelligence had been obtained, and he refused to accept payment for the information, but he kept a steady stream of intelligence flowing to Israel, much of it critical in limiting the number of attacks from Gaza and crucial in halting the flow of arms to the West Bank.

Two years later, evidence from satellite photographs provided through Wiseman indicated a reactor near Aleppo, Syria, was being used by that government to develop nuclear weapons. With targeting information obtained from the photographs, the Israeli Air Force attacked and destroyed the site. Syria filed a protest with the United Nations, claiming the facility was a pharmaceutical factory.

Though not formally accused, rumors circulated throughout the Middle East that the U.S. had provided Israel with information necessary for the attack. In response, the CIA conducted an investigation. Access logs for three intelligence databases linked the information to Wiseman. The following day, he was arrested by the FBI. Citing provisions of the Patriot Act, he was held without charges and without benefit of an attorney.

Wiseman's case attracted the attention of Israeli politicians and quickly became a popular cause among Israeli citizens who viewed Wiseman as a hero. Not long after his arrest, Esther Rosenberg was hired by the Israeli government to defend him and given the task of winning his release. So far, her efforts had proved unsuccessful.

After what seemed like a lengthy wait that morning, the door finally opened and Wiseman appeared. Accompanied by two guards, he stepped into the room and waited while they unlocked the manacles from his ankles. He smiled over at Esther as the cuffs were removed from his wrists. "Have a good drive up this afternoon?"

"Yes," she replied. "Traffic wasn't too bad today."

"Good."

The guards collected the chains and cuffs and retreated to the hall. The man who had accompanied Esther turned to a metal panel on the wall beside the entrance. He took a key from his pocket and unlocked it, revealing a box with a phone inside. "When you are ready to leave, pick up this phone. Someone will answer. We will come for you. You cannot exit the room on your own. Understand?"

"Yes. I've done this before," Esther replied.

The guard stepped outside and closed the door. When he was gone, Esther turned to Wiseman. "Shall we sit?"

"I do a lot of sitting around here," Wiseman chuckled. "But sure."

They took a seat at the table. Esther sat sideways on the bench. Wiseman sat with his forearms resting on the tabletop and looked her in the eye. "Is the prime minister safe?"

"As far as we know."

"Did they capture the men who did it?"

"All three are dead," Esther replied.

"What happened?"

"One of the missiles blew up. Supposedly it was sabotaged."

Wiseman arched an eyebrow. "But no one has claimed responsibility."

"Not yet." Esther leaned closer. "The missiles were Russian Kornets."

"Anti-tank missiles."

"They have been using them recently against a number of targets besides tanks. Where would they have obtained them?"

"Where did they obtain them?" Wiseman had a look of incredulity. "You know where they obtained them. They are Russian missiles. Where do you get Russian missiles?" He answered his own question. "They get them from Russia."

"But how did they get them?"

He had a troubled look. "Someone asked you to ask me this?"

"Yes."

"Do they not have people who can answer these questions?"

"I'm sure they do," Esther replied. "I suspect someone at the center in Beersheba already thinks they know the answer. They're just hoping you agree with their conclusion. Your support would give them the upper hand in an intra-agency dispute."

"Well," Wiseman said gruffly. "I'm glad to help but I don't like being a pawn."

"But you have an idea."

"Yes." He sighed. "I know how the Palestinians obtained them. There is really only one source for the Kornets themselves."

"Demetrius Nilus?"

"Yes." Wiseman nodded his head slowly. "And his nephew, Leonid Malenkov. Since Adnan Khashoggi was forced out of the business, they have been the primary source of illicit arms in the Middle East." Wiseman paused a moment. His voice softened. "You are certain the prime minister is safe?"

"As far as we know, he escaped without a scratch."

"Has anyone considered this might have been an inside job?"

Esther shrugged in reply. "If someone on the inside wanted him dead, they could have done it long before now. Why do you ask?"

"This was a great opportunity to kill him and make it look like it was the work of Hamas." Wiseman fell silent again, as if lost in thought, then changed subjects. "They still have not charged me?"

"No," she replied. "They have not."

"How long can this go on?"

"Indefinitely, I'm afraid."

Wiseman gave her an ironic smile. "They do not see the contradiction?"

"Which is?"

"Our country, dedicated to individual liberty and freedom, incarcerating one of its citizens indefinitely, without due process."

"They are scared."

"Why? What does America have to fear from me?"

"I know," she nodded. "But they don't see it that way."

Wiseman sighed. "I think you are right." He rubbed his hand across his jaw. "Isn't there something you can do to get me out of here?"

"Not really. Not through the courts. I've talked again with the Justice Department. The person I normally see is no longer there. Someone else has taken his place."

"Great," Wiseman rolled his eyes. "I've outlived the Attorney General."

"Not him," Esther chuckled. "Just his staff."

"Is this new person sympathetic to our cause?"

"I think she might be, after she reads your file."

Wiseman's eyes brightened. "A woman?"

"Yes," Esther nodded. "Rather attractive, too."

"But is she compassionate?" Wiseman rubbed his jaw again. "We need a compassionate soul. Brains and beauty are wonderful to behold, but this situation calls for a decision from the heart." He rubbed his jaw once more.

Esther's forehead wrinkled in a frown. "Is there a problem with your jaw?"

"Not my jaw," he said, shaking his head. "It's my tooth."

"How long has it been this way?"

"Two or three weeks."

"Did you tell someone?"

"Yes," he nodded. "But they do not care about my tooth. Too much trouble to move me to a clinic."

"You need to see a dentist."

Wiseman looked away. "The Russians are so shortsighted," he said with disgust. "They have their own problems with Islamic terrorism, yet they sell sophisticated weapons to Jihadists in the Middle East, thinking this won't come back to bite them. It's all about short-term gain for them, isn't it?"

"It's not about the wisdom of selling arms."

"You're right. It's about trying to pry the U.S. out of the region.

They think that peace will only make it more affordable for the United States to continue its involvement in the region. War, they hope, will eventually cost us more than we're willing to pay."

"Are they right?"

"Maybe," Wiseman nodded. "We are not a patient bunch. Nilus is patient. And it's finally giving him a chance to do what he has always wanted to do—arm one of Israel's neighbors with the power to annihilate the entire country."

"No American president would ever let that happen."

"I used to think that, too. Now I am not so sure."

Esther shifted positions on the bench. "Is there another source for the missiles?"

"No." Wiseman shook his head. "There are many smuggling routes. But the Russian Kornets came from Nilus." His eyes darted away. His hand ran lightly over his jaw. "And Nilus...is trouble." He glanced back at Esther. "You must keep your people focused on him. And watch out. He's arrogant but he's not stupid. There could be more to this than meets the eye."

Esther glanced at her watch. "You think others are involved?"

"I think it makes no sense for Russia to sell to Hamas."

Esther stood. "My time is up." She pointed to Wiseman. "I think there is more to that jaw you keep rubbing than just a sore tooth, too." She turned to the box on the wall and picked up the phone. "I'll make arrangements to have someone take a look at it."

CHAPTER 9
WASHINGTON, D.C.

STEVE TAYLOR SAT AT a conference table on the third floor of the Justice Department building. Gathered around the table were representatives of a dozen federal agencies discussing security along the U.S.-Mexican border. Taylor attended the meeting as a spokesman for the Defense Intelligence Agency.

Born in Yuma, Arizona, Taylor had been immersed in cross-border conflict since birth. His uncle, Tommy Praetor, had been sheriff of Yuma County in the 1960s and '70s. Back then life had been different. People crossed from Mexico without a visa, worked a few days, then went home. No one cared. But in the late 1970s, things began to turn ugly. Drug dealers saw lax border security as an opportunity to smuggle heroin and cocaine into the United States. When it began, the federal government seemed unconcerned. So Praetor took things into his own hands. He developed a special squad of deputies and outfitted them with surplus Army equipment and assault rifles purchased from a Mexican gun dealer. After four weeks training in the desert, they began raiding houses and businesses on both sides of the border.

Drug dealers as far away as New York felt the sting of short supply created by Praetor's bare-knuckles approach. But markets in the U.S. were too lucrative for the drug cartels to ignore. They responded by hiring mercenaries from South America, outfitted with Russian-made weapons and supported by intelligence from members of the Mexican police. Within months, Yuma County was on the verge of a full-scale war. Then Praetor went missing. Three days later his body was found in the desert five miles east of Picacho Road, staked to the ground near the base of an organ pipe cactus. He had been shot once at close range, but the coroner was unable to determine whether he had died of the wound or of the mutilation inflicted by hungry coyotes.

The death of his uncle had a galvanizing effect on Taylor. Only twelve years old at the time, he remained the compliant, obedient child he'd always been, but deep-seated anger simmered just beneath the boiling point. Late at night when no one was looking, he would wipe tears from his eyes as he thought about his uncle and resolved to avenge his death by ridding the world of those responsible for his brutal murder.

After high school, Taylor attended Arizona State University. By then, the desire for vengeance against a handful of drug dealers had grown into hatred of all Hispanics. As a college freshman, those views became quickly evident. Before the first semester ended, Taylor was approached by Walter Raymond, a fellow student, who invited Taylor to join his study group.

Though they often studied together, the group was actually a campus chapter of the Holy Western Empire, a loosely organized confederation of white supremacists. Over the next three years Taylor was schooled in what Raymond saw as the core issue beneath all of America's ills—a worldwide Jewish conspiracy. Jews, Raymond argued, were the reason the federal government did little to curb the flow of drugs across the border from Mexico.

"Jews control the government and they want as many Americans using drugs as possible. It undermines our morality and creates a sense of lawlessness that they can exploit to gain control over us. They own the banks, the motion picture industry, radio, and television. And they control the advertising agencies. They tell you what to buy and give you the financing to make it happen. Drugs and sex are tools they use to keep everyone in place, oblivious to the manipulation and content to follow their orders."

Raymond's words fell like water on the parched ground of Taylor's angry mind. In that twisted logic Taylor found the organizing principles he needed to reconcile his mind with his conscience, to mesh the notion of revenge with a sense of justice and righteousness he'd always believed were his. The problem was bigger than the Mexicans. Behind the scenes, the Jews were pulling the strings. There was no way to rid the world of Mexicans without first getting rid of the Jews.

Because the study group was only an informal gathering, Taylor's association with the Holy Western Empire was never widely known. Several friends knew of his relationship with Walter Raymond, but none of them knew the Holy Western Empire existed.

During his senior year at Arizona State, Taylor took the Foreign Service Examination. He scored high enough to attract attention and was recruited by the Army. A background check turned up nothing that raised any concern. He enlisted without a problem. After a six-week course at Fort Knox, he was assigned to the Defense Intelligence Agency. When his enlistment ended, he was retained as a civilian analyst. He'd been there fifteen years.

That afternoon at the Justice Department meeting, Taylor sat with his hands folded in his lap, staring blankly into space, his eyes fixed on nothing at all. Out of sight, beneath the table, his fingers felt along his left hand and came to a ring. Made of gold, it had a set inlaid with red opal that formed a Maltese cross. He slowly twisted the ring, round and round, as his mind returned to the morning they told him about his uncle. It was summertime, and he'd been sitting on the back porch eating a candy bar he'd bought from the store down the street. His mother came to tell him …

Just then, someone from across the table spoke up. "Anyone care for more coffee?"

The voice jerked Taylor's mind back to the present. "Yeah," he replied. "I'll have a cup." He scooted back his chair and made his way around the end of the conference table. As he reached for the coffeepot, his cell phone received a text message. He took out the phone and read the message on the screen. "Rosenberg with Wiseman this PM." Taylor frowned and returned the phone to his pocket.

CHAPTER 10
ARLINGTON, VIRGINIA

LATER THAT SAME AFTERNOON, Paul Bryson left his office and drove across the Potomac River to Wilson Boulevard in Arlington. Just past Tenth Street he turned into the parking lot at Arlington Community Church. Since his arrival in Washington as a freshman congressman, he had attended services there almost every Sunday. Stuart Palmer, pastor of the church, had grown up in Lake Jackson, Texas. He and Bryson were friends.

Bryson parked the car near the rear entrance to the church and went inside. He made his way down the hall to the sanctuary and took a seat near the back. Stained-glass windows lined both sides of the room with scenes depicting events from the life of Christ. Sunlight streamed through the images, casting an array of color across the empty pews and filling the room with soft natural light. Bryson let his eyes roam from window to window, focusing on the story behind each scene. As he did, he thought of Esther and the events of the past year.

When he married Linda he made a commitment for life. As they had grown together, their relationship moved beyond the simple love of a man and a woman. They were best friends, confidantes, the completion of each other's mind and personality. In the weeks and months following her death, he'd been certain he would never love anyone else.

Then he met Esther. He hadn't meant to fall in love, but there she was and they hit it off, and before he knew it he was seeing her almost every night. At first it seemed natural and right and he'd never thought once about whether she as a Jew and he as a Christian could make a life together. But now things were serious and the differences between them seemed more real than before.

Just then, a door opened down front near the altar rail. Stuart entered the sanctuary carrying a silver candelabrum. He set it on the altar table and stepped back to check its position. Bryson watched in silence, amused at the way Stuart seemed to labor over finding the exact place for the candles. Finally satisfied, Stuart turned to leave. As he did, their eyes met. Stuart started up the aisle in Bryson's direction. "Didn't see you back here," he said with a smile. They shook hands. "How are you?"

"I'm fine," Bryson replied.

"Missed you Sunday."

"Yeah," Bryson sighed. "Just too lazy to get out of bed."

"Everyone needs a day off."

Bryson looked at him with a broad grin. "Do you get a day off?"

"Not really," Stuart replied, shaking his head. "How's Tom enjoying life at the University of Texas?"

"Rather well from what I hear. I'll be in Austin next weekend. Hope to see him."

Stuart chuckled. "I remember those days." They were silent a moment. Stuart crossed his legs and rested his hands in his lap. "So, what brings you out here?"

"Just needed a moment to collect my thoughts."

"This is a good place to do that. Something on your mind?"

"Yeah," Bryson said quietly. "I've been seeing someone."

"Great!"

"It is great. But it's unsettling, too. It feels like I'm cheating on Linda."

"I can see how it would feel that way. You were with her for a long time. Who are you seeing?"

"Esther Rosenberg. She's a lawyer with a firm downtown."

"She's Jewish?"

"Very much so."

"You say that like it's a problem."

"I don't know." Bryson glanced in Stuart's direction. "Is it?"

"What do you mean?"

"Don't people say Christians and Jews shouldn't marry?"

"I don't know what they say, but I think what they mean is Believers and nonbelievers shouldn't marry. Does she respect your beliefs?"

"I think so. We've never really talked about it."

"Maybe you should."

Bryson nodded. "I guess maybe we should."

CHAPTER 11
KRASNOYARSK, RUSSIA

DEMETRIUS NILUS STOOD NEAR the window and looked out into the darkness. Sixty-five years of age and heavily jowled, his barrel chest heaved up and down in time with his long, deep breaths. Dark circles ringed his bulging bloodshot eyes. Above them were bushy unkempt brows that matched the graying hair atop his head. In his hand he held a tumbler filled with Turi vodka, which he sipped as he stared into the night.

The mountain ledge on which his home was perched, high above the Yenisey River, afforded a panoramic view of Krasnoyarsk, a city of a million people. But at night that wonderful view disappeared behind a strictly enforced blackout. Every evening as sunset approached, the light-keeper and his deputies set out on patrol through the streets, reminding everyone that compliance with the blackout was mandatory, on pain of death. Since August 1969, no one had been executed for violating the order, but the patrols and their nightly chants were engrained in the city's culture and continued unabated.

The city of Krasnoyarsk had been under that nightly blackout since construction began in 1949 on Russia's first nuclear reactor. Efforts to obscure activity at the site ensured the location's secrecy until a U-2 flight photographing a tank convoy moving toward the Kazakhstan border accidentally captured the reactor on film. That original reactor was no longer in use but Krasnoyarsk remained home to the most critical components of Russia's nuclear program. As a result, it was a closed city. No one from the outside could get in, and no one on the inside could get out, without a special passport and travel document issued only on the specific authorization of the Army's chief regional commander, General Demetrius Nilus.

The son of a successful Russian businessman, Nilus came to the Russian Army by choice. His family's wealth and position in Russian society would have allowed him to easily escape the rigors of military service. Instead, he chose to serve and had enjoyed a long career in the Russian Army. Born at the height of the Cold War, he entered service as a lieutenant fresh from Moscow University and spent his first years in the Ural Mountains training with a special winter corps. From there, he was posted to a secret listening station on the northern tip of the Svalbard Archipelago, a string of islands in the Arctic Ocean officially under Norwegian jurisdiction. The base was operable for two years until it was discovered by a whaling ship.

When the base was decommissioned, Nilus was given his choice of assignments. He volunteered for duty at Krasnoyarsk. Since then, he had logged no official travel beyond the two-mile security perimeter that encompassed the city. Many thought his service there was a noble gesture, a son of privilege surrendering a bright and promising future to defend the country that made his privilege possible, but Nilus had a far more sinister motive.

After a moment gazing out the window, Nilus checked his watch. It was a quarter to eleven. "Almost time," he whispered. He took one last sip from the glass and turned away from the window.

As he moved across the room, he set the glass on a table near an overstuffed chair and continued on to a polished oak desk on the opposite side of the room. In a deliberate, unhurried manner, he took a seat at the desk and slid the chair up close to a well-worn laptop. With the press of a button, it whirred and crackled as it booted up the operating software.

While the computer loaded its programs, Nilus rested his hands in his lap and glanced down at his fingers. On his left hand he wore a gold ring inlaid at the top with red opal in the shape of a Maltese cross. Nilus had received it at the Knights Castle on Rhodes in a ceremony to honor his grandfather, Sergei Nilus, and to commemorate the anniversary of Sergei's book *The Protocols of the Learned Elders of Zion*. Thinking about that day made Nilus' chest swell with pride.

Seated in his chair at the desk, he let his eyes scan along a bookshelf on the opposite side of the room, near the window. As his eyes roamed over the third shelf his gaze fell on the leather binding of a first-edition copy of the book. It had been given to him by his grandfather just a few days before his death.

"There are things in here you must know," his grandfather had told him, the words coming in short, breathless gasps as he lay upon his bed. "Things about the Jews no one wants to discuss. I believe they are not as they appear and they mean to see our undoing." He thrust the book into Nilus' hands. "You must not let them get away with it. You must bring them to their knees. The world must be rid of them all."

Fabricated in 1897 under the direction of Pyotr Rachovsky, chief of the foreign branch of Czar Nicholas II's secret police, *The Protocols of the Learned Elders of Zion* had been Sergei Nilus' crowning achievement. Russia had enjoyed an era of broad economic and social expansion. The peasants and working class, quick to seize on the opportunity afforded by that expansion, had begun to agitate for economic reform, including expanded private ownership of land and greater civil liberty. The monarchy had been slow to respond and the growing tension plunged the nation into a period of great uncertainty with the very real possibility of armed revolution. To avert open warfare, Nicholas II sought to shift public anger onto Russia's largest immigrant group, the Jews. For that, he turned to Pyotr Rachovsky, and he in turn to a struggling writer from Moscow named Sergei Nilus.

For six months Sergei scoured the royal family's library, dredging up medieval myths and legends—the use of Christian blood to celebrate the Passover, human sacrifice, and anti-Semitic tales of a global Jewish conspiracy bent on obtaining world domination. Carefully he pieced those legends and lies together in a single work written as though it were an instructional manual for a clandestine, diabolical Jewish leadership. The book became the most powerful work of Sergei's short literary career.

Less than three months after *The Protocols* was published, Russian Christians, incited by what they had read, unleashed an intense and horrifying campaign of violence upon the Jews, one that led to deaths at such an alarming rate even the czar was appalled. Though many later refuted its claims, the book's power endured and spread. New translations appeared in England, France, Poland, and the United States, carrying its message and influence to an even more receptive audience. From the words on those pages, Hitler was spurred to greater and greater atrocities in his attempt to eliminate Jews from Europe. And even now, Muslims across the Middle East treated the fictitious book as absolute truth, second only to the Koran.

Demetrius Nilus smiled as he thought again of the effect that one single volume had on the course of world history. "To think, my grandfather did all that. With one pen and a few pieces of—"

Just then, the screen flashed blue as the web browser opened. Nilus leaned forward and placed his fingers on the keyboard. Working quickly, he typed in the Web address for an online blog known as *Daily News and Information*. He scrolled through the headlines until he came to an article about Iran's nuclear program. "Iranian Reactor Languishes," Nilus mumbled as he read the title. "This is the one." He clicked on the title and waited while the article opened. When the page was loaded, he scrolled his way toward the bottom and found a section designated for reader comments.

"Iran's need for reactor fuel is a matter about which we all should be concerned," Nilus typed, "especially in the West." He chuckled to himself as he continued typing. "The West should supply the fuel before Iran turns to black market sources." When he was finished, he pressed the Enter key and watched as the message was posted to the comments section.

Moments later, a response appeared. "The West should do the same with Pakistan so access and use can be controlled for peaceful purposes."

As Nilus read those words, a broad grin broke over his face. "So glad you were awake tonight," he whispered. "You shall make my life far more comfortable than you will ever know." He scooted back from the desk. "This calls for a drink."

Nilus rose from the chair and started across the room toward the table where he had left his glass. Halfway across the room, he took his cell phone from his pocket and typed in a text message. "Ready for immediate delivery." Then he scrolled down his contacts list to the entry for his nephew, Leonid Malenkov, and pressed the button to send the message. When the screen indicated the message had been sent, he slipped the phone into his pocket. He continued across the room to a table near the window, picked up the bottle of vodka, and refilled his glass. As he lifted the glass to his lips, an alarm dinged from the laptop computer. Nilus took a sip from the glass, then returned to the desk.

With a click of the mouse he opened the email account. In it he found a message that read, "Release the four angels who are bound at the great river Euphrates." A frown wrinkled Nilus' forehead. "Just when things were about to get easy," he sighed. "They go and do this."

CHAPTER 12
INNSBRUCK, AUSTRIA

LEONID MALENKOV WATCHED from the rear seat of a Mercedes sedan as the buildings moved slowly past. In spite of the car's size, his long, slender frame was an awkward fit and he sat with his knees against the back of the front seat. As the car wound through the narrow streets, he remembered the first time he had seen the city. He was only seven but even then he knew that one day he would make it his home. Now, at the age of thirty-one, he was living that childhood dream in ways he'd never imagined.

Born in Prague, Leonid had enjoyed a privileged life. His father, Otto, was a direct descendant of Vratislav II, the first king of Bohemia, a region that once encompassed Prague and most of what is now the Czech Republic. Though the Premyslid dynasty, of which he was a remnant, had long since declined, and the last vestiges of the Bohemian kingdom had faded from sight, the notion of Bohemian royalty remained.

Otto Malenkov used that family influence to establish a banking business and developed a reputation for discretely managing the accounts of foreigners seeking to hide their wealth from the prying eyes of government. One of his most lucrative accounts was that of Victor Nilus. Victor had two children, a daughter named Anastasia and a son named Demetrius. Demetrius Nilus joined the Soviet Army. Anastasia Nilus married Otto Malenkov and soon gave birth to a son.

In spite of the distance between them, Leonid Malenkov and his uncle became close. Nilus visited often in his sister's home, taking young Leonid for long rides and regaling him with stories of life in the army. When he took the post at Krasnoyarsk, their time together was more limited but they managed to communicate through cryptic letters and occasional phone calls. Once, Nilus even slipped Leonid into the closed city, hiding him in the trunk of the car, much to the boy's delight. Slowly, carefully, one small piece at a time, Nilus shared the family secret with Leonid, its belief in *The Protocols* and the family's dedication to the cause of eliminating the terrible Jewish conspiracy. By the time he was an adult, Malenkov was thoroughly and irrevocably indoctrinated.

A few blocks down the street, the Mercedes came to a stop outside an apartment building located at the edge of Innsbruck's oldest neighborhood. Malenkov pushed open the door and stepped out. Without a word, he slammed the door shut and started across the sidewalk. The doorman, wearing a dark green jacket with gold piping on the sleeves, reached to open the door. Malenkov brushed past him without so much as a nod or a smile.

Inside, Malenkov crossed the lobby to the elevator and pressed a button for the sixth floor. As the elevator rose, his cell phone received a new text message. He took the phone from his pocket and checked the screen. "Ready for immediate shipment." Malenkov pressed a button to verify the sender's identity. "Uncle Demetri," he smiled to himself. "You know how to make my day."

Moments later, the elevator doors opened. Malenkov slid the cell phone into his pocket and walked quickly to the far end of the hall. There, he came to the door of his apartment, a three-bedroom suite that filled the eastern half of the sixth floor. He took the key from his pocket and as he slipped it into the lock, the door swung open. Malenkov's heart skipped a beat. His eyes opened wide, his ears were alert for the slightest sound.

Moving cautiously, he leaned past the doorframe and called out, "Hello? Anybody there?" A rustling sound came from the right. Malenkov shoved the door with his hand, swinging it wide, then turned in the direction of the noise. "Who's there?"

Just then a tall, slender woman appeared from around the corner near the kitchen. Malenkov's shoulders relaxed. "Irina," he smiled. "I thought you were in Paris."

"I was," she beamed. "But we finished early, and I missed you."

Malenkov pushed the door closed behind him and slipped his arm around her waist. "And how was it?"

"It was good." Irina draped her arms around his neck. "But not as good as you." She leaned forward, pressing her warm, moist lips to his. For a moment, Malenkov was lost in her embrace. Then, just as quickly, he remembered the message on his phone. He pulled away with a smile. "One minute." He raised his index finger, wagging it in a plea for patience. He moved his hands to her hips and held her at bay as he backed away. "Stay right there. This will only take a moment." Malenkov hurried down the hall.

Irina folded her arms across her chest and cocked her head to one side in a defiant stance. "If this is about business," she called, "I am going to be angry."

He glanced back at her. "It will only take a minute."

"Leo," she growled impatiently.

At the end of the hall Malenkov turned right and darted into his study. Across the room were three windows. In front of them was a writing desk. On it was a laptop. He dropped into a chair behind the desk and opened the computer. Almost instantly, the screen was loaded and ready. Seconds later, he logged on to *The Huffington Post* Web site.

At the top of the page he clicked on the entertainment tab and scrolled down to a story about indoor snow skiing in Dubai. Beneath the story he located the comments section and typed in a message. "Indoor snow skiing is a waste of time. The best places to ski are in Iran, though they are outdoors and can only be enjoyed in winter. I especially like the slopes at Dizin. Great skiing and no Americans. And in the fall it's a great place for a quiet retreat. In fact, I already have reservations there for later this week." He clicked the button to post the message and waited. The screen refreshed with the comment at the bottom of the page. Malenkov closed the computer and stood. As he did, Irina appeared in the doorway.

"This was about business, wasn't it?"

"Everything is about business," Malenkov grinned.

Irina arched an eyebrow. "Everything?"

CHAPTER 13

BEERSHEBA, ISRAEL

OREN COHEN SAT IN the control room at the Mossad operations center. At sixty-one, Cohen had enjoyed a long and distinguished career, first as an officer in the Israeli Defense Force, then as an operations officer with Mossad. There he quickly gained a reputation as a man with a brilliant mind and uncanny intuition. He also was one not afraid to make a decision.

Much like the operations center at the Pentagon, the one at Beersheba had a large flat screen that covered one wall. Half the screen showed images from a camera mounted outside Malenkov's apartment building. The other half displayed information from a computer monitor.

An operator, Tzipi Levanon, was seated near Cohen turned in his direction. "We're in."

"Show me where he's been."

She pressed keys on the keyboard. "He went to this site." The image on the screen changed, showing the front page of *The Huffington Post*.

"Just this one?"

"Yes," she replied.

"What did he do there?"

Levanon's fingers clicked across the keys as the image changed. "He posted a message in the Reader Comments section of an article about an indoor snow skiing facility in Dubai."

"We have it?"

"Yes. It's right here on the site."

"Let me see it." She scrolled down to it. Cohen leaned over her shoulder and read it aloud. "Indoor snow skiing is a waste of time. The best places to ski are in Iran, though they are outdoors and can only be enjoyed in winter. I especially like the slopes at Dizin. Great skiing and no Americans. And in the fall it's a great place for a quiet retreat. In fact, I already have reservations there for later this week." Cohen leaned back in his chair. "Get me a copy. And the article he responded to, also."

She nodded in response. A moment later, an assistant brought the copies to Cohen. He skimmed the first. "This article about indoor skiing in Dubai…Is he saying no to Dubai?" Cohen looked over at the operator. "Have they offered him anything?"

"They have no reactor fuel to offer."

"But could they broker it?" Cohen's eyes widened. He pointed to the article. "He is saying no to skiing in Dubai and he is saying there are no Americans in Iran."

"Are you suggesting Dubai has attempted to broker a deal for the Americans to supply Iran with reactor fuel?"

"Perhaps." Cohen slumped back in his chair. "Malenkov works with his uncle, Demetrius Nilus. What do we have on him?"

Levanon typed a command on the keyboard. Moments later, the display on the screen changed to the *Daily News and Information* home page. "He has visited this site."

"Do we have access to Nilus' computer?"

"No. We still have not been able to get past their security system. But we can track him when he comes out."

"We are certain it is him?"

"Yes." Levanon gestured toward the screen. "There's a posting on the comments section to an article on *Daily News and Information*. The user name is Protocol24."

"And we have confirmed that user is Demetrius Nilus?"

"Yes."

"What did he say?"

"There is an article here about Iran's nuclear program. The article is entitled 'Iranian Reactor Languishes.' Protocol24 said, 'Iran's need for reactor fuel is a matter about which we all should be concerned, especially in the West. The West should supply the fuel before Iran turns to black market sources.'"

"And we think Malenkov was responding to that?"

"No, sir. He was responding to a comment on Protocol24's posting."

"Which was?"

"A user from Pakistan said, 'The West should do the same with Pakistan so access and use can be controlled for peaceful purposes.'"

"Pakistan has its own program."

"They still need fuel. They can't produce their own uranium."

"So Malenkov sees these two comments and adds a comment on *The Huffington Post,* telling those in the loop where he will be."

"Yes, sir."

"Interesting." Cohen laid the articles on a nearby table. "Tell operations to monitor the resort at Dizin."

"I'll take care of it right away."

CHAPTER FOURTEEN
LAS VEGAS, NEVADA

THE FOLLOWING MORNING, Pete Rios arrived at his office on the eighth floor of Bromley Tower, an office building located on Reno Avenue a few blocks off the Vegas Strip. From the windows behind his desk, he had a clear view of the city and the desert beyond.

On the personnel chart, Rios was the manager of the Department of Energy's Nevada Field Operations. That title gave him an office in the gleaming steel and glass building, but since September 11 he rarely had the opportunity to enjoy it. Most days, he spent his time at the agency's command center, a secure facility two levels beneath the parking lot of a single-story building on the western edge of town. There he performed his job as head of the Nuclear Emergency Support Team, known simply as NEST to the few who were privy to its existence.

Created by executive order in 1985, NEST was an obscure Federal agency charged with the sole responsibility of monitoring and responding to nuclear threats against the nation. For that purpose, Rios had at his disposal a cadre of scientists and technicians from both the public and private sector. When force was needed, he could draw on any asset necessary.

Rios hung his jacket on a coatrack in the corner of the office and walked to his desk. As he took a seat, there was a knock at the door. "Come," he commanded without looking up.

A young man dressed in a gray suit with a white shirt and muted blue tie entered the office. In his hand was a leather folder. He stepped quickly to the desk. "Sir, the morning brief from Washington."

"Thanks." Rios took the folder. "That will be all." The young man turned away and closed the door behind him as he disappeared from the room. When he was gone, Rios opened the folder.

Unlike the President's Daily Brief, which covered a wide array of security threats, the NEST Director's Brief addressed only nuclear threats. Items in it were prepared for Rios by a number of intelligence agencies and assembled by staff working for the Director of National Intelligence. Each morning it was delivered by courier from Washington.

Rios scanned a summary memo, then leafed through each of the articles included in the brief. Several involved satellite observation of enrichment facilities in Burma, a growing area of concern, and in Pakistan. One of the last pages included photographs of a reactor in Iran and information gleaned from items posted on two Internet blogs. Rios found the report intriguing.

Following the attacks of September 11, the National Security Agency had increased its attempts to collect information traveling over the Internet. To do that, they installed servers and related equipment at key locations in the U.S. and throughout the world. By tapping into fiber-optic trunk lines, they gained access to virtually all Internet traffic.

For over a year, the agency had tracked postings on Internet blogs made by a user in Russia under the name Protocol24. Many of those messages included follow-up comments added by a user in Pakistan identified as NewYork912 and by a user believed to be operating from Iran with a dynamic Internet protocol address. The most recent activity involved messages posted on the *Daily News and Information* site regarding the need for reactor fuel in Iran and Pakistan.

"Seems a little obvious," Rios mumbled as he read the report. "A little too obvious to be real." He turned the page. "But we can't really afford to take any chances."

At lunch that day, Rios gave a redacted version of the daily briefing memo to Randall Morris, the deputy director in charge of daily operations at NEST's command center.

Easily the oldest person in the Las Vegas office, Morris had been with the agency since the beginning. He had spent a lifetime in clandestine intelligence and had been ready to retire when the president asked him to help with NEST. Morris couldn't say no. His broad network of political connections and encyclopedic knowledge of covert operations proved invaluable in maintaining NEST's viability as a distinctive player in the intelligence community.

Morris glanced at the report. "You want us to investigate this?"

"Put somebody on it," Rios replied. "Don't make a big deal about it. Let's see what we can find."

"The Russians have been heavily involved in Iran's nuclear program. Think they want to branch out into Pakistan?"

"I don't know. I'm more concerned about who the Pakistan connection really involves. If it's the Pakistani government, that's one thing. But if their Inter-Services Intelligence is involved, we could be dealing with some dangerous extremists."

"I'll get someone on it this afternoon," Morris replied.

CHAPTER 15
FORT MEADE, MARYLAND

ANTHONY WISEMAN SAT NEAR the window enjoying his morning cup of hot tea. He held the warm liquid in his mouth and let the heat from it soothe the throbbing pain of his tooth. As he sat there, he thought of a day long ago when he was a young boy. He'd climbed with a friend to the top of a scrubby oak. Then his foot slipped from a branch and he slid down the tree trunk. He'd kept from falling but his chest was scraped and bloody and his jaw was bruised. When his mother asked what happened he'd told her they had played soccer with some older boys and one of them pushed him down. From the look on her face he could tell she didn't believe him, but she didn't ask any questions. She was like that. Giving her boys space to be boys in the hope they would grow up to be men capable of caring for themselves. She knew they'd need—

Across the room there was a sound at the door. Moments later, it opened and four guards entered. With them came Steve Taylor.

"Mr. Wiseman, I understand you have a problem with a tooth?"

Wiseman rubbed his hand across his jaw. "It's a little sore."

"We're going to take you to the medical ward and let a dentist have a look."

The guards stepped forward. One of them motioned for Wiseman to stand. He set the teacup on the table and rose from the chair. The guards secured his legs with manacles and placed his wrists in cuffs. Then one of them slipped a black hood over his head. "Is this really necessary?" Wiseman protested.

A guard took him by the arm. "Afraid so. Come this way, please."

With a guard guiding him, Wiseman shuffled across the room. He heard the door open and felt the air change around him as he stepped out into the hallway. His footsteps echoed off the walls. Soon they came to an elevator. The guards guided him inside and rode with him. From the feeling in his stomach Wiseman was sure they were going down.

When the elevator doors opened, the guards guided him along another hallway to yet one more room. Wiseman heard a door close behind him and then someone removed the hood. He blinked and squinted as his eyes adjusted to the light.

In front of him was a dentist chair. Taylor pointed in that direction. "If you'll have a seat, Mr. Wiseman, the dentist will be in shortly."

With the guards helping him, Wiseman took a seat in the chair and leaned his head against the headrest. In a few minutes a man and woman appeared. Tall and slender, the man was dressed in cotton scrubs over which he wore a white lab coat. He moved across the room to a sink and washed his hands, then turned in Wiseman's direction. "My name is Dan Miller. I understand you are having some pain."

"Yes," Wiseman replied.

"Where?"

"Right side of my jaw."

Wiseman opened his mouth. Miller peered inside, then leaned away. "I need x-rays to confirm it, but I believe you have an impacted wisdom tooth that has abscessed."

"Impacted?"

"Growing sideways." Miller gestured with his hands. "Not uncommon. Most people have their wisdom teeth extracted in early adulthood. Those who don't can have the trouble you're experiencing."

"What will it take to fix it?"

"We'll get it out." Miller backed away from the chair.

An x-ray machine was suspended from a nearby wall with a long, articulated arm. The assistant covered Wiseman with a lead-lined apron, pulled the head of the machine over to the chair, and pointed it at Wiseman's jaw. "Don't move," she directed as she stepped behind a shield before pressing a button on the control panel. The machine made a clicking sound, followed by a low hum. An image appeared on a screen to one side of the control panel. Miller leaned over it, studied it a moment, then pointed. "That right there is your trouble." He glanced back at Wiseman. "Can you see it?"

"I see the teeth. I can't see the problem."

"All that white around the tooth is inflammation. That's where the pain comes from."

"You can take care of it now?"

"We'll get you fixed up. Don't worry about a thing." Miller moved to the opposite side of the room and returned with a syringe. "We'll just numb this place...."

"You'll put me to sleep?"

"No. Not quite. Just make you drowsy."

"Is that really necessary?"

"We have to cut the gum away from the tooth, then pry it loose from the bone. It's a little more difficult than simply extracting a tooth."

Wiseman flinched as the needle punctured his skin. A few minutes later, he felt his mental processes slow. It became more difficult to form words, and keeping his mind on a single thought was almost impossible. Finally he gave up and closed his eyes. Miller stepped closer, nudged open Wiseman's mouth, and began working on his tooth.

Sometime later, Wiseman felt a sting in his right shoulder. His eyes popped open. Miller glanced down at him. "Hold still. I'm almost finished."

Wiseman closed his eyes, but the pain in his shoulder persisted and he wondered why a problem with his tooth would cause his shoulder to hurt, but he couldn't make his mind form the thoughts long enough to ask the question.

CHAPTER 16
IRAN

MOSHE WEISS STEERED HIS CAR through Tehran's heavy afternoon traffic. Just past Azadi Square, he turned left onto a service road that wound around the east side of Mehrabad Airport. Once the city's official international airport, it had been replaced by a newer, more modern facility but Mehrabad still received all domestic flights and remained the country's busiest airport.

At the far end of the runway, Moshe parked near the corner of a hangar owned by an Iranian construction company. He sat there in the shade and watched as planes took off and landed. Ten minutes later, he saw what he'd come for.

Out to the west, a Learjet made its final approach toward the runway. Moshe watched as the aircraft touched down, stopped short at the first taxiway, and turned toward the hangar. A few minutes later it rolled to a halt on the tarmac fifty yards from where he sat. The plane's engines whined to a stop and the door opened. A stairway then extended from the jet's fuselage and a man appeared in the doorway. On his right shoulder he carried a leather bag.

Moshe lifted a small spyglass to his eye and focused the lens. "Leonid Malenkov. What brings you here?" he whispered to himself. Through the lens he saw Malenkov adjust the shoulder strap of the bag.

A Mercedes sedan came from the opposite side of the hangar and coasted to a stop near the foot of the stairway. The driver hurried to the passenger side and opened the rear door. Malenkov came slowly down the steps. As he stooped to enter the car, his shoulder bumped into the driver. Moshe grinned as he watched through the lens. In the instant their shoulders touched, the driver slipped a writing pen into Malenkov's bag.

"Let's see if this works," Moshe mumbled.

He laid the spyglass aside and picked up a radio from the seat beside him. A small earpiece was connected to it by a thin white wire. He slipped the earpiece into his right ear and adjusted the volume on the radio.

Moments later, the car moved away from the plane and turned onto the service road not twenty yards from Moshe's location. Through the earpiece he heard the voice of the driver.

"You had a good flight?"

"Yes," Malenkov replied. "How long will the drive take?"

"About two hours."

"Very well," Malenkov replied. "I should like to enjoy the ride in silence."

Moshe shook his head at the arrogance in Malenkov's voice. "I shall enjoy seeing him taken down."

As the Mercedes moved out of sight, Moshe started the car and backed it from its parking place. Two hours later they arrived at the Dizin resort. The driver held the door for Malenkov and assisted the bellman with the luggage, but from all that Moshe Weiss could see, Malenkov gave him not even a single coin as a tip.

* * *

The following morning, Malenkov appeared downstairs in the main lobby of the resort. He walked to a restaurant in the east wing of the hotel and took a seat in the corner. A few minutes later Hossein Jiroft made his way to the table and slid onto a seat across from Malenkov.

Thin and wiry, Jiroft was Iranian but had spent most of his life in Oman. He returned to Tehran a few years earlier to take a position at Tehran University. There he came under the influence of Shiraz Moussa, leader of a Nizari sect that flourished on the university's campus.

Meanwhile, Moshe Weiss sat in the cab of a food-service truck parked at a loading dock behind the restaurant. A radio receiver lay on the seat beside him. With it, he connected to the listening device in Malenkov's shoulder bag. Moshe pressed the earpiece into his ear and adjusted a knob on the radio. Then he heard Malenkov's voice.

"We are meeting alone this morning?"

"No," Jiroft replied. "He will be here shortly."

There was the tinkle of glass and the sound of a utensil against a plate. A waiter appeared and took their order. Then Malenkov spoke again. "Here he is now."

A chair scraped against the floor as someone scooted back from the table, followed by the rustle of someone standing, and then Malenkov continued. "Sahab. So good to see you. I wasn't sure you got the word."

Moshe had a somber look. Sahab was none other than Sahabzada Ayub, a senior official with Pakistan's Inter-Services Intelligence agency. His presence meant the meeting was not simply about fuel for a nuclear reactor. Something much more sinister was in the works.

"Yes," Sahab replied. "We have been monitoring the Web sites constantly. Hoping to hear from you."

The Web sites, Moshe thought. *They have more than one. A network. A cluster of fringe groups communicating through comments left on otherwise nondescript social networking Web sites. The possibilities were intriguing. If they could—*

A waiter appeared at the table. There was the sound of dishes and utensils again. Then Jiroft spoke up. "So, we can make a deal?"

"You get right to the point."

"I think we should keep things simple."

"I agree."

"The same terms as last time?"

"Yes. This is the bank account."

"Switzerland is still safe?"

"You have concerns?"

"There have been reports of intrusions in their system by the Americans."

Jiroft looked determined. "We prefer a bank in Luxembourg."

"It is already arranged with the Swiss," Malenkov countered. "This is our arrangement. If you would like to find another source, you certainly have that option."

There was an uneasy silence, then Sahab replied, "We can accept it."

"And you?"

"Yes," Jiroft replied. "We will agree to the financial arrangements."

There was a pause, then Malenkov spoke. "You have other concerns?"

"I am wondering about the quality."

"The quality? You question the quality?"

"I question whether the plutonium you offer us is as bad as those missiles you sold us for the job in Ramallah."

"I am offering you weapons-grade plutonium, salvaged from Russian bombs. It is refined, pure, and ready to use. With this, your weapons systems will leap into the next century." There was a loud clank, followed by the scoffing tone of Malenkov's voice. "Quality. You should examine the quality of the people you recruit. Not the quality of the goods I supply." There was another pause. Then Malenkov's voice. "We are in agreement?"

"Yes," Sahab replied.

"As you wish," Jiroft added.

"Good." Malenkov's voice was till tense. "When half the money is deposited, we will start the shipment. When the other half arrives, the ship will reach the dock."

"How will you deliver it?"

"We will transport the containers overland to Makhachkala. There they will be placed onboard a freighter to Bandar Anzali."

"Bandar Anzali?"

"We will deliver two containers to that point. I trust you can get the material from there to its final destination."

"That will not be a problem."

"Well, then, all is agreed?"

"Yes."

"We have a deal."

Outside in the truck, Moshe felt his skin tingle at what he'd heard. This wasn't a discussion about uranium to use as fuel in civilian reactors. This was about plutonium for weapons production. Moshe took the earpiece from his ear. "I must report this at once."

CHAPTER 17
RHODES

IN THE KNIGHTS CASTLE, Antonio Belisconi pushed a broom across the floor inside the Hall of Saints. He glanced around at the rich wood paneling that lined the walls. "The hallowed walls of the Twenty-Four," he whispered to himself. "The Council has met in this room, right where I'm standing, for more than a thousand years." He let his eyes scan the walls. "I wonder what they would say of their Order now."

A third-order Knight of Grace, Belisconi was a layman from Catania, Sicily. An artist by training, at the age of twenty-six he contracted meningitis, which left him deaf and unable to use his right hand. Desperate to regain his artistic talent, he searched all of Italy for a doctor who could help him. Then a friend took him to Father Umberto Magdilani at San Biagio Church. Father Magdilani sprinkled him with Holy Water and prayed for him. Belisconi was instantly restored.

To show his gratitude, Belisconi sought to enter the priesthood. He submitted to routine examination by the Archbishop of Cantania and was set for admission to the seminary in Palermo, but Father Magdilani suggested he apply to an order that would admit him as a layman. "There you can do your service to God and listen to His voice. Perhaps He has more for you than can be accomplished within the confines of the priesthood." Magdilani suggested the Order of Malta.

Belisconi was admitted to the Order as a donat, the lowest level of lay participation. He was assigned to a hospital in Germany where he cleaned rooms, washed linens, and helped prepare meals. Later, he was sent to an orphanage in Bangladesh where he worked cleaning toilets and washing clothes. At each of those locations, he learned to ignore his surroundings, to accept his lowly position as an act of service, and work as unto God. In the course of that work, he proved his commitment to a life of service and established himself as a man of honor. He also learned things about the Order that deeply troubled him. On a rare visit to Sicily, he discussed those issues with Father Magdilani over tea at a café in Cantania.

"They are an authority unto themselves," Belisconi complained. "They submit to no one."

"Many of us are troubled by the Order's reliance upon its own sovereignty."

"Others are aware of this?"

"Yes."

"They have their own bank, their own code, their own army."

"We know," Magdilani nodded.

"Generals and diplomats from countries around the world come to them."

"You are right."

"They take pride in their sovereignty and exert authority as though they are accountable to no one. And," he wagged his finger, "the things they do with that authority are not the work of a Holy Order. Has no one tried to expose them for who they really are?"

"We have been watching them, but we have never had anyone on the inside willing to help us."

Belisconi lowered his voice. "I would be willing to help."

"You would be risking your life."

"I have but one life to give," Belisconi replied. "I should prefer to give it for something, rather than nothing." He focused his eyes on Magdilani. "I cannot look the other way."

Not long after that, Father Magdilani contacted his cousin Phaedon Michail Damaskinos, the Archbishop of Milos, the lone Catholic prelate with liturgical authority over the Island of Rhodes. At Damaskinos' request, Belisconi was assigned by the Order to the Knights Castle. There he worked hard at being an obedient knight, and at keeping his eyes and ears open for useful information.

In the Hall of Saints he moved around the table, sliding each chair from its place. With the chairs aside, he made a second trip around the table, sweeping beneath it. When he reached the far end, he noticed a small scrap of paper lying on the floor. He stooped down and picked it up. It was crumpled in a tight wad, which he carefully unfolded. On it was the name *Demetrius Nilus*. He stuffed the scrap of paper in his pocket and made yet a third trip around the table, sliding the chairs back in place. When he was finished he left the room and swept his way up the hall.

A few minutes later, he turned the corner toward the Grand Master's office. Giovanni's desk sat to one side of the office door. Across from it was a desk for the Grand Master's secretary. Giovanni stood at his desk and typed a text message on his Blackberry. Across from him, the secretary rose from his chair and disappeared down the hall in the opposite direction. Belisconi pushed the broom along the base of the far wall. With his head down, he watched Giovanni from the corner of his eye.

An alarm dinged on Giovanni's Blackberry. He glanced at the phone, mumbled something to himself and laid it on the desk. The secretary poked his head around the corner and called to him. Moments later, Giovanni disappeared in that direction. When they were gone, Belisconi moved to the desk and picked up the phone.

Without warning, the door to Busca's office opened and Busca stepped out. "Giovanni," he called in a loud voice. His eyes darted from side to side, searching. Belisconi dropped the Blackberry into his pocket and continued sweeping. Busca glanced in his direction. "Have you seen Giovanni?"

"He stepped around the corner," Belisconi replied.

Busca moved away from the door and made his way around the desk. "Giovanni," he called again. "Where are you?"

Giovanni appeared at the corner. By then, Belisconi was at the stairwell. He picked up his broom and hurried down the steps.

CHAPTER 18
RHODES

DEEP INSIDE KNIGHTS CASTLE, three floors beneath the Hall of Saints, Carmine Russo, aide to the prelates of the Military Vicariate, sat in the corner of a room known to the Order as The Dungeon. Once used to hold prisoners, it had been converted to a secure meeting room not unlike the situation rooms at the Pentagon and the White House. Located underground, with the castle above, and surrounded by thick stone walls, it presented a formidable obstacle to anyone who attempted to eavesdrop on activities conducted inside. Recent additions of electronic cloaking capabilities made it even more secure.

A long, slender conference table occupied the center of the room. Made of oak, its smooth top was polished to a glossy shine. Around it sat thirteen high-backed leather chairs perfectly positioned an equal distance apart. Overhead, small spotlights shined down on each of the chairs, giving the occupants an eerie luminescence.

Ignacio Spoleto sat at the end of the table near the door. Gathered around him were the twelve prelates of the Military Vicariate, a group of men designated to implement the Order's military policy. Each of them had been appointed to the Vicariate by the Grand Master but they all served at the discretion of Spoleto. And once appointed, their business was solely their own. Not even the Grand Master could question how they executed policy.

Spoleto rose from his place at the head of the table. "Gentlemen, we are gathered here today to consider execution of the Order's decision regarding American Jews."

Father Galena, seated at the opposite end of the table, spoke up. "We discussed at our last meeting the possibility of using devices obtained from Chinese sources. Is that still our intention?"

"Busca was pressing for us to use our Russian friends."

"He mentioned it to me three or four times," someone volunteered.

"I wonder about the relationship between Busca and Nilus," another mused. "They seem far too close for the good of the Order."

"I am worried that he has already contacted the Russians and set the plan in motion through them."

"He would not be so bold," someone glowered.

"He would not be so stupid."

"Do you have evidence, or is this merely your own worries and suspicions?"

"I have no evidence."

"Busca does not decide how we pursue our obligation. He has no say in this matter. He is the Grand Master, not a dictator."

"But can the Chinese provide a reliable device?"

"They have been far more successful than either the Russians or the Americans in miniaturizing their nuclear weapons. Their suitcase bombs are two kilotons and new. Those from Russia and America are half that strength and more than two decades old."

"Very well," Spoleto interrupted. "We will use the Chinese to supply the bombs, through unofficial channels, of course."

"How many?"

"Four suitcase bombs," Spoleto replied. "Placed at the targets we selected earlier."

"That will make an impact."

Once again, the conversation moved around the table. "It will destroy the U.S. economy."

"Can we live with that?"

"A necessary consequence for ridding the world of those Jews," someone offered. "And for prying America from their grip. We will be doing them a favor."

"Germany will be the world's controlling economy once again."

"Not the Chinese?"

"I think it will be the Chinese."

"They agree with you."

Galena spoke up. "The Chinese believe that America is now only a consumer nation. They see themselves as both a consumer and a producer and view their economy as self-sufficient. With America out of the way, they believe they will be the world's supreme economic power."

"Have we built strong alliances in China to safeguard the interests of the Order?"

"We were building them, but Busca has curtailed activity there."

"The Chinese are delusional about their place in the world, but let them live with their delusions, so long as the devices work and they can keep quiet."

"Regardless of who ends up on top, this will bring a change in the world order."

"Do we care about the world order? We are members of the Kingdom, not some political nation."

Halfway down the table, a hand went up. "I would note, however, that the Chinese are rather unpredictable."

"As are their weapons."

"Have we considered the possibility of failure? Could the bombs be traced back to the Chinese, and to us?"

"No. The materiel cannot be traced directly to the supplier. And we have members in the United States who are committed to the strategy. They will do everything in their power to see that our plan succeeds and that the Order is protected after the attacks. If we can get the bombs to them, no one can stop us."

"That is an interesting situation," Galena suggested. "Both a blessing and a curse. Busca and Giovanni have relied far too heavily on the Americans, and while they may ensure our success, they can also ensure our failure."

"Perhaps we should consider every eventuality," Spoleto suggested.

"Any failure will fall at our feet."

"We must all work together to make it successful."

"But we must protect our anonymity."

"Yes," Spoleto interjected. "The anonymity of the Order must be protected. At all costs."

Spoleto rapped the table with his knuckles. "We are agreed, then? Our Chinese connections will supply the bombs and deliver them to America. Our members in America will place them at the target sites and, on a predetermined signal, make certain they detonate." Spoleto scanned the table, looking each of them in the eye. "We are agreed?" The Twelve pushed back from the table and stood. Spoleto continued. "Then we are in accord."

The Twelve replied in unison, "So be it."

Spoleto caught Russo's eyes and gave him a nod. Russo rose from his chair and quietly left the room.

CHAPTER 19

IRAN

LATE IN THE AFTERNOON, Jiroft left the Dizin Hotel and strolled around the grounds. Near the ski lift he took a seat on a secluded bench. A few minutes later, Malenkov arrived. Jiroft looked up at him as he approached. "They failed," he said with a dour look.

Malenkov took a seat beside him. "One of them failed," he countered. "Two of them worked perfectly. You did not have to bring that up in front of Sahab."

Jiroft gave him a sullen look. "Because of your failure, three of our men are dead."

"It was not a total loss. The talks have been canceled. The region is in disarray."

"They were good men," Jiroft insisted. "Because of your stupid mistakes, the prime minister is still alive and America is more committed than ever to the protection of Israel."

Malenkov crossed his legs. "I did not sell them with a guarantee."

Jiroft leaned away. "Will the plutonium we discussed today work better than your missiles?"

Malenkov looked at him. "What would you like me to do?"

"Make it right," Jiroft demanded.

"You would like a replacement? Recruits are becoming more difficult to find. Mistakes are costing us an advantage."

"That was a risk you assumed." Malenkov smiled at Jiroft. "What about something else?"

"You have more worthless junk you wish to dump on us?"

"What about a suitcase bomb?"

"Suitcase bomb," Jiroft scoffed. "That is only one more Russian myth."

"This myth is a reality."

"And what power do these suitcase bombs possess? The same weak impotence of your missiles?"

"These are one-kiloton bombs."

"Kilotons." Jiroft shook his head. "You make up words no one understands so that you sound important."

"A mile," Malenkov said. "Set one off in a city, and they will level everything for two kilometers in all directions."

Jiroft was silent, then he cut his eyes in Malenkov's direction. "Perhaps you will make the missiles right by supplying the plutonium for free."

Malenkov folded his arms across his chest. "What if the suitcase bomb was located inside the United States?"

"What good does that do me? My people are committed to the fight against Israel," Jiroft snapped. "An attack against America does me nothing now."

"You think that hitting the Great Satan does nothing to help you against the Little Satan?"

"Ask Saddam Hussein what good it did him to help al-Qaeda. Ask the men lost in the mountains of Afghanistan. America's time will come, but first we will slaughter the Jews."

"And if there was a way to get this suitcase out of America, would that make a difference for you?"

"Please." Jiroft was even more indignant. "Talk to me when you are serious." He stood. "We will buy your plutonium because that is what I was sent here to do. But there will be no more sales of other items until this matter is resolved."

Malenkov's tone changed. "I am serious. And it can be yours to do with as you like, for free. Will that set things right?"

Jiroft stood. "Show me such a suitcase bomb, and then we will talk about your debt."

CHAPTER 20
JERUSALEM

TWO DAYS LATER, Zalman Rabinovich, deputy director for Mossad, stepped from a car onto the sidewalk at the western gate to Hebrew University. He made his way across the street to the Aroma espresso bar and took a seat at a table near the back. A few minutes later the front door opened and John Somerset, the cultural attaché from the U.S. Embassy, stepped inside. Somerset took a seat at the table across from Rabinovich.

Somerset looked nervous. "A little strange meeting here in the open, isn't it?"

Rabinovich smiled. "In the heart of danger is where we shall find safety."

"I trust Prime Minister Roham is well."

"Yes," Rabinovich nodded. "He survived the incident with no harm at all."

"And I assume you had something in particular you wanted to see me about."

Rabinovich scooted his chair closer to the table and leaned forward. "We have obtained certain information." His voice was low. "Information of critical importance to our countries."

Somerset's eyes darted to the side, checking their surroundings. "And what sort of information is that?"

"You are familiar with Leonid Malenkov?"

"Yes," Somerset nodded.

"We have reason to believe he sold the missiles to the Palestinians. The missiles used in the attempt against the prime minister."

"And how do you know this?"

"Two days ago he traveled from his home in Austria to a resort outside Tehran."

"Dizin?"

"Yes."

"While there, he met with two men. Hossein Jiroft and Sahabzada Ayub."

"We have been tracking Ayub."

"You were aware of his visit to Iran?"

"Yes. But we have limited capability inside Iran."

"The meeting was arranged under the guise of discussing the sale of uranium for reactors in Iran and Pakistan."

"What was the real subject?"

"Weapons-grade plutonium."

Somerset was stricken. "You are certain of this?"

"Yes." Rabinovich reached inside his jacket and took out an envelope. "They have been communicating through posts left on various Internet Web sites." He handed the envelope to Somerset. "You will see what I mean from these notes."

"How does this connect Malenkov to the attack on the prime minister?"

"Leonid Malenkov has an uncle—Demetrius Nilus. He's been funding his retirement by selling off Russian military hardware. While Malenkov was there, he had a conversation with Jiroft about the missile failure."

"I don't suppose Jiroft was in an agreeable mood."

"No," Rabinovich said, shaking his head. "He was not and even threatened their arrangement for the plutonium. But Malenkov offered him a very enticing deal as a way of making up for the problem with the missile."

"What was that?"

"He offered Jiroft a suitcase bomb."

The color drained from Somerset's face. "Are you serious? Can he deliver it?"

Rabinovich leaned even closer. "That is the worst part. He says the suitcase is already in the United States."

Somerset took a deep breath and leaned away from the table. "You are certain of this?"

"As sure as one can be in our line of work."

Somerset turned away, his eyes fixed on the wall at the opposite side of the room.

"But there is one more thing," Rabinovich continued. "I have been instructed to tell you that Israel will not allow the delivery of the plutonium to either of these countries. Under any circumstances. Even if it means a confrontation with Russia."

CHAPTER 21
RHODES

ANTONIO BELISCONI SPENT HOURS searching the contents of Angelo Giovanni's Blackberry. He read the messages and scrolled through the contacts list. Though many of the names sounded familiar, he had no way of knowing which ones were important. Most of the names on the list were written out in full, but others were noted only by a phrase or single word, and some had no notation at all. He was certain the information was valuable—Father Magdilani would be delighted to receive it—but Belisconi was unsure how to retrieve the information from the phone and send it to him in a useable format.

As he continued to study the phone, Belisconi was also keenly aware that time was running out. Giovanni wasn't the smartest person in the Castle, but he wasn't dumb, either. He would eventually determine the last time he knew where the phone was located, work backward from that point, and figure out who was present when the phone went missing.

In desperation, Belisconi took the phone to a computer store in Falirakion, a town located a few miles south of the apartment where he lived on Eden Roc Bay. A young clerk in the store listened thoughtfully to Belisconi's predicament.

"With the right cord," he nodded, "you could connect the phone directly to your computer and copy the files straight to your hard drive. But I don't have a cord that will fit the port on this phone."

"Anything else I can do?"

"Oh, there's always something else." The clerk's eyes danced as he reached under the counter. "You can use this." He held up an electronic device wrapped in plastic packaging.

Belisconi frowned. "What's that?"

"This is a Segus slotted zip drive."

"And it does what?"

The clerk had an amused smile. "You don't know much about this, do you?"

"Not really."

"Well, it works rather simply." The clerk turned the phone over and pointed to a cover on the back. "You open this cover. It will pop off." He glanced up at Belisconi. "Inside you will find a SIM card. It's a little bigger than your thumbnail, but not much."

"How do I know which thing it is?"

"It will say 'SIM' on the back." Belisconi nodded. The clerk continued. "You pop that SIM card out with your thumbnail." He reached under the counter once more and brought out a second package that held a thin plastic device about the size of a credit card. "You stick the SIM card into this. It's a SIM card adapter." He pointed. "There's a clip on the back that will hold the SIM in place."

"Then what?"

The clerk gestured with the adapter in his hand. "Slide the adapter card with the SIM card attached into the zip drive."

"Okay."

"Connect the zip drive to your computer with a USB cord."

"What's a USB cord?"

The clerk reached under the counter once more and brought out another package. "This," he replied, gesturing with the package. "Once you get all that connected, you'll still need a program to actually read the SIM card, but there are tons of those available as freeware."

"Freeware?"

"Free software. Just do a quick Internet search and you'll pull up a zillion sites that offer free programs. Find one that lets you read SIM cards, download it to your computer, and you're in business."

Belisconi gestured to the three packages that lay on the counter. "How much is all of this going to cost?"

The clerk pointed to the Blackberry. "Not as much as replacing that phone. And you'll be up and running in just a few minutes." Belisconi gave him a skeptical look. "Really," the clerk insisted. "It's not nearly as complicated as it sounds. You'll see."

Belisconi returned to his apartment and set the electronic gear on a desk that stood along the wall opposite the door. He took his laptop from a leather satchel, set it on the desk, and raised the screen. While the computer booted up, he moved across the room to the stove and put on the kettle for a cup of tea.

As the kettle heated, Belisconi sat at the desk with the Blackberry facedown in the palm of his hand. Using his thumbnail, he pried open the cover on the back and flipped the SIM card from its pocket. Pinching it carefully between his thumb and forefinger, he lifted the card from the phone and gently inserted it into the SIM card adapter. With the card securely attached, he slid the adapter into a slot on the zip drive.

Just then, the kettle whistled. He rose from the desk, took the kettle from the stove, and prepared a cup of tea. After a sip or two, he returned to the desk and connected the zip drive to the laptop with the USB cord.

"Let me see if this works."

Just as the clerk had suggested, a quick search of the Internet located a freeware program that allowed him to read the SIM card. He downloaded the program and copied the card to a file on the laptop. When he was certain he could read the copy on the laptop, he disconnected the zip drive and returned the SIM card to Giovanni's cell phone. Then he turned on the cell phone and scrolled down the contacts list, comparing the list on the phone to the list he'd copied to the laptop. Satisfied they were the same, he switched off the phone and laid it aside.

Belisconi paused for a moment and took another sip of tea as he thought about what to do next. He could email the file to Father Magdilani, or he could send it directly to Archbishop Damaskinos. Either way, sending the file with an email would create a trail that led back to Belisconi's computer. *They will know it came from me. My email address will be attached to it. And who knows where that email will eventually end up.* At the same time, sending it to Damaskinos destroyed any sense of deniability for the Archbishop and it would link him to Belisconi and the disappearance of Giovanni's cell phone. Giovanni would know the Archbishop was suspicious about the Order's activities.

Better to send it to Father Magdilani. He will know what to do with it and if it creates a trail back to me, that is how it must be.

Belisconi moved the cursor across the computer screen to an icon for Outlook Express and opened the program. In the email box he created a brief message to Magdilani, then attached the file that held the contents of the SIM card from Giovanni's phone. As he moved the cursor to send the message, Belisconi heard the apartment door creak open behind him. Before he could move he felt the cold hard steel of a pistol barrel pressed against the back of his head.

"Do not turn around," a voice behind him said.

"Who are you?"

"Where is the cell phone?"

"Right here." Belisconi took it from the desk with his left hand and held it up. "I was going to return it tomorrow."

"That will not be necessary."

Belisconi sat motionless, awaiting what he knew was certain to come next. Behind him, he heard a rustling noise and felt the gun slide low near the base of his skull. Moving gently, almost imperceptibly, Belisconi pressed his index finger against the computer mouse and felt it click beneath the pressure. An instant later, he heard the sound of the pistol as it fired.

His eyes opened wide as the bullet burst into his skull and ripped a path across his brain. He blinked as it reached the bone of his forehead and exploded out the front, spewing blood across the laptop keyboard. As his head pitched forward, a dialog box on the screen indicated the email had been sent. By then he was dead.

CHAPTER 22
WASHINGTON, D.C.

THE FOLLOWING MORNING, Paul Bryson looked out the window and stared down at the Potomac River. From his office on the eighth floor of the Watergate Building, he had a commanding view of the river and the Virginia suburbs on the opposite side. As he stood there enjoying the view, he thought of Esther and a smile came to his face. In his mind he saw her eyes, dark and mysterious, peering out at him, her auburn hair cut just below her ear, the angle of her jaw as it sloped down to her narrow chin. In his heart he wanted to throw his calendar out the window and run off to find her. They could go for a ride or a walk. Have lunch or just sit and watch the world go by. But right then he had clients from Lexar Technologies, waiting for him on Capitol Hill. They were scheduled for a meeting with key senators about details of a defense proposal. Lexar needed their support and the business that support could bring. Bryson needed the consulting fee. He glanced at his watch. "I'm late," he sighed.

Reluctantly, he turned away from the window and took a folder from his desk. He shoved it into a leather briefcase that sat on the floor. He grabbed a pen and legal pad from the drawer and added them to the case, then snapped it shut. With the case in hand, he stepped from his office, made his way down the corridor, and pressed a button for the elevator.

From the eighth floor, he rode down to the underground garage beneath the building. His car was parked on the second level. When the elevator doors opened, he started toward the far side of the floor. As he came around a support column, he saw Steve Taylor leaning against the front fender of his car.

When terrorists struck the Pentagon on September 11, Bryson's wife died in the horrific explosion that followed. At the time, Taylor, whose desk sat only a few feet from hers, was on the other side of the building. She died. He survived. At first, the irony of that coincidence drew the two men together and they met regularly for coffee or lunch to console one another. Bryson found solace in hearing firsthand accounts of the explosion and response. Taylor sought relief from the guilt he felt at not being the one who died. Later, both men slowly picked up the pieces of their lives. The incident became more difficult for them to discuss. Over time, their friendship faded.

As Bryson approached the car, Taylor moved away from the fender and stood up straight. "I was just on my way to see you." He patted the hood of the car and smiled. "Saw your car. Got lost in remembering those conversations we used to have."

Bryson found Taylor's comment odd, but kept his thoughts to himself. "What's going on, Steve?"

The two men shook hands. Taylor looked nervous. "I just wanted to see you before you go the Hill." His eyes darted away. "Give you a heads-up."

"Oh?" Bryson was puzzled. "About what?"

The smile left Taylor's face. "I understand you've been seeing Esther Rosenberg."

"Yes."

"That's not good, Paul." Taylor shook his head. "Not good at all."

Bryson was offended by the sudden intrusion into his privacy, but he did his best to hide it. "What's wrong with me seeing her?"

"Lexar provides critical technology to the Army."

"And?"

"And you have several other clients that do business with DoD."

"What's your point, Steve?"

"Come on, Paul. You know what I mean." Taylor lowered his voice. "Esther Rosenberg represents Israel."

Bryson unlocked the car. "She has some clients from Israel, I think."

"For crying out loud." Taylor's voice became more emphatic. "She's a spy, Paul."

"She's not a spy." Bryson opened the car door and tossed his briefcase to the far side of the front seat. "She's a lawyer, Steve. An American lawyer. Just because she's Jewish and loves Israel, doesn't make her a spy!"

"She's a spy. And I don't think the General Counsel's office would like it if they find out you're seeing her."

The hair on the back of Bryson's neck bristled. "What business is it of theirs who I see?"

"Okay." Taylor raised his hands in a defensive gesture. "I'm just saying." He dropped his hands to his side. "As a friend." He looked Bryson in the eye. "This may cause you some problems. Probably not at the meeting today, but in the very near future."

"Are you threatening me?"

"No, Paul. I'm trying to help you."

"Did somebody send you over here to tell me this?"

"No." Taylor held up his hands in protest. "Nobody sent me. I didn't come here to start trouble. I'm just here as a friend." He backed away. "That's all."

With that, Taylor turned and started across the deck toward the stairway. When he reached the doorway he glanced back at Bryson. "I'm just saying, Paul, you need to do something about this."

Bryson dropped into the front seat of the car and put the key in the ignition. With a twist of his wrist, the SUV's engine came to life. He pulled the door closed and switched on the air-conditioner. The cool air felt good against his damp skin. For the first time, he realized his hands were trembling.

"The nerve of that guy," he whispered. "I should have punched him."

From the parking deck, Bryson steered the car onto Virginia Avenue and drove east. Near the White House, he turned onto Constitution Avenue. By the time he reached the Washington Monument, he began to consider what Taylor had said.

Perhaps Taylor was right. Perhaps seeing Esther wasn't good, on several levels. Their relationship could never work out long term. "She's Jewish," he said to himself. "I'm Christian. I'm a Believer, she's not." He shrugged his shoulders. "Well, that's not exactly right. She believes in God, but she doesn't think Jesus is the Christ."

As the car continued east, his thoughts became a prayer and as he prayed he thought again of how odd and awkward it was to find Taylor in the parking garage.

They hadn't seen each other in years. And yet there he was, standing by the car, waiting for him. For what? Warning him like they were old friends? Had he heard something? Was trouble really brewing? And was Steve Taylor the kind of person whose advice he would seek or accept as a guide for his life?

"I don't think so," Bryson whispered to himself. "I like Esther. I enjoy being with her. Something inside me comes to life when I'm with her." He turned in front of the Capitol building and searched for an open parking spot. "They can take all my business if they like." He found a space and brought the car to a stop. "I'll go home to Texas a happy man."

CHAPTER 23
LAS VEGAS, NEVADA

THAT SAME DAY, the NEST Director's Brief included a report of Mossad's eavesdropping on Malekov's meeting at Dizin, Iran. As Rios turned to the third page, he picked up the telephone receiver and pressed a button on the keypad. A moment later, his assistant answered.

"Yes, sir?"

"Get me a car," Rios grumbled. "And tell Morris to meet me at the command center right away." He hung up the phone without waiting for a reply.

A few minutes later, a car arrived in front of the building. The driver held the rear door open as Rios came from the building and climbed inside. He read the remainder of the report while they rode. Ten minutes later, he arrived at the command center.

Unlike situation rooms at other government agencies, the NEST command center was not designed to accommodate curious operatives or interested government officials. Instead of a spacious showplace, the room was crowded and cramped. Large flat screens lined all four walls and every bit of available floor space was filled with computers, monitors, and workstations operating software developed for the specific purpose of collecting and monitoring information from every facet of daily life, both in the United States and in countries around the world.

Manned around the clock, the command center regularly monitored several incidents each day, many of them serious threats to national security.

Randall Morris was waiting in the corridor outside the center when Rios arrived. "What's up?"

"You remember I asked you to have someone look into those postings NSA found on Internet Web sites?"

"Yes."

"Who did you give it to?"

"Jeff Howell."

"Good. I like the way he works."

"Something new happen?"

Rios handed Morris the report of Malenkov's conversation with Jiroft. Morris read it quickly. "Think Malenkov was telling the truth?"

"I don't know. But I don't want to be the one who gets this wrong."

"So where do we go from here?"

"Let's get into it a little deeper."

Rios pushed open the door to the command center. Morris followed him inside but lingered near the back of the room. Rios made his way to an operator seated at a workstation near the center of the room. "Punch up a map of the Caspian Sea."

The operator pressed keys on his keyboard and pointed to the right. "It's on the big screen."

Rios studied the map a moment. "What do we have in the area?"

The operator shuffled through some papers on the desk and scrolled through several screens on his monitor. "Not much, sir. CIA has a pursuit team in Baku. Navy has an Orion on station there. Nearest NSA post is in Tbilisi."

"That's it?"

"Yes, sir. Other than what we have in Iraq and Afghanistan."

Rios studied the map a moment longer, then pointed to the next screen. "Put up a profile of Leonid Malenkov." Seconds later, Malenkov's picture appeared on the screen along with a summary of information about him. Rios glanced back at the operator. "What do we have on Sahabzada Ayub?"

"Not much." A picture of Ayub appeared on a screen. "Pakistan intelligence official. Born in Karachi. Educated at St. John's College in London."

"What about Hossein Jiroft?"

A picture appeared on another screen. "Iranian. Born in Tehran. Ties to a dozen extremist organizations. Appears to be a government operative. CIA suspects he coordinates terrorist activities. Implicated in the bombing of our embassy in Spain. Thought to have been involved in the Christmas Day attempt in Detroit. Helped facilitate the plot to use UPS packages to deliver bombs to the U.S."

Rios studied the screens a moment, then turned back to the room. "Okay," he said loudly. "Let me have your attention a moment." Analysts seated around the room looked up at him. "We have a developing situation in the Middle East." He stepped to the screen showing a picture of Malenkov. "I'm sure you're all familiar with Leonid Malenkov. He and his uncle, Demetrius Nilus, have been selling Russian weapons to the highest bidder for years. Three days ago Malenkov met with operatives from Iran and Pakistan." Rios pointed to the other screens. "He met with these two men, Sahabzada Ayub and Hossein Jiroft. Ayub works for Pakistani intelligence. Jiroft acts as a middleman for the Iranian government. He coordinates government support for Hezbollah, Hamas, Palestinian Islamic Jihad and a long list of other Islamic fundamentalist organizations. They met in Iran supposedly to discuss sale of fuel for reactors in Iran and Pakistan. What they actually discussed was the sale of weapons-grade plutonium."

"Jeff Howell has been analyzing this for us." Rios turned to him. "Jeff, why don't you answer that question."

"I wouldn't discount the uranium angle just yet. For the past several years Iran has been getting uranium through Africa from the Chinese. Until recently, Pakistan got its fuel from us. We pressured the Chinese to end their support of Iran's program. To get them to agree, we had to withdraw our support for Pakistan. Both countries have been searching for new sources. Their diplomats have pushed the issue with a number of countries and their operatives have been working the black market."

Someone spoke up. "Any contact with North Korea?"

"They've tried, but the North Koreans have steered clear of Pakistan. China has let them know that any assistance they give to Pakistan will cost them their Chinese support. The North Koreans depend on China completely. The Russians see this as an opening for them to become a bigger player in the region."

Ken Aycock spoke up. "So, what about the plutonium? Think there's anything to it?"

"Russia certainly has weapons-grade plutonium. And they have it to spare. Malenkov's uncle, Demetrius Nilus, is commanding officer over their largest nuclear weapons decommissioning facility. Has control of an enormous stockpile."

"But don't we have observers there?"

"Yes. But that hasn't prevented problems in the past. And," Rios continued, "there's even more to the story. As you are aware, there was a recent attempt on the life of the Israeli prime minister. He survived because one of the Russian missiles used in the attack failed. Apparently, those missiles had been purchased by Jiroft from Malenkov. At the meeting in Iran, Jiroft confronted Malenkov about the failure. Malenkov offered to make it good by supplying Jiroft with a suitcase bomb." Rios paused a moment. "A suitcase bomb he claims is, or very shortly will be, in the United States."

A groan went up from the room. "Impossible."

"Not as tough as it seems," Howell offered.

"How? How are they going to get a suitcase bomb—assuming one exists—into the United States?"

"Trawler off the coast of Florida," Howell suggested. "Swim it ashore. Bring it in with a diplomatic mission. Get it to an oil rig in the Gulf of Mexico, bring it in from there on a crew boat."

"They could have smuggled one in years ago," someone added. "In the 1970s, before we had any effective countermeasures."

"Or, it could be one of ours," someone chuckled.

"Okay," Rios called out. His face was serious. "First of all, this is not a joke. I know you all think the suitcase bomb was an idea from the 1980s that everyone tried and abandoned because the thing is just too heavy. But we can't exclude the possibility that this is real. Myth or not, our job is to take serious threats seriously. I expect you to do your homework. There are a thousand ways this could go down. I need you to check your sources. And then double-check them. We have to assume Malenkov isn't just blowing smoke here." The room fell silent. Rios gestured with both hands. "Get busy." Suddenly the room came alive with activity.

Rios glanced across the room and caught Howell's eye. Howell came from his desk and met Rios at the operator's workstation near the center of the room. Rios leaned close and lowered his voice. "I want you to dig into Malenkov." He tapped Howell on the chest as he spoke. "Find out everything there is to know about him. Phone logs. Girlfriends. His mother's shoe size. Whatever there is to know about him."

"Right," Howell nodded.

"We need it quickly. They're up to something and we have to figure out what it is before we have a catastrophe on our hands."

Howell returned to his desk. Rios turned to the operator. "Contact Interpol. Ask them to flag Jiroft's passport. Ask them for assistance in locating him. We need to know where he is now, but we also need to know where he's been."

"Yes, sir."

"And tell the Navy to have their Orion patrol the Caspian Sea."

"Not much space for that, sir. Russia claims most of it as theirs."

"I don't care what the Russians claim. And I'm not *asking* the Navy for help. This is NEST. Tell them to do it."

"Yes, sir."

Rios moved to the back of the room and stood near Morris. "Think there's anything to it?"

"I think our people are working in the right direction. Howell gave a rather thorough account of where things are. More in that two-minute sketch than most people in Washington know about the situation."

"The Middle East is so fractured. Difficult to know which direction the wind's blowing, even when it's hitting you in the face."

"Interesting that we still have people, even right here in this room, who are skeptical that the Russians have suitcase bombs."

"Not a program anyone wants to talk about. Especially after the trouble at Rocky Flats."

"That was bad," Morris nodded. They were silent a moment, then Morris spoke up again. "Are we calling this a threat?"

"Not yet. We need to fill in the details a little better. Once we announce this, everyone will want in on it."

Morris grinned. "You're learning."

"You taught me well," Rios smiled. "Build this thing one step at a time."

"Any idea how you'd stop them from delivering the plutonium?"

"I'm working on a plan. But it isn't our call in the end. The president will have to make that one."

CHAPTER 24
WASHINGTON, D.C.

ESTHER ROSENBERG SAT ON A BENCH inside the synagogue
at Sixth and I streets. Empty and quiet, she found it peaceful and invit-
ing. When she was a young girl, she attended Sabbath services near her
home because her parents made her join them. Now she came to pray,
meditate, and remind herself the cause to which she was devoted was
God's and that He was in control. But that day she came not because
of issues with Israel, but because of Paul and the struggle with their
differences.

As she sat there, staring blankly at the bimah, she remembered a
time when she was in high school, struggling with God and His will for
her life. One day, Rabbi Feldman saw her sitting on a bench very much
like the one in which she was now sitting. They talked awhile about
many things and then she told him of her frustration. "I don't know
what to do about college and which way to go. I pray, but God doesn't
speak."

Rabbi Feldman took her hand and turned it palm up. "This is you,"
he said, pointing to the center of her palm. "This is your life and all the
choices you could make." He drew an imaginary circle around the edge
of her palm. "God already knows the outcome of each of those choices,
but he has given us the amazing gift of free will. He has respected us

in that way. It is part of His image in which we were created. He knows the outcome, but you must choose. The more you know Him, the more you learn from Torah, the better your choices will be. But here's the important part—He knows your heart. And as long as you pursue Him, He will work within the context of your choices to do His will."

"So it's not just about picking the right one."

"No. There are many obviously wrong choices. And there are many obviously good ones. You should strive to pick the best, but you cannot wait for the perfect. God alone knows that. Only He is perfect."

The memory of that moment brought a fresh sense of hope to Esther. Whether she continued to see Paul—whether they married or not—was not a life-or-death decision. God would not abandon her because of her choice. He would not—

A buzzing sound from her cell phone interrupted her thought. She took it out and checked the screen. A text message appeared as a single word. "Jefferson."

She closed the phone with a sigh. "They always call me in the middle of something else."

Esther walked out of the synagogue and crossed the street to her car. She got in behind the steering wheel and started the engine. As she drove away from the curb, she glanced in the rearview mirror. A dark blue sedan pulled out from a parking space behind her. Unfazed, she made her way over to 14th Street.

At the Tidal Basin she turned onto Ohio Street and rode around to the Jefferson Memorial. As she turned into the parking lot, the blue sedan moved to the lane beside her and sped past. She found a parking space and brought the car to a stop, then got out and strolled leisurely toward the memorial, doing her best to attract as little attention as possible. Reuben Brody was waiting for her near the statue. He glanced around, checking. "They followed you?"

"Yes." Esther rolled her eyes. "You do this like it's some big secret. You ought to just come to my office."

"Seriously." He glanced over his shoulder behind them. "They shouldn't be following you like that. I could have someone speak to them."

"Don't bother." She dismissed him with a wave of her hand. "They've become like old friends. What did you want?"

"You saw Wiseman? How is he?"

"Okay, I think. Having some trouble with a tooth but they were supposed to fix it."

Brody turned away from the statue and led her slowly toward the back of the rotunda. "What did he say about the missiles? Any ideas on who supplied them?"

"He says Demetrius Nilus is the source. Probably sold them through his nephew, Leonid Malenkov."

"That's what the operations center thinks." His eyes darted away from her. "We told the Americans most of what we know about Malenkov's meeting in Iran."

Esther shook her head. "I don't like it."

"If the threat is credible, they need to know."

She looked up, as if reading the inscription along the top of the wall. "We have a habit of forgetting our friends."

"Couldn't be avoided. The U.S. is still our closest ally, and we need their help. We can't face our enemies without them."

"Well," she grumbled. "They can't keep their mouths shut."

"I know, but we had no choice. We had to tell them. And besides, telling them forces them to choose."

Esther looked Brody in the eye. "What if they do not choose wisely?"

"We will worry about that later. Any realistic chance of getting Wiseman released?"

"We're making progress. Time has helped. The change in personnel at Justice has been good."

"He's been in there a long time."

"Too long. But there isn't much we can do through the legal system."

"He is still our greatest expert on these matters. Detained all this time, and still his depth of knowledge about the people involved is unsurpassed."

"He's smart, that's for sure."

"Which is why I wanted to see you." Brody moved from the rotunda to the grassy lawn. "We have information from our source at Rhodes."

"Rhodes?" Esther frowned. "We have a source on Rhodes?"

"Had," Brody emphasized. "He was murdered. But he managed to send an email. Rather cryptic."

"Which was?"

"'They are releasing the four angels.'"

"That's it?" Esther looked over at him. "That's the message?"

"Yes," Brody nodded. "Any idea what that means?"

"That was the entire message?"

"Yes."

"Strange," Esther shrugged. "I have no idea what it means."

"Cohen and the operations center in Beersheba would like your input on it. So, see what you can find out. And keep working for Wiseman's release. We need him free." Brody turned away and started back toward the memorial rotunda. Esther continued on to her car.

CHAPTER 25
LANGLEY, VIRGINIA

BRYSON'S MEETING ON CAPITOL HILL went off without any mention of Esther or the concerns Taylor had raised earlier that day. When the meeting was over, Bryson returned to his car for the drive back to the office. As he steered through traffic he replayed that conversation with Taylor over and over in his mind. And once again doubts began to surface about Esther and the nature of her work. Could she really be a spy? And what do spies do, anyway? She was a lawyer. She went to court, appeared with executives for testimony before Congress, and interceded on their behalf with government agencies.

Still, he had the nagging sense that more was at stake. Taylor hadn't shown up in the parking garage by accident and what he said was more a threat than friendly warning. "Steve Taylor doesn't care whether I lose business or not." He was up to something, and Bryson wanted to know what was really happening. When he reached the office, he picked up the phone and placed a call to Doyle Thompson.

Thompson had grown up in Sylvester, Georgia, a small town in the southern half of the state not far from Albany. After graduating from high school he attended the University of Georgia as a National Merit Scholar and majored in European History. During his senior year, he was recruited by the CIA. He began working for the Agency as an analyst at its headquarters in Langley, Virginia. At the same time, he enrolled at Georgetown University and obtained a master's degree in Middle Eastern History.

After three years at Langley, he was sent overseas and posted to the U.S. Embassy in Beirut, Lebanon, as a political officer. Three years later, at the height of the Lebanese Civil War, the embassy staff evacuated the city. When everyone else left, Thompson stayed behind with a Marine Corps Scout Sniper platoon that had been assigned to the CIA as a Counterterrorism Pursuit Team—a platoon comprised of two-man sniper teams that patrolled the city in search of targets among Hezbollah leadership. Thompson continued to work as an analyst, reading and analyzing captured documents, but the lure of covert operations overtook him and soon he was fully engaged in an effort to bring all the CIA's resources to bear on the situation in Lebanon.

Thanks in part to Thompson's efforts, an uneasy peace brought an end to the war in Lebanon. Thompson was sent to Saudi Arabia as the U.S. began a buildup for the Persian Gulf War. He remained in Riyadh for three weeks and then mysteriously disappeared, later to surface among the Kurds in northern Iraq. With a penchant for insinuating more authority than he had, Thompson established a supply chain through Turkey that delivered food and weapons in support of Kurdish separatists. Using a few well-placed phone calls and the right government forms, he established a satellite link that gave the Kurds access to the U.S. aerial surveillance system. Through it, the Kurds acquired real-time battlefield information and a decided advantage over Saddam Hussein's army. By the time the Americans had liberated Kuwait, the Kurds had formed their own parliament and were governing themselves. Three days before they were to declare formal independence, the CIA station chief in Ankara discovered their plan. Thompson was hastily removed and Kurdish leaders were forced to abandon their move to form a separate state.

With a record of success, but a growing reputation as a rogue agent, Thompson was sent to Kampala, Uganda, where it was assumed he could do no harm. Within weeks of his arrival, he made contact with rebel leaders who were using Uganda as a base for attacks into the Congo. Thompson's seemingly unlimited supply of weapons and information quickly won the leaders to his side. Then, with their trust and allegiance secured, he began to divert rebel units from civil war in the Congo to attacks on foreign interests operating in the region. Thompson rather quickly focused their attention on Chinese companies that were mining gold and drilling for oil. His plan was to stage a rebellion among laborers that would render the Chinese effort unprofitable. Those plans fell apart when a rebel lieutenant leaked Thompson's plan to assassinate a visiting Chinese vice premier.

The evidence was dubious, but to avoid an international incident Thompson was quietly recalled to Langley and assigned to the Middle East analyst group. He languished there, chained to a desk and given only limited tasks, until a Congressional subcommittee chaired by Bryson turned its attention to a covert CIA program designed to target and eliminate terrorist leadership inside Pakistan. Bryson's interest in the program put him in touch with the CIA's Middle East analysis group, where he met Thompson. The two became friends and, working together, saved the program from numerous budget-cutting attempts. Thompson remained with the analysis group but his successful work with the subcommittee and his newfound clout in Congress brought fresh life to his career.

When Bryson called that day, Thompson readily agreed to meet for lunch. They met at Sweet Leaf Café on Chain Bridge Road not far from CIA headquarters. Bryson was waiting when Thompson arrived.

"Thanks for coming."

The two men shook hands, and then took seats opposite each other at a corner table. Thompson picked up a menu. "How's business?"

"It's good," Bryson replied. "I think."

"Oh?" Thompson peered around the menu with a puzzled look. "Something wrong?"

"I'm not sure. That's part of the reason I wanted to see you."

"I'll help if I can." Thompson laid aside the menu. "What's up?"

A waiter appeared and took their order. When he was gone, Bryson continued. "Do you know Steve Taylor?"

"Works at the Pentagon? Yeah, I've met him a few times."

"He came to see me today."

"Trouble with some of your Defense clients?"

"He seems to thinks so."

"What about?"

"For the past few months I've been seeing a woman named Esther Rosenberg."

"The lawyer?"

"Yes. You know her?"

"Everybody knows Esther Rosenberg." Thompson took a drink of water. "She's a good lawyer."

"Taylor thinks she's a spy."

"Interesting."

"Anything to it?"

The waiter appeared again and set glasses of iced tea on the table. They waited until he was gone, then Thompson picked up the conversation.

"We used to have titles for people. Called them things like cutouts, NOCs, double agents." Thompson chuckled. "Even triple agents." He sighed. "Those were the days when things were neatly organized. Everyone followed the rules and then went home to the family at night. Seemed more like a game than a life-or-death struggle." He wiped his mouth with a napkin. "We used to hear about guys in Europe meeting their Soviet counterpart at a dinner party and discussing their latest escapades over drinks and a cigar."

"Think it really happened?"

"I don't know," Thompson shrugged. "But it made for a good story." He took a sip of iced tea. "Esther Rosenberg is not a spy. She might be talking with Mossad from time to time. In fact, I'd be surprised if she wasn't. But Esther isn't out there breaking into buildings or stuffing her purse with classified documents. She doesn't have access to anything the Israelis don't already have."

"But you think she's working for them?"

"That makes it sound more sinister than it really is."

"What do you mean?"

"Suppose she represents a client. Mossad has a question that client can answer. She conveys the question. Gets an answer. Gives it to Mossad. That sort of thing."

"So why did Steve Taylor come to see me?"

"What did he say to you?"

"That Esther was a spy. That my relationship with her would cause a problem at DoD for some of my clients."

"They might be worried that she would get you to give her some piece of information, but it wouldn't be a military secret. Your clients aren't going to give you that kind of stuff. You would have information about your client's business practices—jobs they're bidding on, how much money they've made. That information might be of use to an Israeli company that wanted to compete against your client." He shrugged his shoulders again. "But that would be a matter between you and your client, not an issue between you and DoD." He rested his hands on the table. "I doubt this is really about Esther being a 'spy' or any of that."

"Then what's it about?"

"She represents Anthony Wiseman?"

"Yes."

"I think it's probably about that. Taylor's probably worried she'll actually get the U.S. Attorney to release him."

"Why does Steve Taylor care about Wiseman?"

"Because Wiseman is a Jew," Thompson said flatly.

A frown wrinkled Bryson's forehead. "What do you mean?"

"Steve hates Jews."

"Steve? Why?"

"I don't know. But he does. And he especially hates Wiseman because he thinks he sold us out."

"Wiseman didn't sell us out."

"That's what Taylor thinks. A lot of others agree with him, too."

"How do you know that?"

"I've been in this business a long time." Thompson gave Bryson a wry smile. "I know things."

CHAPTER 26
KRASNOYARSK, RUSSIA

DEMETRIUS NILUS STOOD at the front window and stared out at the mountain rising up behind his house. Often, when he was still young and full of energy, he had wondered what it would be like to climb to the top of the mountain and gaze into the valley on the opposite side. But the mountain crest was the boundary line for the secure region. Even from the window where he stood he could see the silhouette of a guard post outlined against the sky at the very top. The guards who manned it were under separate control from the Kremlin. They would never permit him to see over the crest. But they could not keep him from dreaming about it.

A few minutes later, a black Volga sedan turned into the drive and came to a stop in front of the house. Nilus stepped outside and waited as the driver got out of the car and opened the rear door.

From the house on the mountainside, Nilus rode down the winding road to the streets of Krasnoyarsk. He sat quietly in back and watched as the buildings moved past. On the far side of town, the car turned through a gate. Guards stationed there snapped to attention as the car rolled by. Nilus acknowledged them with a tip of his head.

Beyond the gate were rows and rows of warehouses. They drove slowly past them, the driver scanning the buildings until they came to one marked with the number 21. The driver steered the car to the right and came to a stop near a door at one end of the building. As he turned to grasp the door handle, Nilus grumbled from the backseat, "Stay put. I will get the door myself."

"It is no trouble," the driver protested.

Nilus threw open the door. "Do as I say," he barked. He stepped out and slammed the car door shut behind him, then moved quickly inside the building.

Warehouse 21 was one of five weapons decommissioning centers in Krasnoyarsk, tasked with disassembling Russia's aged and outdated nuclear weapons. That day, five ballistic missiles lay on workstands positioned down the length of the building. Technicians dressed in white shirts, white pants, and long white lab coats worked carefully and quietly over each one. Cranes overhead moved intermittently, hoisting a warhead from one missile, removing the engine from one, ferrying another to a waiting trailer for final disposal.

As Nilus entered the building, he was greeted by Alexander Koppov, a short, slender man with thin gray hair and watery blue eyes. He had a forced smile as Nilus approached. "General. So good to see you."

Nilus ignored the greeting. "You have the items?"

"Yes," Koppov replied. "They are in the back."

"And they are ready for shipment?"

"You would like to see them?"

"Of course."

Koppov led the way across the building to a door on the far side. Yellow and black signs warned of a radiation hazard. Koppov paid them scant attention as he pushed open the door and stepped inside.

Beyond the door was a separate room. Spotlessly clean, it was thirty feet wide and ran the length of the building. In it were two nuclear containment casks, each roughly the size of a railcar. Koppov and Nilus walked slowly past them. Koppov glanced back with a somber look. "You would like me to open one and see the contents for yourself?"

There was a twinkle in Nilus' eye. "You can do that?"

Koppov turned sullen. "Don't be ridiculous."

"Ahh, Koppov, you never joke."

"This is not a joking business."

Nilus looked around once more, his eyes scanning the casks. "You are right about that. If you say they are ready, I believe you, and if you are wrong, our Persian friends will kill us both." He threw back his head and laughed. "So if you say they are ready, I say let them go. We will both live together, or we will both die together."

Koppov had a thin, tight smile. "Always with a joke."

"Yes," Nilus chuckled. "You should relax." He tapped his fist playfully against Koppov's shoulder. "After all, you work in a facility that could explode at any moment." Nilus laughed again. "Better enjoy life while you can." Koppov turned away. Nilus took a deep breath to gather himself, then his face turned serious. "You have arranged for shipment?"

"Yes," Koppov replied. "By rail to Makhachkala. Then a freighter will take them to Bandar Anzali." He took a clipboard from a peg on the wall and thrust it toward Nilus. "All we need is your signature authorizing their removal."

Nilus reached inside his jacket for a pen. He held the clipboard with one hand and signed the form on it with an exaggerated motion. When he was finished, he looked up at Koppov. "Now," he sighed. "What about the other items?"

Koppov tucked the clipboard under his arm and gestured with a nod. Nilus followed him from the room and across the warehouse to an office. When they were inside, Koppov pushed the door closed.

Nilus looked worried. "Is there a problem?"

"No." Koppov shook his head. "There is no problem." He moved to the opposite side of the room and swung open the door to a closet.

"They are all right here." He stepped back to reveal four cases, each the size of a large suitcase, stacked neatly inside.

Nilus moved closer, his eyes wide, his mouth open. "You keep them in your office?"

"What better place?"

Nilus glanced at Koppov. "But your office?"

"Would anyone suspect they were here?"

"I suppose not. But is it safe to have them here?" He gestured with a sweep of his arm. "Where you sit and work every day?"

"They are completely safe," Koppov assured him. "They leak no radiation. Otherwise, they would be easily detectable and useless as a weapon of surprise."

Nilus ran his hand over his face. "Are they ready for delivery?"

"Yes. But for that," Koppov smiled, "we need no papers."

A grin spread across Nilus' face. "Oh, Koppov." He wagged his finger playfully. "You are trying to make a joke."

Koppov shrugged. "I do the best that I can."

"You do well." Nilus ran his hand over one of the cases. "Very well. These came from the center at Snezhinsk?"

Koppov had a dour look. "You would really like to know?"

"No," Nilus replied. "I suppose not."

"You have someone reliable to transport them?"

"Do not worry about that." Nilus took a cell phone from his pocket. "I will arrange transportation for these myself. And it will only take a moment." He typed a text message on the phone, then scrolled down the contacts list to a number for someone named Semion, and pressed Send. A moment later, the phone beeped indicating the message had been sent. Nilus looked up with a smile. "Now it is done."

Koppov folded his arms across his chest. "You are certain this will work?"

"I am certain." Nilus reached inside his jacket to put away the phone. When he withdrew his hand he held a plain white envelope.

"Here," he said, handing it to Koppov. "If my jokes do not put a smile on your face, this should do the trick."

Koppov took the envelope from him and tore open the end. Inside was a large stack of U.S. currency. He looked up at Nilus and slowly smiled.

CHAPTER 27

MOSCOW, RUSSIA

THAT EVENING, YURI IVANOVSKY sat at a table near the back of Fabrika, a popular Moscow nightclub. Known to most simply as Ivan, he had grown up in Odintsovo, a city of a hundred thousand, not far from Moscow. As a young man, he enjoyed wrestling and had been selected for a high school that would train him for a career in competition. He had done well but at the age of nineteen he was injured and unable to continue. Alone, with no place to live, he took a job washing dishes in a restaurant. One of the cooks took pity on him and let him sleep at night in the storeroom.

While working there he met Georgy Bulganin, a small-time boss in the local Bratva, the Russian Mafia. Bulganin gave him a job collecting delinquent loans, where Ivan's athletic skills and muscular physique proved very useful. Before long, his reputation for producing income, rather than broken legs, caught the attention of more powerful men. By the age of twenty-three, Ivan was boss of a crew under Semion Mogilevich, one of the most powerful crime figures in the world.

Seated with Ivan that night at the club were six young girls. Recently brought to Russia from Bosnia, they had been lured by the promise of a career in the entertainment business. In Moscow, they were placed in apartments, furnished with new clothes, and provided with the finest that Russia had to offer, which they were told to enjoy while arrangements were made for "training." They were kept that way until they grew bored and complained, then they were presented with a bill for their expenses—exorbitant charges for transportation, clothing, meals, and housing. Unable to pay, they were forced to work off the debt in Mogilevich's nightclubs. Ivan glanced around the table at them. Soon this newest crop of women would find their duties included more than merely waiting tables as barmaids.

Just then he felt his cell phone vibrating inside his jacket. He took it from his pocket and glanced at the screen. An icon indicated a text message was waiting. He pressed a button on the phone and the message appeared. It read simply, "Outside." Reluctantly, he rose from the table. "Ladies," he announced. "I am afraid our fun will have to wait for another time."

"But you promised a night of dancing," one of the girls protested.

Ivan smiled. "I am sure you will dance until dawn." He leaned over and kissed the girl seated to his left. "And you will learn more than you ever dreamed possible about the pleasures of Russian entertainment."

He crossed the dance floor and made his way to the front entrance of the club. A doorman held open the door as he stepped outside. Parked at the curb was a black Mercedes sedan. Ivan stepped to the rear door, pulled it open, and crawled onto the backseat.

Seated on the opposite side was Alexander Kalashov, Semion's closet confidante. As Ivan closed the car door, Kalashov nodded to the driver. The car started forward. Ivan glanced across the seat. "We have trouble?"

"No." Kalashov shook his head. "We have opportunity." He patted Ivan on the leg. "Semion thought it should be yours."

"And what would he have me do?"

"Have you ever been to Krasnoyarsk?"

Ivan chuckled. "Has anyone ever been to Krasnoyarsk?"

"We have arranged a visit there for you."

CHAPTER 28
WASHINGTON, D.C.

FROM THE JEFFERSON MEMORIAL, Esther drove west along the Potomac River. By then it was late in the afternoon. Instead of returning to the office, she continued on toward Georgetown. As she drove, she thought about her conversation with Brody and the request for assistance in determining the meaning of the message they had received from Rhodes.

"They must have dozens of analysts at Beersheba. All of them trained to figure out these things. I'm just a lawyer."

Still, Esther was intrigued by the request for help and by the notion that Mossad actually had contacts inside the Order of Malta. She had first become aware of the Order and its anti-Semitic views as a teenager when her synagogue sponsored a conference on tolerance and social issues facing Jews in America. Representatives from the Anti-Defamation League gave a detailed account of the Order and its agenda. Later, while lobbying Congress for passage of hate-crimes legislation, she'd learned even more through contact with lawyers from the Southern Poverty Law Center who schooled her on the coordinated activities of American hate groups.

Any operative Mossad might have in the Order would almost certainly have come through the Catholic Church, and that most likely required the consent of the Vatican. Cooperation from Catholic leadership seemed like a good sign. *Perhaps they are serious about reining in the Order. Maybe now,* Esther thought, *they are making a concerted effort.*

When she arrived at the townhouse, Esther set her laptop on the dining room table. With a few keystrokes, she reached an Internet search engine and entered the phrase, "release the four angels." Seconds later, a list of several thousand entries appeared on the screen. Most of them pointed toward a quotation from the ninth chapter of The Revelation to John, the last book in the Bible.

She rose from the table, walked to the living room, and scanned a bookshelf. "I'm sure I have a Bible here somewhere." When her search of the shelves came up empty, she slipped on a jacket and walked down the street to a bookstore on the corner. Half an hour later, she returned with a Bible in her hand.

She sat at the table with a cup of hot tea and turned to Revelation. For the next twenty minutes she read and reread the ninth chapter, stopping to make notes on a legal pad. Finally she laid the book on the table beside the laptop and leaned back in her chair.

This phrase comes from a quotation about war. A cataclysmic war. And it happens in the Middle East. She picked up the Bible once more and read the passage out loud. "Release the four angels who are bound at the great river Euphrates." She scanned through the rest of the paragraph. "They come from the Middle East. They have been detained there—and are released there. Doesn't necessarily mean the war occurs there. But that's where the angels have been held." She thought about it a moment. "And they were set free to kill a third of mankind."

She leaned back once more. "A third of mankind. Earth's population is nearly seven billion now. A third would be over two billion people." She closed her eyes and ran her fingers through her hair. "There would be dead bodies everywhere." She leaned forward and quickly flipped through the remaining pages of the book. Images of corpses lying bloated in the sun filled her mind. "It would be impossible to dispose of that many bodies."

After a while she pushed back her chair from the table and stood. "Maybe it doesn't mean an actual number. Just a way of saying it will be really bad." She folded her arms across her chest and paced back and forth. "And I don't need to know what it means in terms of Christian theology. I need to know what the sender meant by using that phrase.

"Four angels. Angels. Messengers from God. Four messengers. Four messengers bringing devastating destruction." Her eyes opened wide. "Four armies?" She raised her hand, pointing with a finger in the air. "Four attacking forces. Four attacks with devastating consequences. A messenger with a message derived from Christian scripture."

She collapsed in the chair. "Someone is planning four attacks. They are imminent and will be apocalyptic in nature. And they are meant to send a message." She tapped a finger on the tabletop. "This can only mean a nuclear explosion. Four nuclear explosions." She turned away from the table. "But who could deliver that kind of strike?"

The Knights of Malta were large but not that large. They would need help. She ticked off the countries with nuclear capability. Russia and China could do it...Pakistan, India. Launching a straightforward attack would require participation by one of those four nations. But why would they help the Knights of Malta? What advantage would that bring them? Her eyes were wide again.

"They don't need official approval. They just need people in critical positions. And they have members in governments around the world."

By midmorning, Esther was certain her analysis of the email message was correct. *Release the four angels* was a signal that would set in motion a plan to launch four attacks—four devastating attacks. She was also certain that analysts in Israel had already reached that same conclusion, which left her wondering why Brody had asked her to review the message.

"And to get an answer for that," she smiled, "I have to play Brody's spy game."

Esther picked up her iPhone from the table and pressed the Twitter icon. When the application was loaded and ready, she logged on to

Twitter as Mary Smith. At the home page, she typed in the message "Starbucks twenty minutes," and sent it to a user @CarolinaBlue.com. Once the message was sent, she closed the application, picked up her purse, and started for the door.

From the townhouse she walked up the street to the Starbucks on M Street. At the counter she ordered a mocha frappe and bought a copy of *The Washington Post.* Coffee in hand, she took a seat at a table near the window and scanned the front page of the newspaper.

A few minutes later, Reuben Brody entered. He ordered a cup of coffee and stood near the counter while he waited. Esther watched him from the corner of her eye and did her best not to laugh as he surveyed the room, checking the faces of the people seated around the café. He smiled politely when the barista handed him a cup of coffee, then joined Esther at the table by the window.

She gave him an amused look. "Why do you do that? Walk right past me without saying a word."

"I wanted to see who was here before I acknowledged you."

"You think someone's going to shoot us while we sip coffee at Starbucks?"

"You never know who might be watching."

"They're always watching, Reuben. And they already know we talk."

"It's the way I am." Brody took a sip of coffee. "What's on your mind?"

"Four angels are the four horsemen."

He looked puzzled. "Of the apocalypse?"

"Yes," Esther replied.

"That is a Christian prophecy. What do they say it means?"

"Depends on who you talk to. But that isn't our problem. We aren't concerned with the ultimate interpretation of prophecy. All we need to know is what that phrase meant to the person who sent it, and those who received it."

"So, what are you saying?"

"The message was a signal."

"Yes, but a signal for what?"

"Four attacks."

"What kind of attacks?"

"Bombs, I think. Big bombs. Possibly nuclear. I know this sounds crazy, but the quote is from a passage in the Book of Revelation. It's a prophecy about the end of time. The Four Horsemen unleash apocalyptic devastation. The four pending attacks will be big."

Brody propped an elbow on the table. "Where would these attacks take place?"

"I don't know." Esther leaned away. "With the Order of Malta involved, I'm sure it will have something to do with us."

"Israel?"

"Maybe. Jews, for sure."

"Impressive." Brody leaned closer. "Your analysis fits perfectly with that of the center at Beersheba. But we need to know when and where this is going to happen."

"I don't know that," she groused. "I have no way of knowing it. You're the one with access to that kind of information."

"We need your ideas."

"On the timing?"

"Yes. And the location."

"What's this all about?"

"Cohen thinks Wiseman still has access to contacts that can help us. He thinks those contacts can provide us with information we need."

Esther shook her head. "Anthony is completely cut off from the outside world. He has no access to anything except the newspaper."

"And you," Brody smiled. "He has access to you."

Esther frowned. "What are you saying?"

"They would like you to get the names of Wiseman's contacts. People on the inside who agree with him and his effort to help."

Esther shook her head. "I don't think he would ever divulge that information."

"He might if you asked him."

Esther looked away. "It will take time," she sighed.

"Unfortunately, time is something we have very little of."

Esther looked at Brody. "Why do they ask me these questions?"

"Which questions?"

"Why did they ask me for my ideas about the message? Someone at Beersheba knows at least as much as I do about this. I have no better information than the general public."

"But you are the only one with access to Wiseman." Brody took another sip of coffee. "And you have a long history with these issues."

Esther took a sip from her cup. "I can't see Anthony without making an appointment."

"You should make the call."

"And there's one more problem."

"What's that?"

"I'm supposed to go to Texas with Paul this weekend. You want me to cancel that and try to see Wiseman earlier?"

"No." Brody paused to take a sip of coffee. "If you cancel the trip it will look suspicious. The Americans might notice."

"They already have."

"Follow your normal schedule, but work quickly." Brody took one last sip of coffee, then rose from his seat at the table and walked out the door.

CHAPTER 29
WASHINGTON, D.C.

THE NEXT MORNING, Paul Bryson drove downtown for breakfast with Tom Russell, president of Wenfield Industries. They met at the Liaison Hotel. Bryson arrived early and took a table near the window.

Wenfield Industries was a large corporation with divisions in heavy equipment, oil field services, and technology. Their technology unit held lucrative defense contracts to supply sensitive parts for a missile guidance system in one of the Army's newest battlefield systems. The company's headquarters was located in Houston and it had a large production facility in Dallas.

Russell and Bryson had been friends a long time. When Bryson entered politics, Russell had been instrumental in obtaining financial support for his first congressional race and he had remained a loyal donor throughout Bryson's congressional career. When Bryson quit, the company hired him as a consultant. They were one of his best clients.

A few minutes after Bryson arrived, Russell appeared at the doorway. Bryson waved him over to the table. They ordered breakfast and drank coffee while they talked.

"I'm glad you could meet me this morning," Russell began.

"Something wrong?"

"I had a meeting at the Pentagon yesterday."

"I didn't realize that was on the schedule. I would have been there if I'd known. What was it about?"

"It wasn't about anything you're working on," Russell replied. He took a sip of coffee and looked at Bryson. "They were asking about you."

"Me?" Bryson was puzzled. "What did they want to know about me?"

Russell leaned back from the table and rested his hands in his lap. "They wanted to know if we ran a security check on you before we hired you as a consultant."

Bryson frowned. "Why were they asking that?"

"They think you have ties to someone in Israel that might be a security risk."

Bryson's shoulders slumped. "Steve Taylor was at that meeting?"

"No," Russell shook his head. "Just Andy Cardwell and Ben Waldrop."

Bryson leaned back in his chair. Cardwell was Secretary of the Army. Waldrop was his general counsel. "Why would they call a meeting about something like this?"

"They're concerned, Paul. Really concerned. And they're the primary source of business for our technology unit."

"This isn't about me or some supposed security risk. This is about Esther Rosenberg." Bryson took a sip of coffee. "You know Esther. And you know she's not a spy."

"Yeah," Russell nodded. "I know Esther. And I know the Pentagon, too."

"There's nothing to it."

"Look, Paul," Russell leaned closer. "What you do with your private life is your business, but this company is my business. I can't afford a problem with the Army. I can't make my quarterly numbers without them."

Bryson set his cup aside. "What are you saying?"

"We're going to do a background investigation on you. Straight up. By the numbers. Exactly like the regulations say. And if we determine there's a security risk, we'll have to take our consulting business elsewhere."

Bryson felt his jaw muscles flex. His neck grew tense and his cheeks were warm. "Tom, we've known each other a long time. You know the only thing you'll find is Esther."

"I don't make the rules." Russell leaned back once more. "You may just have to choose between her and making a living."

"That's an easy choice." Bryson took his napkin from his lap, laid it on the table, and stood. "Forget the background check. I'll refund the balance of your retainer."

CHAPTER 30
WASHINGTON D.C.

BRYSON LEFT THE LIAISON Hotel and drove down Constitution Avenue. As he did, his mind replayed the conversation with Russell. "I don't believe this!" He banged the palm of his hand against the steering wheel in frustration. "This is all about Esther. And the reason it's about her is because of Anthony Wiseman. They think because she represents Wiseman, she's working for Israel." With the windows rolled up, his voice was loud and emphatic. "A man I don't even know is shaping my business. My future." For the first time, Bryson realized he knew nothing about Wiseman. Not where he was from, his birthplace—nothing. "But I know where to go to find out something about him."

At the next cross street he turned right and doubled back toward Capitol Hill. A few minutes later, he steered his car into a parking deck near the Capitol and made his way to the Library of Congress.

As a former congressman, Bryson still held research privileges at the library. He dug an identification card from his wallet and swiped it at the entrance, then made his way to the reception desk. A few minutes later, he was seated before a computer terminal in a booth on the second floor. With a few strokes of the keyboard, pages of information appeared on the screen.

While working at Naval Intelligence, Wiseman had completed

a graduate degree at Harvard and became an adjunct faculty member at the Naval War College. Gradually, he developed a reputation as an expert on Middle Eastern history and affairs. He spent four summers conducting research at the Jewish Historical Documentation Center in Vienna, and produced several notable papers on anti-Semitism, which received wide publication. With the help of library staff, Bryson located those papers.

Two of the papers were short summary articles dealing with the present identity and work of South American organizations that were responsible for hiding Nazis after World War II. A third article was longer and more intriguing.

Entitled "Influence of a Lie," the article showed how the book *The Protocols of the Learned Elders of Zion* lay at the root of modern anti-Semitism. It traced the book's influence beginning with the pogroms in Russia, through Hitler and the Nazis, to current radical Muslims. At the same time, the article followed the lineage and legacy of the book's author, Sergei Nilus, across several generations of the Nilus family, ending with Demetrius Nilus and his nephew, Leonid Malenkov. Bryson was astounded by what he read.

Nilus had been recruited by the Communist Party while attending technical school in Leningrad. After graduation he joined the Soviet Army, where he was sent to officer's school. Naturally suited to the army's highly structured organization, he was quickly promoted through the ranks. Along the way, he was assigned to the nuclear program where he rose to the rank of general and held command of the nuclear facilities in Krasnoyarsk.

Malenkov, his nephew, was born in Moscow but attended school in Austria, where he continued to live. He was believed to control a fortune worth many millions of dollars, but his primary occupation was as an arms dealer. His customers were Islamic terrorist organizations in the Middle East and Central Asia. Most of the arms he sold were Soviet-era equipment and munitions made available to him by his uncle from aging and unprotected Russian military stockpiles.

For the next several hours, Bryson read everything he could find about Nilus and Malenkov. Finally, a librarian handed him a one-page article. "This is the last thing we have."

The article was a brief account of a visit to the Soviet Union by Yasser Arafat. During that visit he toured the Kremlin, attended the annual May Day parade, and took an excursion to the city of Chelyabinsk. Included with the account was a photograph of Arafat standing with Soviet Prime Minister Alexie Kosygin. Behind them was a young Demetrius Nilus, dressed in an Army uniform, and next to him was a man identified in the photo caption as Shiraz Moussa.

Bryson studied the photograph a moment, then looked up at the librarian. "Can you make a copy of this for me?"

"That is a copy. You may keep it."

"Thanks," Bryson nodded as he turned back to the computer. He spent the remainder of the afternoon searching for information about Nilus' relationship to Arafat and details about Moussa.

CHAPTER 31
KRASNOYARSK, RUSSIA

DEMETRIUS NILUS STARED across the desk at Ivan. "They tell me you can do the impossible."

"I have had some success," Ivan shrugged.

"You enjoy it," Nilus chuckled. "I can tell."

"I enjoy the challenge," Ivan smiled.

"Semion tells me you have friends in many places."

"There is usually someone willing to accommodate our efforts." Ivan crossed his legs. "What about you?" He gestured to the room where they sat. "You have done well for yourself."

"Yes." Nilus rested his hands in his lap. "I suppose I have." He had a satisfied look. "By most measures."

Ivan propped an elbow on the armrest of the chair. "But you did not bring me all the way out here to discuss our mutual accomplishments."

Nilus scooted his chair closer to the desk. "We have some packages for delivery to the U.S."

"And what do these packages contain?"

"That, I cannot tell you." Nilus hunched forward, his elbows resting on the desktop. "These packages must be delivered without detection." He raised his finger for emphasis. "And without any connection to us."

"To you."

"To all of us. No one must know where they came from or who delivered them or how they arrived."

"You ask much."

"If it was easy, we would have given this task to someone else."

"You want me to bear total responsibility?"

"But in a way that no one may discover. The trail must stop with the delivery."

"These are sensitive packages."

"Yes," Nilus nodded. "They cannot pass through port inspection or be subjected to any analysis, external or otherwise."

"I am to deliver them without knowing the contents?"

"Yes. Any attempt to open them would produce devastating consequences."

Ivan looked away. "You ask a lot."

"Can you do it?"

"Yes," Ivan nodded. "It can be done. How soon do you want them delivered?"

"There are four items. They must travel separately and be delivered immediately."

Ivan raised his chin slyly. "And what do I receive for taking on this responsibility?"

Nilus twisted the Maltese ring on his finger. "This you will do for the pleasure of the wealth you have already obtained." Ivan's eyes focused on the ring. Nilus continued, "And you will do it to preserve our way of life for yourself, for your children, and your children's children."

"Well." Ivan's mouth turned up at the corners, forming a thin smile. "If this means killing Jews, I do not mind."

CHAPTER 32
WASHINGTON, D.C.

BRYSON LEFT THE LIBRARY of Congress and walked to his car. On the way, he took his cell phone from his pocket and placed a call to Doyle Thompson. "We need to talk."

"Okay," Thompson replied. "You want to do lunch tomorrow?"

"I was thinking now would be better."

"All right," Thompson said, his voice suddenly serious. "There's a parking lot where Glover Road turns into Rock Creek Park. Meet me there in half an hour."

Bryson pressed a button to end the call and turned onto Pennsylvania Avenue. Half an hour later, he arrived at the parking lot off Glover Road. Thompson was waiting for him as he came from the car.

"What's so urgent?"

"It's not urgent," Bryson replied. "I just need some answers."

Thompson led them to a picnic table a few yards away. "About what?"

"About Esther. Anthony Wiseman. And Steve Taylor."

Thompson wheeled around in Bryson's direction. "You called me all the way out here for that?"

"It's important, Doyle."

"Important?" Thompson raised his hands in frustration. "Just marry her and get it over with."

"This isn't about me and Esther." Bryson took him by the arm. "It's more than that."

Thompson looked puzzled. "What? What are you talking about?"

"I had lunch with a client this morning."

"Tom Russell," Thompson nodded. "I heard."

"How did you hear about it?"

"I hear a lot of things," Thompson shrugged.

"They're dropping me."

"I know."

"You said Esther wasn't a spy."

"I said she wasn't a spy," Thompson wagged his finger. "I never said that dating her wouldn't cause you a problem."

"This isn't just about Esther."

"I told you that already."

"I did some checking."

"Checking?" Thompson frowned. "On what?"

"Demetrius Nilus and Leonid Malenkov."

Thompson shoved his hands in his pockets. "What did you find?"

"They've made a fortune selling Russian military gear to just about everybody in the Middle East."

"Yeah." Thompson's voice took a sarcastic tone. "Tell me something new."

Bryson reached in his pocket and took out a copy of the article describing Arafat's visit to Moscow. He pointed to the photograph. "Recognize those two?"

Thompson had a quizzical look. "Yasser Arafat and Alexei Kosygin?"

"No." Bryson pointed again. "The two men standing behind them."

Thompson took the picture from Bryson and looked at it more closely. "That's Demetrius Nilus on the right."

"And the other man?"

Thompson cut his eyes at Bryson. "What are you after, Paul?"

"The man standing next to Nilus is Shiraz Moussa."

"Like I said, what are you after?"

Bryson took the photograph from Thompson. "Do you know where this picture was taken?"

"Why do you care?"

"It was taken in Chelyabinsk, Russia."

Thompson looked away. "And your point is?"

"Chelyabinsk has a lot of heavy industry and one of the things they make is rocket launchers." He moved around to catch Thompson's eye. "Arafat wasn't there to take a tour of the city's parks. He was there with Kosygin to make a deal for missiles."

"Arafat is dead," Thompson grumbled.

"And the man who was with him, Shiraz Moussa, has taken his place."

"Moussa isn't head of the Palestinian Authority."

"But Moussa is the political and spiritual successor to Arafat's Fatah movement."

"Arafat had no spirit," Thompson growled. "Look, what do you want from me?"

"Militants in Ramallah attacked the Israeli prime minister. They did it with Russian-made rockets. I think if you looked deep enough you'd find that Moussa arranged for the missiles. And if you kept digging you'd find that he bought the missiles from Malenkov and Nilus."

"What's that got to do with you and Tom Russell?"

"Tom dropped me because the Pentagon is threatening his defense contracts—because I'm his lobbyist and they don't like my association with Esther. But no one at the Pentagon knew I was seeing her until Steve Taylor told them. And Taylor knows what I just told you about those missiles. That's why he's upset."

"You think Steve Taylor had something to do with the missiles?"

"I think Taylor knew about that attack on the prime minister before it happened."

"That's a serious allegation, Paul." Thompson looked over at Bryson. "Are you hinting at treason? And how does it relate to Esther, and Taylor making trouble for you at the Pentagon?"

"Wiseman." Bryson nodded. "Taylor is afraid Wiseman will figure it out. And when the Israelis find out someone at the Pentagon was involved in an attack on their prime minister ..." Bryson's voice trailed off. "Well, it won't be pretty."

"And you think Taylor sees Esther as Israel's link to Wiseman."

"She's the only reliable link they have to him."

CHAPTER 33
DES MOINES, IOWA

LATE FRIDAY AFTERNOON, Charlie Silliman came from the hangar and looked to the north, out past the end of the runway and beyond the tangled interchange for the highway. In the distance, barely visible even in the cloudless Iowa sky, a Boeing 767 banked to the left and lined up for a landing. Charlie slipped his hands in his pockets as he watched the blue and white Aeroflot jet slowly descend. In his mind he wondered what the people onboard were like. He'd never seen anyone from Russia. "I've spent my whole life right here in Iowa. Never been farther away than Chicago, and then only for a weekend." He shielded his eyes against the glare of the setting sun. "We only went there to see…"

"Charlie," the radio squawked.

He unclipped it from his belt and pressed a button. "Yeah. What do you need?"

"Secret Service would like for you to move away from the hangar."

"Move away?" Charlie glanced around to see a man dressed in a black suit standing at the far side of the hangar door. "This is where I work," Charlie protested.

"They want the area cleared."

"Right," Charlie sighed.

All morning he'd worked with the advance team, showing them every inch of the hangar—the storm water drains outside, the towing tractors, all the ground equipment. Even the restrooms and the storage space upstairs over the office. Now they wanted him out of the way.

He turned aside and started across the tarmac toward his pickup truck. As he walked in that direction, he keyed the microphone on the radio. "Okay if I sit in the truck?"

"Negative," the operator replied.

"Negative?" Charlie raised his free hand in a gesture of frustration. "Now you're starting to sound like one of *them*."

"No can do," the operator chuckled.

"That's better," Charlie cooed. "But why not?"

"They want you to move it to the parking lot back here behind the office."

"The guy's standing about thirty yards away. Why can't he just yell at me?"

"Not part of the SOP for this Op."

"Oh, no," Charlie laughed. "They've taken out your brain and inserted a recording of government gibberish."

"They have radios, Charlie," the operator explained. "Earphones in their ears. Microphones on their wrists. They use them all the time. It's just the way they work. Bring the truck back here and have a cup of coffee."

"Now, that I can do."

Charlie climbed inside the pickup and laid his radio on the seat. He slammed the door shut, started the engine, and drove around to the back of the hangar. At the corner of the building, he turned the truck into a parking space that faced the runway and switched off the engine. He sat there behind the steering wheel and watched as the airplane touched down, then zoomed past the terminal on the far side of the airport. A few minutes later, it appeared on the taxiway, turned toward the hangar, and gently rolled to a stop near the building.

From his seat in the pickup truck, Charlie had a clear view of the airplane. Through the windows he saw faces peering out. He imagined that in the aisle behind them, others worked to take baggage from the overhead compartments. Gradually, they would move toward the front of the plane. Then the passenger door opened and the steps came out.

A Secret Service agent appeared near the plane with a ramp attendant from Hangar One. Working together they secured the steps and put the guardrails in place, then waited as passengers made their way to the ground.

One by one, people onboard the plane appeared in the doorway, gazed out on the Iowa countryside, and lumbered down the steps to the pavement below. They lingered there, talking excitedly among themselves, as if waiting for direction about what to do next.

Before they were finished unloading, three black SUVs came from the hangar and parked near the steps. When they were in place, a limousine appeared from the left. It rolled across the hangar apron and came to a stop near the gathering crowd. A moment later, the rear door of the car swung open and a man dressed in a dark gray suit stepped out.

"Well, look at that," Charlie whispered to himself. "That's the Secretary of Agriculture. No wonder the Secret Service was all over this place."

While the passengers gathered near the SUVs, a cargo door opened in the belly of the airplane's fuselage. Ramp agents moved a baggage conveyor into place. Charlie watched as they scrambled inside the plane and began unloading suitcases.

"That's Billy and Pete," he groused. "Why do they get to be out there and not me?"

In quick, well-practiced motions, Pete placed luggage on the conveyor and sent it down to the ground. From there, Billy moved it to a cart parked just a few feet away. Suitcases, cardboard boxes, and a briefcase or two. Then an aluminum case appeared on the conveyor. Two men dressed in black suits hurried forward, pointing and gesturing with both hands as they worked their way through the crowd. Just as the case neared the bottom of the conveyor belt, Pete reached for it to lift it off. One of the men elbowed him aside and grabbed it by the handle. He snatched the case from the conveyor belt and hurried with it toward one of the waiting SUVs.

As he came near the vehicle, the rear door opened. He shoved the case inside and closed the door. Then the SUV peeled away from the others parked near the plane and started across the tarmac. At the hangar, it turned left toward the parking lot and passed within a few feet of the pickup truck where Charlie sat. He watched through the side window as the SUV reached the street, turned left, and sped down the airport drive. Charlie turned sideways in the seat and followed it with his eyes as it reached the airport exit, turned left again, and disappeared up the ramp to the interstate.

As the SUV moved out of sight, the radio squawked. "Charlie."

"Yeah?"

"The guys from Hangar One want you to show them where to park the plane."

"Ask the Secret Service. I can't go out there."

"They'll be gone in a few minutes. When they leave, you can drive out there and show Billy."

"Pete's out there. Let him decide."

"Charlie." The voice on the radio had a parental tone.

"Yeah," Charlie sighed.

"Come get some coffee."

"Okay, Martha," he groused. "I'll be there in a minute." Charlie pushed open the door and stepped from the truck.

CHAPTER 34
LAS VEGAS, NEVADA

PETE RIOS SAT IN THE CORNER of the NEST command center, his feet propped up on an empty trash can, arms folded across his chest, head back, eyes closed. Suddenly, a computer warning beeped. Rios swung his feet to the floor and stood.

"What was that?"

An analyst spoke up. "A U.S. Navy Orion has detected a ship on the Caspian Sea."

"What's the ship's name?"

"*Morning Star*. Looks like it sailed from Makhachkala."

"Best guess on where it's headed?"

"Based on its size and course, analysts at CIA think it's headed for Bandar Anzali."

Rios rubbed his hands over his face and wiped his eyes with his fingers. "Any idea what it's carrying?"

"Nothing confirmed yet. They're just now getting pictures from the plane."

Rios took a deep breath. "We need to find out what it's carrying."

The operator at the center of the room spoke up. "We have a live feed from the Orion now." She pointed to a screen on the wall.

An image appeared of the freighter as it sailed the Caspian Sea.

Cargo doors that lined the top of the deck were closed, obscuring any view of the hold. Rios watched a moment, then turned to the operator. "Any way to get readings from the air? Maybe check the trailing wind?"

"They've done that already and found nothing."

"Has the White House seen this?"

"The situation room has these same images."

Rios continued to study the image on the screen. "What are they saying about it?"

"None of the analysts know of a way to find out what's in the ship."

"Any response from Israel?"

"No, sir."

"Do we know if this ship is following a regularly scheduled route?"

"I'll check."

A door to the room opened, and Randall Morris appeared. "Found something?"

"A ship," Rios pointed. "On the Caspian Sea."

"Does Israel know about it?"

"I don't know."

"If they know about it, and haven't responded, then we could assume it's not the shipment of plutonium Malenkov was talking about."

"And if it is?"

"If it is, Israel will sink that ship, and there's nothing we can do to stop them."

"That would solve a lot of problems—if it's really a shipment of plutonium."

"Any attempt on our part to stop it would be an act of war. We don't have the authority to do that. And you don't have enough information to make a recommendation to the president."

"Right." Rios glanced in Morris' direction. "Not our problem?"

"Not yet."

"Sir," the operator called out. "The ship is following a previously scheduled route. Times are not always exact, but it makes this run once or twice each week."

"Okay," Rios replied. "Tell the Navy to continue the Orion over-flights." He looked at Morris. "We'll have to hope it's not what it could be."

CHAPTER 35

EAST TEXAS

SATURDAY MORNING, Bryson and Esther came from the house and sat in a swing at the far end of the porch. Off to the left, a grassy lawn sloped toward the driveway and down to the creek on the opposite side, rose through the pasture, and disappeared beyond the cows grazing in the distance. To the right, a grove of pecan trees stood in neatly spaced rows, their gray branches bare in the autumn sunshine, the ground beneath them littered with dried brown leaves.

Bryson settled into place in the corner of the swing. He propped his left elbow on the armrest and wrapped his hand around the swing chain. His other arm rested along the back of the swing. Esther leaned against his side. Her head rested against his shoulder. "I could sit here all day," she sighed.

"Sometimes I do," Bryson replied.

"Do we really have to go tonight?"

"I'm afraid so."

"Isn't their ranch near Austin?"

"Yes."

"How will we get there?"

"Bert's sending a helicopter."

"Oh, yeah. You told me that before. He has a ranch?"

"Rancher. Oilman." Bryson gently pulled her closer. "He owns a large piece of Ingram Industries."

"They have a nice ranch?"

"Very nice. It'll be fun."

She snuggled closer. "This is all the fun I want."

"Really? How long would you like to sit here?"

She looked up at him. "Paul, what are you asking me?"

"We aren't young anymore, Esther."

"Have you talked to your children? Don't you think you should do that first? At least talk to your daughter?"

"I wanted to know what you thought."

"I think you're wonderful. But we are very different." She rested her hand on his knee. "And you know what I mean."

"Is that a problem?"

"I can't stop being Jewish, and you can't stop being Christian."

He nuzzled his cheek against her hair. "I would never ask you to stop being who you are. And I don't think you'd ask me to, either."

"But how would that work? I go to Temple every Friday. And you go to church every Sunday."

"We could begin worship on Friday evening and end it on Sunday night."

She slapped his thigh. "I'm serious. You think Jesus is the Messiah. I don't."

"I know. But I also believe it all works out in the end."

"What does that mean? We can all just 'believe' and it doesn't matter what or who we follow?"

"No. I'm not saying that. I'm saying, I believe Jesus is the fulfillment of ancient prophecy. You say the prophecy hasn't been fulfilled yet. But we both believe in the God of Abraham, Isaac, and Jacob."

"I don't know. It seems like a stretch. We are not like some. I don't just call myself a Jew and you don't just call yourself a Christian. We actually believe and put feet to those beliefs."

"Think of the arguments we could enjoy."

She slipped her arm around his waist. "I'd rather think of other things we could enjoy."

* * *

Shortly after lunch, a Bell helicopter touched down to a soft landing in the pasture near Bryson's house. The side door opened and Bert Driskell stepped out. Tall and lean, he was the quintessential Texan—rawboned and tanned, with a weathered complexion. He gestured with a wave. Esther and Bryson hurried from their place by the fence, ducked instinctively as they passed beneath the whirring rotors, and climbed aboard.

As they took their seats, Bert handed them each a headset. When they had them on, he gave them a smile and tapped the headphones with his finger. "Only way to hear yourself think in a helicopter."

"You're right about that," Bryson nodded.

Bert turned to Esther. "First time in Texas?"

"Yes," she nodded. "And my first time in a helicopter."

"Well, sit back and enjoy the ride." Bert raised his hand in a gesture to the pilot. The engine began to whine, followed by the thump of the rotor blades as they beat against the air. Slowly the helicopter rose from the ground. Esther looked down as the pasture and house receded beneath them.

Two hours later, the helicopter landed on a grassy knoll behind the main house at Lago Vista Ranch, a ten-thousand-acre estate near Round Rock, a few miles north of Austin. Bert led them inside the house and upstairs to the second floor. He pointed to a room on the left. "Esther, you can freshen up in here. Bathroom's through that door." He pointed across the room. "Should have towels by the sink. If you need anything, just let us know. We can get you whatever it takes to make you comfortable."

Esther drifted into the bedroom. Bert took Bryson by the arm. "Come over here a minute." He guided Bryson to another bedroom across the hall. "I've passed the word that this is more than just a social occasion."

"What do you mean, Bert?"

"I know we talked about it as a way to honor you for your years of service, but I also know you still have some campaign debts you haven't resolved." There was a twinkle in his eye. "And you might want to run for something else sometime."

"So, what did you do?"

"I put out the word that they should come ready to participate."

"You know I don't like asking for money."

"You won't have to ask." Bert patted him on the back. "I already have." He turned toward the door and stepped out to the hallway. "Make yourselves at home," he called. "Come on downstairs when you're ready."

By evening, the grounds around the main house came alive with activity. To the left, a brick chimney stood at the far end of a large swimming pool. In front of the chimney, three men worked a grill loaded with cuts of beef. Catering stations arranged around the pool offered chicken and an array of vegetables and desserts. Across from the pool, a band played on a stage that overlooked a dance floor specially constructed for the event. And all of it was awash in a sea of people.

With Esther at his side, Bryson came from the house and moved effortlessly through the crowd, introducing her, laughing, and reminiscing about dreams and accomplishments from the past. They ate, and drank, and talked the evening away.

A little before eleven the crowd began to thin. Esther slipped upstairs to her room. Bryson found her there a little while later. She stood near the window with her cell phone, listening to voice messages. He crossed the room and stood behind her, his hands resting on her shoulder.

"You looked wonderful tonight."

"Thanks," she nodded with a smile. He leaned over and kissed her. She took the cell phone from her ear and pressed a button, then turned to face him. He slipped his arms around her and pulled her close. "We never finished our conversation from the porch."

"I know," she sighed. "But I think it's going to have to wait a little longer."

He leaned away. "What's wrong?"

"I need to get back to Washington."

"Tonight?"

"No." She shook her head. "But I need to be back by Monday morning."

"Okay. What's up?"

She pushed his arms away and closed the bedroom door. "Someone at the CIA wants to talk to Wiseman. I have no idea who it is or what it's about, but I don't want them to talk to him without me there."

Bryson had a sinking feeling in the pit of his stomach. His eyes darted away. "I think I know what it's about."

Esther had a puzzled look. "What?"

Bryson gestured to the bed. "Sit down and I'll tell you."

Esther took a seat on the edge of the bed and listened while Bryson told her about his conversation with Tom Russell, what he learned at the Library of Congress, and his conversation with Doyle Thompson. She shook her head in disbelief. "They really want to drop you as a consultant because of me?"

"Like I said, it's not about you. It's about Wiseman and Steve Taylor, and everything that happened in Ramallah."

"No." She shook her head once more. "It's about more than that."

"More than that?" Bryson frowned. "There's more going on than just an attempt on the prime minister's life?"

"Yes," she nodded.

"Like what?"

"I'm not sure I can tell you."

Bryson took a seat beside her. "Look, I don't care about my business. I want to help. Whatever it is, I want us to do it…together."

She squeezed his hand. "I'm not sure this is ever going to work between us."

"Why not?"

"Being with me is already costing you business. If you go much further with this, you could lose it all."

"I'd give up a thousand businesses to be with you. And besides, Tom Russell isn't my only client."

"But he's your biggest."

"Well," Bryson shrugged. "Good things come at a price." He looked her in the eye. "I'm not letting Tom Russell or Steve Taylor or anyone else decide my future." He gave her a smile. "Our future."

Just then, there was a knock from the hallway. The door opened and Bert leaned inside. "You two okay in here?"

"We're fine."

"You can spend the night if you like." He gestured with his thumb over his shoulder. "I can have them make up the room across the hall for you, Paul."

"Thanks," Bryson replied. "But we'd better get back to Longview."

"Okay. I'll tell Keith to get the chopper ready." He gave Bryson a satisfied look. "It was a good night."

"Yes, it was."

"No. I mean it was a *good* night."

"We raised some money?"

"I'll send you a check next week."

"Great," Bryson grinned. "I really appreciate what you've done for me."

"My pleasure." Bert backed away. "Come downstairs when you're ready."

When he was gone, Esther turned to Bryson. "What kind of money is he talking about?"

"Campaign money."

She had a look of concern. "You're running for office again?"

"No." He shook his head. "Just paying off old campaign debts." He took Esther's hand. "We need to finish our conversation."

"We can do that later." She stood. "Right now we'd better head downstairs."

CHAPTER 36
COOS BAY, OREGON

SHORTLY BEFORE MIDNIGHT, Gaines Whitaker stepped into the wheelhouse of the Golden Harvest, a sixty-foot steel-hulled crab boat tied up at the dock in Coos Bay, Oregon. Born a few miles inland, Gaines took his first ride on a crab boat at the age of ten. He'd been on the water for every crab season since.

With him that day was his cousin, David Moore, and two hired hands, Juan and Jose, neither of whom spoke a word of English.

David leaned through the doorway with a worried look. "What about the Mexicans?"

"They won't talk. All you got to say is 'green card' and they'll get really forgetful, really fast."

"I don't like having them around."

"They worked out of Port Orford last year."

"So they've been living around here all this time?"

"Nah." Gaines shook his head. "I think they work the season up here, then head to Florida to pick oranges or something."

"Well, all I'm saying is, I ain't going down for no loudmouth Mexicans."

"Nobody's going down," Gaines assured him. "We're going—"
An air horn sounded from the dock, interrupting him. Gaines glanced

down at his wristwatch to check the time, then grinned at David. "We're not going down. We're going crab fishing." He flipped three switches on a panel to the right, then pressed a button on the console by the boat's wheel. The deck of the ship rumbled beneath his feet and thick black smoke belched from the exhaust stacks as the engines came to life.

An hour later, the crew of the Golden Harvest began laying its first run of crab pots, circular traps made of wire mesh. They loaded the traps with squid for bait, then dropped them over the side. A red buoy attached by rope to each trap bobbed on the surface to mark the location.

By four that morning, the crew had set all four hundred of the boat's traps. Normally, they would have set them in a circle, arriving at the first pot just as they set the last, but that night they set them in a line and continued in a westerly direction long after the last trap was in the water. Juan and Jose hosed down the work area, then returned to the cabin. They were soon fast asleep on bunks in a room behind the kitchen. David went up to the wheelhouse and stood near the front windows, staring out at the open water of the Pacific.

"Think anyone will notice?"

"You seem really worried."

David glanced over his shoulder. "I ain't never done nothing like this before."

"Me neither," Gaines replied. "But we both need the money."

"I know."

Gaines checked the screen on the GPS, then took a navigation chart from a cubby hole beneath the console. He traced a path across the chart with his finger to check their location. "Better get ready." He glanced around warily and lowered his voice. "Maybe we can catch it before they wake up."

David opened the wheelhouse door and stepped out on the deck. He made his way past the cabin to the stern of the boat and scanned the water. A few minutes later, he spotted a red buoy floating on the waves. The boat's engines slowed as they drew near. When they were within a few feet, David used a long pole with a grappling hook on one end and caught hold of the buoy. He dragged it up to the hull and fastened the line from the buoy to the line from the boat's hydraulic hoist. With it secured to the hoist's rope, he slid a handle forward to engage the lift gears. Slowly, the hoist spool wound the rope as it reeled in the line.

Moments later, a large square trap appeared at the surface. David pulled back the lever to stop the machine. The trap lay just beneath the surface of the water. He reached over with the grappling hook and pulled it to the edge of the boat.

"Don't drop it." David jumped at the sound of the voice. Gaines put a hand on his shoulder. "Didn't mean to scare you. But it's no good to us if it goes to the bottom."

"I got it," David growled. He wrestled the trap to the side of the boat and handed the pole to Gaines. "Hold it steady."

In the dark water he saw the shining surface of an aluminum case floating inside the trap. David leaned over the side of the boat and opened the trap door. He reached inside, took hold of the handle on the case, and lifted it out. Using both hands, he heaved it onto the deck and set it near the hoist spool.

Both of them stood there, hands on hips, staring at it. Finally David spoke. "Hope it's waterproof."

"Not our concern. They're paying us to get it. We got it."

"Doesn't look like much."

"Looks like ten thousand dollars to me," Gaines replied.

David gave him a startled look. "I thought you said five."

"That's your share." Gaines picked up the case. "Fifty-fifty. Isn't that what we said?"

"Yeah," David laughed. "But I thought we were talking about splitting five. Not ten."

Gaines grinned. "You have a problem with making twice as much as you thought?"

"No." David's face went cold. "But I have a problem with that." He pointed toward the cabin. Standing at the door were Juan and Jose.

"Never mind them," Gaines replied. "Drop that trap and let's get busy." With the case in hand, he moved toward the cabin door. As he came near, Juan and Jose stepped aside. "Trabajo," Gaines barked as he pushed his way past them. "Trabajo."

Juan and Jose pulled on their jackets and started out to the deck.

CHAPTER 37
ALEXANDRIA, VIRGINIA

SUNDAY MORNING, Steve Taylor awakened early. He prepared breakfast for his wife and children, then the family rode together to the Methodist church on Old Dominion Boulevard. They took a seat in a pew to the right of the center aisle, halfway to the front. A little after ten, the organist appeared and took a seat at the console behind the pulpit. Precisely at ten thirty, the choir entered from the foyer for the worship service. Behind them, dressed in a flowing black robe, came the pastor.

For an hour, Taylor did his best to pay attention. He recited the creed, participated in the responsive readings, and followed along with the hymns. He dozed off once or twice during the sermon, but a jab of an elbow from his wife brought him back before he began to snore.

When the service was over, Taylor took his family to the Chart House, a seafood restaurant at the foot of Cameron Street. They enjoyed a view of the Potomac River while they ate. On the way home, Taylor felt his phone vibrating in the pocket of his jacket. He took it out and glanced at the screen. An icon blinked indicating he'd received a text message. He pressed the icon and the message appeared.

"Rosenberg Wiseman Monday AM."

His wife glanced at him from across the seat. "Work?"

"Yeah." He returned the phone to his pocket. "Sorry about that."

"It's okay," she nodded. "I don't mind."

"No," he shook his head. "A deal's a deal. No work on Sunday."

She reached across the seat and took his hand. "And no work yesterday, either."

He arched an eyebrow. "That was fun."

"I told you it would be good to spend more time at home."

"You were right," he replied.

"But if you need to take the call, go ahead."

"No," he smiled. "It's nothing."

"Good." She gave him a knowing look. "I like it when your afternoons are free."

A short while later, Taylor turned the car into the driveway and brought it to a stop near the walkway to the back door. He hustled the children inside and called after them as they hurried up the stairs. "Change your clothes."

He looked over at his wife. "Did you bring in the newspaper?"

"It's lying in the yard."

"I didn't see it when we drove up." He moved to the front door. "I'll go get it."

"Don't be long," she smiled.

Taylor opened the front door and stepped outside. The newspaper lay in the grass near the street. As he started toward it, he took his cell phone from his pocket. He scrolled down to the text message he'd received on the way home and pressed a button to reply. Working quickly with his thumbs, he typed a response. "Remove her name from tomorrow's list." He read it once, then pressed a button to send it. A moment later, the phone alarm dinged and a message appeared confirming the text had been sent. He shoved the phone in his pocket, stooped over to retrieve the newspaper, and turned back toward the house.

CHAPTER 38
FORT MEADE, MARYLAND

On Monday morning, Esther arrived at Fort Meade a little before eight. She was cleared through the main gate and drove across the base to the building off Cooper Road near Burba Lake. As usual, she parked in a space near the sidewalk and walked to the front entrance.

A guard met her as she crossed the building lobby. "I'm sorry, ma'am. I can't let you in today."

"But I'm here to see my client."

"Yes, ma'am. But I can't let you in the building. Not today."

"You haven't even asked my client's name."

"You're here to see Anthony Wiseman. They called from the gate."

"Well, I called yesterday and they said I could see him."

"I'm sorry, ma'am. Not today."

"This won't do," Esther said furiously. "I need to speak with someone else. Who's your supervisor?"

"Just a minute." The guard stepped to a nearby office and picked up the phone.

A few minutes later a man dressed in a navy blue suit came from around the corner. "Ms. Rosenberg," he smiled politely. "I'm Roy Dawson. Head of security. I'm sorry for any misunderstanding. There's been a change in plans."

"What kind of change in plans?"

"I'm afraid I can't discuss that." He gestured toward the door. "I'm sure if you will just—"

"I'm here to see my client," Esther insisted.

"He's not available."

"Look, someone from Langley wanted to interview him this morning. That can't happen without me in the room. I object to anyone interrogating my client without my being present. I am his attorney. He is represented by legal counsel and I demand to be allowed in the room."

"I'm sorry," Dawson replied. "The prisoner is not available today." He stepped to the door. "You'll have to leave."

Esther squared her shoulders. "Not without seeing my client."

"You'll have to make an appointment."

"I made an appointment for today."

"You'll have to make another one. On another day."

Esther's voice was tense. "I demand to see my client!"

The guard appeared in the hallway behind her. Dawson glanced in his direction. "Ma'am, if you don't leave, I'll have to ask the guard to take you into custody."

Esther glanced at the guard who now stood just a few feet away. She took a deep breath and slowly exhaled. "This isn't right and you know it," she fumed as she moved past Dawson and stepped outside.

CHAPTER 39
FORT MEADE, MARYLAND

ON THE OPPOSITE SIDE of the base, Doyle Thompson arrived at a nondescript building near Cochrane Road. He was met there by Colonel Jimmy Gillespie. "Good morning, Doyle."

Thompson acknowledged him with a handshake. "Been a while since I've seen you."

"They keep me busy," Gillespie replied. He pointed over his shoulder. "We have your man down here."

Thompson followed Gillespie up the hall. Gillespie glanced back in his direction. "You got the release from Justice saying it's okay for you to see him?"

"Oh," Thompson gasped with a snap of his finger. "Forgot to bring it. Can I send it to you tomorrow?"

"Sure," Gillespie replied. "Just paperwork anyway."

Near the back of the building they came to an office suite. A door to the right was secured with a biometric locking system. Gillespie placed the palm of his hand on a screen and waited while a scanner checked his prints. When the scan was completed the system unlocked the door. He pushed it open and waited while Thompson stepped inside.

In the center of the room was a metal table with four chairs. A single light fixture hung from the ceiling. Anthony Wiseman sat at the far side of the table. Thompson looked in Gillespie's direction. "I'll call you when we're finished."

"Sure thing," Gillespie nodded. He backed out of the room and pulled the door closed. When he was gone, Thompson took a seat across from Wiseman.

"My name is Doyle Thompson."

"Graduate of the University of Georgia," Wiseman replied. "Spent time in Beirut. Worked with the Kurds in Iraq. Now they have you sitting at a desk."

A faint smile turned up the corners of Thompson's mouth. "I see you've kept up, even in here."

"I do the best I can," Wiseman replied. "But I knew about you before I arrived at this place."

Thompson slid his chair to one side and crossed his legs. "I need to ask you a few questions, Mr. Wiseman."

Wiseman folded his hands together and rested them on the table-top. "Where's my attorney?"

Thompson's eyes darted away. "I thought it might be better if we talked alone today."

Wiseman shook his head. "She won't like it."

"I won't ask about your legal case."

Wiseman leaned back from the table and moved his hands to his lap. "How much longer will they keep me here?"

"That's for the Justice Department to decide," Thompson shrugged. "I don't know anything about that."

Wiseman cocked his head to one side. "But you have friends at the Department of Justice."

"I know a few people," Thompson nodded.

"A telephone call to one of them might help."

"Yes." Thompson nodded again. "I see your point."

"Good," Wiseman smiled. "Now, what did you want to talk about?"

"The missiles used in the attack against Prime Minister Roham were Russian Kornets."

"Take you this long to figure that out?"

Thompson ignored Wiseman's sarcasm and continued. "Mossad has confirmed that they were supplied through an Austrian arms dealer named Leonid Malenkov."

"Okay."

"He sold them to an Iranian named Hossein Jiroft."

"And you have been tracking Jiroft?"

"Yes. As has Mossad."

"And where is he now?"

"Still in Iran, we think."

"But that still leaves you with the missing link—how the missiles got from Jiroft to the rooftop in Ramallah."

Thompson gave Wiseman a thoughtful look. "What do you know about Shiraz Moussa?"

Wiseman leaned back in his chair. "I wondered when someone would get around to him."

"You know of him?"

"Arafat's bodyguard? Yes. Certainly. I know of him. He used to follow Arafat everywhere he went. Carried his luggage. Held the door. Occasionally substituted as a security guard when necessary."

"Any idea where he might be now?"

"Ramallah. Perhaps Gaza. He moves in and out of the West Bank and Gaza. Doesn't stay anywhere long." Wiseman gave a thoughtful nod. "But I am sure you'll find him in Ramallah. Life is much easier there."

"You know this for a fact, or just your best guess?"

"I'm in here." Wiseman gestured with a toss of his hand. "I have no fresh intelligence. But I cannot imagine him being anywhere else right now. Ramallah is his power base." Wiseman let his eyes bore in on Thompson. "Shiraz Moussa is a dangerous man."

"How so?"

"When Arafat died, Moussa became the de facto leader of the Fatah movement. Many thought that movement died with Arafat, but it is very much alive and well. Only it's different now."

"In what way?"

"Arafat loved politics but cared little for religion. He used Islamic rhetoric to inflame the Arab masses, but he had no faith. Not in Allah or anyone else, except himself. Moussa is quite different. For him, Islam is everything. He has figured out that Fatah will only be able to compete with Hamas and Palestinian Islamic Jihad by being perceived as a religious movement itself. They call themselves the *Jund Ansar Allah.*"

Thompson thought for a moment. "Army of the Faithful?"

"Very good," Wiseman said slowly. "Army of the Supporters of Allah." He leaned forward. "Jund Ansar Allah gets all their arms through Jiroft from Malenkov."

"You are sure of this?"

"Very sure." Wiseman smiled proudly. "I wrote an article about Malenkov and Nilus." Wiseman lowered his voice. "Malenkov's uncle, Demetrius Nilus, is a general in the Russian Army. Head of one of their most secret and important nuclear programs. Just before the Russian Revolution, Demetrius' grandfather wrote a book called *The Protocols of the Learned Elders of Zion.* It was a hoax about how Jews were conspiring to take control of the world. Everyone in Czarist Russia believed it was the truth and used it to justify a Russian holocaust. Hitler believed it was true, too, and used it to justify the systematic extermination of six million Jews. Perhaps many more."

"And this somehow relates to Moussa?"

"Today, many Muslims believe the book is absolutely true." Wiseman tapped his finger on the table for emphasis. "*The Protocols* is read every day in mosques and has become required reading for students in their madrasahs. They have convinced the adults it's true and have engrained it in the minds of their children."

"So let me get this straight." Thompson had an ironic smile. "A book about a worldwide Jewish conspiracy is really the work of a worldwide anti-Semitic conspiracy? It seems a little—"

"Paranoid?" Wiseman interrupted him. "Hatred of the Jews has been handed down from generation to generation. Some hated us for religious reasons, others because they think we know some secret about how to get wealthy. You know I'm right. We have people who think like that in our own country."

"I'm sure there are people here who don't like Jews, but—"

"I'm not talking about racists and bigots. I'm talking about people who are seriously committed to the violent extermination of all Jews."

"And there are organizations like that in America?"

"Yes. Absolutely."

"What organizations?"

"Are you familiar with the Holy Western Empire?"

"Sounds like a name I've heard before."

"The Order of Malta?"

"Come on." Thompson dismissed him with a wave of the hand. "Don't start all that Catholic anti-Semitism argument. The Church doesn't believe that anymore."

"The Pope has renounced the Church's official position, but the Order of Malta isn't under the Pope's authority. He doesn't set policy for them. They set their own policy and they are absolutely convinced *The Protocols* is true."

"That doesn't have much to do with the attack on Roham, or Moussa, or the Jund Ansar Allah."

"Oh, but it does." Wiseman tapped his finger on the table once more. "This is where you CIA guys fall short. You have sophisticated technology and access to anything you desire, but you don't have patience."

"Patience?"

"Patience to connect the dots."

"What dots?"

"*The Protocols*, Demetrius Nilus, Malenkov, Arafat, Moussa, the Order of Malta."

"And how do they connect?"

"They are all committed to one goal—bringing an end to the Jews."

"Perhaps Nilus, Malenkov, and Moussa." Thompson shook his head. "But not the Order of Malta."

Wiseman's eyes were alive with anticipation. "Demetrius Nilus is a member of the Order of Malta."

Thompson frowned. "You are certain of this?"

"Ask your contacts with Mossad." Wiseman had a knowing smile. "They'll confirm it."

"Interesting."

"More than interesting. This is a serious threat."

"How so?"

"Members of the Order of Malta look just like you and me. Even now you're skeptical that they could be involved in such a plot." Wiseman smiled. "It's the perfect cover."

"Which means?"

"Which means they have operatives living inside your country that are able to move at will without raising any suspicion. They can come and go without need of a visa. They travel freely without detection. They are a threat from within, from one of your own—precisely the kind of threat your security system is not set up to recognize or equipped to handle."

CHAPTER 40
ALEXANDRIA, LOUISIANA

LISA WADE SQUINTED against the morning glare and watched as a Gulfstream jet turned from the taxiway and started toward the apron. She winced at the sound of the engines as the plane turned to the left and came to a stop fifty yards away. She glanced at the cameraman. "You ready?"

"Yeah. I'll hit the light when he starts down the steps."

She ran her fingers across the corners of her mouth and picked up the microphone. "Just make sure you get shots of him. We can film the cutaways later." She tugged at her jacket and adjusted the waistband of her skirt.

"Here we go." The cameraman pointed. "They're opening the door."

Through the plane's open doorway Lisa caught a glimpse of a tall, slender man dressed in a dark gray suit. "That's him," she said, pointing. "Vasily Gerashchenko."

"Yeah," the cameraman nodded. "That's him."

She had seen pictures of Russians before, with large features and heavy jowls, but this man was trim, athletic, and handsome. He came quickly down the steps to the tarmac. The cameraman switched on the light. Lisa followed him as they jockeyed for position.

A reporter from New Orleans bumped into her shoulder. Lisa nudged him with her elbow and moved into position. When Gerashchenko stepped to the pavement, she thrust the microphone toward him. "Mr. Gerashchenko, good morning, do you expect Dubov Oil to have a permanent presence in Louisiana?"

"Yes," Gerashchenko nodded. "We have made many explorations in the great state of Louisiana and have found the people most receptive to our overtures. We look forward to a long and productive relationship with your community."

"Will you open an office here in the Alexandria area?"

"That is why I am here today. To determine suitable locations and approve final arrangements."

"So we can expect an announcement before you return to Russia?"

"I hope to make an announcement soon."

"Are facilities here at England Airpark under consideration?"

"You have a lovely facility. Perhaps we can find something suitable here."

"How many employees do you expect to hire for your operations in Louisiana?"

"No determination has been made about that yet. We are only in the beginning stages of developing the Dry Prong field. But I expect to have many employees working there soon."

Around midmorning, Lisa met with a technician in an editing room at the station. They edited together Gerashchenko's answers with the cutaways of her questions. When the basic piece was in place, Lisa checked her watch. "We still have time before the noon show. Let's look at the other tape we have from the airport."

The technician punched a button on the console, and images appeared on the editing monitor. A view of the plane landing came first, followed by several shots of the crowd gathered at the foot of the steps. After a minute or two, the screen jumped to a different angle. Gerashchenko stood in the foreground, still answering questions, but behind him a man came from the airplane carrying a large aluminum case. He moved quickly down the steps, slipped past the crowd, and disappeared from view.

Lisa pointed to the screen. "Who was that?"

"I don't know," the technician replied. "I saw him in another shot when we were editing the piece." He pressed a button and the image on the screen went black. Then a long view of the tarmac appeared with three black SUVs parked behind the spot where Lisa had been standing for the interview. The man with the case emerged from the crowd and entered one of the SUVs. Moments later, the SUV made a sharp turn to the right and drove away from the airplane, leaving behind the crowd with the reporters and Gerashchenko standing at the steps.

"That's strange."

"Yeah," the technician replied. "Would be interesting to know who he is and what was in that case." He pressed a button and went back to the edited report. "Are you doing this from the newsroom?"

"No. It's a complete report."

"Then we need to add the signoff at the end. Grab the microphone and we can record it now."

CHAPTER 41
WASHINGTON, D.C.

AT LUNCH, BRYSON went to the gym. He was jogging on a treadmill when his phone rang. He pressed the Bluetooth on his ear to answer. The call was from Esther.

"Something's wrong," she said bluntly.

"Where are you?" Bryson steadied himself with a hand on the rail of the treadmill. "Are you okay?"

"They wouldn't let me see him."

"See who?"

"Anthony. I was on the list to see him this morning. They told me yesterday I was on the list. I was supposed to be there when he met with the CIA. But they wouldn't let me see him."

"Who wouldn't?"

"The guards. Some guy who said he was in charge of security."

Bryson pressed the button to stop the treadmill. "They wouldn't let you on the base?"

"They let me on the base. But they wouldn't let me see Anthony."

He stepped from the treadmill and moved to the corner of the room. As he walked, he took his cell phone from his waist, unclipped the Bluetooth, and pressed the phone to his ear. "What did they do?"

"They ushered me from the building."

"Why?"

"They wouldn't say. They just kept saying he wasn't available."

"This is crazy." Bryson did his best to hide the guilt he felt inside. He knew what happened. Thompson was out there talking to Wiseman alone. A sense of betrayal stabbed him in the stomach. "Let me make some calls."

"Who are you going to call?"

"Just give me a few minutes."

"Paul," she insisted. "Who are you going to call? I really need to know. This isn't something you can fix."

"I'll make a call and call you back."

Bryson pressed a button to end the call and headed to the locker room. He picked up his gym bag, wiped off with a towel, and started toward the elevator. Five minutes later, he was seated at his desk, still dressed in gym shorts and T-shirt. He snatched the receiver from the cradle and punched in a number. Doyle Thompson answered the call. Bryson charged right into the conversation.

"Why did you do it?"

"Do what?"

"You met with Wiseman without Esther being present."

"I didn't say she couldn't be there."

"Well, someone did. She was on the list to see him this morning. When she got there, they let her on the base but wouldn't let her in the room."

"I had nothing to do with that."

"You need to talk to her."

"Why?"

"Because it looks like you used what I told you against her. Because we are all supposed to be on the same team. Because it's the right the thing to do."

"Okay," Thompson replied meekly. "I'll see her. Pick a time."

"This afternoon?"

"All right. Meet me at the Iwo Jima Memorial. Four o'clock."

"We'll be there," Bryson replied as he headed back to the locker room. On the way, he phoned Esther and arranged to pick her up at her office.

An hour later he was showered and ready. He rode down to the parking garage and walked toward his car.

CHAPTER 42

GLACIER, MONTANA

DAVID CHESNEY SAT atop his horse and scanned the mountain-side. Unable to detect anything out of the ordinary, he took a pair of binoculars from his saddlebag and brought them to his eyes. He adjusted the focus and scanned the slope just below the ridge. He was about to put them away when he caught a glimpse of something moving through the trees. He steadied the binoculars with both hands and adjusted the focus.

"I see him now," he mumbled. "A horse and two mules." Chesney looked a little longer, letting his eyes check the details of the rider's clothing. "Not a ranger." He tilted the glasses down and zoomed in on the horse. "Don't see a rifle. Doesn't appear to be a hunter." He looked back at the rider's face. "Not sure who he is." He returned the glasses to the saddlebag. "But I'm gonna find out."

For two days, Chesney had roamed the Lewis Range east of Cosley Lake, searching for a man riding a horse and leading a string of mules. Some said he had two. Others said it was three. Hikers had first reported seeing him two weeks earlier, a little south of Waterton Lake, near the Canadian border. No one paid much attention but after reports of mule deer carcasses along the trail, someone at headquarters decided it was time to locate the mysterious traveler and investigate his activities.

Chesney, who worked from the Belly River Station, was sent to do the job.

Now atop the ridge, he rubbed the heel of his boot against the horse's flank and started down the mountainside. Fifteen minutes later, he reached a dry creek bed at the bottom of the slope. He drew the horse up short and listened. Behind them, on Flannigan's Ridge, a northern breeze rustled through the trees. Down the hollow to the right, a mule deer ambled along the creek bed. High above, an eagle soared on a thermal updraft, its wings spread wide, its eyes trained on the woods below, searching for prey. Chesney cocked his head to the right and listened with his left ear.

At first he heard nothing, but then he caught the tinkle of a bridle chain. He held his breath and listened again, straining to catch the slightest noise. And then he heard the tinkling sound again.

"Come on," he whispered, and patted his horse's neck. "They're up the mountain. In the glade that overlooks Beecher's Draw." He nudged the horse with his heels and started forward.

Moving carefully and quietly, Chesney worked his horse to the left through the dense forest. Slowly, methodically, he passed wide of the glade, being careful to keep well out of sight. When he was half a mile beyond it, he turned back and approached from the west side, then brought the horse to a stop near a large oak.

Uncharted on official maps, the glade was known to rangers and hikers as Ordway's Meadow, named in honor of John Ordway, a sergeant in the Lewis and Clark Expedition. About two acres in size, it sat on a ledge formed by a natural cut in the face of the mountain. It was bounded on one side by a sheer rock face and on the other by the slope toward the hollow below.

Sixty yards away, on the opposite side of the meadow, a sorrel mare and two mules grazed on the leaves of a wax bush. The mare was saddled but her reins hung free. The mules, tethered with a rope to the mare, were packed but not heavily. Each load was covered with a canvas tarp.

From his place in the shadows of the forest, Chesney scanned the tree line on the far side. "I don't like it," he whispered to himself. "I don't like it at all."

He dismounted the horse and tied the reins to a low-hanging tree branch, then stared out at the meadow once more. With practiced caution, he let his eyes scan from tree line to tree line, searching for the slightest hint of human presence. When he found none, he started across toward the mules. With each step he listened intently for the sound of a human footstep coming from the edge of the forest, the bolt of a rifle sliding slowly in place, or the brush of a jacket sleeve against a leafless branch.

When he reached the opposite side, he moved first to the horse and gently ran his hand over its neck. The horse seemed not to notice but kept on eating from the wax bush. Carefully, quietly, Chesney moved past the horse to the mules.

The first one paid him no attention as he lifted the canvas tarp. Beneath the cover he saw a leather bag, two rifles, and an aluminum box the size of a large suitcase. It had a handle at the top fitted between two latches. On the lower right corner were two words that appeared to be written in Russian. Chesney pushed back the tarp a little farther for a better look.

Then he heard the crunch of twigs. He turned to see a man standing at his side. Pistol in hand, his eyes bore in on Chesney in an emotionless blank stare. He was dressed in blue jeans with a flannel shirt and heavy jacket. Atop his head he wore a cowboy hat and he looked like any other man traveling the mountains by horse, but when he spoke he revealed a heavy European accent. "Step back from the animal." He gestured with the pistol. "Slowly."

Chesney let go of the tarp and held both hands wide apart. "I am a National Park ranger," he said slowly. "Put that pistol away and we can talk."

The man ignored Chesney's plea and gestured with the pistol. "Move back farther, please."

Chesney took another step backward and turned again to face the man. "I can let you—"

Without warning, the man placed the muzzle of the pistol against the side of Chesney's head and squeezed the trigger. Chesney felt the heat of the bullet as it sliced through his brain. His arms and legs went numb, then his knees buckled and he slumped to the ground. He caught a glimpse of the eagle, its wings still spread wide against the updraft, and he heard the sound of hooves as the horse and mules lurched aside. Then his eyes closed and life slipped from his body.

CHAPTER 43

ROSSLYN, VIRGINIA

THAT AFTERNOON, BRYSON picked up Esther at her office. She climbed in the SUV and looked across the front seat at him.

"Where are we going?"

"Iwo Jima Memorial. To see Doyle Thompson. My friend at the CIA."

She reached across the seat and touched his hand. "You don't have to do this."

"Yes, I do. I told Doyle about Wiseman. That's why he went out there to see him. That's why they wouldn't let you into the meeting. I should have told *you* my ideas, instead of him."

"He's agreed to see me?"

"He's agreed to see us. This involves me now. First Steve Taylor with his threats. Now Doyle. Something's going on. I'm going to find out what it is, one way or the other."

"Will he speak candidly with both of us there?"

"He'll talk. And he means well. But you never know whether you're getting the entire story."

"I'm used to that," she smirked.

Near the end of Constitution Avenue they turned onto Ohio Drive and started across the Arlington Bridge over the Potomac River. A few minutes later, they turned in to the Marine Corps Memorial. Thompson's car was parked near the Iwo Jima monument. Bryson parked nearby and opened the door for Esther.

"Come on, I see Doyle over there." He pointed to a grove of trees across the way.

Esther stepped from the car. "How do you know Doyle Thompson?"

"He briefed our committee a few times." Bryson closed the car door and took her arm. "We worked together on several pieces of legislation."

"I see," she grinned. "You could tell me more, but then you'd have to shoot me?"

"Something like that."

They walked together across the parking lot and found Doyle seated on a stone bench beneath a large chestnut tree. He smiled up at them from his seat. "Like my office?" He gestured to the lawn around them.

"Nice view." Bryson took a seat on the bench. Esther sat beside him. Thompson wasted little time with introductions. He turned to Esther and got right to the point. "I understand Anthony Wiseman is your client."

"Yes. And I understand you talked to him yesterday without my being present."

Thompson frowned. "I didn't know you were there to see him."

"Please." Esther rolled her eyes. "You couldn't hear me talking to Roy Dawson in the hall?"

"Where were you?"

"In a building down near Burba Lake. Off Cooper Road."

"We didn't meet there." Thompson placed his hands at the edge of the bench. "Did you call ahead?"

"Yes," Esther said sharply. "They put me on the list Sunday morning."

"Then I don't know what happened," Thompson shrugged. "I'll check on it and find out."

"What did you talk about?"

"The attacks in Ramallah."

"Not his pending case?"

"No."

"What specifically did you talk to him about?"

"We were interested in what he might know about a general in the Russian Army named Demetrius Nilus."

"What about him?"

Thompson glanced away, as if thinking. After a moment, he looked back at her. "This conversation must remain absolutely secret. No leaks. No hints. Nothing dropped in casual conversation."

"Sure," Esther nodded her head up and down slowly.

Thompson continued. "General Nilus and his nephew, Leonid Malenkov, have been selling Russian arms to terrorists in the Middle East. We're all but certain they supplied the missiles used in the attack on Ehud Roham during his trip to Ramallah."

"Anthony wouldn't know much about that."

"Perhaps not," Thompson nodded. "When I asked him about it, he told me a lot about Nilus' connection to something called the Order of Malta."

"One of the oldest, most anti-Semitic organizations in the world," Esther added. "They are responsible for the deaths of millions of our people."

"That's what I've been told."

"It's one of his many areas of expertise. What else did you discuss? This is all information you already had."

"I asked him about Shiraz Moussa."

"So, you were fishing."

"Yeah," Thompson nodded. "I was fishing."

"For what?"

"The Israeli government has informed us that they intercepted a conversation with Malenkov involving suitcase bombs. The man to whom Malenkov sold the missiles for the Ramallah attack complained that one of them failed. He was quite upset. Malenkov offered to supply him with a suitcase bomb to set things right."

"Such a sense of honor among thieves."

"According to Malenkov, the suitcase he offered is either already in the U.S. or very soon will be." Thompson looked back at Esther once more. "No one has been able to confirm that any cases actually exist."

Esther sighed. "I think they exist. And I think they will be used very soon."

"What makes you say that?"

She looked away for a moment and shifted positions on the bench. "I'll give you the same condition you gave me." She made a slicing gesture with her hand. "No disclosure. And you'll agree to keep me informed of what you find."

"Fair enough," Thompson nodded.

Esther took a deep breath, then began. "We had a source inside the Order of Malta. A carefully cultivated source who managed to gain access to a cell phone used by the Grand Master's assistant."

"The Grand Master?"

"Head of the Order. There was a message on that phone which had been sent to a number of recipients. So far, no one has been able to determine who those recipients were, but the message was rather ominous." She glanced down at the ground. "'Release the four angels who are bound at the great river Euphrates.'"

"That was the message?"

"Yes."

"An apocalyptic war."

"Perhaps in prophecy, but I don't think they're talking about war."

"Then what?"

"Four catastrophic attacks."

"Four suitcase bombs?"

"Precisely."

"Do you have any information to back that up, or is this just a theory?"

"We have the conversation we overheard with Jiroft—that's the man you were talking about. The one who was complaining about the missiles."

"That conversation was about a single suitcase."

"I think Malenkov has more, and they're in play."

"And the Order of Malta is somehow involved?"

"They are obsessed with destroying us."

"So, where would they use these bombs? Jerusalem?"

"If Malenkov had a suitcase bomb already in Jerusalem, he would have told Jiroft about that one. Not one in the United States." Esther crossed her legs at the ankles. "I think all four are right here. In the U.S."

Thompson shook his head slowly in disbelief. "I don't see how."

"Plenty of options," Esther shrugged. "Order of Malta has thousands of members here. Russian mafia."

"Sounds a little farfetched."

She gave him an amused look. "For someone who plotted to kill the Chinese premier?"

"Vice premier," Thompson corrected. "And no one ever proved the plot actually existed."

"You can't afford not to take this seriously."

"We're taking it seriously," Thompson assured her. "But no one knows where to begin." He stood and took a pair of sunglasses from the inside pocket of his jacket. "And I have been here too long. I have to go now." He slipped the sunglasses on and started toward the parking lot. "I'll be in touch."

When he was gone, Esther looked over at Bryson. "That guy is a little weird."

"He is a little flakey, but he makes things happen." "Think those cases really exist?"

"They exist, all right. The question is where?"

CHAPTER 44
WASHINGTON, D.C.

NOT LONG BEFORE SUNSET, Steve Taylor drove to the Old Dominion Boat Club. Located on the Potomac River at the foot of King Street in Alexandria, the club had been organized to promote boating and physical fitness among federal government employees. Taylor had joined in hopes of obtaining a slip at the club's marina. After a long wait, he finally had been allocated one. He used it to moor his lone indulgence—a nineteen-foot Sea Ray boat.

That afternoon, he parked his car in a lot near the club and made his way onto the pier and out to the slip. The boat bobbed gently on the waves. The sun was still an hour from disappearing below the horizon. It would be a great time to take a ride. He glanced at his watch and sighed. This was movie night at home. Everyone would be waiting for him. Being late wasn't an option.

But there was time to enjoy a few minutes of fresh air and autumn sunshine. He climbed into the boat, stretched out on the rear seat, and propped his feet on the gunwale. Before long, his eyes were closed and he was lost in thought.

A few minutes later, he heard the sound of approaching footsteps. He opened his eyes to see Chad Loring coming down the dock. From the smile on his face, Taylor was sure he had good news.

Loring held on to a post on the dock and stepped into the boat. The boat rocked from side to side as he took a seat behind the steering wheel. "Want to crank it up and go for a spin?"

"Yes," Taylor replied. "But I don't have the time. What brings you all the way over here?"

Loring spun the seat around to face Taylor. He leaned forward and propped his elbows on his knees. "Does the name Doyle Thompson mean anything to you?"

"Vaguely familiar." Taylor did his best to appear aloof. "CIA?"

"Yes."

"What about him?"

"Rosenberg and her boyfriend, Paul Bryson, just spent the afternoon talking to him."

Taylor opened his eyes. "Where did they meet?"

"Iwo Jima Memorial."

Taylor frowned. "What were they doing out there?"

"Talking."

"About what?"

"Lot of things. Didn't make much sense to me," Loring shrugged. "Malta and horses and a Russian general."

Taylor was suddenly alert. "What did they say about it?"

"I don't know." Loring reached into his pocket. "But I got it all right here." He took out a flash drive and tossed it to Taylor. "Recorded it from the car. You can listen to it yourself."

"Good." Taylor slid the flash drive into his pocket. "I'll listen to it tonight. Did they see you?"

"Come on," Loring needled. "This isn't the first time I've done this." Loring turned back to the steering wheel. "Sure you don't want to take this thing out for a ride?"

"I'd love to." Taylor swung his feet from the gunwale and stood. "But there isn't time now." He brushed dust from his pants. "Got to get home."

"No point in having it if you don't use it."

"I use it," Taylor insisted. "But it's getting too cold for the family to enjoy. I need to take it out of the water. Can't leave it out here all winter."

"You taking it out today?"

"Nah. I just came down here to relax for a minute." Taylor pointed toward the dock. "You better get going."

"Right." Loring rose from the seat and stepped onto the dock. "Let me know if you need any help with the boat."

That evening, after the children were in bed and his wife was asleep, Steve Taylor made his way to the basement and took a seat at his desk in the corner. A laptop computer was there and he raised the cover, then loaded the audio player. When the program was ready, he connected Loring's flash drive to the USB port and listened to Doyle Thompson's conversation with Esther and Bryson. What he heard told him the Order's plan was in serious trouble.

When he finished listening, Taylor used his cell phone to send a text message to Angelo Giovanni. That message read simply, "Compromised."

The reply came almost immediately. "Extent?"

"Source and objects discovered," Taylor responded.

A few minutes later, his cell phone vibrated. Giovanni responded with, "Thanks."

Taylor thought it an odd answer but he was apprehensive about saying more. The NSA scanned all international telephone traffic for keywords. Telling Giovanni the details would raise the risk of being discovered. Reluctantly, Taylor stood and crossed the room to the basement steps.

As he reached for the switch to turn off the light, his phone vibrated again. A message appeared from Giovanni.

"How?"

Taylor took a seat on the bottom step and typed an answer. "Supplier conversation with third party." He pressed a button to send the message. Then he added another message. "And insider."

When thirty minutes passed and Giovanni still had not replied, Taylor turned out the basement lights and went upstairs.

CHAPTER 45
GLACIER, MONTANA

WHEN DAVID CHESNEY failed to report at his appointed time, the ranger on duty at the station on Belly River tried to reach him by radio and cell phone. Those attempts were unsuccessful but raised no alarm. Deep gorges and high mountains made reception spotty in many areas. But when three days passed without any contact, the duty officer at the ranger station notified park headquarters.

That afternoon, rangers and Border Patrol agents launched a search with teams on the ground and in the air. A few days later, a Border Patrol helicopter pilot spotted a horse standing alone in Ordway's Meadow. Within the hour, Scott Marshall assembled a three-man ranger team and set out from the Belly River station. Early the next morning they reached the hollow at the base of Lewis Range near Cosley Lake.

Jim Olinger and Joe Forton, two newly hired rangers, accompanied Marshall on the search. Neither Olinger nor Forton had much experience in the mountains but Olinger was a former Green Beret, and Forton had recently graduated from Auburn University, where he played linebacker on the Tiger football team. Athletic and tough, they were rapidly becoming some of the best rangers working the rugged terrain of northern Montana.

Marshall pointed to the mountain. "We'll go up the slope to the left and come in from the west." He adjusted the straps on his back-pack and pulled them tight against his chest. "I have no idea what we're dealing with. So be careful. Keep your eyes open. Make as little noise as possible."

Olinger glanced over at him. "Think we'll find him alive?"

"I don't know," Marshall replied. "Keep your pistol handy."

Olinger patted his waist. "Got it."

With Marshall in the lead, the three men crossed the hollow and started up the mountain. An hour later they stood at the western edge of the meadow. Chesney's horse lingered on the far side, still saddled, the reins dangling from its bridle. "I don't like this," Olinger whispered. "If there is some lunatic with a gun up here, anybody crossing that meadow would be an easy target."

"I don't like it either," Marshall said tersely. "But we don't have much choice." They stood in silence a moment longer, then Marshall glanced at Olinger and gestured to the right. "Work around the down-hill side." He turned to Forton. "You work the uphill side. And keep quiet."

Forton reset his cap atop his head. "Which way you going?"

"Straight across," Marshall replied.

Olinger moved to the right and crept along the downhill slope with the meadow above him to the left. Forton moved to the high side and worked his way carefully above the meadow, his eyes focused on the woods around him, doing his best to make certain he wasn't seen.

Marshall waited a few minutes to give the others time to get in posi-tion, then started across the meadow toward the horse. He approached without incident and took hold of the reins. "Easy now," he cooed. "Just gonna tie you off to a branch." He looped the reins over a tree branch and tied them in place, then eased along the horse's flank. "Where's David?" He spoke quietly to the horse with a calm, confident voice. "You seen David around here?" He ran his hand over the horse's hip and checked the saddle. The horse stomped her hoof and moved to one side. As she moved, Marshall glanced down and saw the ground at his feet had been churned soft and embedded with heavy hoof prints. Leaves that littered the ground nearby had a dusting of snow stained brown with what appeared to be dried blood. Marshall moved the horse farther away and knelt for a closer look. And then he saw the trail of dried blood leading into the woods.

Head bent over, his eyes alert for details, he followed a series of drag marks on the ground and smears on the saplings. Then, twenty yards down the slope, he came to a clump of twisted flesh and torn, bloody clothing. Olinger appeared at his side. "Find something?"

Marshall pointed and swallowed hard to keep from vomiting. Olinger turned away. A few minutes later, Forton appeared. The three of them stood there, staring silently at the remains of Chesney's body. Finally Forton spoke. "What happened?"

"Cougar," Marshall sighed. "Black bear. Who knows?"

"Why'd it get him and not the horse?"

Marshall turned away. "Let me show you something." He led them back up the slope to the meadow and pointed to the ground near the horse. "What's that look like?"

"Like that horse has been standing here a long time."

"The reins were loose when I got here," Marshall said. "I tied her to the tree."

"So," Olinger said slowly. "What are you saying?"

"Maybe when whatever got David came along, the horse wasn't here."

"Then how did the ground get so churned up?"

"The horse was tied to the tree," Forton spoke up. "She must've pulled free when something spooked her."

"Maybe," Marshall agreed. "But maybe David found the guy he was looking for right here. I think we should treat this as a crime scene. We need to preserve everything just like it is until we can get some investigators in here."

Forton took a cell phone from his pocket and glanced at the screen. "No reception out here. No way to call anybody."

"We'll have to hike out far enough to call." Marshall took a quarter from his pocket. "First one to win three stays with the body. The other two make the hike to find cell phone reception. Call it in the air." He rested the coin on his thumb to toss it, but before he could flip it in the air, Olinger grabbed his wrist. "You ain't gotta flip for it. I'll sit with him."

CHAPTER 46
FORT MEADE, MARYLAND

A FEW DAYS LATER, Esther Rosenberg returned to Fort Meade. She was admitted to the base and escorted to Wiseman without incident. They met around a conference table in the building off Cooper Road.

"I understand you talked to Doyle Thompson?"

"Yes," Wiseman replied. "Where were you?"

"Somehow my name was taken off the visitor list."

"What happened?"

"I don't know. But I don't like it." She paused to take a breath. "I called Paul and told him about it. He knew Thompson and arranged a meeting so I could talk to him."

"So," Wiseman smiled, "you're still seeing Paul Bryson?"

"Yes." Esther's eyes darted away.

"I thought that was just a date to some reporter's dinner or something."

"Well, that led to dinner a few nights later, and that—"

Wiseman folded his arms across his chest. "You like him."

"Yes." Her eyes darted away again. "I do."

"He sounds like a good man." Wiseman scooted closer to the table.

"He is," Esther nodded. "But he's also a Christian."

Wiseman had a kind look. "Esther, I've known you a long time now ..."

"Not that long."

"It seems like a long time." He rested his elbows on the table. "You should live life today, while it's here. Tomorrow may not get here."

Tears filled her eyes. "I know."

"Trust me." Wiseman reached across the table and took her hand. "Not as a client, but as a friend."

"We'll see." She withdrew her hand. "What did Thompson ask you?"

"Questions about Demetrius Nilus, Malenkov, and he wanted to know about Shiraz Moussa."

"What did you tell him?"

"I told him about Moussa and his connection with Jund Ansar Allah."

"Did he believe you?"

"Yes. But I'm not sure he believed me about the Order." He rocked the chair on its back legs. "How does he seem to you?"

"A little over the top with the spy persona."

"Think we can work with him?"

"I hope so."

"And Paul introduced you to him?"

She nodded. "He keeps insisting on being involved."

"He'll lose his business."

"I think he would be happier without it."

"As long as he has you?"

"Yes," she smiled sheepishly. "That's what he tells me."

"That's a good sign."

"Perhaps." Esther changed the subject. "Reuben Brody wants the names of your contacts. People you know in Naval Intelligence, other agencies, who would be willing to work with him."

Wiseman shook his head. "Is he crazy? They would lose their jobs. I would never get out of here. What kind of question is that?"

"I know."

Wiseman's frustration grew into anger. "I've already given them my life. I never asked for anything in return. And I'm not even asking for anything now, after I've lost everything."

"I told him as much."

"And still he wants names?"

"He said to ask."

"Well, you asked." Wiseman shook his head. "They sit in cubicles all their lives and never go in the field."

"Sometimes I think politics plays as much a part of their work in Beersheba as it does everywhere else."

He had a faraway look in his eyes. "I know what you mean."

Esther pointed to his jaw. "How is your tooth?"

"It's good." He suddenly returned to the moment. "They pulled the one that was hurting."

"Anything else you need?"

"To be free."

"I'm working on it."

CHAPTER 47
PINEDALE, WYOMING

EARLY IN THE MORNING, Calvin Dixon turned his pickup truck from the highway and let it coast to a stop in the parking space outside the Wrangler Café. He opened the door and stepped from the cab into the crisp morning air. As he slipped on his hat, he glanced in the bed of the truck. The corner of an aluminum case protruded from beneath a blue tarp. He reached over the side of the truck and pulled the tarp back in place then set a sack of horse feed on the edge to hold it there. Satisfied the case was out of sight, he adjusted his hat and turned toward the café.

"Good morning, Cal," a waitress called to him as he entered. Calvin nodded to her, took off his hat and sat down near the back of the room. From the chair where he sat he could see outside to the truck without being obvious. The waitress came to his table. "Having your usual this morning?"

"Yes, ma'am," he smiled. "My usual."

She set a cup at his place and poured it full of coffee. "Two eggs over easy, steak medium, with home fries."

"And don't forget the toast this time."

"Okay," she grinned. "I won't forget the toast."

As she moved away from the table, a blue Ford sedan rolled to a stop in the space next to Calvin's truck. A man dressed in blue jeans and a work shirt got out of the car. He moved nonchalantly to the bed of the truck, reached over the side, and lifted out the aluminum case.

The waitress appeared at the table. "You know that man?"

"Yeah," Calvin replied, his eyes focused on the scene in the parking lot. "I've met him a time or two."

The man in the parking lot carried the aluminum case to the back of the sedan. He opened the trunk, placed the case inside, and slammed the trunk closed. With the case in the car, he came inside the café and took a seat at the table with Calvin. The waitress appeared at his side.

"Having breakfast?"

He pointed over at Calvin. "I'll have whatever he's having."

"Sure thing."

When she was gone, he looked across the table at Calvin. "We're attracting too much attention doing it this way."

"Relax," Calvin replied. "The more obvious we are, the less people will notice."

CHAPTER 48
KRASNOYARSK, RUSSIA

THE NEXT EVENING, Demetrius Nilus sat at his desk and once again waited while the computer booted up its operating program. He took a sip of his drink and glanced at a news magazine, but he was distracted and he found it hard to concentrate. This was the day the contacts in America were to report. "I hope Ivan did as he promised," Nilus grumbled. "I should hate to see what would happen if he failed."

A moment later, the computer beeped, indicating it was ready. He logged on to the Internet and went to the Twitter Web site. It took a while to load but when it was up he quickly found the page for a user identified as SellDirect123. The last entry from the user read, "Reliable product delivery is always appreciated."

"It is a package one could die for," Nilus grinned.

Next, he typed in the Web address for MySpace and stared at the screen while it loaded. "These American sites," he groused. "They are always so slow."

Finally, when the site was up and running, he went to the page for a user known as Jake Spoon. The last comment posted by the user stated, "Successful day."

"All is good so far," Nilus mumbled.

At LinkedIn he found a page for someone named Bob Walker. The user picture was that of a politician from the Ukraine, and seeing it always made Nilus uneasy. "These are supposed to be strictly American," he shouted to no one in particular. "Strictly American."

Still grumbling to himself, he scrolled down the page and found the update section, which read, "Thankfully, many delivery systems are better than the Postal Service."

"I do not like it," Nilus growled. "He has a Ukrainian politician on his site and he is complaining about an American government agency. Someone might notice and get angry. Or worse, they might get curious. Like that thing they say ..." He thought for a moment, then his face lit up. "Like a cat. Only his curiosity just might get him killed—all nine lives gone at once," he laughed.

Finally, Nilus went to the last address, the Facebook page for Dona Reynolds, a user who supposedly lived in Atlanta. Dona's status read, "Spent the day looking for our cat. It's not here. The family is very sad."

Nilus felt his heart drop into his stomach. "I was afraid of this," he sighed. He pushed back from the desk. "This is not good. Not good at all."

He picked up his cell phone and typed in a text message that said simply, "4?" Then he pressed a button and sent it to Ivan.

Within seconds Ivan replied, "3."

Demetrius laid aside his cell phone and took another sip of his drink. As he swallowed, the computer beeped once more. He checked the screen and saw an icon indicating he had received a new email. He opened it and found a message from Rhodes that read, "Invoice incomplete. Contact shipper?"

Demetrius typed in a one-word response, "Conference." Reluctantly, he pressed the Send button and waited.

A few minutes later came the reply, "Granted."

He tipped up the glass and drained it to the bottom.

CHAPTER 49
RHODES

SHORTLY AFTER SUNRISE, Carlo Busca came from his office and started down the corridor. Giovanni rose from his desk and followed after him. Busca spoke without looking back. "We have a meeting of the Council."

"It is not on the schedule."

"This is an emergency."

Fear seized Giovanni. He was certain someone had discovered the problem with his Blackberry. He stammered a response. "An emergency?" His voice was unusually loud and excited. "What has happened?"

"Hush." Busca snapped around to face him. "You should know better that to talk like that in the corridor. What if others hear you?"

"Yes, Your Grace." Giovanni bowed his head. "Forgive me. I was wrong."

"We must follow procedures. Even in such trying times as these. Never ask me a direct question and never outside the office."

"Certainly." Giovanni bowed his head lower and kept it there as they continued down the corridor. "How may I serve you?"

"You will sit in the meeting." Busca glanced again in his direction. "And stand up straight," he complained. "You'll only draw attention to us if you act like that and others will ask questions."

They turned the corner and came to the Hall of Saints. Giovanni reached past Busca and pulled open the door. He moved aside and let Busca pass, then followed him into the room. The Twenty-Four were already seated at the conference table. They rose as Busca entered. He acknowledged them with a wave of his hand. "Be seated, please."

The men took their seats. Busca stood at the head of the table. "Gentlemen, I regret to inform you that what we feared most has occurred. One of the angels has failed to reach its destination."

Father Penalta looked stricken. He glanced at Spoleto, then back to Busca. "What happened?"

Spoleto stood. "What 'angel' are we talking about?"

The room became deathly quiet. Busca looked indignant. "Father Spoleto, we are discussing the matter we authorized earlier, against the Jews in America."

"The Military Vicariate has not yet formulated the final details of its execution of that directive. We are only now contacting our sources."

All eyes turned to Busca. "I was under the assumption that authority had been given to me."

"Yes," Spoleto nodded. "Authority was given, but that authority was given to the Military Vicariate. Are you saying that you have taken upon yourself the execution of the Council's directive?"

"We have discussed this matter at length in a number of sessions," Busca argued. "Action was authorized in our last meeting."

"The Grand Master has no authority to execute directives regarding military matters." Spoleto gestured to those seated around the table. "Even this Council, which sets policy for the entire Order, has no authority to execute its own directives in military matters. The Rule creating our Order separated the two functions. Those functions, having been separated from the beginning, cannot be merged by a directive of this body. It would take a directive from the entire Order to do such a thing, and even then it might not be possible."

Busca was obviously shaken. "I...I am the Grand Master. I hold plenary authority."

"All authority is limited by the Rule that authorizes our existence. Yours included."

"We are sovereign."

"Yes," Spoleto nodded. "We, the Order, are sovereign. But you, the Grand Master, are not."

Uneasiness descended over those seated at the table and they began to murmur. Busca rapped the table with his knuckles. "We must have silence," he snapped. The Twenty-Four turned to him with an imperious stare. Busca cleared his throat and softened his tone. "Perhaps I have exceeded the intent of the Council."

Someone at the far end of the table spoke up. "What, exactly, has been done?"

Busca's face turned to stone. "I have executed the Council's directive, and you now ask me for details?"

"Yes," someone else replied. "A full accounting."

Busca's hands trembled. "Very well," he said finally. "Following the Council's most recent meeting on the matter of the Jews, I notified our Russian contacts and instructed them to put the plan in motion."

"And what, exactly, was the plan they put in motion?"

"I do not—"

Four delegates rose in unison from the table and in unison said, "Call for the deposition."

Busca's face turned pale. A demand for deposition called into question the veracity of a delegate. It was, in effect, an accusation that one had not told the truth and required the consent of four delegates. By rule, such a demand superseded all business before the Council while the delegate in question was examined on the matter at issue. Busca, being Grand Master and the delegate against whom the demand was raised, could no longer chair the meeting. That duty fell to Spoleto.

Spoleto, still standing, glanced around the table. "The deposition having been demanded by four, let us proceed."

Spoleto then took official control of the meeting. "I repeat the question raised by the Council in its demand for deposition. What was the plan?"

Busca sank to his chair. "A coordinated attack against the four cities in America with the highest Jewish population."

"And what was the means?"

"Four Russian suitcase bombs."

"How were they acquired?"

Busca gave Spoleto a sullen look. "From General Nilus. As we have discussed many times."

"And when is this attack to take place?"

"The plan is in motion. It has its own timetable."

"You cannot stop it?"

"It is compartmentalized. No one is to know the identity of all the operatives."

Spoleto continued. "And one of these suitcase bombs is now missing?"

"Yes," Busca replied. "Four were sent. Three have arrived. Our supplier has asked for a conference."

"And you agreed to a conference?"

"Yes," Busca nodded. "I agreed."

Murmuring began once again. Spoleto interrupted, "A conference for a failed execution of the Council's order in military matters cannot properly come before this Council."

"That is a matter for the Military Vicariate," someone murmured.

"This is most irregular," another whispered.

Spoleto rapped the table with his knuckles. The room fell silent. Spoleto continued. "When is this conference to take place?"

"The general is on his way to meet us now."

Spoleto was silent a moment, then looked across the table at the four delegates still standing. "Satisfied?"

"Yes," they replied, and took their seats.

Spoleto turned his attention to those seated at the table. "It seems we must await the arrival of General Nilus to discuss this matter further and reach a conclusion about the action we must take. But I see no other option than to authorize the Military Vicariate to contain the matter of the missing case."

"Agreed," several said at once.

"And then a formal inquiry when this matter is at rest."

"Agreed," several more said in a strong voice.

Spoleto glanced down the table to Busca. "Your Excellency, the Twenty-Four are unanimous."

"Very well," Busca replied. His voice wavered. He took a moment to collect himself, then continued. "All in favor signify your vote by the usual manner."

In unison, the delegates pushed back their chairs from the table and stood.

"Any opposed?" The room fell silent. Busca rapped the table with his knuckles. "So be it."

Then the delegates responded together, "In the name of the Father, and of the Son, and of the Holy Spirit. Amen." And with that, the meeting adjourned and the men made their way from the room.

When they were gone, Busca glanced at Giovanni, who was still sitting in the corner. Their eyes met and Busca nodded. Giovanni rose from his chair and stepped outside. As he walked up the corridor, he took out his cell phone and entered a text message.

CHAPTER 50
MOSCOW, RUSSIA

A LITTLE BEFORE NOON, Nikolai Trepov climbed the steps outside St. Basil's Cathedral off Red Square. Since the age of seven he had gone every day to pray, usually at Vespers in the evening after the work of the day was done. But this day, he had time at noon and his evening was already filled.

When he reached the top of the steps, he pulled open one of the massive doors and quietly made his way through the narthex to the nave. A crowd was gathered there already and Nikolai had to squeeze into a spot near the back. He stood there, self-conscious at having arrived late, with his hands folded together and resting at his waist.

A priest stood near the icon wall. With him were the deacons and two altar boys, each with a thurible holding the incense. They swung them back and forth while the priest recited the liturgy. The air was filled with sweet-scented smoke.

Nikolai followed along with the service until they reached the anaphora, then he felt his cell phone vibrate inside the pocket of his coat. He glanced around nervously to see if anyone noticed. There weren't supposed to be any calls that day. While the priest continued with the litany, Nikolai slid the phone from his pocket and turned it to one side so he could see the face. On the screen was an icon indicating he had received a text message. He recognized Giovanni's number immediately.

With a sigh, he slid the phone back into his pocket and nudged the man beside him, gesturing for space to ease past. The man frowned at him and stepped back. Nikolai turned sideways and slipped by. As he moved through the doorway, he glanced over his shoulder to see the priest glaring at him. Nikolai ignored him and crossed the narthex toward the door.

Outside on the street, he took the phone from his pocket again and pressed a button to view the text. The message read simply, "Employment terminated." He pressed another button to scroll down the screen and came to a photograph of Yuri Ivanovsky. He exited from the message and returned the phone to his pocket.

* * *

Oren Cohen sat in a control room at the Mossad operations center at Beersheba. Tired and bored, he rubbed his eyes and leaned his head against the top of his chair. Just then, a computer alarm beeped. He glanced across the room toward Tzipi Levanon who was seated at a workstation a few feet away. "Anything new?"

"We have intercepted a text message."

"Who is it from?"

"The cell phone on Rhodes."

Cohen sat up straight in his chair. "Who is he contacting?"

"A cell phone in Moscow. The number is not registered, but our database indicates it is assigned to Nikolai Trepov."

Cohen scooted his chair closer. "You are sure of this?"

"Yes."

"Show me the message."

Levanon pressed a button. The text message and photograph appeared on the screen. Cohen studied them a moment. "We should inform the Americans."

"CIA?"

"No," Cohen replied. "Forward this information to NEST."

"NEST?" She frowned. "We can send it to them directly, without going through Langley? But why NEST?"

"Never mind why," Cohen snapped. "Just do as I say."

CHAPTER 51
NEW ORLEANS

A BLACK SUV ROLLED SLOWLY down Laurel Street. Gennady Pomarov saw it from the bedroom window. He was downstairs and waiting when it turned into the driveway. As it came to a stop he pushed open the screened door, crossed the porch, and stepped onto the front lawn.

When Pomarov reached the SUV he jerked open the back door and found the aluminum case sitting on the backseat. Without a word to the driver, he took the case, slammed the door closed, and walked back toward the house. The SUV backed into the street and drove away.

Pomarov lugged the case through the living room and down the hall to the back bedroom. He laid it on the bed and backed away, his eyes fixed on the case, keenly aware of the power it held.

Alim Solonik appeared in the doorway. A short man, he had big, muscular arms, a wide barrel chest, and a large round belly that hung over the waist of his pants. A cigarette dangled between two fingers of his left hand. He raised it to his lips and took a long, slow drag on it, then slowly let the smoke escape through his nostrils. "I see the package has arrived," he said finally. The words in Russian came effortlessly from deep inside and rumbled up through his throat.

"Yes," Pomarov replied. "It is here." He pointed toward the case.

"You would like to inspect it?" He leaned forward and stretched out his hands to grasp the latches.

"No!" Solonik barked. He paused and lowered his voice. "Do not touch it."

Pomarov looked back with a smile. "You are worried it will blow up?"

Solonik moved the cigarette from his mouth. "I am worried it will blow up here."

"It must be armed first." Pomarov spun around and took a seat on the edge of the bed.

"It was armed when it left Russia." Solonik propped his arm against the doorframe. "You know the way to the synagogue?"

"Yes."

Solonik took another drag from the cigarette. "They told you about the delay?"

"I will be long away when it goes off."

"Not too far." Pomarov looked worried.

Solonik laughed. "We do not want someone to find it before it has time to explode."

Pomarov chuckled. "Can you picture the rabbi finding it?"

Solonik joined him in the ironic humor. "He picks it up. What is this? And then *boom*, it goes off in his hands."

Pomarov glanced over at the case. His face turned cold and hard. "Either way, he will never know what hit him."

They fell silent. Solonik took another drag from the cigarette. After a moment, he dropped the cigarette to the floor and rubbed it out with the toe of his shoe. "Get ready." He glanced over at Pomarov. "You slept last night?"

"Yes."

"Good. Miami is a long way." Solonik turned away from the door. "Soon you must be going."

CHAPTER 52
RHODES

ANGELO GIOVANNI LEFT HIS DESK outside Busca's office and made his way down the hall. With the cell phone recovered he could breathe a little easier, but there was always the possibility Belisconi had compromised the information it held, contacts and numbers and messages that no one should ever see. If they became public, the damage to the Order could mean his own execution. That must never happen and already he was at work arranging events to put himself in the best light. Part of that plan involved Father Spoleto.

By the day's schedule, Spoleto was set for a meeting in the chapel. Giovanni glanced at his watch. That meeting would begin within the hour. If he hurried, he might be able to catch Spoleto on the way.

He walked quickly down the Corridor of St. John the Divine toward the grand staircase. As he turned the corner at the end of the corridor he saw Spoleto headed in his direction. Giovanni lingered there, waiting. Moments later, Spoleto passed his station.

"Good afternoon, Your Grace."

"Yes," Spoleto replied. "It has been an excellent afternoon."

"I was wondering if I might have a word with you."

"Certainly." Spoleto came to a stop. "Are you on an errand from Father Busca?"

"No." Giovanni glanced around nervously. "I come on my own accord."

"Very well." Spoleto gestured toward the stairway. "Perhaps you should join me for a brief walk in the courtyard."

Giovanni trailed behind as Spoleto made his way down the stairs. Three flights below, they came to a heavy wooden door. Spoleto pushed it opened and held it as Giovanni followed him outside. When they were in the courtyard, Spoleto glanced back at him. "Now, tell me what is on your mind."

"As you know, I have spent many years in the service of Father Busca. He has all my loyalty, second only to God and the Order."

"As it should be."

"Yes. And that is why I have come to you." Giovanni took a breath, then continued. "The Military Vicariate is now mobilized for execution of the Council's most recent decision."

"And all is going according to plan?"

"Yes. But I am worried about Father Busca."

"Oh?" Spoleto stopped and turned to face Giovanni. "And how is that?"

Giovanni looked down at the ground. "I am not certain he is up to the task of leading the Order in such trying times."

"That is a serious charge. What makes you say such a thing?"

"I hear him. In his office." Giovanni looked up. "Talking to himself. He sounds like a madman."

"That is not such a bad thing." Spoleto smiled. "I talk to myself sometimes, too. What does he say?"

"This is not like the musings of someone deep in thought. He has conversations. First in one voice, then in another, and when he speaks his face actually changes."

Spoleto had a troubled look. "Surely, you must be mistaken. There must be others in the room with him."

"No." Giovanni shook his head. "I see everyone who comes and goes. Every visitor must pass by my desk first." He looked away once more. "And I have checked, just to make certain."

Spoleto arched an eyebrow. "You were spying on him?"

"Only for the good of the Order," Giovanni said quickly. "I assure you."

"And how did you accomplish this without being noticed?"

"There is a small hole in the wall, around the corner from my desk."

"A hole?"

"Yes, sir. An ancient one, I suspect. From it one may see directly into the office with a clear view of the wall where Father Busca has his desk."

"And you have seen him in these…conversations?"

"Yes," Giovanni nodded. "I have watched him as he talks with himself."

"Hmm. I see." Spoleto had a thoughtful look. "I appreciate you coming to me." He dismissed Giovanni with a gentle wave of his hand. "I will keep this under my own counsel." He had a sober expression. "As a confession."

"Yes, sir." Giovanni nodded. "Thank you." He turned to leave. Then Spoleto called after him, "You will keep our conversation to yourself, as well?"

Giovanni bowed his head. "Certainly, sir." He turned away and walked quickly toward the door.

CHAPTER 53
ASTANA, KAZAKHSTAN

NABAPAV DAULENOV WATCHED from the cab of the fuel truck as the Learjet taxied from the runway to the hangar. A man wearing an orange vest came from the hangar and guided it to a stop near the tie-down hooks at the left of the building. As the engines slowly whined to a stop, Daulenov put the truck in gear, let out on the clutch pedal, and started forward toward the plane. He brought the truck alongside the wing and carefully positioned it next to the fuel cap, then climbed from the cab.

He pulled a hose from a rack beneath the truck and attached one end to the nozzle on the tank. With the other end, he moved beneath the wing, opened the plane's fuel filler cover and attached the hose. As he moved back to the truck, he glanced up at the plane. Leonid Malenkov appeared in the doorway.

A car came to a stop near the plane. Malenkov came down the steps toward the car. When he reached the tarmac, he took his cell phone from his pocket and glanced at the screen. His face turned grave as he stared at it.

Daulenov turned a valve on the truck and began pumping fuel into the wing of the aircraft. The sound of the pump motor drowned out Malenkov's voice, but Daulenov could see he was talking loud and fast to the driver. The driver raised his hands in a gesture of frustration, jabbed the air with his finger, and placed his hands on his hips. Malenkov held the phone in one hand and gestured to it with the other as if to indicate someone had called or sent a message he could not ignore.

Malenkov turned away from the car and started back up the steps. A man dressed in a pilot's uniform met him at the doorway and the two men exchanged words. Then the pilot nodded in submissive agreement. Malenkov disappeared inside the plane. The pilot came down the steps and across the tarmac toward Daulenov. He smiled as he came closer.

"Can you fill it all the way?"

"If someone will guarantee payment."

"I will guarantee payment."

"I do not know you." Daulenov gestured toward the hangar. "Check with someone inside."

The pilot turned away and started toward the building. A few minutes later, a woman appeared at the hangar door. In her hand she held a paper, which she waved in Daulenov's direction. From the look on her face he knew it was authorization to fuel the plane.

Half an hour later, Daulenov disconnected the hose from the wing of the plane and replaced it in the rack beneath the truck. He climbed into the cab and drove the truck back to the hangar. He parked alongside the building and went inside. A woman at the desk handed him three forms. He signed them and handed her a ticket indicating the amount of fuel he had loaded.

"Looks like that guy changed his plans."

"Yeah."

"Where was he going?"

"Russia."

"Where in Russia?"

She frowned. "What do you care?"

"Was it within the plane's range?"

"It's a Learjet," she replied. "It has a three-thousand-mile range."

"So, was it going to Moscow?"

The woman sighed and opened a desk drawer. She took out a form and glanced at it. "Krasnoyarsk," she said with a smile. "If you must know, it was going to Krasnoyarsk."

"Okay," Daulenov replied. "Now I can fill in my forms correctly."

He tossed the documents on the counter and stepped outside. At the far end of the building, he took a cell phone from his pocket and entered a text message. He waited for a note indicating the message had been sent, then closed the phone and returned it to his pocket.

CHAPTER 54
CHICAGO

SAVELY TOLKALINA SAT in the Mercedes and listened to the radio. From his parking space at the corner of the fifth floor he had a clear view of anyone who entered the deck. Cars coming up from the street passed him to the right. People arriving from below entered the floor from the elevator to the left. Next to it was a staircase. He could see them all. No one would catch him by surprise. The angle of the car obstructed the view of the space to his left, which meant arriving cars would pass it by, leaving it open.

Fifteen minutes later, a dark blue SUV came slowly up the ramp. Savely caught the driver's eye. He turned the SUV into the open space.

Savely opened the car door and stepped out. With one step, he reached the SUV and jerked open the rear door. On the backseat he found an aluminum case. He grabbed the handle and lifted it out, then slammed the door shut. The driver backed out of the space while Savely set the case on the rear seat of the Mercedes. In less than a minute he was back behind the steering wheel. He waited a moment for the SUV to get a head start, then followed it down the ramp to the street.

Savely drove north to Lincolnwood. At Howard Street he made a left and turned into the driveway beside a stone house. He parked the car in the garage, took the case from the backseat, and walked toward the house. As he came through the back door, Vitali Safronov was seated at the kitchen table, reading the newspaper. He wore dress slacks with a white cotton T-shirt and spoke without looking up. "You had no trouble?"

"None."

"They did not question you?"

"No. The driver said nothing. I am certain he knew if he opened his mouth on our turf he would not speak again—ever."

Vitali moved the paper aside and glanced down at the case. "Set it in the bedroom." Savely carried the case across the kitchen and down the hall. "The front bedroom," Vitali called. "I don't want it anywhere near me."

"Have you heard from Ruslan?"

"He is on his way."

"Good. We must get it to New York before Friday."

Vitali picked up the newspaper. "Everything is set for their Sabbath."

"A sacrifice," Savely chuckled.

"A human sacrifice," Vitali called, this time even louder. He folded the page of the newspaper. "This time we do it right," he said to himself quietly. "We kill every Jew in New York City and most of their American friends."

CHAPTER 55
KRASNOYARSK, RUSSIA

A CAR WAS WAITING on the tarmac when Malenkov arrived at the airport. He hurried down the steps from the Learjet and ducked into the backseat. Ten minutes later, he was at Nilus' house. They sat near the desk and shared a bottle of vodka while they talked.

Malenkov looked perplexed. "What was so important you had to take me away from our business in Kazakhstan?"

Nilus looked grave. "I must travel to Rhodes."

"Rhodes?" Malenkov frowned. "Greece?"

"Yes."

"But travel is forbidden for you." Malenkov looked puzzled. "Russian authorities will never approve it. You cannot leave Krasnoyarsk. You have not been allowed to leave since…I know of no such time."

"I must go," Nilus shrugged.

"But how? The Kremlin will allow you to leave?"

"I do not intend to ask." Nilus took a drink from his glass. "The Black Knights have agreed to see me."

"Black Knights?"

"The Twenty-Four Elders of the Order of Malta."

Malenkov's countenance turned somber. "You cannot simply refuse them?"

"Three of the cases arrived at their destination." Nilus had a thin, pained smile. "One of them did not."

"I thought the cases were already delivered. We discussed this weeks ago—how to get them to America without detection, the immunity of special diplomatic missions." Malenkov dropped his hands against his thighs in a gesture of frustration. "We even discussed who could arrange such a trip."

"We discussed the possibility," Nilus corrected. "They did not send the orders until just a few days ago."

Malenkov shook his head. "You should have never trusted the mafia."

"Ivan is a knight."

"Ivan is a crook," Malenkov retorted. "He will hold that case over our heads, over all our heads. We are now at war with ourselves."

"You do not understand." Nilus gestured with his hand. "The case will be found. The order will be executed. The Elders will see that it happens."

Malenkov gave him a doubtful look. "They cannot reach the mafia."

"They can reach anyone," Nilus insisted. "Anyone."

"I do not think so."

Nilus leaned closer. "You remember Nicholas II? The Romanovs?"

"Yes. Of course."

"What happened to them?"

"They were executed by Bolsheviks. Everyone knows that. Gunmen on orders from Lenin took them to the basement and shot them."

"That is what the history books say."

"Is it not what happened?"

"The Romanovs were killed, but not on orders from Lenin." Nilus set his glass on the table and turned it between his fingers while he spoke. "They were killed *because of* Lenin."

"Because of him? What are you talking about?"

"Nicholas was under orders from the Twenty-Four Elders to

execute key Red leaders. They were all Jews and they were taking control of Russia. Our national treasury went from the wealthiest in the world to nearly empty. At the time Nicholas took the throne, Russia was the most powerful country in the world. Then the Jews started their revolution and were on the verge of destroying everything. The Elders decreed their removal, but Nicholas would not execute the decision. The men who entered the basement that night were not Bolsheviks on a mission from Lenin, they were assassins sent by the Order of Malta to terminate Nicholas for his failure to carry out their command."

"That is preposterous."

"It is the truth." Nilus took hold of the bottle and poured his glass full of vodka. "And that is what will happen to Ivan if that fourth case does not show up."

"You are certain of this?"

"As certain as I am alive." Nilus took a drink and swallowed it. "You must go to Moscow, find Ivan, and find out what happened to that case. I must go to Rhodes and beg for our lives."

"*Our* lives?"

"They know you work with me. We will both be under suspicion. We must appear to be working diligently to bring the matter to a successful conclusion."

"Three were delivered?"

"Yes. And that will help. But we must appear to be diligent. If we are making progress, perhaps they will give us time. Especially if they think we can reach a successful conclusion quickly."

CHAPTER 56
MOSCOW, RUSSIA

VITOLD TREPOV PARKED THE CAR on a side street next to the Cosmopolitan Center, an office building in the city's entertainment district across from the Fabrika nightclub. He switched off the engine and took a leather satchel from the seat beside him. With the satchel in hand, he slid from the car and walked to a service entrance in back of the building. He climbed the steps to a loading dock, made his way inside to the freight elevator, and rode to the top floor. On the opposite side of the floor he came to a stairway that led to the roof. Moments later, he stepped outside and gazed down on the city below.

From atop the building he could see all the way to Red Square. The Kremlin stood like a fort and across from it were the familiar domed heads of St. Basil's. He could have stood there longer, enjoying the panoramic view, but there was work to be done and little time to waste.

Trepov pushed the stairway door shut and moved across the roof to a billboard with neon lights that faced the street below. Standing behind the frame of the sign, he was obscured from view but had a clear line of sight to the main entrance of the Fabrika. He knelt by the sign, set the leather satchel at his side, and opened it.

From inside the satchel he took out the stock and body assembly of an SA80 assault rifle. He clicked the barrel into place, twisted the silencer onto the muzzle, and loaded a magazine into the slot near the trigger. He reached inside the satchel once more for the scope and attached it to the top of the body near the front of the stock.

With the rifle prepared, Trepov glanced down at the street and waited. A few minutes later, a black Mercedes came into view. He followed it as it rolled down the street and pulled to a stop in front of the nightclub. Trepov raised the gun and pressed the butt of the stock against his shoulder. He leveled the barrel in the direction of the club and brought the scope to his eye. With the rifle steadied against the frame of the sign, he placed the crosshairs of the sight on the Mercedes.

The rear door of the car opened and a woman stepped out, followed by Ivan. Trepov moved the crosshairs from the Mercedes and brought them to rest on the woman's back. Through the scope he saw she was laughing and smiling as she moved from the car to the sidewalk. They were about to pass from view beneath the entrance canopy when she abruptly stopped. Ivan appeared in Trepov's sights as he stumbled into the woman. Trepov's finger curled around the trigger to squeeze off a shot but Ivan quickly moved to the right to step around the woman. As he did, he paused to say something to her. A scowl wrinkled his face and he raised his hands in a gesture of frustration. Trepov adjusted his aim, placed the crosshairs on Ivan's chest, and calmly squeezed the trigger.

Through the scope he saw Ivan's eyes open wide. His arms dropped as he clutched at his chest with both hands. A red blotch soaked through the shirt. Now his head was fully exposed. Trepov moved the crosshairs to Ivan's forehead and squeezed the trigger once more. Ivan's head snapped backward, then jerked forward as blood splattered onto the sidewalk. Above the traffic noise, Trepov heard the woman scream.

CHAPTER 57
KRASNOYARSK, RUSSIA

LATE IN THE AFTERNOON, Malenkov came from Nilus' house. The car was waiting outside. He climbed in back and rode silently through the streets of Krasnoyarsk. What he'd heard that day left him shaken and he stared out the window, thinking again of the conversation.

The notion that the Order of Malta could extend its reach so far had never occurred to him. Princes, kings, and presidents were subject to their decisions. Even his own uncle, a general in the Russian Army, was leaving a closed city to travel a quarter of the way around the world to beg for his life. *If they can reach a general, in a closed Russian city, then how safe can I possibly be?*

A few minutes later, the car turned in at the airport. It made its way to the hangar and came to a stop alongside the Learjet. The fuselage door stood open with the stairway extended. Already the engine on the opposite side was up and running. Through the cockpit window Malenkov saw the crew seated inside. A tall, leggy woman dressed in a business suit stood just inside the plane, awaiting his arrival.

Malenkov reached for the door handle, then hesitated. For the first time in his life, boarding an airplane wasn't automatic. *If I get on that plane, I'm handing my life to the pilot. Will he take me where I want to go, or follow directions supplied by someone I've never even seen before?*

"Ahh," he growled out loud. "I'm going crazy." He stepped from the car and hurried up the steps to the jet. As he settled into his seat, the woman he'd seen earlier appeared again at the galley near the doorway. She pressed a button to retract the stairway, then pulled the door closed and latched it in place. When an indicator light above the door turned green, she took a seat and fastened the belt around her waist.

Malenkov glanced out the window and watched the ground crew move the chocks from the plane's wheels. Moments later, the plane started forward, turned onto the taxiway, and rolled slowly to the end of the runway. The pilot's voice spoke over the intercom. "We are cleared for immediate takeoff."

Without stopping, the plane turned onto the runway and picked up speed. Before it reached the first turnout, the nose lifted and the plane rose into the air. Malenkov rested his head against the back of the seat and closed his eyes. Soon he was fast asleep.

* * *

With Malenkov on his way, Nilus called for his car and driver. An hour later, he arrived at a warehouse on the opposite side of town. He pushed open the car door and glanced up at the driver. "Do not wait for me."

"You will call when you are ready?"

"I will have a ride home later. It will be late. There is no reason to ruin your evening."

"Yes, sir." The driver smiled and nodded. "Thank you."

Inside the building, a truck was parked near a roll-up door at the far end. Nilus made his way past it to a restroom near the warehouse office. Hanging on a peg behind the door were a pair of work pants, a work shirt, and a heavy coat. Nilus closed the door and locked it, then changed his clothes. Ten minutes later, he emerged looking like any other workman in the city.

He stepped to the passenger side of the truck, pulled open the door, and climbed inside the cab. A driver was seated behind the steering wheel. Nilus acknowledged him with a nod. The driver started the engine. Two men appeared at the roll-up door and opened it. As the door rumbled overhead and out of the way, the truck started forward. Nilus reached under the seat and took out a cap. He placed it atop his head, propped an elbow against the window, and closed his eyes. By nightfall, they were almost to Kemerovo.

CHAPTER 58
PORTLAND, OREGON

GRAY LIGHT OF A CLOUDY DAY drifted through the opaque window behind Nikolai Elson, outlining him in a surreal glow. Brad Ramsey shifted uneasily in his chair and waited for a response. When Elson finally spoke, the words came with a heavy Russian accent. "So, you think she is cheating us?"

Ramsey was the manager of Barely Here, a strip club located on Denver Avenue. For three weeks he'd been monitoring the nightly receipts, and every night the cash register had come up short. "Yes, sir, Mr. Elson. I'm sure she is."

"You know this for a fact?"

Ramsey cleared his throat. "I saw her put in a twenty and take out a hundred."

"How many times?"

"She did it three times."

"And that made us three hundred short for the night."

"Yes, sir." He tried to do the math in his head but he was nervous. "Close to it. For that night."

"She did this every night?"

"I didn't see her every night, but every night we were two hundred fifty to three hundred dollars short."

Elson reached in the drawer for a pack of cigarettes. He took one out, poked it in his mouth, and lit it. "You are certain it was Anna Milkova?"

"Yes, sir. Positive. I know her."

A young man entered from the doorway behind Ramsey. He crossed the room and came behind the desk, then leaned close to Elson's ear and whispered something. Elson looked up at him with a smile, then over at Ramsey. "We will see to it that she is no longer here." He stood and dismissed Ramsey with a wave of his hand. "That is all."

"Yes, sir." Ramsey rose from his chair and stepped out to the hallway. He paused there and listened to the conversation in the office.

"It is here?"

"Yeah."

"Finally," Elson replied. "There is not much time."

"You want it in here?"

"No." Ramsey heard Elson scoot his chair back from the desk. "Show me that Jew killer. I want to kiss it with my own lips."

The words struck a nerve with Ramsey. He moved quickly down the hall to the corner near the dance floor, then lingered there out of sight. A moment later, Elson and the young man left the office. Ramsey heard their footsteps as they walked up the hallway toward the back door. When the door banged closed, he hurried to an open window near the restroom where he watched and listened.

A gray Honda Accord was parked a few feet away. A second man stood beside it. Elson nodded to him.

"It is in the trunk?"

"Yes."

"And our friends in Coos Bay?"

"They will give us no trouble."

"Good." Elson gestured toward the car. "Open it."

The young man unlocked the trunk and raised the lid. Through the opening, Ramsey saw an aluminum case lying inside. Elson gazed down at it, then leaned over and kissed the top. When he raised his head from the trunk, he had a broad grin. "You know what to do?"

"Yes."

"You will have it in Los Angeles before Friday?"

"Yes."

Elson stared at the case a moment. "Everything is scheduled for Friday. You must get it in place before Friday night, when everyone comes to temple."

"I will," the young man assured him.

"And then you must be far away. Just drive," Elson said with a wave of his hand. "Drive…East. Drive east on the interstate. But not too fast. You don't want to get stopped. We have given you enough money to take care of things for a while."

They stared at each other a moment, then Elson draped an arm across the young man's shoulder. "I will tell your mother, when the time is right."

"Okay."

"She will be proud of what you have done." He slapped the young man on the back. "We shall rid the world of many Jews, and strike a blow at their protectors." He withdrew his arm and squared his shoulders. "And when the dust settles, the entire West Coast shall be under our control." They embraced again, then the young man pulled free and opened the car door. He crawled behind the steering wheel and placed the key in the ignition. Elson came around the car behind him and leaned through the open door. He handed the young man something, kissed him on the cheek, then backed away and closed the door. The engine started and the car moved toward the street.

CHAPTER 59
MOSCOW, RUSSIA

WHEN MALENKOV LANDED in Moscow he stepped from the plane and walked alone to a nearby hangar. A Hyundai sedan was parked there. He opened the door, slipped behind the steering wheel, and felt with his hand along the bottom edge of the dash. Beneath the steering column he found a key taped in place. He peeled it from the column, inserted it in the ignition, and started the car.

From the airport, Malenkov drove straight to Ivan's apartment. If things were as serious as Nilus suggested, there was little time to waste with formalities. He parked on a side street and watched the building. When nothing appeared suspicious, he left the car, crossed the street, and entered the lobby. He rode the elevator to the fourth floor and stepped cautiously into the hall. Slowly, with hesitant steps, he made his way to the left.

When he reached the apartment, he found the door ajar. He eased it open wider and called out, "Hello. Anyone home?" He listened intently for the slightest noise. After a moment, he pushed the door all the way back and stepped inside.

From the doorway he could see the apartment had been searched thoroughly. A table lay on its side. Chairs were out of place. Papers and pillows were strewn about the room. He glanced inside the kitchen to find the cabinet doors open. Dishes and plates sat on the counter. Down the hallway he found the bedroom in disarray. But there was no sign of Ivan.

Malenkov was unsettled by what he'd found but now he knew his uncle was correct. The Order had the power to reach anyone. He needed to locate Ivan, now more than ever. He turned from the bedroom, retraced his steps past the kitchen, and stepped outside to the hallway.

He left the apartment building and drove across town to the Fabrika. The club was just opening for the evening when he arrived. Out front near the entrance the outline of a human body was painted in white on the sidewalk. In the middle was written the simple phrase, "Party on!" Malenkov thought it odd, but the Moscow club scene wasn't known for its restraint or understatement.

At the bar inside he ordered a shot of vodka and glanced around, checking to see if Ivan was there. When he saw no one familiar, he caught the bartender's attention. "Is Ivan in today?"

The bartender gave him a strange look. "You haven't heard?"

"Heard what?" Malenkov knew what was coming next and his heart raced at the thought of it.

The bartender leaned closer. "Ivan is dead."

A wave of panic coursed through Malenkov's body. He pushed it aside and did his best to appear unfazed. "What happened to him?"

"Someone shot him." The bartender gestured toward the door. "Didn't you see the markings on the sidewalk?"

"He was shot here?"

"Yes. Just outside," the bartender nodded. "Very upsetting."

"How did it happen?"

"Not sure. He was getting out of the car. Shot came out of nowhere."

The bartender's description did little to ease Malenkov's nerves. A shot from nowhere—an assassin with a long-range rifle—a professional job. He tipped up his glass, sucked out the last drops of vodka, and turned to leave.

CHAPTER 60
FLAGSTAFF, ARIZONA

SKIPPER ALLEN SAT on a Coca-Cola crate outside Kurt and Shorty's Garage. Located on U.S. Highway 66, the garage had once been a busy place. Back in the day, the gravel lot around it was filled with trucks and cars waiting to be repaired. Transfer trucks were their specialty and they were open twenty-four hours a day, seven days a week, every day of the year except Easter, Mother's Day, and Christmas. But that was before the interstate took all the traffic. Now all that was left of those days was a mountain of used tires piled behind the building and oil stains on the parking lot.

From his place across the road, Skipper watched as a blue Ford sedan turned from the highway and rolled to a stop outside Thornton's Café. The driver stepped from the car and disappeared inside the building. A few minutes later, a green Chevrolet pickup rattled and rumbled as it turned from the pavement and came to a stop alongside the Ford.

As the dust settled around the truck, the driver's door opened and a slender man stepped out dressed in khakis and a T-shirt. He slammed the door closed and walked around to the driver's side of the Ford. Without so much as a glance in the window of the café, he opened the door and got in behind the steering wheel. A moment later, he backed the car from the parking space and turned it toward the road. He waited there a moment for a car to pass, then pulled onto the highway.

"That was a drop," Skipper said to himself. He took a sip of Coca-Cola and belched. "Drugs, most likely." He took another sip, swished it around inside his mouth, and swallowed. "Drugs or drug money."

Before he finished drinking the Coke, the door of the café opened. A man stepped out, slipped on a pair of sunglasses, and walked to the Chevrolet pickup. He opened the door and climbed inside the cab. Skipper watched as the man started the engine and backed it away from the building. At the edge of the parking lot it blended into traffic without stopping and soon disappeared down the road.

Skipper tipped up the bottle and drained it dry. "Could be the CIA." He wiped his mouth on his shirtsleeve. "But I think it was drugs."

CHAPTER 61
RHODES

DEMETRIUS NILUS GLANCED out the window of the Gulfstream jet at the blue water of the Mediterranean shimmering in the bright sunshine. He took one more sip from his glass, then leaned back and closed his eyes. In spite of a lifetime in the Russian Army, he still hated flying.

The plane banked sharply to the left. Nilus gripped the empty glass with one hand and took hold of the armrest with the other. Something bumped beneath his feet. The sound of the air flowing past the fuselage changed. He opened his eyes and glanced out the window to find the wing flaps were down.

A voice spoke softly at his side. "General, we are preparing to land. May I take your glass?" Nilus cut his eyes to the left and saw the young woman standing in the aisle. He handed her the glass, gripped the armrest with both hands, and squeezed his eyes tightly closed. Moments later, the wheels touched down on the runway. He opened his eyes and relaxed his grip.

At the end of the runway, the plane turned toward a nondescript hangar on the far side of the airport. It taxied inside the building and came to a stop as the engines slowed and grew quiet. Nilus unlatched his seat belt and stepped into the aisle. He took his jacket from an overhead compartment and slipped it on, then adjusted the cuff of the sleeves and fastened the buttons on the front. Hat in hand, he started up the aisle toward the front of the plane. By the time he reached it, the stairs were down and the door was open.

A car was parked nearby. He made his way down the steps and walked briskly to the car's rear door. The driver was standing near the rear fender. As Nilus approached, the driver opened the door. Nilus crawled inside and settled into place on the seat.

Five minutes later, the car moved from the airport grounds onto a road that ran along the coast. Nilus watched out the window as the sea moved slowly past, but in his mind he concentrated on the meeting that lay ahead. Busca was not a difficult man. They had met before and he had found the Grand Master a practical man. But Busca did not have the final say in the matter. Nilus' fate, and that of his nephew, lay with the Council—the Twenty-Four Elders—the Black Knights.

Near the tip of the island, the car turned from the coast road onto a winding driveway that led up from the sea. Around a curve, the Knights Castle came into view. Its size alone cast an imposing presence over the landscape. Even though he'd seen it before, Nilus was impressed by the ancient structure's majestic simplicity.

The car came to a stop under a canopy at the entrance. A doorman stepped to the car and opened the rear door. Nilus climbed out, straightened his jacket, and turned to enter the building. In the main corridor, he was met by Angelo Giovanni. "General," he smiled. "I trust you had a good flight."

"There would have been nothing I could do about it if it were bad," Nilus growled.

A little way down the corridor, he felt his cell phone vibrating in his pocket. He took it out and glanced at the screen to see he had a new text message. "Arrived late," it read. "Discussion already concluded." Nilus exited the message, returned the phone to his pocket, and took a deep breath. Things were more serious than he expected.

On the opposite side of the castle they came to a set of large wooden doors. Giovanni paused there and rapped on the door. A voice inside called in response, "Enter." Giovanni pushed open one of the doors and held it aside. Nilus stepped forward into the Hall of Saints.

Seated around the table were the Twenty-Four members of the Council. Busca stood at the end with his back to Nilus. He turned in that direction and gestured with his left hand. "General, so good of you to join us." Nilus made his way toward the table. Busca pulled out a chair to his right and stepped back to make room. "Sit here." Nilus felt like a schoolboy taken to task over a playground fight, but he had little choice but to obey. He made his way to the chair and took a seat.

With Nilus seated to his right, Busca began. "General." He kept his eyes focused on the men seated at the table. "We understand one of the angels has not yet arrived at its destination."

"That is correct," Nilus replied. "Three were delivered. One is as yet unaccounted for."

"You were using an approved shipping method?"

"Yes."

"And all arrangements were made?"

"Yes."

"Have you contacted your shipping agent?"

"I have attempted, but I was informed just now that he is no longer in business."

"This is most unfortunate."

"Yes," Nilus agreed. "It is."

Busca cut his eyes in Spoleto's direction. Spoleto stood. "General, what do you propose to do about this matter?"

"I am sure there are others who have acquired his business. I intend to pursue the matter with them."

Spoleto seemed unmoved. "And is there any assurance you can locate his successors?"

"He has many business relationships. I am certain we can find others who know of the details."

Someone across the table took a deep breath. "That is helpful, and troubling at the same time."

"If the details are known by one," someone added, "they can be known by many."

"The trouble will only spread," another suggested.

Busca spoke up. "The general has been successful in the past. He has a most thorough knowledge of the transaction details. Perhaps we should work with him on this matter." For the first time, Busca turned in Nilus' direction. "But we will expect prompt and successful resolution."

"As will I," Nilus agreed once more.

Busca looked back to the Council. "We are in agreement?"

"Yes," they replied.

"Signify your decision in the usual manner."

In unison, the men pushed back their chairs from the table and stood. Nilus moved to stand. Busca laid his hand on Nilus' shoulder to keep in him place.

"Any opposed?" The room fell silent. Busca let his gaze roam around the table once more, looking every man in the eye. When he had gone all the way around, he rapped the table with his fist. "So be it."

They responded together, "In the name of the Father, and of the Son, and of the Holy Spirit. Amen."

Their work concluded, the delegates filed from the room. When they were gone, Busca looked over at Nilus. "You have three days."

"I am not sure I can—"

Busca did not wait for the reply. He stood abruptly and walked from the room.

Giovanni was waiting when Nilus came from the Hall of Saints. Nilus followed him down the corridor across the castle to the entrance. The car was parked beneath the canopy. He ducked inside and took his place on the rear seat. Before the door was closed, two men rushed forward and squeezed in next to him on either side. They held him in place while the driver reached over the seat with a syringe. He stabbed the needle of the syringe in Nilus' leg and depressed the plunger, injecting a clear substance into his thigh. As Nilus faded into unconsciousness, the driver turned to face forward and the car sped away.

* * *

Inside the Knights Castle, Giovanni raced down the corridor to Busca's office. He burst through the doors without knocking and rushed toward the desk. Busca leaped to his feet. "What is the meaning of this intrusion?"

"General Nilus has been taken," Giovanni shouted.

"What?"

"Just now," Giovanni gasped breathlessly. "They took him."

"Who took him?"

"Two men. They were waiting for him by the car. The driver was with them."

"The driver? Our driver?"

"I did not get a good look at him. I don't know if he was ours, or someone else."

Busca slumped into his chair. "It is Mossad," he sighed. Then slowly he raised his head. His eyes flashed with anger. "Those stupid Jews have taken him."

"What shall we do?"

"Where is Malenkov?"

"He was spotted at Ivan's club in Moscow, but he left before he could be apprehended. No one knows for certain where he is."

"Find him," Busca barked. "Find him now." He slammed his fist against the desktop. "This very minute."

"Yes, sir," Giovanni replied. "I shall alert the others." He turned to leave the room.

"No," Busca called after him. "Not a word to the others. We shall settle this ourselves."

"As you wish, Your Grace." Giovanni bowed once, then opened the door and stepped out to the corridor.

CHAPTER 62
LAS VEGAS, NEVADA

AT THE NEST COMMAND CENTER, someone called out to Rios, "Sir, you'll want to see this."

"What?" Rios came from across the room. "What is it?"

"Satellite images from Rhodes."

"What do you have? Put it on the screen."

The large screen on the wall flickered. Then an image appeared of a car speeding up the road near the airport. It careened around a hangar and screeched to a stop on the tarmac beside a jet.

Rios stared at the images. "Is this live?"

"Yes, sir."

Randall Morris appeared at Rios' side. "What's happening?"

"Mossad agents apprehended Demetrius Nilus."

Morris frowned. "Apprehended him?"

"Yeah. Apparently he was attending a meeting at Knights Castle."

"That's pretty bold," Morris added. "Snatching a Russian general."

"They'll never get away with it," Rios sighed.

"You're right. Russia may never acknowledge it, but they *will* retaliate."

"Let's watch this," Rios said, pointing to the screen.

He and Morris stared up at the screen as men pulled Nilus from the car, placed a hood over his head, and hustled him aboard the waiting jet. As Nilus disappeared inside, the stairs began to retract. Before they were all the way up, the plane started forward. Someone closed the door. When the jet reached the end of the taxiway, it turned onto the runway without stopping and accelerated for takeoff. Moments later, it was in the air.

"Okay," Rios said finally. "Let's confirm what just happened."

Ken Aycock, an analyst seated near the back of the room, spoke up. "Mossad's operations center at Beersheba has notified the prime minister that they have Nilus."

"All right." Rios closed his eyes a moment and covered his face with his hands. "Has anyone alerted the FBI?"

"No, sir."

Rios' eyes popped open. "Do it," he ordered. "And tell them to put the rendition team in Tel Aviv on standby."

"Tel Aviv?" Richard Weavil, an analyst on loan from the CIA, was doubtful. "Will they take him to Israel?"

"Where else are they gonna go?" Rios turned to the operator at the center of the room. "Contact the State Department. Tell them what's happened and have them alert our embassy in Athens. Rhodes is a Greek island. I doubt Mossad filed a flight plan before they went in there. The Israelis may need some help. I want our ambassador ready if they do."

"Right."

Rios continued calling out directions. "And see if the Israelis will allow us to interrogate him."

"The FBI or the CIA?"

"I don't know," Rios acknowledged. "I hate working with either of them, but we don't have much choice now. We need to find out what he knows about this suitcase, and they're the best we have to do the questioning."

"Yes, sir."

He leaned over the operator's shoulder and lowered his voice. "Have the CIA pick up the nephew."

"Malenkov?"

"Yeah. Tell them to find him now and take him into custody. We need him alive."

Morris appeared with a cup of coffee and nudged Rios' elbow. "Here." He handed Rios the cup. "Better start drinking this. Might be a while before we get out of this room."

Rios took a sip. "We need to know what Nilus was doing on Rhodes. It must have been big to get him out of Russia. When was the last time he left Krasnoyarsk?"

"It's been a while," Morris replied. "But that's a red herring. Keep your eyes on the task at hand."

"Which is?"

"Protecting the United States from a nuclear threat. Let somebody else unwrap the details of Nilus' life. We need to find out whether there really is a Russian suitcase bomb on U.S. soil."

"Nilus is bad news."

"He's like his grandfather. But that's not the point right now. Focus on the suitcase."

"I'd like to talk to Nilus."

"Well, if you insist, perhaps the Israelis will let you."

Rios had a curious look. "You think so?"

"You could always ask."

Rios took a sip of coffee. "Maybe later. Right now we need to find Malenkov."

CHAPTER 63
RHODES

THREE FLOORS BENEATH the Hall of Saints, Ignacio Spoleto gathered the men of the Military Vicariate into The Dungeon for an emergency meeting. When they were all seated, Spoleto scooted his chair up to the end of the conference table.

"Gentlemen, we face a grave situation," he began. "As you are aware, following the Council's decision regarding action against the Jews in America, Carlo Busca usurped our authority and initiated his own plan to execute the Council's directive. That plan included suitcase bombs provided by the Russian general, Demetrius Nilus. And, as you are also aware, one of the items used in that effort did not reach its destination. Demetrius Nilus appeared before the Council today to account for the failure. At Carlo Busca's insistence, the Council granted Nilus leave to locate the missing case."

"He should have been shot on sight."

"Along with Busca."

"Busca is an idiot."

"You should be careful of the way you speak against the office of Grand Master."

"I do not speak against the office, but against the man. He has lost his mind. He knew full well what he was doing and he did it brazenly."

Spoleto rapped on the table. The room grew quiet. Spoleto continued. "Just now, as Nilus was leaving the Castle, he was abducted by what we think were agents from Mossad who waited for him by his car."

The news stunned them and they sat in silence staring blankly at each other. Then Father Galena banged his fist on the table. "This is impossible," he blurted. "How did they find him?"

"I do not know, but they were waiting for him by the car. Right outside," Spoleto explained. "Not ten minutes ago. The car was still beneath the canopy."

"This is an outrage!" a man seated across the table shouted.

"How did Jews even get on the property, much less near the car?"

"Busca's incompetence has allowed them to invade the castle."

"To invade our sovereignty."

"Do we know where they have taken him?"

"They drove him to the airport and put him on a plane." Spoleto gestured with both hands in a matter-of-fact expression. "As far as we are able to determine, he is being taken to Israel. We assume he will be held in Jerusalem."

"This will surely alert the Americans."

Father Galena spoke again. "Did Greece authorize the flight?"

"There has been no response from the Greeks," Spoleto answered. "I doubt they even know this has happened."

"We have Jews using the Americans for cover while they buy the world." Galena's voice reflected the frustration they all felt. "A suitcase bomb on the loose and available for sale to the highest bidder. And now we have Jews on the grounds of our own estate."

"This lies at the feet of Busca."

Heads around the table nodded in agreement.

"We must act quickly."

A man seated next to Spoleto leaned forward. He spoke with a measured, determined voice. "No one—not the Americans, not anyone—must be allowed to connect any of this to the Order."

They all nodded, and someone murmured, "The Order must survive, intact and unscathed. We can fight the Jews another day."

"Yes," Spoleto interjected. "And it is now our duty—the duty of the Military Vicariate, under the authority of the Rule—to see that the Order of Malta endures."

"At all costs. And we must do it now," Galena added. "All vulnerable points must be identified and neutralized."

The room fell silent as Galena's words sank in. They all knew what he meant and they all knew it would happen quickly.

Spoleto stood and rapped the table with his knuckles. "We are agreed, then? The Military Vicariate shall act by any and all means necessary to contain this situation and neutralize its effects?" The Twelve pushed their chairs back from the table and stood. Spoleto continued. "Then we are in agreement. Extreme action is authorized."

The Twelve replied in unison, "So be it."

As the men filed from the room, Spoleto looked down the length of the table. Galena caught his eye with a knowing look.

CHAPTER 64
WASHINGTON, D.C.

THE PHONE ON THE NIGHTSTAND beside Esther Rosenberg's bed rang, jarring her awake. She rolled onto her side and checked the number. The call was from Brody. She picked up the receiver. "It's the middle of the night. I thought we weren't supposed to actually talk on the phone."

"This can't wait. Come downstairs."

Esther rolled from bed, pulled on a dress, and walked out to the street. Brody's car was parked at the curb. She got in on the passenger side. Brody turned on the radio and leaned near her. "We took Demetrius Nilus," he whispered.

Esther's eyes were wide with surprise. "When?"

"A few hours ago."

"From Krasnoyarsk?" She frowned. "How did we get anyone in there? And how did they get him out?"

"Not there." Brody shook his head. "We took him from Rhodes."

"Rhodes?" The frown across Esther's forehead deepened. "He was at Rhodes?"

"Yes," Brody nodded. "He was at Knights Castle, attending a meeting of the Twenty-Four."

The look on Esther's face changed to one of concern. "Something big has happened."

"Yes," Brody nodded. "Something very big. He would not have left Krasnoyarsk for just any meeting. Any idea what it is?"

"I don't know," Esther shrugged. "But I'm sure it wasn't good. He wouldn't have risked leaving Russia just to discuss a success. Too many people want him. Mossad. The Americans. Probably others. If he left Krasnoyarsk, it was only because something went wrong." She looked in Brody's direction. "What does the center at Beersheba think?"

"That's why I came to see you."

Esther rolled her eyes. "Why would they ask me?"

"I just bring the questions and convey the answers."

She smiled at him. "I'm beginning to doubt whether you actually work for them."

Brody looked worried. "Why would you say such a thing?"

"Because you bring me these impossible questions. I'm an attorney. I live in Washington, D.C. I don't have access to this kind of information and neither do my clients."

"But already you have met with people from the CIA."

Suddenly Esther felt manipulated. "So this is what it was all about? Using me to get to Paul and to Doyle Thompson?"

"Don't be ridiculous," Brody scoffed. "We have been working together since long before you knew either of them. And yes, it is about exploiting your friends and contacts. But that is what it has always been about and you know it. You had no problem doing this when Ephraim was alive."

"That was uncalled for." Esther's eyes blazed with anger. "How dare you use him to manipulate me."

"Esther," Brody said softly, "I'm not trying to manipulate you. What I am telling you is the truth. You're only upset because of the nature of your relationship with Paul. We have always—"

"The nature of my relationship!" she shouted.

"Shhh." Brody gestured with his hand. "Not so loud. Someone will hear us."

"The nature of my relationship—"

Now it was Brody's turn to interrupt. "Look, I know you care for him. And I know that presents certain problems for you."

"Problems? Are you giving me advice now?" She reached for the door handle. "I don't have to—"

"Yes, you do," Brody snapped. "You have to listen to me."

"Why?"

"Because this is serious. Yes, the center at Beersheba has resources you don't have. But you're in America with high-level contacts and this is a serious situation. Right now, based on what you and I have developed and through sources in other locations, the center at Beersheba is convinced the Order of Malta has launched an attack against the U.S., possibly focusing on Jewish targets. It looks like that attack will target locations. No one knows where, but they're pretty sure it's big. Potentially nuclear. Now, something has happened. Something went wrong. And we need help from wherever we can find it." He paused a moment and looked her in the eye. "This is serious, Esther. Ask Wiseman what he thinks. Ask Paul. Ask Doyle Thompson. But see what you can learn. Everyone is checking their sources and calling in favors on this one."

CHAPTER 65

RHODES

LATE THAT EVENING, Spoleto left his office and took the staircase down to the ground floor. At the base of the stairs he met Father Galena waiting in the corridor. The castle's main kitchen was located around the corner. Together, they made their way inside it.

In back, they came to a worktable near a large black stove. On the table was a serving tray with a teapot and a plate that held six shortbread cookies. A napkin was folded beside the plate with a spoon resting on top. Next to the napkin was a small bowl with cubes of sugar and beside it, a tiny pitcher filled with milk. Drops of condensation covered the outside of the pitcher. Steam rose from the spout of the teapot. Galena picked up the tray, rested it on the palm of his hand, and followed Spoleto back toward the door.

From the kitchen they returned to the staircase and made their way without incident to the fourth level. A wide corridor led along the north wall of the castle. It was lined with paintings hung in elegant frames. The floor was made of granite tile inlaid with onyx and white marble in an intricate pattern of crosses, snakes, and eagles. Spoleto and Galena paid no attention to any of it as they walked quietly to the corner, then turned left. Fifty feet farther they came to a solid oak door with a latch at one side and a lock above it. Spoleto rapped on the door with his knuckles. A moment later the door opened, and Carlo Busca appeared. The color drained from his face when he saw them.

"Gentlemen," he said quietly. "I wondered if you would visit me tonight." He stepped back from the door and waited as they entered.

Beyond the door was a foyer that opened into a living room. A sofa sat to the right with a coffee table in front. Galena moved past them with the tray and set it on the table. Spoleto pushed the door closed and locked it. Busca had a look of panic. "Does it …" His voice trembled as he tried to speak. "Is…is there no other way?"

"I am afraid not," Spoleto replied.

"But I have done my best," Busca cried. "I have done my best."

"And you will be justly rewarded," Spoleto calmly assured him.

Galena moved the cup from the tray and set it on the table. Spoleto gestured in that direction. "Perhaps a little tea to soothe your nerves."

"Yes," Busca nodded. "One last cup." He turned toward the table. "I have always enjoyed a cup in the evening." He was trying to be brave. "With a shortbread cookie."

Galena stood with his back to them and poured tea into the cup. As Busca reached for it, Spoleto brought a syringe from his pocket. With a flick of his thumb he flipped off a cap that covered the needle, then plunged it into Busca's flesh at the top of his shoulder, just to the left of his neck. As the needle sank all the way into the muscle, Spoleto moved his thumb to the plunger.

Busca winced in pain as the contents of the syringe emptied into his body. With his left hand he groped for Galena and stumbled forward. In a raspy voice he called out, "Will you not even look at me?"

Before Galena could answer, Busca clutched his left arm and gasped for breath. His eyes were wide with fear. Spoleto backed away toward the door. Galena moved quickly to the left as Busca doubled over, vomited the contents of his stomach onto the tray, and collapsed. He lay on the floor by the coffee table and groaned. His legs twitched and his eyelids fluttered. Then he was motionless and quiet.

Galena looked over at Spoleto. "Is he dead?"

"Heart attack," Spoleto replied. He stooped over, picked up the cap from the syringe, and replaced it on the needle. "Classic symptoms." He slid the syringe into his pocket. "Place the call." Spoleto unlocked the door. "Tell Father Penalta we need him."

CHAPTER 66
PORTLAND, OREGON

BRAD RAMSEY SAT AT THE TABLE in the kitchen of his two-bedroom home. His right hand gripped a bottle of Maker's Mark bourbon whiskey. A cigarette rested on the edge of an ashtray. The end of it smoldered, sending a swirl of smoke slowly into the air. He raised the bottle to his lips and tipped it up for a long, full drink. The smooth liquid burned as it slid down his throat.

A cell phone sat on the table beside the ashtray. Lying beside it was a phone book and next to the book was a picture of a young girl standing with an older man outside a synagogue. Visible behind them was a Star of David on the wall above the door of the building.

Ramsey took the cigarette from the ashtray, placed it between his lips, and took a drag from it. He held the smoke in his lungs, then let it escape through his mouth. He checked his watch one more time. It was nine o'clock. "They ought to be in the office by now," he mumbled.

He reached for the phone book, took it by the corner, and pulled it across the table toward him. He dropped it onto his lap and turned to the blue pages. With his finger as a guide, he scanned down the page and found an entry for the FBI. He picked up the cell phone and punched in the number, then pressed a button to place the call. Someone answered on the third ring. "FBI. How may I direct your call?"

Ramsey stared blankly into space, but in his mind he saw Anna Milkova. She was standing near the register when they appeared, two men at either end of the bar. One blocked her way, the other came behind the bar and caught hold of her elbow.

"Mr. Elson would like a word with you."

A look of fear swept over her. "I didn't do anything," she protested. But it did her no good.

Together, the two men escorted her from the bar and up the hallway to Elson's office. Thirty minutes later, Ramsey watched as they carried her thin, limp body out the back door. Through a window in the hall by the men's room he saw them drop her carelessly in the back of a van. Then they climbed in front and drove away.

In his heart, Ramsey knew they'd do the same to anyone who turned on Elson—even him.

The voice on the cell phone spoke again, this time with a hint of impatience. "FBI. May I help you?"

Ramsey pressed a button to end the call and laid the phone on the table. He lifted the bottle to his lips and took another drink, then picked up the cigarette.

CHAPTER 67
PHOENIX, ARIZONA

A BLUE FORD TAURUS WOUND its way up Camelback Mountain. Twisting and turning, the car's engine raced through the short stretches, then slowed to an idle at the turns. Rashid Al-Hasan watched from behind a boulder near the top of the mountain and trained his binoculars on the car.

At the end of Fifty-Fourth Street, the car turned right onto San Miguel Avenue, then made a sharp turn into the third driveway on the right. The driveway was steep and narrow and led to a rambling one-story house. Built in the 1950s, it had a flat, angular roof with a wide overhang that kept the windows in perpetual shade. The car chugged up the driveway and rolled to a stop near a three-car garage. One of the doors was open and through it Rashid could see a large SUV parked inside.

Rashid watched as the driver exited the car and walked inside the garage. He hesitated near the SUV, as if searching for something, then backed away, opened the side door to the house, and disappeared inside. Rashid moved down the hillside to the back of the house and made his way around to the garage. He paused there and removed an automatic pistol from the waistband of his jeans. He took a silencer from his pocket and screwed it in place on the barrel. With the pistol at his side, he opened the driver's door of the SUV and looked inside. A remote control for the garage door was clipped to the sun visor. He unclipped it and stuck it in his pocket, then quietly closed the door and moved to the rear bumper. He waited there, motionless and silent.

Moments later, the door to the house opened and Pavel Nayfeld appeared. In his hand he held a tumbler from which he sipped as he talked. "And you are certain this is the case?"

"Yes," the driver replied.

Nayfeld gestured with the tumbler toward the trunk of the car. "Then let us have a look." He stepped closer. "They must think we are stupid to waste such an opportunity on the Jews. This is our ticket to whatever we want."

As they moved toward the car, Rashid stepped out from behind the SUV. Nayfeld's eyes were wide with surprise. "Rashid, what are you doing here?" A frown wrinkled his forehead. "I told you never to come to my house."

Without a word in reply, Rashid raised the pistol from his side, placed the muzzle against Nayfeld's head, and squeezed the trigger. Nayfeld's knees buckled. The tumbler slipped from his hand, bounced on the concrete garage floor, and smashed into pieces. Ice and liquid splattered in a circle around Nayfeld's crumpled body.

The driver stood a few feet away, eyes wide, mouth open. Before he could react, Rashid pointed the pistol in his direction and squeezed the trigger. A bullet struck the driver in the stomach. He clutched his abdomen with both hands and doubled over in pain. Rashid stepped closer, placed the muzzle against the driver's temple, and pulled the trigger again. The driver fell face-first onto the concrete floor.

Moving quickly, Rashid stooped over the driver and took the car keys from his right front pocket. He found a cell phone in the left pocket and dropped it on the floor. With the heel of his shoe, he stomped it to pieces.

As he turned to leave he saw Nayfeld's hand twitch. Without hesitating, he placed the pistol at the back of Nayfeld's head and squeezed the trigger. Nayfeld's body jumped as the bullet tore through his skull, then lay motionless.

Satisfied they were both dead, Rashid stepped outside to the driveway and pressed a button on the remote. The garage door rattled and creaked as it slowly descended. When it was in place, he opened the trunk of the Ford. He smiled when he saw the aluminum case. "Yes," he whispered to himself. "Allah is with us." Rashid closed the trunk lid and moved quickly to the driver's door. He pulled it open, crawled inside behind the steering wheel, and backed the car away from the house.

CHAPTER 68
RHODES

THAT EVENING, SPOLETO VISITED Carmine Russo in his private residence on the first floor of the Knights Castle. They stood in the kitchen and drank a cup of hot tea while they talked.

"This transition may be difficult," Spoleto began. "But whatever happens, we remain under a holy obligation to preserve the integrity of the Order."

"Yes, sir," Russo agreed.

"Busca relied on contacts in America."

"Very much so," Russo nodded. "Giovanni was in touch with them often."

"You are aware of this?"

"Yes. Giovanni has put me in contact with them."

"Including Steve Taylor? He told you about Steve Taylor?"

"Yes. I have communicated with him."

"Be very careful about what you say to him," Spoleto cautioned. "And to Giovanni. These are the same people who got us into this trouble."

"I understand."

Spoleto took a sip of tea and swallowed. "You must get close enough to Giovanni to find out what they were doing, but you cannot allow him to influence you." Spoleto took another sip of tea and changed the subject. "Have you located Malenkov?"

"He is staying at a hotel in Luxembourg," Russo answered. "Apparently he is too scared to return home."

"We have people in Luxembourg."

"Yes. They have been contacted."

"Good. You know what to do," Spoleto said.

Russo nodded. "It is done."

"Good." Spoleto set his teacup aside. "We must never involve the Council or the Vicariate directly in these matters. We must stay within the bounds of our authority, but the fewer who know the specifics, the better."

CHAPTER 69
LUXEMBOURG

MALENKOV STOOD AT THE WINDOW of his hotel room and stared out at the city below. Darkness had fallen hours before but he seemed not to notice. In his mind, all he could see was the outline of the body on the sidewalk outside Ivan's nightclub in Moscow. If they killed Ivan for a botched delivery, what would they do to him? And if the Order didn't get him, Jiroft and the Jund Ansar Allah would make him pay for the missile that misfired and the lives they lost during the attack in Ramallah. He took a deep breath and sighed. "We have idiots for clients."

Behind him there was a knock on the door. He turned away from the window, crossed the room, and stared out through the peephole. A maid stood outside the door with towels in her hand. Malenkov unlocked the door and pulled it open.

As he stepped aside to let the maid enter, three men appeared behind her. She scuttled away as the men rushed into the room. Malenkov stumbled back from the door. One of the men grabbed his arm. Another pinned down his feet, lifted him from the floor, and slammed him on the bed. When he tried to scream, the third man shoved a wadded washcloth into his mouth. Malenkov shook his head from side to side in panic, doing his best to spit out the cloth, but to no avail. A body bag appeared beside him on the bed. The third man flattened it out and unzipped it.

In his hand he held a roll of duct tape. He stretched out a length and pressed it against the back of Malenkov's head, then brought it across his mouth and wound it tightly, making two or three passes. The men holding Malenkov's feet and hands picked him up from the bed and laid him on top of the body bag. The third man taped his ankles together, then his hands. Then they stuffed him inside the body bag and zipped it closed.

In the darkness of the bag, Malenkov was overtaken with panic. The washcloth in his mouth left him unable to swallow. Saliva collected at the base of his tongue and he was certain he would drown. Then he felt someone's hands near his ankles. Someone else caught hold of the bag near his shoulders. He was lifted from the bed and a moment later felt his hip bang against the door, then the men were running with him, his body jostling up and down in time with their steps. Tears flowed down Malenkov's cheeks as he thought of what they might do to him.

CHAPTER 70
LAS VEGAS, NEVADA

AT THE NEST COMMAND CENTER, Pete Rios stood with his arms folded across his chest, his eyes once more focused on a flat-screen monitor that hung on the wall. On the screen were video images from a camera mounted atop the pistol of a CIA agent. The camera tracked the agent's path as he moved up the steps, then down the hall toward an apartment door. A hand checked the doorknob, then a foot kicked open the door. The camera moved from side to side as the man entered, checked the hallway and turned the corner. Others rushed past him and soon the room was filled with people. The sound of their voices crackled through the command center from a speaker that hung near the monitor.

"Nothing here," someone whispered.

"Bedroom's clear," a voice called.

"Are we in Innsbruck or some trash house in Reno?" Rios shook his head in disbelief. "Did we confirm this is Malenkov's apartment?"

"Yes, sir," Jeff Howell answered. "That's his apartment."

Rios threw up his hands in frustration. "And wasn't he supposed to be there?"

"Yes, sir," Howell replied. "CIA assured us he was inside the apartment."

"That's right." Rios turned in Howell's direction. "Didn't they say they had a visual on him?"

"Yes, sir."

"I hate working with these guys," Rios groused. "They're worse than the FBI."

A voice came from the speaker by the screen. "Door was locked. No sign of forced entry. Windows are all closed and locked."

"There was no forced entry?" Rios yelled at the screen. "You guys just kicked down the door." He threw his hands in the air once more and pointed with his finger. "*You* were the forced entry." He turned to the operator seated at a workstation near the center of the room. "Okay." He ran his hands through his hair and took a deep breath. "Okay. Who's controlling this team?"

"Langley."

"Who at Langley?"

"Winston Smith," the operator replied.

"All right. Tell Winston Smith I want them to collect whatever they can find. Computers, notes, papers, documents. Do a complete inventory of the place. Did they find a computer?"

The operator pointed to an image on the monitor. "There's one sitting right there on that desk."

Rios glanced in that direction. "Have them take it to the CIA station in Berlin. I'm sending someone over there to analyze it. I want to know everything that's ever been on that hard drive." Rios moved to a nearby desk. "And make sure nobody touches the power switch on that computer until our guy gets there."

Suddenly there were shouts from the speaker. On the screen, men hurried down the hallway. The camera jostled up and down. There were images of the floor, then the ceiling, then the wall. Rios shouted at the screen again. "Can we see what's going on? Don't they know we need to see?" He kicked a trashcan and sent it tumbling across the room. "What's the point of having the camera if they don't know how to use it?"

"There," someone called. "We can see it now."

Rios looked up at the screen. Images of a bedroom appeared, with a woman lying in bed. She had a terrified look on her face and she held a comforter close, pulling it up to her neck.

"She's saying something. Can we hear it?"

The woman's voice, with a thick European accent, came from the speaker. "Wer sind Sie?" She sounded scared and nervous. "Was wollen Sie?"

"That's German," Rios frowned. "Anyone speak German?" He glanced around the room. "Anyone?"

Richard Weavil spoke up. "She's saying, 'Who are you? What do you want?'"

"Yeah," Rios replied. "That's what I'd like to know. Who are you, lady?" On the screen, a man appeared beside the bed. Rios pointed to the screen. "Where did she come from?" When no one answered, Rios shouted in frustration, "Can we at least get a translation of this conversation?"

The man near the edge of the bed spoke to her. "Who are you?"

The voice of a translator answered on the audio stream. "I am... Irina Spechlovich."

"Why are you here?"

"I stay here...when I am in town."

"Where is Malenkov?"

She shook her head. "I do not know any Malenkov."

"You're sleeping in his bed." The man's voice was stern and insistent. "Where is he?"

"Okay," she nodded. "I know him, but I have not seen him."

"When was the last time you saw him?"

"Several weeks ago. I have been away. I just got back into town last night. He was not here when I arrived. I assumed he would be, but no."

Rios turned to the operator. "Tell them to hold her at a secure location."

"You want the Innsbruck police to take her into custody?"

"No," Rios replied sharply. "Don't tell Austrian authorities anything about it. Have the CIA hold her at one of their safe houses."

"Very well." The operator relayed the message. A moment later she caught Rios' attention. "Langley has a safe house. Who do you want to conduct the interrogation?"

"I don't want an interrogation right now. I want her out of the way so she can't contact Malenkov. We'll have the FBI check out her background. I want to know more about her before we let them interrogate her. Tell them just to hold on to her until they hear from us."

CHAPTER 71
VIENNA, AUSTRIA

MUD SPLATTERED THE TOPS of Werner Ranek's boots as he trudged across the construction site. A week of rain had sent everyone home early and turned the ground into an oozing mess. "Rain, rain, rain," he muttered. "Good for the farmers. But bad for us."

At the age of fifty-five, Werner had spent a lifetime in construction, first as a laborer, then bucking rivets on steel girder projects, and finally as a welder. It had been a long and backbreaking career, much of it dangling high above the ground with nothing but the safety lanyard around his waist to protect him from falling. But that was when he was younger. Now he worked in the fabricating yard and left the high work to others.

A large steel box stood in the middle of the fabricating yard. Next to it was a trash bin and around it were scraps of steel tossed carelessly aside. Werner stooped to pick up a piece. "Young people," he growled. "They know nothing about work and even less about keeping the job site clean." With his head down he caught a whiff of an odor that wrinkled his nose. He glanced around, curious. "What is that smell?"

He sniffed the air, turning this way and that. Finally, following the scent, he moved closer to the trash bin and lifted the lid. A swarm of flies rushed at his face. Werner let go of the lid and stepped back, swatting with both hands and raking them away from his nose and mouth. The lid banged closed.

A foreman approached. "What is the matter with you?"

"The bin is filled with flies."

"Flies?" The foreman gave him an amused look. "What are you talking about?"

"Lift the lid and see for yourself."

The foreman raised the lid. Again, flies rush out in a swarm. Not as many as before but still they buzzed around the foreman's head. He dropped the lid and stepped back, fanning his face with his hand. "I think there is something dead in there."

"Dead?"

"Yes," he nodded his head slowly. "It is a body, I think."

Werner stepped back to the bin. "Take the other side of the lid." He gestured to the foreman. "We will lift it together. We can throw it all the way back and maybe the flies will go away."

Reluctantly, the foreman moved to the other side of the bin. They each grabbed a corner of the lid and flipped it all the way back. Flies swarmed from the bin. Werner and the foreman hurried out of the way and watched from a safe distance.

After a few minutes, the flies were gone. Werner stepped to the bin and peered over the top. The foreman inched closer but lingered behind him. "See anything?"

"Yeah." Werner blanched. "I see a head. Right there by that cardboard box."

The foreman walked up and looked over Werner's shoulder. A man's head lay in the trash beside a cardboard bolt box. The face was pale, the eyes open wide, the stub of the neck brown with bloodstains. "No," the foreman gasped. He turned away, bent double at the waist, and vomited on the ground. With his head still down, he called to Werner, "Where is the rest of the body?"

Werner looked inside the bin once more. "I see an arm and a leg."

"But not the rest of him?"

"No, I do not see the rest." He backed away from the bin. "You should call someone."

CHAPTER 72
WASHINGTON, D.C.

BRYSON AND ESTHER sat at a corner table in Clyde's, a restaurant in the Georgetown section of Washington, D.C. With a busy schedule and all that was happening she hadn't seen him in almost a week. Bryson smiled at her from across the table.

"How is your steak?"

"Fine."

"Did you talk any more to Doyle?"

"No."

"How is Wiseman?"

"Fine."

"What have you heard from—"

"Look, Paul, I'm not sure this is such a great idea."

"You wanted to eat somewhere else?"

"No. Not that. I mean us."

"What about us?"

"I can't be the wife you once had, and you can't be the husband I once knew. And I'm not sure either of us can get past all that and relate to each other as we are."

"Esther, I'm not trying to—"

Esther's phone rang. She reached inside her purse, glanced at the screen, and sighed. "I have to take this." She pressed a button to answer the call and stepped away from the table. When she returned she looked over at Bryson. "I have to go. I can get a cab."

"No, Esther." Bryson shook his head. "I realize we're both a little tense tonight, but I'm not giving up. I'll drive you." He stood, took his wallet from the pocket of his jacket, and dropped some money on the table. "Come on." He took her by the elbow and escorted her through the restaurant.

As they walked to the car Esther slipped her hand in the crook of his arm. "They found Malenkov's body," she said in a low voice.

"Where was it?"

"Vienna."

"Do you have to go there?"

"No."

"So where am I taking you?"

"The office."

"Does Doyle know about this yet?"

"I don't know." Her voice sounded irritable and she withdrew her hand from his arm. "How would I know that?"

"I was just asking," he replied. "What's wrong?"

"Nothing. It's just...It feels wrong."

"What feels wrong?"

"Me, even talking about this with you."

"Because I'm not Jewish?"

"Because I care for you and it feels like I'm manipulating you. Like I'm being manipulated. Like everyone wants something and I—"

Bryson slipped his arm around her waist and drew her close. He leaned forward and kissed her. She drew back. "What are you doing?"

"Kissing you." He leaned forward and kissed her again.

She drew back once more. "Why are you kissing me?"

"I don't care if I'm being manipulated. I love you. You don't have to manipulate me. Just ask me, I'll tell you anything I know. Introduce you to anyone I know. Take you anywhere you need to go." He leaned forward and kissed her once more. This time she kissed him back.

* * *

As Bryson dropped off Esther at her office, his cell phone rang. The call was from Doyle Thompson. "We need to talk. I know it's late, but I have something to show you."

"Okay. Where did you want to meet?"

"Your office."

Half an hour later, Bryson met Thompson in the lobby of the building and led him upstairs to his office. Bryson took a seat behind the desk. Thompson pulled a chair up to the opposite side. He took a document from the pocket of his jacket and handed it to Bryson.

"A forensics team took this from Malenkov's computer. It's an email from him to someone named Ivan. Sent a few months ago but they are discussing a project they refer to as The Four Horsemen."

Bryson took the document from Thompson, scanned it quickly, and laid it on the desk. "Malenkov is dead."

Thompson looked surprised. "How did you know that?"

Bryson shrugged. "Word gets around." He leaned back in his chair. "Did the CIA kill him?"

"No. NEST wanted him alive. A team went in to get him at his Innsbruck apartment. He wasn't there."

Bryson looked at the document once more, then handed it back to Thompson. "Are you sure I can look at this stuff?"

"Yeah," Thompson nodded. "Sure. Why not?"

"Isn't this classified?"

"Ahh...you know. Didn't you have a clearance?"

"When I was a member of Congress." Bryson leaned forward. "I'm not a member of Congress now, Doyle. You could get arrested for taking these documents from the office." He leaned away. "I could get arrested for looking at them."

"Listen," Thompson said. "We are facing a national threat. I'm just working a source."

"That's what I am now? A source?"

"No. You're a friend, helping another friend."

"So, what did you mean by source?"

Thompson looked Bryson in the eye. "Demetrius Nilus."

Suddenly Esther's comment about feeling manipulated made more sense. Bryson felt the muscles in the back of his neck tighten. His chin thrust forward. His palms were damp. "Look." He took a deep breath. "I don't mind helping, but this has to be up-front all the way."

"What do you mean?"

"I mean, if I'm going to take you to Esther to get to Nilus, she has to be present when you talk to him."

"Okay," Thompson nodded. "I assumed she would be. You could be there, too, for all I care."

"No funny stuff. No dropping in to see him the night before and doing the meeting ahead of time. No whisking him away unannounced for a meeting at some undisclosed location."

"Why are you telling me this? I don't have access to him. The only way I get access to him is through the Israeli government."

"I know you," Bryson grunted. "They gave you a little wiggle room in Africa, and you were about to assassinate a Chinese leader. If they'd left you in Beirut, you would have taken control of the entire country."

"They sent me to do a job. I did my job."

Bryson leaned forward in his chair. "I'll take you to Esther with this. But if you burn her, I'll find a way to make you pay. I may not be as good at this as you are, but I'll find a way. You understand?"

"I understand."

CHAPTER 73
PORTLAND, OREGON

BRAD RAMSEY TURNED his 1972 Ford Torino onto Powell Avenue and glanced in the rearview mirror one more time, just to make sure no one was following. The street was crowded with morning traffic. Cars moved from lane to lane behind him as drivers jockeyed for the best position to negotiate the morning commute. No one seemed to pay him any attention.

A few blocks later, he came to a Sinclair service station in Gresham, on the east side of town. Ramsey lifted his foot from the gas pedal and turned the car from the pavement. He was miles from Elson's club, but as the car rolled across the parking lot he wondered whether he was far enough away to be safe.

A pay phone stood beside a power pole at the edge of the lot. Ramsey steered the car toward it and came to a stop a few feet away. He climbed from the car and glanced around nervously, checking one more time. When he reached the booth, he took a cell phone from his pocket and checked the number he'd called a few days earlier for the FBI. Then he lifted the receiver from the pay phone, dropped in four quarters, and dialed the number. As before, someone answered on the second ring.

"FBI. May I help you?"

Ramsey cleared his throat. "I wanted to talk to someone about something I overheard."

"Just a moment."

Seconds passed, then a male voice came on the line. "This is Donnie Brown."

"I wanted to talk to someone about something I overheard."

"Okay," Brown replied. "What did you hear?"

"I heard two men talking about taking a Jew killer to Los Angeles."

"A Jew killer? What's that?"

"I don't know, but it was in an aluminum case in the trunk of a car."

"You saw it?"

"Yes."

"So, who are you? Who am I talking to?"

"I don't think I should tell you that just now."

A computer-generated voice interrupted them. "Please deposit one dollar for the next five minutes."

Brown spoke quickly. "We need to talk. Can you meet me?"

"Yeah," Ramsey replied. But before either of them could say more, the phone beeped and the call ended.

Ramsey hung up the receiver and glanced around again, suddenly more nervous than before. He was certain someone was watching but as he checked in every direction he saw no one suspicious. A woman sat in a car near the gas pumps at the service station. Her back was to him and the angle of the car made it impossible for her to see him. A man was filling the car with gas, but he faced the opposite direction and his head was turned toward the pumps. Still, Ramsey couldn't shake the uneasy feeling and found it hard to resist the urge to run, but that was the last thing he needed to do. Running would only call attention to himself. Instead, he took a deep breath, shoved the cell phone into his pocket, and walked slowly toward the car.

CHAPTER 74
WASHINGTON, D.C.

BRYSON CALLED ESTHER and arranged a meeting with Thompson at her office. They arrived there a little before ten that morning. An assistant met them at the front desk and escorted them to a conference room. Esther joined them a few minutes later.

"So, what's this about?"

"Doyle has information," Bryson began. "It came from the computer in Malenkov's apartment. He's trying to figure out what it means and would like to talk to General Nilus."

"Oh?" Esther gave them both a curious look. "What did you find?"

"Emails. Client records. Transaction notes."

"And why are you bringing this to me?"

Thompson smiled across the table at her. "I'd like to talk to Demetrius Nilus. I thought if I showed you what we have, you'd be interested in helping."

"I have nothing to do with Demetrius Nilus."

"But you have contacts in the Israeli government."

"You should take this up with your own office. I'm sure they know how to get in touch with the embassy or whoever one contacts to arrange a meeting about something like this."

The expression on Thompson's face turned serious. "If I send a request up the chain, it will get lost before it gets two feet past my office door. You know that." He leaned forward and rested his arms on the table. "I need your help."

"What makes you think I can help?"

"Like I said, you know the people who can get me to Nilus."

"Even if Israeli authorities agreed to give you access to him, they can't make him talk to you."

Thompson nodded. "I understand."

Esther gave him a skeptical look. "And you're willing to travel all the way to Israel, just to hear Nilus refuse to talk to you?"

"I am willing to travel all the way to Israel to get in the room with him."

Esther thought for a moment. "If they agreed, they would never allow you to talk to him alone."

"I don't mind. You can be present if you want." He gestured toward Bryson. "Bring Paul if you like. I just need to talk to him."

"And you can't get this through the CIA?"

"NEST controls this now. If I send in a request to talk to Nilus, it will go to some guy in Las Vegas who will say no to me and then send in the FBI, and they'll botch the whole thing." He hunched forward. "This is important, Esther."

"I know this is important," Esther replied. "But I don't work for the Israeli government. They're not my client."

"But you do have a client that the Israelis care about. And you've been working for a long time to get him released. Helping us with this would go a long way toward making that happen."

Esther had a wry smile. "Doyle, I've played this game before. And I know enough about you to know that you can't do anything to gain Anthony Wiseman's release. All you can do—"

"What about a swap?" Bryson interrupted.

Esther frowned. "A swap? What are you talking about?"

"A swap," Bryson repeated. "Swap Wiseman for Nilus."

Esther grinned. "Anthony would be delighted, but I doubt the Israelis would go for it. And I doubt anyone else on the American side would go for it, either."

Bryson pressed the point. "If we did a swap, how would we generate it? How would we get it moving?"

Thompson's eyes were alert. "I could do that."

Esther folded her arms across her chest and let her eyes bore in on Thompson. "How?"

"If I told the director of our group that the Israelis were open to the idea, and I had someone who could put the pieces together on the Israeli side, I think the idea would have enough legs to stand on its own. They would send the idea up the chain and get it approved without someone ruining it or just saying no."

"This would have to go to the president. Do you think he would agree?"

Thompson nodded his head slowly. "When NEST explains to him who Nilus is, he'll jump all over it."

Esther was quiet for a moment, then she pushed back her chair and stood. "Sit right here." She let her hand slide over Bryson's shoulder as she moved away from the table. "I'll be back in a few minutes." She paused at the door. "Do either of you need something to drink?"

"Gin and tonic," Thompson smiled.

"I can get you a bottle of water." Esther looked at Bryson. "Coca-Cola?"

"Yes. Thanks."

A few minutes later, an assistant entered with their drinks. Bryson and Thompson sat at the conference table and waited. In a little while, Esther returned. She stood near the end of the table and spoke to Thompson. "You're sure you can do this?"

"Yes."

There was a twinkle in her eye. "Then do it."

"They'll agree?"

"They're interested," she smiled.

"How high does the interest go?"

"High enough."

CHAPTER 75
RHODES

CARLO BUSCA WAS ACCORDED a funeral with all the pomp and reverence due his position as Grand Master. After the service, the Twenty-Four Elders met in the Hall of Saints and elected Ignacio Spoleto as Busca's replacement. He took over Busca's office and installed Carmine Russo as his assistant. As a result, Giovanni lost his position at the desk by the office door.

The following day, Giovanni was summoned to Spoleto's office. Giovanni arrived expecting to meet Spoleto. Instead, he found the office empty and a secretary waiting for him.

"Father Spoleto would like to talk with you."

"Very well," Giovanni answered. He glanced inside the empty office. "Where shall I meet him?"

"He is waiting for you at the retreat cottage."

"Should I go now?"

"Yes. He is spending a few days there, collecting his thoughts and making plans." The secretary smiled. "I am certain he has a role for you."

"Good," Giovanni nodded. "I am ready to serve wherever I'm needed. Father Spoleto is a great man."

The secretary turned away. "I am sure you will find working for him to be an adventure."

Giovanni made his way from Spoleto's office and hurried downstairs to the castle's main entrance. As he came out, he found a car parked beneath the canopy. A doorman stepped quickly ahead of him and opened the driver's door. He held it while Giovanni got in behind the wheel. When Giovanni was seated inside, the doorman pushed the door closed and saluted with one arm placed briskly across his chest, a gesture reserved only for those of highest rank in the Order. The sight of it sent a smile across Giovanni's face. *Perhaps this will be good, indeed.*

From the castle, Giovanni drove along the coast road toward Stegna, a town on the southern end of the island. The Grand Master's retreat cottage was located on a bluff that overlooked the town and beach. Giovanni had been there only once before, shortly after Busca had taken office, where he had been informed he would be the new Grand Master's assistant. He felt certain this day would be just as momentous. He would not be Spoleto's assistant—that was a position reserved for Carmine Russo—but he would be named to an important post. Perhaps clerk to the Council. Or, he grinned, maybe a seat on the Military Vicariate.

Near the town of Archangelos, Giovanni turned left, toward Stegna and the ocean. At the coastline, the road made a sharp turn to the right. It was late by then and he could see the cottage in the distance, outlined on the cliff against the purple sky of a setting sun. The beach in the foreground, with sailboats tethered at their mooring, made the moment seem like a scene from a beautiful painting. Then, just beyond the marina, the road moved away from the beach and passed through a cut in the mountains. Through the gap lay the village of Stegna framed by the mountains and the sea and beach. Giovanni felt as if he were living a dream.

* * *

From the cottage on the cliff, Ignacio Spoleto had a clear view of the beach and village below. Through a large picture window he could see all the way to the marina and even beyond it to the place where the road made the turn near the coastline. It was a beautiful scene, with the setting sun and the blue water of the Mediterranean.

Standing beside Spoleto that evening was Carmine Russo. In his hand, Russo held a cell phone. With the index finger of his free hand, he entered a number to make a call.

Spoleto kept his eyes focused on the village below and the road that ran along the coast. He nodded toward the window. "That is his car? You are certain?"

"Yes. He's just now coming through the cut in the mountain. Past the marina."

"You are certain? If you are wrong, it could be tragic for others."

"I am not wrong."

"We cannot do this in the village."

"I understand."

"Very well, then." Spoleto clasped his hands behind his back and turned away from the window. "Let it be done."

Russo pressed a button on the cell phone to send the call. Almost instantly, an explosion rattled the windows of the cottage. Spoleto turned to look over his shoulder. Behind him, on the road through the cut in the mountain by the shore, an orange fireball rolled into the sky, followed by thick black smoke. Beneath the smoke, flames engulfed the twisted remains of Giovanni's car.

CHAPTER 76
LAS VEGAS, NEVADA

WHEN THE INFORMATION from Malenkov's apartment was forwarded to the CIA, it was analyzed and added to a database accessible by NEST and other intelligence agencies. That database already included information supplied by Mossad from the meeting at Dizin, notes and addresses gleaned by Antonio Belisconi from Giovanni's cell phone, emails intercepted later from Knights Castle, and phone records for Malenkov and Nilus that had been hacked from telecommunications systems in Austria, Luxembourg, and Russia.

As evidence of a threat mounted, Rios and his team of analysts mined information in the database using complex algorithms and matrices to extract details previously missed and relationships not made apparent by earlier efforts. When they had exhausted those techniques, they turned to basic Boolean searches and just plain hunches to squeeze every nuance and innuendo from the information they had obtained. Then Rios turned their attention toward arriving at some answers.

"We need to piece some of this together." He glanced at Morris as if looking for confirmation that his judgment was correct. Morris nodded in agreement. Rios moved to a spot near the operator at the central workstation and looked around the room. "So," Rios continued, "let's think through our information. Begin at the beginning. What do we know about Demetrius Nilus and his nephew, Leonid Malenkov?"

"Arms dealers."

As analysts offered suggestions, an operator created a list of topics on one of the screens.

"Nilus had access to Russian weapons. Malenkov had access to clients in the Middle East. They sold Russian weapons to Middle East terrorists."

"And plutonium."

"Right," Rios agreed. "But let's not get sidetracked with the plutonium aspect. We don't have any good information on what's happening with that right now. Let's stick with the suitcase bomb idea from the conversation at Dizin. What else do we have on Nilus?"

"He was taken into custody by agents from Mossad while he was visiting with the Order of Malta."

"What is Nilus' connection with the Order of Malta?"

"*The Protocols of the Learned Elders of Zion.*"

"Like Scripture for the Order of Malta."

"And every other anti-Semitic organization."

"Okay," Rios interrupted. "Nilus is the heir to his grandfather's legacy. He hates Jews. That same hatred is the central creed of the Order of Malta. So we have an anti-Semitic Russian general working with his nephew to sell Russian arms to a long list of anti-Semitic organizations. The Order of Malta is one of those organizations. What did they sell them?"

"We don't know."

"Yes, we do," Howell spoke up. Everyone turned in his direction, waiting to hear. "They sold them the four angels."

"What do you mean?"

"Why else would the command to release the angels go to Nilus?"

"But what are the four angels?"

"The text message said, 'Release the four angels who are bound at the great river Euphrates.' That's a reference from prophecy about the end of time. The four horsemen of the apocalypse."

"And you think that's a reference to some kind of weapon?"

"Look," Howell began, defending his position. "Malenkov offered Jiroft a suitcase bomb—one he said was already in the United States. I don't think he would offer it to him if he didn't really have one. Jiroft is the kind of person who would kill him over that if it turned out to be a lie. He was already upset about the missile. A lie on top of it would have pushed him over the edge. Malenkov knew that."

"Go ahead," Rios said, encouraging him. "Take it further. So what?"

"What if Malenkov was robbing Peter to pay Paul?"

"What do you mean?"

"What if the four angels were four suitcase bombs. And Malenkov, the cocky young nephew, thinks he can lay one of those cases off on Jiroft to get out of trouble, without anyone knowing about it. Only the case was already spoken for. Part of a coordinated attack directed by the Order of Malta. The fourth suitcase didn't arrive as planned, somebody at the Order found out what Malenkov did, and had him killed."

"Explains why General Nilus left a closed Russian city for perhaps the first time ever. He went to Rhodes to placate an angry client."

"He went to beg for his life."

"And the only reason they didn't kill him is because he's their arms dealer."

"But why would the Order of Malta be involved in an attack using suitcase bombs?"

The room fell silent. After a moment, Weavil spoke up. "I know," he said quietly.

Rios turned to him. "Well, please, Richard, tell us."

"They hate Jews."

"And that's enough?"

"It's the one thing they all have in common," Weavil explained. "Nilus, Malenkov, their customers in the Middle East, Jiroft, the Order of Malta—they all hate Jews. We dress it up by calling them anti-Semitic, but the truth is they all hate the Jews."

"It accounts for more of the information than anything else we've said here today."

"Four angels. Four horsemen. Four suitcase bombs," Rios recounted. "But how do we get from that idea to actual targets on the ground? If we assume Richard is correct and the bombs are meant for Jewish targets, where are those targets likely to be? Remember, we are talking about bombs that will flatten as much as two square miles."

Aycock spoke up. "What are the four places with the greatest population of Jews?"

An analyst across the room spoke up. "If we're talking anywhere in the world it's Jerusalem, New York, Tel Aviv, and Los Angeles."

"What about just in the United States?"

"The top four cities in the U.S. ranked by Jewish population are New York, Los Angeles, Miami, and Philadelphia."

Rios glanced around the room. "So, four suitcase bombs, sold by Russian arms dealers to an anti-Semitic organization, targeting the four cities with the highest Jewish population." The room fell eerily silent. "Is that where we are?"

Aycock slowly nodded his head. "I think so."

"That's the best we have so far," Weavil added.

Rios looked at Morris. "What do you think?"

"A little theoretical, but it's the only way to stay ahead of an attack. If you wait for solid confirmation of what's actually going on, you'll be watching a mushroom cloud rise over the targets."

Rios turned back to face the others in the room. "Okay. This is a national nuclear emergency and a NEST priority. Four bombs, believed to be nuclear, have been smuggled into the United States. They are bound for undetermined targets in New York, Los Angeles, Miami, and Philadelphia. I want all the information you have on this prepared for a presidential briefing. Start writing it up."

Rios looked back at the operator. "Get me a plane. Notify the

White House chief of staff that I'm on my way. I need to meet with the president as soon as I arrive."

"You want an appointment tomorrow?"

"No. I want to brief him now. Tell them to interrupt his schedule, wake him up, whatever they have to do, but I need to see him as soon as I arrive." Rios looked over at Morris. "Want to come with me?"

"No," Morris said, shaking his head. "I've been to the White House enough. You go. I'll stay right here and keep things moving until you get back."

"This could be big."

"Yes," Morris nodded. "It could be devastating."

"Or," Rios shrugged, "it could be a long walk off a short pier."

Morris had an ironic smile. "That's our job. We take that walk so no one else has to."

CHAPTER 77
LAS VEGAS, NEVADA

LATE THAT AFTERNOON, Rios boarded a Gulfstream jet from a private hangar at the Las Vegas airport and settled into the leather seat. Moments later, the plane lifted from the runway and rose into the sky. Once airborne, he took a briefing book from his satchel and opened it on his lap. He understood the nature of the threat, but he wanted to be ready for any questions the president might raise about the details.

An hour later, he received an email transmitted over the plane's secure Internet link. That message read simply, "CIA contacts say an offer to swap Wiseman for Nilus would meet with a favorable response." Rios stared out the window into the darkness of the night as he thought of what that might mean.

Though they had never met, Rios knew about Wiseman. He had supported the initial effort to detain him but as details about what Wiseman had done became clearer, continuing to hold him made less sense, especially in light of Israel's interest in his release and the strategic nature of U.S.–Israeli relations. Yet the FBI and Naval Intelligence had proved unrelenting in their opposition to his release. Now, with the opportunity to end the Wiseman affair, Rios was favorable to the notion, but a swap brought a fresh set of problems. If the swap actually occurred, the United States would have custody of a Russian general.

Unless the U.S. could assure Russia he would be released, detaining him could become a major international incident. They would need to placate the Russians by suggesting this was conceived as a way of getting Nilus home, while not offending the Israelis by instantly releasing him.

Rios propped his chin in his hand. *Giving everyone a way out, while saving face, is going to be difficult.* The fact that the press had not yet learned of Nilus' detention, and the lack of response from Russia, gave them a window of opportunity, one that was rapidly disappearing. *We need to resolve this now. Tomorrow might be too late.*

Two hours later, Rios arrived in Washington, D.C. He was met at the airport by a limousine that drove him straight to the White House. Though it was late, the president was waiting in the Oval Office with Tyler Davis, his chief of staff, and Liston Cook, his National Security Advisor. The president sat quietly while Rios gave him the details of what they'd uncovered so far. When he finished, the president leaned forward and rested his elbows on the desk.

"You have what you need to respond to this threat?"

"Yes, Mr. President. We do so far."

"Anything else you find that you need let me know and we'll make certain you receive it."

"Yes, Mr. President." Rios couldn't tell from the response whether the president understood the gravity of the moment or not. "This is a national nuclear emergency, Mr. President."

"I understand that, Pete. But we have no specific details about exact targets, and while I appreciate the seriousness of the threat, I can't very well order the evacuation of our four largest cities. That would only worsen our situation and hamper our ability to find the bombs, if they exist. It would also reveal the sources of our information. Not to mention the panic that would ensue. We'll have to solve this without going public. I'll make certain you have the resources you need, but we need to keep this quiet."

Rios nodded. "Very well, Mr. President."

"Don't you agree?"

"Mr. President, I see your point. But I think we should deploy mobile radiation detection units in each of these cities."

"Okay," the president nodded. "I agree." He turned to Davis. "You can take care of that?"

"Yes, Mr. President," Davis nodded. "I'll have an order prepared for your signature."

The president looked back at Rios. "Now, I understand the CIA has received an indication from the Israelis that they're interested in discussing a swap for Demetrius Nilus. Was your office aware of that?"

"Yes, sir, I received a message about that a short while ago."

"Apparently, this is just now developing. What do you think about it?"

"I think Nilus could be very helpful, if he's willing to talk. But having him in our custody presents a potential problem for us with Russia."

"I agree," the president nodded.

Cook spoke up. "The Russians have not responded yet. That gives us a little room to work."

"But not for long," Davis added. "Capture of a Russian general by Mossad agents is a big story. They won't be able to keep it quiet for long."

The president looked to Rios. "Why are we still holding Wiseman?"

"He was accused of giving classified intelligence reports to the Israelis."

"Aren't they our allies?"

"Yes, sir. But we had restricted the kinds of things we were sharing with them because of concern over what they might do with the information."

"You mean we were worried that if we gave them information that showed a threat, they would act in their own best interests first, without considering our position on the matter?"

"Something like that."

"And Wiseman was giving them the information anyway, after we limited their access. Wasn't that several years ago?"

"The FBI has refused to allow his release," Davis replied.

"They can't stop us from swapping him."

"No, sir." Rios shook his head. "That comes under your prerogative as president."

"Where is he being held?"

"Fort Meade."

"How would we do this?"

Cook spoke up. "We would need to do it in a way that lets the Russians know we don't intend to hold Nilus."

"But still gives us time to talk to him," Rios added.

The president smiled. "We'd have to ultimately return him to Russia. Will Israel object to that?"

"I don't see how they could," Cook shrugged. "If they turn him over to us, we would have the authority to do whatever we think is best."

"Wiseman is still a U.S. citizen?"

"Yes, sir."

"Does he want to go to Israel? Does he know he can't come back?"

"I think he would want to if it meant a chance to be free."

The president looked back at Rios. "And Demetrius Nilus can tell us what we need to know to stop someone from detonating bombs in New York, Miami, L.A., and Philadelphia?"

"Yes, sir, Mr. President. If he will talk to us."

The president stood. "Then why are we still talking about it?"

Rios rose from his chair. "You'll authorize the swap?"

"If Israel agrees, I will, too." The president pointed at Rios. "You're the lead man on this, Pete. Make it happen." Then he turned to Davis. "Make sure this gets on my desk as soon as we're ready to act."

"Certainly, Mr. President," Davis nodded.

CHAPTER 78
WASHINGTON, D.C.

ESTHER AND BRYSON were cuddled on the sofa, watching a movie, enjoying a rare evening alone in her townhouse. A knock at the door interrupted them. Bryson sat up straight. "Want me to get it?"

Esther stood. "I'll see who it is." She walked to the door and looked out the window. Reuben Brody was standing outside. Esther glanced in Bryson's direction. "It's Reuben. Let me see what he wants." She pulled open the door and stepped outside.

"You know," she began as she closed the door behind her, "this is even more irregular than before."

"You didn't answer your phone."

"I turned it off. We were watching a movie," she sighed. "It's been a tough week."

"Turn it back on." Brody lowered his voice. "The head of NEST just left the White House."

"A briefing? They're finally taking this seriously?"

"It looks like the president will authorize the swap."

Esther smiled. "They went for it?"

"Yeah, Wiseman for Nilus."

"I never thought they'd do it." She folded her arms across her chest and glanced down at the ground. "Now, I'm not sure Wiseman will agree."

"That's why I'm here." Brody looked more serious than usual. "If they ask, you have to make certain he agrees."

"Jerusalem wants this?"

"Roham wants it. The cabinet is divided. Most of them want Wiseman to come to Israel. Three or four want to hold on to Demetrius Nilus."

"That makes the situation interesting."

"You can see him tomorrow?"

"I'm not sure I can get in that quickly."

"Do your best." Brody turned away and started down the sidewalk. As he moved out of sight, Esther stepped back inside the townhouse.

Bryson looked up from the sofa as she entered. "Everything okay?"

"Yeah," she replied. "It's fine. Want some popcorn?"

"Sure."

Esther started toward the kitchen.

CHAPTER 79
WASHINGTON, D.C.

PETE RIOS STEPPED from the West Wing of the White House and ducked into the waiting limousine. He took out his cell phone and called the command center in Las Vegas. Within minutes they gave him Doyle Thompson's cell phone number. Rios called him immediately.

"I understand swapping Wiseman for Nilus was your idea?"

Thompson seemed caught off-guard by the question. "Is this a secure line?"

"Yes," Rios answered. "This was your idea?"

"You could say that," Thompson replied.

"I need to meet with the Israeli ambassador."

"Has the president agreed?"

"The president will agree, if Israel will. Do you know the ambassador?"

"No. That kind of thing gets handled by someone way above my pay grade."

"Look, you're the one who requested the swap. I was in the office when the president gave the go-ahead. He put me in charge of getting it done. You're going to help me."

"I don't know if—"

"Doyle, this is a NEST priority. You're working for me. Whatever

294

happens, I'll straighten it out with your superiors." Rios spoke in a firm and decisive voice. "Set up the meeting."

"I'll see what I can do and call you back."

"No," Rios snapped. "Just set it up and meet me over there."

"At the embassy? I'm not authorized to speak for the CIA."

"The ambassador won't know that."

"But what if he does?"

"Fake it," Rios quipped. "From what I hear, you're pretty good at that."

CHAPTER 80
WASHINGTON, D.C.

ESTHER WAS STILL SEATED on the sofa, watching the movie with Bryson, when her cell phone rang. She didn't recognize the number but answered anyway. The call was from Doyle Thompson.

"The president has agreed to the swap."

She recognized Thompson's voice but was taken aback by his abrupt nature. "Are you supposed to be talking about this on your cell phone?"

"I don't know. There's no time to worry about that now. Pete Rios just called me."

"Who is he?"

Thompson gave a frustrated sigh. "Are you at home?"

"Yes."

"I'll be there in a minute."

"How do you know—" He ended the call before she could finish.

Bryson looked over at her. "Who was that?"

"Doyle Thompson."

"What does he want?"

"He says he's on the way over here. How does he know where I live?"

"Doyle knows lots of things." Bryson pushed himself up from the sofa. "Better get ready. It won't take him long to get here."

"How do you know?"

"I've received those calls from him before."

Minutes later, there was a knock at the door. Bryson opened it to find Thompson standing on the steps. He pushed his way inside and picked up the conversation with Esther where he'd left off on the phone. "Pete Rios is the head of NEST. He flew in tonight from Las Vegas to brief the president."

"Okay," she replied.

"He wants to meet with the Israeli ambassador."

"The president is meeting with the ambassador?"

"No." Thompson had a pained look of frustration. "Rios wants to meet him. The president will agree to swap Wiseman for Nilus. He put Rios in charge of getting it done. Rios found out I was the one who started the ball rolling. So, he called me and told me to arrange a meeting for him with the ambassador." He gave her a cheesy grin. "And now I'm here to get your help."

"When does he want to meet?"

"Tonight." Thompson smiled. "Now! He's on his way over there now."

"To the embassy?"

"Yes." Thompson had a puzzled look. "Is there a problem? You said you could do this. You said, 'Make the call.' That's why I started all this in the first place."

"I know. But the Israeli Cabinet is split. Wiseman is a hero among the hardliners. They're angry that the U.S. has been limiting their access to strategic intelligence and don't understand why he has been held this long."

"They ought to be glad he's going to be released."

"They are glad, but they're offended that they have to swap Nilus to get him."

"Will the prime minister approve it anyway?"

"I'm sure he would. He used the issue in his campaign."

"Campaign?"

"Politics," Esther explained. "They still have elections in Israel."

"Well, we can't solve all of that now." Thompson put his hands on his hips. "Can you set up a meeting with the ambassador?"

"I'll call him in the morning."

"No. Tonight."

"Tonight?"

"Yes. Rios is on his way over there now. The guy's crazy. Told me to set it up and meet him over there." He smiled at her. "You know the ambassador, don't you?"

"Yes," she sighed. "I know him."

"Good," Thompson grinned. "Make the call."

Esther picked up her cell phone from the end table. "I'll make the call, but I'm not making any guarantees." She pressed a button on the phone as she walked down the hall to the bedroom. The ambassador, Rami Eban, had been her friend for a long time. They were on a first-name basis. All she had to do was ask and he would agree to the meeting, but she didn't want Thompson to know that. The call took less than five minutes. When she was through, she sat on the edge of the bed and waited another five minutes, just so she didn't look rushed. Then she opened the door and stepped out to the hall.

She stopped at the hall closet for her coat. Thompson turned in her direction. "He agreed?"

"He agreed to see us." Esther slipped on her coat. "If I were you, I'd let this other guy—Pete Rios—do the talking."

"Hey, it's his meeting. I don't even have to be there."

"Oh no," Esther shook her head. "You're gonna be there. I'm making sure of that." She glanced at Bryson. "Sorry to cut things short before the movie ended."

"I don't mind." Bryson put on his jacket. "But you're not leaving me out now."

"Good," she smiled. "Want to drive us?" She leaned forward and kissed him. "I'd love to have your company."

CHAPTER 81
WASHINGTON, D.C.

THE ISRAELI EMBASSY, located in northwest Washington, D.C., took twenty minutes to get to from Esther's place. Bryson dropped Esther and Thompson at the front gate, then disappeared down International Drive. Esther gave her business card to a guard and waited. He disappeared inside the security office. A few minutes later, the guard returned and opened the gate. Esther and Thompson stepped inside the compound and followed the guard to the front door of the building. "You are going to the third floor," he said. "Elevators are down the hall to the left."

Rios was waiting in the hallway when Esther and Thompson arrived on the third floor. After a brief introduction, he turned to the matter at hand.

"Will they really go for the swap?"

"The prime minister is interested," she replied. "The cabinet is divided."

"What will the ambassador say?"

"I'm not sure that matters. All he can do is relay the message."

Rios pressed the point. "But is he in favor of the exchange?"

"He and Wiseman have become friends of sorts," Esther explained.

"They've exchanged letters and a brief visit. I'm sure he wants to see Anthony released as much as anyone does."

At the end of the hall they came to an office suite. The door was open. Esther glanced inside. The ambassador, Rami Eban, was seated at his desk. She smiled at him from the doorway. "Mr. Ambassador."

He looked up with a smile. "Esther. So good to see you."

"I am sorry for the interruption at such a late hour."

"You are not interrupting me." He came from the desk and took her hand. "Whatever is important enough to bring you out is important for me, too."

While Esther and Eban greeted each other, Thompson and Rios stepped inside the office. Once Esther introduced them, Eban took a seat behind the desk. Esther, Rios, and Thompson sat in front. Rios got right to the point.

"The president will agree to release Anthony Wiseman into Israel's custody, in exchange for Demetrius Nilus. He would like for you to convey that offer. Our interest in Nilus is limited and specific. We have a short window of opportunity in which he could help us, but his help could be critical."

"That is the part that leaves me curious." Eban leaned back in his chair. "What interest does the United States have in a Russian general such as Demetrius Nilus?"

Rios crossed his legs. "We have a few questions we'd like to ask him."

"The FBI would agree to this exchange?" Eban shot a glance toward Esther, then back to Rios. "For quite some time now, they have been reluctant to let Mr. Wiseman go. One might say they have been insistent on keeping him."

"There are other issues more pressing now. We need to talk to Nilus. We think he has information vital to our interests."

"They would not agree to release Wiseman before."

"Sir, the FBI is irrelevant. If the president says yes, then the exchange will occur."

"You understand, this may take some time. Demetrius Nilus is a sensitive subject for many people in our government."

"I understand the issue is sensitive, but we don't have much time."

"You are aware of *The Protocols of the Learned Elders of Zion*? Nilus' grandfather wrote that book."

"I realize that."

"That book has led to the deaths of millions of Jews."

"I understand, Mr. Ambassador, but we are facing a critical situation and time is short."

"Did you know Nilus has orchestrated the sale of nuclear materials to both Iran and Pakistan? Iran would like to wipe us from the map."

"Yes," Rios nodded. "I understand that."

"Not just gas six million in prison camps, but wipe the entire country from existence."

"I understand. But we need to talk to Nilus. Israel needs to get rid of him before Russia responds. None of us wants an international incident right now. You need a plausible reason to let him go. Russia needs him back in a way that saves face for them. We urgently need to talk to him. This swap is a win for everyone."

Eban looked troubled. "The United States intends to turn over Nilus to the Russians?"

Rios nodded. "Right after we talk to him."

Eban shook his head. "I did not know this was part of the deal."

"Mr. Ambassador, I think everyone understands that Nilus has to be returned to Russia. Whether you do it, or we do it. He has to go back."

Eban looked away. "Perhaps you are correct."

"You will transmit our request?"

"Yes," Eban nodded. "I think it is in Israel's best interest to pursue the matter. We would need written assurances—"

Rios cut him off. "Mr. Ambassador, I don't think either of us wants anything in writing on this."

"Very well." Eban stood. "I assume you would prefer an answer quickly."

Rios stood. "Yes, sir. Before morning would be best."

Eban glanced at his watch. "I will see what I can do."

CHAPTER 82
WASHINGTON, D.C.

THOMPSON, RIOS, AND ESTHER walked from the ambassador's office to the elevator. As they rode downstairs, Rios looked at her. "That went well."

"Better than I expected."

Thompson spoke up. "I need a drink."

When they reached the first floor, Esther called Bryson. He met them at the gate with the SUV. She climbed in the front seat. Thompson and Rios lingered on the sidewalk. Bryson glanced out the window. "Where to now?"

"Somewhere to get a drink," Thompson replied.

"I have a car waiting," Rios added. "Let's meet at The Willard. We have a few things to discuss."

Fifteen minutes later, Thompson, Esther, and Bryson were seated at a table in the Round Robin, a bar at The Willard Hotel. It was late, but a few people were still enjoying the evening. Bryson had a cup of coffee. Esther sipped a ginger ale. By the time Rios arrived, Thompson was on his second bourbon. Esther introduced Rios to Bryson.

"I thought you looked familiar. We attended a few meetings together on the Hill."

"Yes," Bryson nodded. "You briefed our committee on a couple of programs."

Rios smiled. "I remember you wanted to know why nuclear threats were handled by the Department of Energy rather than the Department of Defense."

"And no one could answer my question."

"They still can't. We're an odd fit for that department." The bartender looked in their direction. Rios shook his head, then turned back to Bryson. "But being there, instead of at one of the intelligence agencies, gives us more autonomy. It's easier to tell them what to do when we're not part of their organizational chart."

"I can imagine."

Esther gestured in Bryson's direction. "He's actually the one who suggested swapping Wiseman for Nilus."

"Oh?"

"Thompson and I go back a ways," Bryson explained. "I was trying to help everybody out."

Rios glanced in Esther's direction. "I see."

Just then Esther's cell phone rang. She glanced at the screen to check the number, then gestured for them to be quiet. "This is him," she whispered.

Everyone at the table fell silent as she took the call. When she finished, she switched off the phone and smiled over at Rios. "They took it."

"Israel?" Rios looked surprised. "They responded already? How did they do that so quickly?"

"It's morning in Israel. Everyone is already at their offices." Esther took a sip of ginger ale. "It's done."

"Then we should get moving on this right away."

"Yes." Esther reached across the table and took the drink from Thompson's hand. "They want to talk about details. We need you sober and sharp."

"They want to talk again tonight?"

"No. First thing in the morning."

"Okay." Rios pointed to Thompson. "You work for me on this. Meet with them in the morning and set up the exchange. There's no point in trying to bring another team up to speed on this now. We're going to do this ourselves."

Esther frowned. "Ourselves?"

Rios gestured around the table. "The four of us." He looked at Thompson. "You're covering the logistics—getting the plane for Wiseman, and getting one for Nilus."

"We're bringing him over in our plane?"

"Yes. I'll have an FBI rendition team from Jerusalem bring Nilus over here. When the plane arrives with him on board, we'll send Wiseman to Israel." Rios looked over at Esther. "You're Wiseman's attorney. Is that okay with you?"

"Only if I go with him."

"You want to accompany him back to Israel?"

"I don't want him traveling alone. And certainly not with FBI agents. Just Wiseman and me." She glanced at Bryson. "And Paul."

Rios thought for a moment. "Okay," he said finally. "You two take him over. I'll call you tomorrow and tell you when and where." Rios stood and shook Bryson's hand. "Paul, good to see you again." He turned to Thompson and tapped him on the shoulder. "Come with me. We have work to do."

When they were gone, Esther leaned close to Bryson. "How long has it been since you were in Jerusalem?"

"A few years." Bryson sighed. "This seems like something from a movie. Or a comedy show."

"Happening too fast?"

"Too thrown together. None of us has the authority for any of this."

"You're used to reading it in a novel. Novels make sense. Life never does." She leaned away. "Rios is the head of NEST. Once he declares a nuclear emergency, he's in charge. Whatever he says goes. And he's right about the swap. As long as the president approves it, no one can stop it." She took Bryson's hand. "If you don't want to go, you don't have to. I didn't mean to volunteer you."

Bryson looked her in the eye. "I wouldn't miss it."

CHAPTER 83
PORTLAND, OREGON

IN THE MORNING, Brad Ramsey drove the Torino to Gresham, a town on the west side of Portland. He turned into the parking lot at the WinCo grocery store and parked the car about halfway between the store and the street. He sat there awhile, doing his best to make certain he wasn't followed and that no one was watching. When he was sure he was safe, he took his cell phone from the pocket of his jeans and once more called the FBI. The receptionist connected him to Donnie Brown.

Ramsey began talking as soon as Brown picked up. "We spoke yesterday about the Jew killer. The call was cut short. Meet me in the parking lot outside the WinCo on Burnside Road."

"In Gresham?"

"Yeah."

"Take me thirty minutes to get over there."

"I'll be waiting."

Ramsey clicked off the cell phone and slid low in the seat. He took a package of Camel cigarettes from his pocket and poked one in his mouth. He smoked it while he waited and watched through the windshield as cars came and went from the store. In a little while, a late-model gray Chevrolet sedan turned from the street. Ramsey followed it as it moved slowly toward him.

"That's him," he mumbled. "Gotta be. Ain't nobody but a government employee gonna drive a car like that." He rolled down the window, flipped the cigarette on the ground, and casually waved his hand. The Chevrolet came to a stop in a nearby space. Brown got out of the car, walked to the Torino, and got in on the passenger side.

"I take it you're Brad Ramsey." He pulled the door closed.

"Yeah."

"What's this all about?" Brown asked.

"I work for Nikolai Elson. You know him?"

"Runs a strip club. Barely Decent or something like that."

"Barely Here."

"Yeah. What about him?"

"I was in the office the other day. A guy came in. Elson sent me out so they could talk. I didn't know the guy, but we've been having some trouble lately so I waited around the corner to hear what they were talking about."

"What kind of trouble?"

"Employees stealing out of the cash register. Handing booze over the counter without anybody paying for it. That kind of thing."

"What were they talking about?"

"The guy said, 'It's here.' Then Elson said, 'Let me see that Jew killer. I want to kiss it.' Elson got up from the desk and followed the guy to the hall. I wondered what he was talking about when he said 'Jew killer,' so when they went outside I walked down to the door and watched. There's a window back there and I could see out to the parking lot behind the building."

"This was during business hours?"

"No. This was in the morning. Sometime around ten, I think. We don't open until afternoon."

"All right. You went to the back door and looked outside. What did you see?"

"There was a car parked near the door. Elson and this other guy walked over to it and opened the trunk. I could see inside it."

"It was backed into the parking space?"

"Yeah. Kinda parked sideways. In the trunk there was one of them aluminum cases, like bands use to put their stuff in when they travel. Only this one was pretty big. Not as big as the trunk but pretty big. Elson leaned over and kissed it."

"Kissed the case?"

"Yeah."

"Then what happened?"

"They talked a little and I heard him say—"

"Heard who say?"

"Elson. I heard Elson say it had to be in L.A. by Friday and how everyone would be proud of him for getting rid of a bunch of Jews."

"You're certain it was Elson who said this?"

"Yes."

"And he was talking about killing a bunch of Jews in L.A."

"Yes."

A red Mercedes turned into the parking lot. Ramsey followed it with his eyes. Brown continued. "Any idea where this killing is going to take place? I mean, specifically. Someplace in L.A. you know about?"

"No." Ramsey glanced around, suddenly nervous. His eyes glued to the Mercedes. "I've told you all I heard. The Jew-killer suitcase, L.A., and Friday. That's all I know."

"Why are you telling me this?"

"I …" The Mercedes came to a stop and the car door opened. A woman stepped out and started toward the store. Ramsey's shoulders slumped. "I…didn't like what he said. About Jews. My mother was Jewish. Emigrated from Ukraine before I was born."

"That makes you Jewish."

Ramsey frowned. "What?"

"You said your mother was Jewish, like it didn't apply to you. I was just saying, you're Jewish too. If she's Jewish, you're Jewish."

"Yeah." Ramsey had a nervous smile. "I guess that's right."

"Any idea what was in the case?"

"No."

"Okay." Brown sat quietly a moment, then thrust his hand toward Ramsey. "Thanks."

Ramsey gave him a limp handshake. "That's it?"

"We'll be in touch." Brown reached for the door handle.

Ramsey called after him, "You know how to find me?"

Brown glanced over his shoulder. "That was your cell phone you called from?"

"Yes."

"Keep it on. I'll be in touch."

Brown walked across the lot to the Chevrolet sedan. Ramsey watched him as he got in the car and drove away. "Yeah. Sure," he sighed. "I'll hear from you." He shook his head in disgust. "Shoulda kept my mouth shut before I get myself killed." He started the engine, put the transmission in gear, and drove the Torino toward the street.

CHAPTER 84
WASHINGTON, D.C.

AT SIX O'CLOCK IN THE EVENING, Esther and Bryson were seated in a Gulfstream jet inside a hangar at Andrews Air Force Base. Esther glanced out the window. "You think they'll really bring him?"

"Rios can get anything he wants."

"You think he wants Nilus as bad as he says?"

"I don't know. I've wondered that myself. Seems like a long shot that he would actually talk."

"Unless he was given asylum."

"That would be tempting," Bryson agreed, "if we were living in the Cold War era."

"Like that movie." Esther paused a moment. "I can't remember the name. With Sean Connery and the submarine."

"*Red October.*"

"Yes."

"You watch a lot of movies."

"I enjoy them. Plus they help me think about things."

Bryson took her hand. "Think any more about what we were discussing in Texas?"

"Yes." She smiled at him, then turned back to the window.

"What do you think?"

Just then someone appeared in the doorway. "They're arriving with Nilus."

The whine of an approaching jet engine grew louder. Then the nose of a Learjet appeared at the hangar door. It rolled inside the building and lurched to a stop fifty feet away. The engines fell silent and the stairway extended from the fuselage. Three black SUVs came from the tarmac and parked near the plane. Doors flew open as FBI agents bailed out.

Doyle Thompson came from behind an SUV. When the door of the plane opened, he hurried up the steps and disappeared inside. A few minutes later he reappeared at the top of the steps. Beside him was a man dressed in a gray jumpsuit and white tennis shoes. A black hood covered his head. His hands were cuffed behind his back. Thompson led him by the elbow down the steps and into one of the SUVs. FBI agents who had encircled the plane now hurried back to their cars. Doors slammed closed, and they were gone.

Before Esther could speak, a single SUV appeared in the hangar and came to a stop alongside the Gulfstream. The rear doors opened and Anthony Wiseman stepped out. Dressed in cotton dungarees and a golf shirt, he looked ten years younger than the last time she'd seen him. Rios appeared beside the SUV and walked with Wiseman up the steps and into the airplane. Wiseman grinned at Esther as he ducked inside.

Rios looked over at her. "Satisfied?"

"Yes, and thank you."

Rios stepped away and hurried back to the SUV. An attendant inside the aircraft grabbed a handle to pull the door closed. By the time he had it secured, the stairway was retracted and the jet was moving toward the tarmac.

Wiseman took a seat across from Esther and fastened the seat belt. A wide grin spread cross his face. "Hello, Esther."

The attendant moved down the aisle, lowering the window shades as he went. When he was past them, Esther reached across the aisle and squeezed Wiseman's hand. "How does it feel to be free?"

"I'll let you know when we touch down at Ben-Gurion International Airport."

Her face turned serious. "You understand, you can never come back here."

"Yeah," he nodded soberly. "I understand." Then his smile returned. "But I'll be free."

"Yes. You'll be free."

Wiseman looked past her and gestured with a nod. "Is this Paul?"

"Yes." Esther leaned back and introduced them.

"Glad to finally meet you," Wiseman said with a smile. "Esther has told me all about you."

"And she's told me a lot about you."

"Don't believe much of it," Wiseman chuckled. "I'm not that interesting."

The plane picked up speed and roared down the runway. Moments later, it rose into the night sky. Below them, Washington faded from sight.

CHAPTER 85
WASHINGTON, D.C.

AT HOME THAT EVENING, Steve Taylor received a text message on his cell phone, "Wheels up."

He shook his head in disbelief. "I still can't believe they did it," he muttered to himself.

His wife glanced at him. "What's wrong?"

"Nothing." He rose from his chair and started across the room. "I'll be back in a minute."

Taylor made his way downstairs to the basement and took a seat at his desk in the far corner. Using the laptop, he logged on to the Internet with a software tool that cloaked his computer's IP address. Then, using that program, he logged on to an I2P network that allowed him to send and receive instant messages through additional layers of encryption and anonymity that made his online activity untraceable. When the programs were up and running, he used his cell phone and sent Carmine Russo a text message that read simply, "Now."

A few minutes later, Russo replied to Taylor's laptop through the instant messaging service. "Yes."

Taylor typed quickly. "It went down just as I suspected."

"They swapped?"

"Yes."

"They will never learn. They cannot give their support with impunity. They can die right along with all the others."

"Did you log on to the satellite program like I showed you?"

"Yes."

"Are you in the system now?"

"Yes. I think so."

"Check and make sure. You should be able to track him by now."

There was a pause in the exchange between them, then Russo returned. "Yes. I have him. He's due east of you."

"Good. As long as they don't find the chip, you'll know exactly where he's located."

"Okay."

"Just don't forget, you're using a Pak satellite. So make sure you use those Pashtun responses if you hit any security challenges."

"Okay."

CHAPTER 86
FORT MEADE, MARYLAND

WHILE ANTHONY WISEMAN flew east toward Israel, Demetrius Nilus sat in the backseat of an SUV. A black hood covered his head, trapping his hot, stale breath. Men pressed against him on either side, sitting shoulder to shoulder, leg to leg on the seat. He felt anxious but he was not worried. Americans might treat him rudely, subjecting him to their so-called enhanced interrogation techniques, but they would not kill him. He was a Russian general and Russia would know who did those things to him. Whatever they did to him, Russia would repay twelve times over. The Americans would know that without being told.

Thirty minutes later, the SUV came to a stop. Doors opened. Someone took Nilus by the arm. "Come on," a voice said.

Nilus scooted across the seat to his right and felt with his feet. A hand grasped his ankle and guided it to the ground outside the SUV. "This way," the voice said.

The air was cool against his skin. Instinctively, he tipped back his head and took a deep breath. A hand took him by the arm. "Keep moving. Watch your step."

Someone else spoke up. "Think he understands English?"

"I don't know," the voice beside him replied. "But I don't speak Russian. I'm sure he can figure out the gist of what we're saying."

The hand on his arm pulled back. "Watch your step." Nilus hesitated, felt with his foot, and stepped up to the sidewalk.

A little farther and a door rattled. The air was different against his skin. It was warmer, stuffier. From the echo of footsteps, he was certain they were inside a building. Someone pulled him this way, then that. There was the ding of a bell, then the floor moved. *An elevator,* he told himself. Moments later, another ding. The hand against his arm nudged him forward.

The sounds were muffled now and the floor beneath his feet was soft. *Carpet.* He was certain of it. There was the rustle of movement. To the right, a door closed. Voices spoke but the echo was gone. The hand on his arm jerked him to a stop. They waited, then moved forward again. He banged his shoulder against something hard—a door facing, perhaps. Doors clanked shut behind them. Another door closed. And then someone lifted the hood from his head.

Nilus blinked against the glare and looked around the room. An upholstered chair sat against the wall. Beside it was a small table with a lamp. Next to it was an open door that led to a small bathroom.

In front of him were three windows. Beneath them was a low table. The top of the table was covered with magazines and a paperback book. He stared at it a moment and read the title.

Someone took hold of the cuffs that held his arms behind his back. He leaned forward as they moved his hands, then inserted a key. Moments later, the cuffs fell from his wrists and his arms were free. He brought his hands around to his chest. It felt good to flex his arms.

A man appeared at his side. He was dressed in a gray suit with white shirt and muted tie. Nilus took him for an FBI agent. "You will remain in here." The agent gestured to the right. "The bathroom is over there." He took Nilus by the arm and led him to the left. "The bedroom is over here." Nilus glanced through an open doorway. A large bed occupied the center of the room with a table and lamp on either side. There was a dresser to the right of the door and a closet along the wall to the left.

They want me to relax, he thought to himself. *I can do that just fine. But they should not think that I will cooperate with whatever they have in mind.*

Nilus nodded. "And how long shall I be here?"

"Someone will be in to see you tomorrow."

Behind them the door opened. Nilus glanced over his shoulder and saw the others who'd been in the room were now leaving. The agent turned to Nilus once more. "There are toiletries in the bathroom and a change of clothes in the closet. If you need anything, there's an intercom by the door. Just press the button and someone will respond."

Nilus squared his shoulders. "I am a general in the Russian Army. I would like to go home, now."

"I understand," the agent nodded. "Arrangements have been made." His hand thrust forward. Nilus reached out. The agent pressed something against Nilus' palm.

It was a curious move and Nilus looked down to see what the agent had given him. Then he saw on the agent's finger a ring made of gold. In the center of the top was a Maltese cross made of smooth red stone. Nilus slowly lifted his head. Their eyes met. The agent smiled at him. "Arrangements have been made," he repeated, then moved toward the door and was gone.

When he was alone, Nilus looked down at the object in his hand. It was a round cylinder, smaller than the joint of his middle finger, with a screw top. He opened it and glanced inside to see two small capsules. "Cyanide," he whispered. "Just as I thought."

CHAPTER 87
STEGNA, RHODES

HIGH ON THE CLIFF OVERLOOKING the village and the beach, Spoleto came from the cottage and stepped out to the courtyard behind the house. Carmine Russo sat at a table, reading a book and enjoying the sun. He stood as Spoleto approached.

"Good afternoon, sir. You are finished for the day? Shall I have the cook bring you something to eat now?"

"Not yet." Spoleto gestured with a nod. "Let us take a walk."

A brick wall surrounded the courtyard with a gate in back that led to the garden. When they reached the gate, Spoleto opened it and continued down a narrow path past the plants and early-winter shrubs. Near the center of the garden, the path curved back to the left toward a bench on the cliff overlooking the beach. Spoleto walked slowly in that direction, hands behind his back, head down and silent. Russo kept pace, following half a step behind.

At the cliff, Spoleto paused and looked out at the ocean. "A magnificent view," he said finally.

"Yes, it is," Russo agreed.

They stood there in silence awhile, then Spoleto continued. "You have reached Steve Taylor in America?"

"Yes."

"And he has provided you with all that you need to locate Wiseman?"

"Yes. We are tracking him now."

Spoleto moved his hands from behind his back and folded his arms across his chest. "We have only two loose ends that remain."

"Wiseman?"

"No." Spoleto shook his head. "Steve Taylor and our other contact."

"There is the matter of the missing case. Shall I ask them about that?"

"That is no longer our concern. It will not come back on us now." Spoleto glanced in Russo's direction. "That will be a problem for the Russians to handle."

"I see."

"I understand Nilus is with the Americans now?"

"Yes, sir," Russo answered. "He has been transferred to them."

"Were we able to reach him at his new location?"

"Yes."

"Did he accept the message?"

"The message was given to him. Whether he has followed instructions, I do not know."

"You will make certain that he does?"

"Yes. We can send a second message, if necessary."

"I do not think that will be necessary. I am more concerned about the Americans Busca used. He and Giovanni relied on them far too much." Spoleto sighed and shook his head once more. "They know too much about our business."

"Yes, sir."

"Taylor gave you the codes for the satellite?"

"Yes. We are using the system now."

"You have the responses, as we discussed? In the event their security measures challenge you?"

"Yes."

"Very well." Spoleto turned toward the ocean. A breeze blew his hair back from his forehead. He closed his eyes, lifted his chin slightly, and enjoyed the moment. "It is time to terminate our relationship with the Americans."

"Yes, sir."

Spoleto opened his eyes and looked over at Russo. "You will take care of that?"

"Yes."

"Discreetly," Spoleto added. "I understand one of them has a wife and children."

CHAPTER 88
FORT MEADE, MARYLAND

A LITTLE BEFORE NINE the next morning, Pete Rios arrived at Fort Meade. He was admitted onto the base and directed to a building near Cooper Road. There, a soldier escorted him to an elevator and rode with him up to the top floor. At the end of the hall they came to a secure door. The soldier entered a code on a keypad and pressed his palm against a screen for a print scan. The door opened and Rios stepped inside to a one-bedroom suite.

Demetrius Nilus stood across the room, his back to the door. He held a cigarette, which he lifted to his mouth in constant, nervous motion, taking one drag after another. Gray smoke hung thick in the air. Rios glanced down at an ashtray that sat on the table beneath the window. It was littered with cigarette butts.

"General Nilus, my name is Pete Rios. I have a few questions I'd like to ask you." Still, Nilus did not respond. Rios gestured to the chair. "Perhaps you'd be more comfortable over here, in the chair, where we can talk."

Nilus took one final drag on the cigarette he was holding and let the smoke escape from his mouth and nose. "Questions," he growled. "You Americans always have questions." He dropped the cigarette in the ashtray and took a seat in the chair.

Rios sat on the sofa. "General, as I think you know, we face a very grave situation."

A smile crept across Nilus' face. "Grave," he chuckled. "An interesting choice of words."

"What can you tell me about the four angels?"

"I see you have managed to hack into someone's computer."

"What can you tell me?"

"Nothing." Nilus shook his head. "I can tell you nothing."

"General, your nephew, Leonid Malenkov, has been found dead. The man—"

Nilus' eyes were wide. "What are you saying?"

"You didn't know about Malenkov?"

"Why are you telling me this?"

"The Order of Malta plays for keeps, General. I think you know that already. Ivan is dead. Your nephew's body was found in a trash bin in Vienna. You are next."

"And only you can protect me?"

"Your best chance of survival is in Russia. We can return you there, but we need your help."

"If the Order of Malta is as powerful as you say, why should I help you?"

"Because you won't survive ten minutes on the street."

"What street?" A frown wrinkled Nilus' brow. "What are you talking about?"

"Paris. London. Lisbon." Rios shrugged. "Pick a street." He leaned back and crossed his legs. "Maybe we'll just drop you in Athens. Or make it convenient for everyone and take you back to Rhodes."

"You would not do such a thing," Nilus scoffed.

"I would prefer to return you to Russia. I am not certain what would happen to you there. They got to Ivan without much trouble. But I—"

Nilus had a quizzical look. "Where did they find him?"

"Outside his club."

Nilus looked out the window. Rios uncrossed his legs and leaned forward. "Tell me about the four angels." He rested his elbows on his knees. "Four apocalyptic horsemen. Four bombs. Four attacks. Four cities. Tell me what you know."

"Four nuclear bombs," Nilus mumbled, his eyes still fixed on some imaginary point beyond the window. "They are four nuclear bombs." He turned to look Rios in the eye. "We have suitcase bombs, you know. They are not a myth as many suppose."

"Where are they?"

"Here. In the U.S."

"All four?"

"We sent four."

"What does that mean?"

"It means we sent four," Nilus replied in a sarcastic tone.

"Why did you travel to Rhodes?"

"One of the angels was missing."

"Missing? One of the cases is missing?"

"It arrived in the U.S. but did not reach its destination."

"What was its destination? Which city was it going to?"

"It is useless," Nilus smiled. "This heroic effort of yours. It is useless. You cannot stop us."

"Who? Who can't we stop?"

"We will kill more Jews than Hitler and Stalin combined. Even with the complicity of your President Roosevelt, they did not kill as many as we."

"What are you talking about?"

"Hitler, Stalin, Churchill, even your beloved President Roosevelt, they were all in it together. They did their best to wipe out the Jews, but your American conservative faction intervened." Nilus wagged his finger. "There will be no intervention now." He slipped his hand inside his pocket, then took it quickly out and popped two pills into his mouth. He swallowed them. "Now it is finished."

Rios leaped from the sofa and rushed toward Nilus. "What did you do?" He turned to the door and shouted, "Guard! Guard!"

Nilus' face turned pale. His eyes opened wide and he gripped the armrests of the chair with both hands. Rios took hold of his chin and tried to pry open his mouth. "What did you do?" he shouted. "What did you put in your mouth?"

"It is no use now," Nilus replied, then slumped to the left, slid from Rios' grasp, and flopped onto the floor.

"I don't believe this." Rios knelt beside him and checked for a pulse. "Don't do this," he fumed. "Don't do this." He placed his ear over Nilus' nose and listened. In the silence of that moment he heard the faint sound of breathing. Desperate to keep Nilus alive, Rios lunged toward the door and pressed a button on the intercom. "Guard! This is an emergency," he shouted at the speaker. "Send a medical team."

A voice responded from the intercom, "State your name, please."

"This is Pete Rios. Get up here now!"

"Is anyone else in the room with you?"

"Get up here now!" He scurried back to Nilus' side. "Don't die on me," he growled. Nilus looked up. His lips moved but made no sound. Rios leaned closer. "What? I can't hear you."

Nilus took a deep breath and tried again, this time a little louder. "Pray …" His voice was raspy and barely audible. "Pray for me." Then his head slumped to the right and his arms went limp.

CHAPTER 89
BEERSHEBA, ISRAEL

NINE HOURS AFTER TAKING off from Andrews Air Force Base, the Gulfstream jet with Anthony Wiseman aboard landed in Tel Aviv. It was met by a convoy of SUVs. Esther, Bryson, and Wiseman were escorted by Israeli secret service agents down the steps from the plane into the Masada VIP lounge, where they were welcomed by the prime minister's military secretary. Less than an hour later they arrived at the Mossad operations center in Beersheba.

After a brief celebration and quick introductions, Wiseman was whisked away for an examination at the Soroka Medical Center. When he was gone, Oren Cohen led Esther and Bryson to a conference room, where they ate lunch. Afterward, he took Esther down the hall to his office so they could talk.

Cohen took a seat behind his desk. Esther sat in a chair across from him. He leaned back and laced his fingers together.

"Reuben told you about Malenkov's body?"

"He told me it has been found."

Cohen opened a desk drawer and took out a photograph. He laid it on the desktop and pointed. "This is what they found." Esther winced when she saw the picture.

Pieces of Malenkov's body lay on a medical examination table. His head had been severed at the base of the neck. His arms and legs had been hacked off at the torso. A Maltese cross was carved into his chest. Esther turned the photograph over. Cohen picked it up and dropped it in the drawer. "I think there's little doubt who did this."

"But why?" Esther had a puzzled look.

"They were obviously sending someone a message."

"But to whom? And why?"

"Something went wrong. Very wrong."

"What could it have been?"

"We think something happened with their plan. The one we asked you about."

"Reuben told you my thoughts on that?"

"Yes. And I agree. Four attacks of apocalyptic proportions."

"How would they do that?"

Cohen leaned forward, propped his elbows on the desk, and lowered his voice. "I think they're talking about suitcase bombs."

"Nuclear suitcase bombs?"

"Yes."

"Why do you think that?"

"Malenkov mentioned it to Jiroft and suggested one of them is in the United States."

"That's one. Where are the other three?"

"I don't know."

"Any way to confirm that the case is actually in the U.S.? Malenkov could have been just trying to placate Jiroft."

Cohen reached inside the desk drawer again and took out another photograph. He dropped it on the desk. "This is Hossein Jiroft."

Esther leaned forward for a closer look. "Where was this taken?"

"Sonoita. A town in northern Mexico. Right on the U.S. border."

"When?"

"Three days ago."

"Who took this?"

"Can't say."

"So, you think he's there because he's come to retrieve a suitcase?"

"It's circumstantial, but it adds a layer of plausibility."

"Has anyone from the U.S. seen this photograph?"

"No."

"Why not?"

Cohen rose from his chair and closed the window blinds. Then he came from behind the desk and took a seat next to Esther. She had a puzzled frown. "What are you doing?"

He put his finger to his lips in a gesture for quiet and leaned close to her ear. "We had a source inside the Knights Castle. He was able to gain access to a Blackberry used by the Grand Master's assistant. We received some of the files from that Blackberry. They included emails and text messages sent to contacts of the Order all over the world. One of those contacts was a man who works for the United States government."

"Who?"

"Steve Taylor."

Esther was startled. "Steve Taylor works for the Order?"

"He has been orchestrating the Order's activities in America."

Esther leaned away and propped her head on her hand. "That makes things much clearer."

"So you know this man?"

"Yes."

"But he is not your friend."

"No. Quite the opposite. Have you told anyone in Washington about this?"

"We have not had an opportunity to share the information with someone who would believe us...until now."

"What do you mean?"

"You have met Pete Rios?"

"Yes."

"We want you to convey this information to him."

"How?"

"You will find an appropriate way."

"What about Doyle Thompson? Can I just tell him?"

"No." Cohen shook his head vigorously. "Not him. Don't tell him a word. It must be Rios. Find a way to let him know, quietly and discretely."

"I may not see him again."

"Do your best."

"Why not just tell them directly?"

"They'll ask too many questions about our sources."

"And you don't want to tell them?"

"We are not giving up this source."

"But the contact on Rhodes—the man who sent you this information—is dead. They need to know about Steve Taylor. This is a real threat."

"That's why we need you to do this." Cohen stood. "And you need to do this at the first opportunity."

"Okay." Esther stood. "As soon as I am finished here with Anthony."

"We will take care of Anthony." Cohen gestured toward the door. "He is in good hands."

"Don't you want to talk to him and debrief him?"

"Certainly. We probably already are."

Esther's face was flush with anger. "Not without me being present."

"You're not in the United States now, Esther."

"He's my client," she protested. "I'm his attorney."

"In America that would be correct. Here, you're a tourist." He took her by the elbow and guided her toward the door. "Esther, we are all friends of Anthony Wiseman now. I assure you, nothing will happen to him. Besides, you don't have a security clearance that would allow you to hear the kinds of things we want to discuss." Cohen opened the door and led her down the hall. "Spend the night, then tomorrow the plane will take you back home."

Her shoulders sagged. Tears filled her eyes. After all the years of working to gain Wiseman's freedom—endless meetings, phone calls, and cajoling—the ending seemed anticlimactic. She gave Cohen an imploring look. "Not even a last good-bye to him?"

"I am sorry." Cohen shook his head. "This is how it must be for now. We'll tell him you said farewell."

When she reached the conference room, Bryson was standing on the opposite side of the room, looking at a photograph that hung on the wall. He turned to face her as she entered. "Back so soon?"

"I'm afraid this is going to be a short trip. They want us to start back tomorrow."

"So soon? What happened?"

"Come on." She hooked her arm in his. "I'll try to explain it."

CHAPTER 90
WASHINGTON, D.C.

PHILIPPE JOBERT SAT in Ford's Theatre with Isabelle Clavier, his girlfriend of fifteen years. They watched as their daughter, Corinne, rehearsed on stage for a performance scheduled later that evening. She had appeared in several plays during the summer, but Jobert had been away from home most weekends. He was determined to see her this night. To make up for lost time he came with Isabelle for the afternoon run-through.

Corrine's part in the play was small but Jobert sat with rapt attention, watching her every move. Somewhere in the second act, he felt his cell phone vibrating in his pocket. He ignored it and kept his eyes focused on the stage until Corrine exited to the left.

When she was out of sight, he took the phone from his pocket and glanced at the screen. A one-word message appeared that read, "Assignments." He scrolled down and found a photograph of a man who appeared to be in his early fifties. Beneath the picture was the name Steve Taylor. He scrolled farther down and a second name emerged with a photograph beneath it.

Isabelle whispered in his ear, "Work reaches you even in here?"

Jobert exited the message and returned the phone to his pocket. "Not tonight," he smiled. "Tonight I know nothing but you." He took

her arm in his and nuzzled her cheek. "And Corinne…and the stage."
He kissed her. She grinned. He kissed her again and gazed into her eyes.
"You are the most wonderful woman in the world."

"Do you say that to all the women you meet in the theater?"

"There is only you."

She laughed and rested her head on his shoulder. "You forgot one
thing."

"What's that?"

"Dinner."

"Yes," Jobert nodded. "You, Corrine, the stage, and a lovely dinner
after the performance."

Isabelle sighed. "Then you can think about work."

CHAPTER 91
NEAR PISINEMO, ARIZONA

RASHID AL-HASAN PROPPED his boot against the front bumper of a green Range Rover and leaned back against the hood. He pulled a cowboy hat low over his eyes, shielding them against the glare of the hot Arizona desert. "It'll be a scorcher today," he sighed.

Sixty yards away, a string of mules stood in the shade of a palo verde tree. Two young boys worked with them, fastening the rigging to their backs.

Off to the left, a blue Ford sedan was parked inside a dilapidated shed. A man dressed in blue jeans and a white shirt stood near the rear bumper of the car. He opened the trunk, reached inside, and took out an aluminum case.

Hossein Jiroft stepped out of the Range Rover from the passenger side and stood at the bumper near Rashid. "What will you do with the car?"

"I have a friend in Tucson who operates a recycling plant."

"And the man?"

"Zepeda? He is of no concern."

"Everything is my concern."

"He is a Tohono," Rashid explained. "A man of discretion."

"I cannot afford any problems."

"And I cannot afford to lose the man." Rashid glanced at Jiroft. "Or the boys."

"Why are they so valuable to you?"

"His brother is a member of the cartel in Juarez. They allow us to operate here because of him."

Zepeda came from the shed with the case and started toward the Range Rover. As he drew near, Rashid gave him a nod. "Just put it in the back," he gestured over his shoulder. Zepeda did not respond but continued past them to the back door of the Range Rover. He put the case behind the rear seat and closed the door. Rashid and Jiroft watched as he walked back toward the boys.

The boys brought four leather satchels to the palo verde tree. They arrived back at the tree just as Zepeda stepped into the shade. One by one he took the satchels from them and hooked them on the mule's rigging.

Jiroft pointed. "What's in the satchels?"

"Clothes. A little food." Rashid stood up straight. "Whatever he needs for the trip."

"That looks like a lot to carry for one man."

"Perhaps," Rashid replied. "I do not ask many questions."

"He can cross the border without being detected?"

"He can cross without being stopped."

"What goes on the second mule?"

"Water bags."

Ten minutes later, the mules were loaded and ready. Zepeda climbed on the lead animal and settled into place. The boys handed him ropes for the others and stepped back. They waved and smiled. He acknowledged them with a tip of the hat. Then the mules started forward at a slow, deliberate pace.

Rashid stepped away. "You should get going. You can still make it on time?"

"Yes. I think that will not be a problem."

Jiroft moved around to the driver's door and got in behind the wheel. He pulled the door closed and spoke through the open window. "Do you need a ride?"

"No," Rashid shook his head. "I will take the car to Tucson. Someone will meet me there."

In the distance, Zepeda and the mules were still visible, the dark skin of animals and man silhouetted against the backdrop of a low, barren hillside. Jiroft stared after him. "I am not sure he can be trusted."

Rashid propped his hand against the driver's door and glanced inside at Jiroft. "Do you trust me?"

"Yes," Jiroft replied. "Of course."

"Will I not pay with my life if he talks?"

"Yes."

"Well, then," Rashid chuckled. "You are not the one who should be worried."

Jiroft stroked his chin. Then his eyes moved from Zepeda in the distance to Rashid standing beside him. "You are certain the case will work?"

"Positive. You know where to meet them?"

"Yes."

Rashid reached through the window and squeezed Jiroft's shoulder. "Assalam Alikum."

Jiroft reached for the ignition. "Wa Alikum Assalam." He started the engine, put the Range Rover in gear, and drove away.

CHAPTER 92
LAS VEGAS, NEVADA

A CAR WAS WAITING at the airport when the plane carrying Pete Rios landed. He walked from the Gulfstream jet into the warm night air and opened the back door of the car to find Randall Morris inside. Rios ducked into the backseat. "I thought you were running the center."

"They're doing just fine." Morris waited while Rios closed the car door. "I heard what happened with Nilus."

"It was awful, watching him die right there on the floor. Think the Russians know about it?"

"I doubt it," Morris shrugged. "And anyway, that's for the diplomats to worry about."

"They said it was cyanide."

"Yes, that's what they're reporting."

"Where did he get it?"

"Either he brought it with him, or someone on the inside gave it to him."

"I think he got it after he arrived at Meade," Rios mused. "The Israelis searched him before they put him on the plane and he arrived with nothing but the clothes he was wearing. I don't see how he could have had it with him when he landed at Andrews."

"Then we have a mole," Morris observed.

"But who are they working for?"

"Israel. Russia." Morris took a deep breath. "Order of Malta. Who knows?"

"Israel wouldn't want him dead and neither would the Russians."

"Which leaves the Order."

Rios stared out the window. "We were right. About the four suitcases and the cities."

"He told you this?"

"He told me there were four cities. And he admitted the suitcase bombs are nuclear."

"The four cities are in America?"

"Yes. They sent four cases here. One of them didn't make it to its destination."

"What does that mean?"

"I don't know," Rios shrugged. "That's when he swallowed the pills."

"Have you told anyone this?"

"Only you. Just now. I didn't know who to trust. I just got through the details with the people at Fort Meade, and got out of there."

The car turned from the street into the parking lot at the Frontier Lounge. Rios looked at Morris. "What are we doing here? We need to get to the center."

"You've had a rough few days." Morris patted Rios on the shoulder. "You need a moment to relax."

"We need to get to the center," Rios insisted. "That's what I've been waiting for. We need to tell them what Nilus said and get busy on finding the locations."

Morris ignored him and opened the car door. "Come on. We'll have a bite to eat first. All that will still be waiting for us when we get out there."

CHAPTER 93
WASHINGTON, D.C.

THAT EVENING, TYLER DAVIS, White House chief of staff, attended a reception at the National Gallery of Art honoring the opening exhibition of a Russian art collection. As he wandered through the exhibit, Lobanov Rostovsky, the Russian ambassador, came to his side.

"I was wondering if we might talk now," Rostovsky asked quietly.

"Certainly," Davis replied.

Davis followed Rostovsky down the hall to the East Garden Court, a large room with high ceilings and a garden courtyard in the center. As they entered the room, Rostovsky nodded to the security detail. Three men moved behind them to secure the room. When they were inside, he turned to Davis.

"You and I have a problem."

"Oh?"

"You have something of ours you cannot keep. We have lost something we cannot find."

"That would be an interesting situation."

"What do you suppose we can do about that?"

Davis drew Rostovsky into the center of the room. "What are we talking about?"

"We have learned that four suitcase bombs are missing from our arsenal."

"You guys have been talking about suitcase bombs since the sixties."

"We have them. Both conventional and nuclear. They were being stored at our decommissioning facility in Krasnoyarsk. Your own inspectors have seen them."

"And now they're missing."

"We discovered it two days ago."

"And why are you telling me this now?"

"Under normal conditions, three men have access to them. One is in Moscow. The other two are in Krasnoyarsk. Alexander Koppov and Demetrius Nilus. Koppov is dead. Nilus is missing." Rostovsky arched an eyebrow. "I believe you know something about him."

"I'll have to check on that and see what we know about him. Any idea what happened to your suitcases?"

"It appears Demetrius Nilus was engaged in the sale of arms."

"So you think he sold them?"

"It would seem so."

"This is exactly the kind of thing our countries have been working to prevent."

"Yes."

"We warned you this could happen."

"We are well aware of the risks."

"And it took you two days to inform us they were gone?"

"No. It took us two days to learn that the bombs may be here in the United States."

"Then why did you wait two days to tell us?"

"Mr. Davis, in spite of what you may think, the world is under no obligation to report its business to the Americans. I am informing you now because we have learned details that may concern the safety of your people. I should think you would be grateful."

Davis took a deep breath. "I am," he sighed. "I am very grateful."

He shook Rostovsky's hand. "Now, if you will excuse me, I must tell the president at once."

"Certainly."

CHAPTER 94
ALEXANDRIA, VIRGINIA

THE FOLLOWING MORNING, Steve Taylor awakened well before dawn. He rolled quietly out of bed and dressed in blue jeans and a sweatshirt. Shoes in hand, he tiptoed down the hall to the closet and took a parka from its hangar. At the back door, he paused to put on his shoes, then slipped on the parka and hurried outside to the driveway.

Working quickly in the cold night air, he pulled the boat trailer from its place at the end of the house and hitched it to his SUV. He checked to make sure it was securely attached, then hooked up the lights and attached the safety chains. Finally, he made his way to the driver's door of the SUV and crawled inside.

Thirty minutes later, he arrived at the launch ramp at Old Dominion Boat Club. The parking lot was empty and quiet. Security lights along the pier glowed brightly but otherwise the place was deserted. Only the waves gently lapping the shore broke the silence.

Taylor had no time to enjoy the peaceful predawn moment. A friend had offered the use of a cabin in the mountains of North Carolina. They were scheduled to leave this morning. By evening, he planned for them all to be far from the East Coast and the confusion he was certain would come that weekend. To leave on time, he had to get the boat out of the water and back to the house before sunup. There was little time to spare.

He turned the SUV around in the parking lot and slowly backed the trailer down the launch ramp until the rear bumper was at the water's edge. He set the parking brake and stepped out to make certain the trailer was fully submerged. Satisfied he could drive the boat all the way onto it, he switched off the engine and hurried toward the pier.

At the slip, he unhooked the stern lines, then put his foot on the gunwale and stepped into the center of the boat. The outboard motor was locked in a tilted position with the propeller out of the water. He reached over the cowling and grasped the back of the motor with one hand, then lifted up to relieve the tension on the locking pin. As he reached with his free hand for the pin to release the motor, he felt a jarring blow to the back of his head.

A tingling shock ran down his spine. Both arms went numb and his legs no longer responded. His vision was blurred. The glow of the lights on the pier faded from his eyes. Stunned and unable to move, the weight of his body pitched him headfirst over the transom of the boat and into the icy water of the Potomac River. He floated there for a moment, facedown, arms and legs spread wide apart. In a reflexive action, his lungs expanded, filling completely with water. Taylor's arms trembled. Fingers on his right hand twitched. Then everything turned black.

CHAPTER 95
WASHINGTON, D.C.

BRYSON AND ESTHER arrived back in Washington a little after sunset. The plane landed at Dulles Airport and came to a stop outside the general aviation hangar. A car was waiting for them and took them to Esther's townhouse in Georgetown. Bryson helped her inside, then lingered at the door.

"I suppose I should go home and sleep now," he said with a smile. "But I'd rather go down to the Egg And I and have breakfast."

She glanced out at the sky. "Actually, I think it's dinnertime."

"But my body thinks it's breakfast."

She slipped an arm around his waist. "I'd rather sit on the sofa and watch a movie with you."

"I would, too, but we'd never stay awake for the ending." He leaned over and kissed her. "Besides, I need a shower and if I stay for a movie, we'll doze on the sofa and be useless tomorrow."

"I suppose you're right." She kissed him again. "I enjoyed the trip, even though it was short."

"I did, too."

"This is my life, Paul. Do you think we can work this out?"

"I think we already have."

Just then Doyle Thompson appeared on the sidewalk. "I hate to interrupt you two, but we need to talk."

Bryson turned to face him. "What is it?"

Thompson gestured toward the door. "Let's talk inside."

Esther pushed open the door. Bryson and Thompson followed after her. When they were inside, Thompson began. "Demetrius Nilus is dead."

Esther looked concerned. "What happened to him?"

"Cyanide."

"How? Where did he get it?"

"It looks like someone on the inside gave it to him. The Israelis searched him before they put him on the plane, but he had it when he was at Fort Meade."

"Any idea who?"

"No."

Bryson folded his arms across his chest. "What did the Russians say?"

"We haven't told them yet. But they're looking for him. And they told Tyler Davis that four of their suitcase bombs are missing. They think they are here in the United States."

"The four horsemen," Esther groaned.

Bryson moved his hands to his side. "So, who would have them?"

"I guess that's the obvious question," Thompson replied.

"You misunderstand," Bryson explained. "If Nilus and Malenkov sold them, who would they have sold them to? Can we reverse engineer our way from the sale back to their customers?"

"I don't know, but I have an idea how we could find out. We analyzed Nilus' telephone records." Thompson gave them a knowing look. "He sent at least fifteen text messages to a cell phone in Moscow used by Yuri Ivanovsky."

"Ivanovsky." Esther looked puzzled. "Who is he?"

"Goes by the street name of Ivan," Thompson smirked. "He's a mobster in Moscow."

"Has anyone talked to him?"

"He's dead. Shot outside his nightclub."

Esther leaned against the door. "So, what is Rios doing?"

"He's back in Las Vegas, trying to figure out where those cases are."

"Any good leads?"

"I don't know. They don't talk to me about that kind of stuff."

Bryson chuckled. "I wonder why?"

"Yeah."

There was a twinkle in Thompson's eye as he spoke. Bryson caught it and gave him a quizzical look. "So, Doyle, you said you had an idea how we could find out where the cases are. What are you thinking?"

Thompson grinned. "Chevy Chase."

Esther frowned. "What's in Maryland?"

"Viktor Yursky," Thompson replied. "Supposedly one of the biggest Bratva dons on the East Coast."

"And you want to pay him a visit," Bryson nodded.

Thompson took a deep breath. "I do. You want to come along? It would look better if someone was with me."

"Okay."

"No." Esther shot Paul a look. "You can't be serious."

"He's right," Bryson replied. "He can't go alone."

"Let him get someone from the office."

"He can't tell them what he's doing." Bryson kissed her. "I'll be back in a little while."

"You aren't an operative," she cautioned. "You're brilliant at many things, but you don't know what you're doing with this."

"It's just a few questions," Bryson shrugged. "And I'm tired of sitting behind a desk."

CHAPTER 96
CHEVY CHASE, MARYLAND

TWENTY MINUTES LATER, Bryson and Thompson arrived outside Yursky's home on Connecticut Avenue. The house, a spacious two-story with white siding and a well-manicured lawn, sat back from the street on a large lot. A circular driveway led from the street. Bryson parked the SUV near the front steps and got out. Thompson waited for him on the passenger side. "Let me do the talking," he cautioned.

"Right," but don't go too far."

"What do you mean?"

"You're a CIA agent out on a limb. I'm a civilian out there with you. If this works, we'll look like heroes. If we push it too far, we'll look like idiots."

"I've been called that all my life."

"I haven't," Bryson replied.

"What did they call you?"

"Until recently, Congressman."

Thompson grinned. "Maybe you'll get a new name tonight." He pressed a button to ring the doorbell and stepped back.

There was the sound of approaching footsteps inside, then the door opened and a butler appeared. "May I help you?"

"We're here to see Viktor Yursky."

"Is he expecting you?"

Thompson shook his head. "I doubt it."

"Mr. Yursky only sees visitors by appointment."

Just then, Yursky stepped into the hallway. He glanced at Bryson and Thompson, then looked at the butler. "Juan, who are these people?"

Before the butler could speak, Thompson held up his wallet to show his ID. "We're from Langley."

Yursky came closer. "How do I know that?" He glanced at Thompson's wallet. "Anyone could print an identification card."

Thompson reached in his pocket and took out a business card. "Call your contacts." He handed Yursky the card. "We'll wait."

Yursky turned away and disappeared down the hall. The butler pushed the door closed. Bryson shoved his hands in his pockets. "What do we do now?"

"Wait."

"You actually think he's making a call?"

"Yeah."

"Probably calling the—"

The door opened and the butler appeared once more. "This way, gentlemen." He stepped aside to the let them enter, then led them down the hall to a study. Yursky was seated in a leather chair by a desk near the far corner of the room. As Bryson and Thompson entered, the butler pulled the door closed behind them.

Yursky looked up. "How may I help you?"

"The Russian government has lost four suitcase bombs."

"Nonsense." Yursky was indignant. "Is this a joke?"

"No," Thompson replied. "It's not a joke. A Russian general named Demetrius Nilus took the cases from an arsenal in Krasnoyarsk. They have been brought to the United States. Transportation to bring them here was arranged by Yuri Ivanovsky." Yursky's eyes brightened. Thompson pressed the point. "You know him?"

"The name sounds familiar." Yursky looked away. "But then again, there are many Ivans in Russia."

"Ivanovsky is dead," Thompson continued. "General Nilus was taken into custody. We need to locate those cases."

Yursky rested his hands in his lap. "And you think I know something about them?"

"Mr. Yursky, we're not here about your business, or your taxes, or your drug operation, or how many young girls you coerce into the sex trade every year. We are not the police, or the FBI, or Interpol. We can get them involved, if that's what you'd like, but right now we're more interested in those cases. We have reason to believe they are going to be used on targets in key American cities. Cities where you have significant business interests."

"I have nothing to do with any of this. I am a citizen of the United States. I have not even had so much as a traffic violation in the past... twenty years."

Thompson stepped closer. "You are one of the most well-connected men in America. With a phone call, you can find out where those cases are and the names of the people who have them."

"I am a businessman. I make millions every year. A nuclear explosion in the places you describe would ruin everything I came here to enjoy. Why would I ruin such a great opportunity?"

"The only way you can stop all that from happening is to help us. Have you heard anything about these cases?"

"No." Yursky looked away once more. "I have not."

"We need you to find out."

"You're with the CIA, why don't you find out for yourself? Secrets are your business."

"Okay," Thompson nodded. "We can do that. We'll start shaking down Russians, rounding up people, disrupting business. By morning, every nightclub, drug dealer, and whorehouse on the East Coast will be out of business." He took a cell phone from his pocket. "We'll start with the building on Fourteenth Street." Yursky's eyes opened wide.

"Yeah," Thompson nodded. "Didn't think anyone knew about that, did you?"

"You're bluffing."

Thompson placed his thumb on the button to make a call. "One way to find out."

"What do you want from me?"

"Names, Mr. Yursky. We need names. Before noon tomorrow."

"Before noon?" Yursky laughed. "You two are crazy." He looked at Bryson. "How did you get mixed up with a man so crazy?" Before Bryson could respond, Yursky looked back at Thompson. "I give you the names, you people leave me alone?"

Thompson lowered the phone to his side and slipped it into his pocket. "You have my card. Give me a call before noon tomorrow. Sooner would be better."

* * *

When Bryson and Thompson returned to Georgetown, they found Esther wide awake. She greeted Bryson with a hug and kiss. "Are you all right?"

"I'm fine." He kissed her once more. "Doyle's only half as crazy as they say."

Esther looked at Thompson "What did you find out?"

"Not much yet."

"At least he didn't shoot us," Bryson chuckled.

"Think he can help?"

"I'm sure he can," Thompson replied. "I just don't know if he will. Or if he'll help us in time to be of any use."

"Well, it was actually a good move." Esther looked back at Bryson. "I'm hungry."

"Me, too," Thompson agreed. "Where are we going to eat?"

Thirty minutes later they were seated in the lounge at Citronelle, an upscale restaurant on M Street. While they were eating, Thompson's cell phone rang. He took the call and jotted notes on the cloth dinner napkin. A moment later, he ended the call and looked up at Bryson. "That was Yursky," he whispered.

Bryson looked surprised. "That was fast. What did he say?"

"Three names." Thompson glanced down at the napkin. "Vitali Safronov, Nikolai Elson, and Alim Solonik."

"What about a fourth?"

"Pavel Nayfeld may have one of them, but no one has seen him in several days."

"That's it?"

Thompson leaned over the table toward them. "Do you realize who these four men are?"

"Russian mafia," Esther shrugged.

"Not just Russian mafia. These are the top four Russian dons in the United States. With Yursky they are like the heads of the Five Families in New York for the Italian mob. Even bigger."

Esther gestured to Thompson. "You have to tell someone about this."

"I can't tell anyone." Thompson shook his head. "I'm not supposed to be doing this."

"But you can't keep it to yourself," Esther insisted. "This is a major break. Someone has to find these people. Find out what they know."

Thompson's expression changed. "I'll call Pete Rios. I have his phone number. He gave it to me the other night."

Thompson took out his cell phone. Bryson grabbed his hand. "Wait. What if Yursky is lying?"

"Doesn't matter. We have a lead. A very good lead." Thompson nodded in Esther's direction. "And she's right. We have to tell someone and let them sort it out."

"But what if they're just names to distract us, send us in the wrong direction?" Bryson eased his grip on Thompson's hand. "Better yet, what if they're names of his rivals—people he's trying to get rid of and he's using us to do it?"

"But what if he's right," Esther interjected.

"Yeah," Thompson agreed. "What if he's right?"

"Okay." Bryson shrugged. "Call Rios."

Thompson entered the number. Rios answered on the third ring.

CHAPTER 97
LAS VEGAS, NEVADA

WHEN RIOS' CELL PHONE RANG, he and analysts in the NEST command center were hard at work trying to determine specific targets for the suitcase bombs. In addition to potential sites in New York, Los Angeles, Miami, and Philadelphia—cities they had determined as likely targets earlier based on the concentration of Jewish population—they also searched for locations based on more subjective criteria, but the effort proved futile. Even with the list narrowed to four cities, finding an exact site was all but impossible and as they continued to work, morale in the room lagged.

As he talked to Thompson, Rios stepped to the back of the room. He fished a piece of scrap paper from the trash can and took notes. When he was finished, he switched off the phone, stepped to the operator's workstation, and handed her the paper.

"Put up whatever we have on these four men."

She skimmed over the names on the list and read them aloud. "Vitali Safronov, Nikolai Elson, Alim Solonik, and Pavel Nayfeld."

"Put it up on the screens."

The operator entered the names into the computer system. Seconds later, pictures of the men along with basic information about them appeared on four screens at the end of the room.

Rios studied the screens briefly, then spoke in a loud voice to the analysts in the room. "Listen up." He scanned the room, waiting for their attention. "Change of plans. As we learned earlier, the Russian government has confirmed that four suitcase bombs are missing from their arsenal. It now appears likely the Russian mafia provided transportation for the cases to the United States." Rios pointed to the screens. "These four men on the screen have emerged as prime suspects. We need to know everything about them—where they are right now. Names of their associates. Telephone records. Banking records. Whatever we can get. Put aside what you've been working on, at least for now, and follow the trail on these four men as far as it takes you."

The room was silent. Analysts sat at their desks as if waiting for more. When no one responded immediately, Rios clapped his hands. "Let's go, people! This is a national nuclear emergency." Rios' voice grew louder. "Do whatever it takes to find these men." Suddenly, the room came alive as the analysts went to work with renewed energy.

Ninety minutes later, Rios' team had gathered an array of information on each of the men, but most of it was several years old. He moved from desk to desk and culled through layers of data. "Can't we get anything newer than this?"

"They don't have credit cards."

"And no bank accounts," someone offered. "At least, not in their own names."

"Vehicles are registered to business entities," Weavil replied, "but other people own those companies. It'll take weeks to track them down and connect the dots."

"What about phone records?" Rios was growing more frustrated. "Don't they have cell phones? Does NSA have anything on them?"

"None of them have phones in their own names. NSA has a lot of information about calls and Internet traffic to and from Russia, but nothing we can tie to any of these specific names."

A voice spoke up. "We need to get agents on the street, asking questions."

"We don't have time for that," Rios groused. "This thing is about to—"

"Sir," Jeff Howell spoke up. "There is one interesting piece of information."

"What?"

"An FBI agent in Portland interviewed someone who claimed to have information about Nikolai Elson."

"When? Do we have the report?"

"Yes. I have the record here on my screen. Informant's name was Brad Ramsey."

Rios moved across the room and leaned over Howell's shoulder. His lips moved as he quickly scanned the report. "Jew killer." He pointed to the screen. "What does that mean?"

"It doesn't say."

"Was there a follow-up to this interview?"

"No, sir. This is all they have."

Rios scrolled down the screen. "This interview was done three days ago. Why didn't we have it earlier? Why didn't they send it to us when they did it?"

Howell scrolled back to the top of the page. "No one opened a file on it. It was just done and forgotten."

An analyst spoke up. "We should send the agent back to redo the interview."

"No." Rios hit the desktop with his fist. "This is exactly why I don't like working with the FBI."

"To be fair about it, they probably get a lot of useless calls every day," Howell suggested. "Easy to see how it was just done and set aside. Probably have a lot of other things to do."

"This wasn't a useless interview. This man had information that bears directly on our situation. A simple keyword scan of the report would have shown that." Rios ran his hands through his hair. "There is always someone who doesn't get the latest memo." He took a deep breath. "We don't have time to get the agent up to speed on what we know and then send him back out there to ask the questions we want answered. We need someone who's already involved in this to talk to him and determine what he saw." Rios' eyes opened wide. "And I know someone who can do it." He took a cell phone from his pocket and found Doyle Thompson's number.

CHAPTER 98
WASHINGTON, D.C.

BRYSON WAS SOUND ASLEEP when his cell phone rang. He rolled on his side and checked the screen for the number. The call was from Esther.

"I'm moving slow this morning," she grumbled. "Flying through all those time zones finally hit me."

Bryson rubbed his eyes and tried to get them open. "What time is it?"

"A little after nine."

"Oh." His mind raced as he struggled to remember what he had scheduled for that day. "I didn't realize it was that late. Where are you?"

"At home. I haven't been awake long, either."

Bryson sat up in bed. "Interested in Starbucks?"

"I was hoping you'd ask."

An hour later, Bryson picked up Esther from her townhouse and drove down to the Starbucks café a few blocks away. He parked at the curb and went inside. Esther waited in the SUV and watched through the window as he ordered.

A few minutes later, he came out carrying two cups of coffee. As he opened the door of the SUV, Doyle Thompson appeared on the sidewalk. He moved around Bryson and opened the back door and sat on the rear seat.

Bryson was surprised to see him. "What are you doing?"

"We need to talk," Thompson replied.

Esther took one of the cups from Bryson's hand. He set the other one in a cup holder on the console, climbed inside, and closed the door. He took a sip of coffee and glanced in the rearview mirror to look in Thompson's direction. "Are we in trouble about last night?"

"I got a call this morning from Pete Rios."

"What did he say?"

"The FBI interviewed a guy out in Portland who knew something about one of the names we got from Yursky."

"Which one?"

"Nikolai Elson."

"What did he know about him?"

"He told the agent he overheard Elson talking about something called a 'Jew killer.'"

"A Jew killer?" Esther frowned. "What was he talking about?"

"The report doesn't say. That's why they want us to go out there."

Bryson jerked his head around toward Thompson. "Us?"

"You're the one who started all this," Thompson chuckled. "You called me. Remember? Some theory about Nilus and Shiraz."

"It was just an idea," Bryson sighed. "I didn't know it would lead to all this."

"Well, I'm not going out there by myself."

Esther turned to Thompson. "When do they want you to go?"

"Now. There's a plane waiting at Reagan National Airport."

Esther opened her purse and checked inside, then looked up with a smile. "I'm packed." Bryson took a sip of coffee and glanced at her. She cut him off with a look. "You aren't going out there without me."

He glanced in the rearview mirror at Thompson. "Looks like you have a team."

"Good." Thompson gestured toward the street. "Let's go. The plane's waiting."

* * *

Four hours later, Thompson, Esther, and Bryson arrived in Portland. They rented a car at the airport and drove to Brad Ramsey's house on Charleston Avenue. Thompson knocked on the door. Bryson and Esther waited at the driveway. When Ramsey opened the door, Thompson flashed his ID.

"Mr. Ramsey, I'm from the CIA. We read a report about your interview with Donnie Brown. We'd like to ask you a few questions."

"Are you guys crazy?" Ramsey glanced around warily. "You're gonna get me killed."

"Maybe you should invite us inside."

Ramsey stepped back. Bryson and Esther followed Thompson inside. Ramsey moved to a window and looked outside. "Anybody else with you?"

"No," Thompson replied.

Bryson took a chair from the kitchen table. "You worried?"

Ramsey glanced over his shoulder. "You don't know Nikolai Elson."

"Has he threatened you?"

"He ain't got to threaten nobody to get things done."

Thompson took out a chair and sat beside Bryson at the table. "You told the FBI you saw an aluminum case in the trunk of a car."

Esther wandered around the room, checking the messages taped to the refrigerator door and the contents of the shelves beside it. Ramsey made one more check from the window, then turned to face the table. "If you read the report, you know all I know about it."

"What did it look like?"

"Like I told the FBI, it was an aluminum case. One of those cases like bands use to carry their stuff in. Only, this one was like a big suitcase. It pretty much filled up the trunk of the car."

"And you think it was going to Los Angeles?"

"That's what Elson said. He said it had to be in L.A. by Friday. Everything was set for Saturday."

"Did you hear anything else?"

"He said, 'You must get it in place before Friday night.' And something about everyone coming to temple."

Esther jerked her head around. "He said that?"

"Yes."

"He said they wanted it in place before everyone came to temple on Friday?"

"Something like that."

She looked at Thompson. "We don't have much time. They're going to detonate this bomb at a synagogue. They want it there by Friday so no one will notice it." She looked over at Ramsey. "This Friday?"

"I guess. I don't know. What happens on Saturday?"

"Most temples have services all morning. They're going to—"

Ramsey interrupted. "What are you talking about?" His eyes were wide. "This is about a bomb?"

Thompson ignored the question. "Can you think of anything else?"

"Not really."

"What did the car look like?"

"Silver Honda Accord."

"What year?"

"I don't know." Ramsey was visibly nervous. "The case I saw was a bomb?"

"We can't say."

"Are there more?" Ramsey's forehead wrinkled.

Thompson stood. "We've taken enough of your time."

"You can't just leave me like this," Ramsey protested.

Thompson started toward the door. "We appreciate your time, Mr. Ramsey." He gestured to the others to follow. "We better get going."

They walked in silence from the house to the car. When they were seated, Esther leaned over the seat. "You were in a hurry to get out of there."

"He works for Elson. He told us what we need to know. Whatever we say in front of him just gives him one more thing he has to lie about. The less he knows the better."

Bryson started the car. "Saturday morning at a synagogue in Los Angeles." He glanced back at Esther. "Any idea which synagogue they'd use?"

"I don't know." Esther turned away and looked out the window. "It could be any one of hundreds."

"Well, time is running out. If Ramsey is right, this thing will go down this Saturday." Thompson turned to face Esther. "If you were a terrorist and you wanted to blow up the most significant Jewish location in L.A., what would it be?"

Tears ran down Esther's cheeks. "Wilshire Boulevard Temple," she said quietly. "It's the largest one in the city."

Thompson took the cell phone from his pocket and called Rios.

CHAPTER 99
LAS VEGAS, NEVADA

RIOS WAS STANDING NEAR the back of the command center when Thompson called. Finally, after days of inference and supposition, moments of getting close then feeling it slip away, he finally had something concrete, the information he needed. Something they could respond to with specific action.

"Get me the FBI office in Los Angeles. I need the special agent in charge." He started toward the center of the room. "Did we get those mobile detection units deployed?"

"Yes, sir," someone replied. "Most of them."

Rios pointed toward a screen. "Put up a map of Los Angeles. And show me the Wilshire Boulevard Temple."

The operator at the center of the room pressed a button on her keyboard. "Here it is."

"Any security cameras in the area?"

"We're checking on that now."

"Get me what you can find and put it on a screen."

"There's a traffic camera at every intersection on Wilshire."

"Great! Tap into them and put the images on the wall." He waited while live feeds from the cameras appeared on a split screen. "We're looking for a gray Honda Accord."

Aycock spoke up. "What year?"

"Don't know. Keep your eyes open. Look for anything out of the ordinary. Anything suspicious or out of place." Rios turned back to the operator at the center of the room. "We need to find the largest synagogues in each of the other cities—New York, Philadelphia, and Miami. Find them and get them on a map. We can narrow this down to potential targets."

"We're just guessing," someone complained. "What if we guess wrong?"

"This isn't a guess," Howell countered. "We're using the best information we have to reach a workable conclusion."

"We need more time."

"We don't have time," Howell replied. "This thing will be over by Saturday morning."

"Sir," the operator called. "I have the FBI in L.A. on the line."

Rios grabbed a phone. "This is Rios at NEST in Las Vegas. Who am I talking to?"

"Sarah Brenner. I'm the special agent in charge."

"We have a verifiable nuclear threat in Los Angeles. We need your assistance."

There was a long pause before Brenner responded. "Who are you?"

Rios barked into the phone, "I am Pete Rios. Check your organizational chart."

"But how do I know it's you?"

"Is this your first day on the job? We have to move now. Time is running out."

"What are you talking about?"

"I'm talking about a nuclear bomb at Wilshire Boulevard Temple."

"Is this a drill?"

"Okay." Rios lowered his voice. "I'll make it easy for you. I'm sending someone out there...Jason Hanks. He's coming from the office in San Diego to coordinate this."

"By what authority?"

"This is NEST, Ms. Brenner. We have all the authority we need. I'll have Tyler Davis fax you an order signed by the president."

Rios ended the call and turned to the operator. "Get me the FBI director in D.C. We need to take our four suspects into custody and we need to do it in a way that doesn't send everyone into hiding."

CHAPTER 100
WASHINGTON, D.C.

WHILE RIOS WORKED to locate and intercept the Honda Accord in Los Angeles, Thompson, Esther, and Bryson left Portland and flew east on the return trip to Washington. When they landed, Thompson had a message waiting on his cell phone. He checked the screen, saw it was from Rios, and returned the call. He caught up with the others at Bryson's SUV.

"Esther, they want to know about sites in New York, Philadelphia, and Miami."

Suddenly Esther felt tense and irritable. She knew what Rios needed—hard, definable targets, against which he could take action with a high probability of success. This was no game. They faced an attack with real bombs and the potential for devastating consequences. Finding probable locations in New York and Miami was not a difficult task. Rios could have figured that much out on his own, but Esther knew from her conversation with Cohen that Jiroft was already on the Mexican-American border, most likely to take delivery of one of the bombs. Rios might not figure that part out. She could point him in that direction—Cohen wanted her to talk to Rios—but she had been given strict instructions not to tell Thompson anything.

Thompson grew impatient. "Rios wants to know."

Esther tried to put him off. "Why does everyone ask me these questions?"

"Because you know the best places."

"He has all the resources of the American government at his disposal, and he calls me?"

"Maybe he likes you," Bryson grinned. He opened the door on the driver's side and got in behind the steering wheel. Esther slid onto the front passenger seat.

Thompson climbed in back and leaned forward to talk. "Look, we still have to track down the other three cases. We need to locate them before Saturday morning. If this is a coordinated attack, they'll all go off on Saturday morning." Esther did not respond. Thompson prodded her again. "Come on, Esther. If you had to pick one place in each of those cities, what would it be?" Still she didn't respond.

"Esther, they need an answer. Time's ticking by. Give me one place in New York."

"Okay," she snapped. "The Jewish Center at Brighton Beach."

"And in Miami?"

"Temple Beth Shalom."

"What about Philadelphia?"

"I don't know." She waved her hands in frustration. "I don't know Philadelphia."

Thompson persisted. "If someone asked about the most notable Jewish site in Philadelphia, what would someone from Philadelphia say?"

"They would say you're crazy."

"What site, Esther?"

"Har Zion Temple, but it makes no sense."

"Why not?"

"The current location is in the suburbs. Penn Valley. People are scattered all over. A bomb there would have little impact. And the original Har Zion building is now a Christian church."

"Where else would you put it?"

"Why do you keep asking me these questions?" She banged on the console with her fist. "I am Jewish, but that doesn't mean I know every Jew in the country."

Thompson wouldn't quit. "Where else would you put it?"

"Why not right here in Washington?"

"No," Thompson insisted. "In Philadelphia."

"No one thinks of Philadelphia as a Jewish town. If I was making a statement about Jews or anything else, I'd put the bomb in Washington, D.C."

"But we aren't dealing with that. We're talking about Philadelphia. Where would you put it in Philadelphia?"

Esther turned to face him. "You ask me these questions as if all Jews somehow know each other. As if we're all just one big happy family."

"There is a common experience."

"But there are as many versions of Judaism as there are of Christianity."

Still Thompson would not stop. "So, if you were a terrorist and you wanted to make a statement against Jews, where would you make that statement?"

"I'd make it in Jerusalem."

"That might be so, but the bombs are in America." Thompson took out his cell phone and called Rios to give him the sites.

* * *

Bryson brought the SUV to a stop at the curb near Starbucks and let Thompson out. His car was parked nearby. When he was gone, Bryson reached across the front seat and took Esther's hand. "Are you okay? You were pretty upset back there."

"It just makes no sense. All this guessing at sites and asking me questions about Jews like I speak for all Jewish people."

"So, if you were the terrorist and you wanted to make a statement here, where would you put it?"

"It doesn't matter now. He already made his call."

"It matters to you."

Esther sighed. "Either of two locations," she said finally. "Adas Israel Congregation, or the Temple at Sixth and I."

"Okay." Bryson pulled her hand closer and tucked her arm beneath his. "Those are ours."

She frowned at him. "What are you talking about?"

"Those are our locations. Rios, the FBI, the police—they can cover the others. We'll cover those two."

"We can't cover them both."

"Okay. We'll cover one of them."

"I can't choose," Esther said, shaking her head. "This is ridiculous."

"Then I'll choose," Bryson replied. "And I say it's the temple at Sixth and I streets."

"Why?"

"It's closest to the center of the city. A suitcase bomb exploding there would bring the government to a halt." He leaned forward and kissed the back of her hand.

"I don't know," she groaned. "I'm really tired."

"No problem. I'll drop you off at home and go check it out."

Esther leaned her head against his shoulder. "You are an amazing man, Paul Bryson."

"Think you'll remember that when we're old and gray?"

"I feel old and gray right now." She closed her eyes. He felt her body relax against him.

CHAPTER 101
TEL AVIV, ISRAEL

AFTER A MEDICAL EXAMINATION and thorough debriefing, Anthony Wiseman was taken to a safe house in Ramat HaSharon, a neighborhood north of the Old City and east of the airport. The house sat atop a hill with a view of the surrounding streets. A wall six feet high ringed the property. A gated driveway led to an attached garage in back.

Wiseman arrived there in a specially armored SUV that had tinted bulletproof windows, reinforced door panels, and blast-resistant floor-boards. As they approached the driveway, the gate swung open, allowing them to enter without stopping to wait. The gate closed behind them as they continued past the house. In back, they made a turn into the garage and came to a stop inside. They waited there while the garage door closed, then stepped out.

Guards were posted at the driveway gate and along the wall at each corner. Two agents remained inside the house and two more patrolled the grounds. Wiseman took a shower, ate supper, and relaxed for the evening.

The following morning, he rose early and walked to the kitchen. He found a kettle on the stove and put on water for tea. An agent was seated at a table near a window that overlooked the backyard. Through it Wiseman saw a small courtyard behind the garage. A table and two chairs sat in the shade of an orange tree.

Wiseman gestured out the window. "May I take my tea out there?"

The agent turned to look, then glanced back at Wiseman. "I suppose so."

When the water was hot, Wiseman made a cup of tea. He found pita bread in a cupboard and hummus in the refrigerator. He put it on a plate and grabbed a knife from the drawer. With the cup in one hand and the plate in the other, he walked from the house to the courtyard and took a seat at the table.

The morning was clear, bright, and cool. The shade was pleasant and the scent of citrus lingered among the trees. Two flowerpots sat to his right. The flowers in them had tiny pink and white blooms that gave a sweet fragrance.

Wiseman took a sip of tea and looked around the grounds. It was a nice location, for now, but already it had the feel of a prison. Perhaps Oren Cohen would find a job for him. Something he could do to make a contribution. *I can't just spend the rest of my life sitting here in the shade,* he thought to himself.

He pinched off a piece of bread and smeared it with hummus, then popped it into his mouth. While he chewed that first bite, a ray of sunshine fell across his face. The glare caught him in the eye. He hunched forward enough to lift his weight from the chair and scooted it to the left.

Just then, a bullet zipped past his right ear—so close he heard the sound as the projectile moved by. It struck a flowerpot, sending dirt and shards of clay into the air.

Before Wiseman could react, a second shot struck the table just inches from his hand. Fragments of the bullet grazed his wrist and peppered his cheek. Blood trickled from his jaw.

The back door of the house flew open and the agent who'd been seated in the kitchen charged forward. "Get down! Get down!" He was only ten feet from the house when a bullet struck him in the forehead.

For an instant, his head seemed to stop in midair, suspended above his body while his feet and legs continued forward. Then his head exploded in a halo of blood and flesh and his body fell backwards to the ground.

Wiseman dove to the left. As his knees hit the ground, a third bullet struck the chair where he'd been sitting. He crawled to the corner along the back wall of the garage and pressed himself flat against it. Behind him, agents moved across the grounds in a frantic search to locate the shooter.

CHAPTER 102
PORTLAND, OREGON

A LITTLE BEFORE EIGHT the next morning, Brad Ramsey steered the Torino into the parking lot behind the Barely Here club. He had arrived early to check the previous night's receipts. As he came into the parking lot, he saw a black Mercedes sitting a few spaces from the building. "Great," he sighed. "Nikolai is here already. This can't be good." Muscles on the back of Ramsey's neck and shoulders grew tight.

He parked in the far corner of the lot and made his way to the back door. As he stepped inside and started down the hall, he heard Elson's voice. The office door was closed but Elson was shouting in Russian.

Lights were off in the rest of the club. A neon beer sign over the bar provided the only light. Ramsey found the switch near the end of the hall and turned on the lights. Behind him, Elson's voice still drifted through the office door.

In a moment, the door flew open. Ramsey looked up from behind the bar to see Elson glaring in his direction. "Did you talk to somebody?" His voice was loud and angry. He pointed an accusing finger in Ramsey's direction. "I want to know. Did you talk to somebody about me?"

Ramsey's heart skipped a beat. There was a sinking feeling in the pit of his stomach. Someone saw him talking to the FBI. Even worse, someone saw those people who came to his house. He did his best to control his emotions.

"No." Ramsey shook his head. "I haven't talked to nobody. What are you upset about?"

"That girl." Elson came toward the bar. "They found that girl's body."

"What girl?"

"The one you told me about."

"Anna?"

"Yeah." Elson took a seat at the bar. "Skinny little…Ripped me off and now she's still causing trouble."

Ramsey felt his body relax. His heart rate returned to normal. "I haven't seen her in…three or four days," he shrugged. "Who's asking about her?"

Elson lowered his voice and seemed to relax. "They found her body in the landfill. Now they are asking questions." He gestured toward the bottles that lined the shelves. "Give me a drink."

Ramsey took down a bottle of vodka, filled a glass, and set it on the bar. Elson snatched the glass with one hand and gulped the contents in a single swallow. He slammed the empty glass on the bar. "Give me another." Ramsey filled the glass once more and set the bottle beside it.

Elson looked up at him. "Anybody around here asking about her?"

"No." Ramsey shook his head.

Elson let his eyes bore in. "You sure about that?"

"Yes. I'm sure."

"If I ask around, I ain't gonna hear your name?"

"No."

Elson smiled. "You're a good man, Brad." He took a sip from the glass. "That girl was bad from the beginning. I wondered what you would do when you found out."

"Not much choice. She was stealing. She had to go."

"Yeah," Elson chuckled. "She had to go." He took another sip. "I hear she offered you sex not to tell me what she was doing."

"Well," Ramsey said sheepishly. "Some people are desperate."

"Ahh." The smile on Elson's face spread into a grin. "I can tell," he laughed. "You took the sex and told me about her."

"I didn't say that."

"You didn't have to," Elson roared. "I can see it on your face." He reached across the bar and nudged Ramsey's shoulder. "I knew you were a good man the first time I saw you."

Suddenly the front door burst open. A SWAT unit poured from the street and filled the room. At the same time, the back door flew open and police officers hurried down the hall toward them. Behind them came Donnie Brown and an FBI team.

Officers grabbed Elson, pinned him against the bar, and cuffed his hands behind his back. Others came behind the bar and shoved Ramsey against the counter. His head banged against the countertop.

Brown stood at Elson's back. "Mr. Elson, you are under arrest for the death of Anna Milkova and on charges of interstate trafficking in women. You have the right to remain silent. If you give up that right whatever you say will be used against you in a court of law. You have a right to an attorney. If you can't afford one, the court will appoint one for you and make him available at the time of questioning. Do you understand?"

Ramsey glanced in Elson's direction. Elson looked at him and winked. Brown grabbed Elson by the handcuffs and pulled him away from the bar. "Do you understand?"

"I have nothing to say to you. I demand to speak to my attorney."

Brown gestured to a waiting officer. The officer led Elson out the front door. Brown turned in Ramsey's direction. "Mr. Ramsey, the same goes for you. Do you understand your rights as I've explained them?"

"I ain't got nothing to say, either. I want a lawyer."

"Fine," Brown barked. "Take them both downtown. We'll deal with them there."

CHAPTER 103
THE RIGOLETS, NEAR NEW ORLEANS

KEITH DARNELL SAT with Mike Presley at a table in the Rigolets Marina store. The table was wedged between a live bait tank and a rack of fishing tackle. Dip nets and fishing rods were suspended from the ceiling. Fishermen moved in and out, laughing, talking, and arguing over prices.

In his hand, Darnell held a Styrofoam cup filled with steaming hot coffee, which he sipped lightly as he stared blankly into space.

Presley looked across the table at him. "How do you drink that stuff?"

"What?"

"Coffee with chicory."

"Ancient drink. People been drinking chicory for a long time."

"Cajun drink."

"Been around a long time before the Cajuns got here."

"I can't drink that stuff," Presley scowled. "Always tastes bitter to me."

Darnell smiled. "Are you a mocha frappuccino macchiato type?"

"Not hardly." Presley lifted a bottle of Dr. Pepper from the table and gestured with it in a mock toast. "I'll stick with The Doctor."

"Too early for that."

Presley pointed to Darnell's cup. "Never a good time for that."

Darnell changed the subject. "You know why we're taking this guy down?"

"Washington said to get him," Presley shrugged. "That's all I need to know."

"You ever have any trouble out of him?"

"No. But that doesn't mean much. Not that many Russians live around here."

Darnell took a cell phone from his pocket and checked the screen. A message appeared that read simply, "Now." He took one last sip of coffee and stood. "Time to go."

From the marina, they drove up the highway and over the bridge at Rigolets Pass. Half a mile beyond it, they turned left onto a road paved with crushed oyster shells. A hundred yards off the pavement they came to a house elevated above the marsh on wooden pilings. Police cars were parked there and officers stood nearby. Darnell parked his car in the road. He and Presley got out.

An officer approached. Darnell flashed his badge. "Is he inside?"

"Yeah."

"Anybody with him?"

"Two women and a couple of young guys."

"Any minors?"

"Not that we can tell."

Presley came from the opposite side of the car. "Did you talk to him?"

"No." The officer shook his head. "Just told him to sit tight."

"Okay." Darnell started toward the steps. "We'll bring him out."

The officer called after him, "You want me to send some guys with you?"

"No, we'll be okay."

They made their way up the steps and knocked on the door. A woman answered. Darnell showed her his badge. "I think Mr. Solonik is expecting us." The woman backed away from the door. Darnell and Presley stepped inside.

The house was small and compact. A kitchen was located to the right of the door. To the left was a dining table. Beyond it was a living room with large sliding glass doors that opened onto a deck. The doors gave a view of the savannah marsh and the Gulf of Mexico that lay beyond. Alim Solonik was seated on a sofa, facing the view, his back to the kitchen.

Darnell approached from the left. Presley moved to the right. They came from behind the sofa and made their way in front. "Mr. Solonik, I am Keith Darnell." He gestured with a nod. "This is Mike Presley. We're with the FBI."

Solonik looked up. "Am I under arrest?" His voice had a thick Russian accent.

"Yes, sir," Darnell answered. "You are under arrest."

"What is the charge?"

"You are being held as a person of interest in an ongoing investigation involving matters of national interest." Darnell gestured with a wave of his hand. "Please stand."

Solonik rose from the sofa. Presley cuffed his hands behind his back.

"You have the right to remain silent. If you speak, anything you say may be used against you in a court of law."

Solonik stared out the window. "I have nothing to say to anyone."

"You have the right to an attorney. If you cannot afford one, the court will appoint one for you."

"I want my lawyer." Solonik spoke in a flat, monotone voice. "I do not consent to your presence on my property. This is private property."

"You have the right to have your attorney present during questioning."

"I claim all my rights given to me by the great American Constitution." Presley took him by the wrist and nudged him toward the door. Solonik continued to talk. "I love this country. I want to be an American citizen." They paused at the door while Presley opened it.

As they came down the steps, Solonik renewed his soliloquy. "I have nothing further to say to any of you. I want my lawyer present." At the bottom of the steps he turned to one of the policemen. "Someone call my lawyer."

An officer stepped forward and guided him into a police car. "I ask for asylum. I am being persecuted for my political beliefs." Solonik ducked through the rear door of the car and dropped onto the seat. "I demand strict proof of all charges against me." The officer pushed the door closed and slapped the top of the car. The car started forward. At the end of the road it turned onto the pavement and disappeared down the highway.

CHAPTER 104
WASHINGTON, D.C.

WITH BRYSON OCCUPIED at the synagogue, Esther spent the evening in bed. The next morning, she slept later than normal. It was almost ten when she padded from the bedroom to the kitchen. She made a cup of hot tea and sat on the sofa, alternately sipping it and staring blankly into space. As the tea brought her more awake, she imagined Bryson sitting in the SUV outside the synagogue, waiting for something to happen. He had no idea what he was looking for, but he was there just the same, watching the street for anything that seemed suspicious. On a typical day she would have thought it a gallant gesture of love and devotion, but that morning it seemed a waste of time. "Like looking for a needle in a haystack," she said to herself.

Waves of sadness swept over her and the more she thought, the deeper the sadness grew. With it came the weight of all they'd seen and heard and done. It settled on her shoulders as if to push her through the sofa and bury her beneath the townhouse. Everything they'd done seemed hopelessly futile—jetting to Israel, flying from one end of the country to the other. For what? Three people working on a hunch could not possibly stop such a vast conspiracy bent on wiping them from the earth. And it was certain the perpetrators would find a way to blame the Jews.

She sipped from the cup of tea and let her eyes wander around the room. Before all of this, life had seemed like an adventure, rich and full while she was living it, but now, facing the possibility of death and destruction, everything looked small and insignificant. Ephraim, her years at the Institute, and all she'd accomplished as an attorney. It seemed like nothing. Tears filled her eyes as she stared blankly ahead.

And then her gaze fell on the bookcase near the doorway. On the third shelf from the top there was a ram's horn, burnished by age to a dark brown luster. But this was no mere horn of a ram. This was a sacred shofar, blown in ancient times at Solomon's Temple in Jerusalem, and now at synagogues across the world to mark the beginning of holidays. She'd heard one blown on many occasions and each time the sound of it had filled her with wonder and energized the mystery of the faith she held so dear. As if God himself inhabited the sound of the horn.

The shofar on Esther's shelf was a relic from Hurva Synagogue in Jerusalem. It had been rescued by Moshe Russnak during Israel's fight for independence. Russnak's grandson gave it to Ephraim, and Ephraim gave it to Esther on the day she graduated from law school. *"Today, you have become the Tokea,"* he had said proudly. *"The one who blows the shofar."*

Esther smiled at the memory of that day. She had tried to refuse the gift; women were not qualified under rabbinic law to blow the shofar, but Ephraim had insisted. *"When those who are qualified do not blow it, others must take their place. You will take that place."*

The horn had been on a shelf ever since, first in their tiny apartment and then at each location where they'd moved after that. Once or twice Ephraim had suggested she blow it—when the Israeli Air Force destroyed the Osirak reactor in Iraq and when Israeli troops occupied Beirut during the Lebanon War—but each time she refused. Now she was curious and wondered what sound it made—no two horns sounded the same. The longer she stared at it the more curious she became. Finally, when she could stand it no more, she rose from her seat on the sofa, crossed the room, and took the horn down from the shelf.

A little more than two feet long, it was wide at one end with an opening like the bell of a trumpet. The other end tapered down to no more than an inch in diameter. A hole ran the length of it and carried the sound from the small end along the length of the horn and out the larger end.

Esther's hands trembled as she propped the large end on her left hand and brought the small end to her mouth. Then she took a breath and blew.

A deep, mellow sound came from the horn and sent a shiver down her back. She took another breath and blew once more, letting the sound build louder and louder as she pushed air through the horn. Once again, the sound of it sent chills through her. She blew it a third time and imagined the army of ancient Israel crossing the Jordan River into the Promised Land, the sound of the shofar rising above the din of marching troops, the wonder in their eyes as the walls of Jericho tumbled to the ground.

"I am the Tokea," she whispered. "The one who blows the shofar."

As the words slipped from her lips, the cloud of despair that had settled over her that morning began to lift. She had been a woman of action all her adult life. When she faced a situation, no matter how grave or hopeless, she had faced it by doing something. This was no time for sitting on the sofa and sipping tea. If she wasn't going to join Bryson in his watch at the synagogue, she at least could put the time to good use. She gently returned the shofar to its place on the shelf, picked up her purse, and headed out the door.

From the townhouse in Georgetown, she drove downtown to the office. A stack of files and correspondence waited on her desk and she attacked it with a vengeance. The office might not resemble the battlefields of Jericho, but it was the place from which she worked. If there was more to be done, she was confident she would find it from there.

Just then her cell phone received a new text message. She glanced at the screen and saw it was from Reuben Brody. She pressed a button. The message appeared. "Come to the Mall."

Esther rose from her desk and walked up the hall to the reception-ist. "I'll be back in a minute." She continued to the elevator and rode downstairs to the lobby.

She left the building and walked down to Constitution Avenue. On the opposite side of the street, she stepped onto the lawn of the National Mall. As she strolled through the grass, Brody moved to her side.

"You're looking tired today."

"Thanks for noticing. I've been a little busy lately."

He pointed toward a bench. "Let's sit over here."

They took a seat with their backs to the street, facing the Mall and the Smithsonian complex on the far side. Brody rested his arm along the back of the seat. "We have news from Wiseman."

"How is he?"

"Someone attempted to kill him."

"No! What happened? Is he all right?"

"Relax," Brody soothed. "He's doing well."

"Was he injured?"

"Bullet fragments grazed his cheek and hand. The wounds are not serious."

"Where was he when it happened?"

"Sitting outside a safe house in Tel Aviv."

"Who did it?"

Brody cut his eyes at her. "Who do you think?"

"How did they locate him? Someone on the inside told them where to look? One of our people?"

"No," Brody shook his head.

"Then how did they find him?"

"The doctor who treated him found a small chip in his shoulder."

"A chip?" Esther looked puzzled. "What kind of chip?"

"An RFID chip. Emits a radio signal. Allowed someone to track his location."

Esther arched an eyebrow. "That sounds sophisticated."

"It is. And that's what worries Cohen. The signal can be followed by airborne tracking systems. The U.S. does this with their JSTARS system. All their troops have a similar device implanted in them. An observer viewing the battlefield on a computer screen can see immediately where all their troops are located."

"What are you saying?"

"We didn't implant a chip in Wiseman."

"You think someone at Fort Meade did this?"

"That is the only place where it could have happened."

"And you think someone was tracking him?"

Brody shrugged. "Other countries have the capability."

"So why have you come to me?"

"We want you to get access to Wiseman's medical records at Fort Meade."

"I hate that place now," Esther scowled. "Why me?"

"Because you are Wiseman's lawyer. You can examine the records without attracting too much suspicion. We want to see who was behind this before we raise the issue directly."

Esther sighed and shook her head. "This case will never go away."

Brody stood. "It's important, Esther. You're in a critical position. We need the information. Look at the records and tell me what you find."

CHAPTER 105
PHOENIX, ARIZONA

TOMMY PORTER TURNED the steering wheel to the left and pressed down the gas pedal. The engine whined as the car twisted and turned up Camelback Mountain. At the top, he turned right onto San Miguel Avenue and found the street clogged with police cars and emergency vehicles. He lifted his foot from the accelerator and slowed the car, weaving his way past a line of police cars, an ambulance, and a fire truck. A little farther down the street he brought the car to a stop beyond the third driveway. An officer met him as he stepped from the car.

"Sir, I'll have to ask you to leave. This is a restricted area."

Porter reached inside his jacket and took out a badge. "Tommy Porter." He held up the badge. "FBI."

"Oh." The officer backed away. "Sorry, sir. We've had a lot of sightseers."

"Who's in charge?"

"Detective Bowles. He's up at the house."

Porter walked up the driveway to the house and made his way over to the garage. The door on the right was up. Two bodies lay inside on the concrete floor, both covered with a white sheet. Flies buzzed through the air. Porter waved them away with his hand and stepped closer.

A man dressed in a brown suit came from the garage. "Can I help you?"

"Are you Detective Bowles?"

"Yes. And you are?"

"Tommy Porter. FBI."

"Right. We spoke on the phone."

Porter gestured toward the bodies. "Both of them took gunshots?"

"Yeah. Nayfeld took two to the head. The other guy took one in the gut and one in the head."

"Find a weapon?"

"No."

"How'd you find the bodies?"

"Neighbor's dog got loose. They followed it up here. Doors were down. The dog was scratching and barking. They couldn't get him to leave. Then they smelled the odor. Called us."

"You sure it's Nayfeld?"

"You want to see for yourself?"

"Not really. But I have to verify the identity of these bodies."

Bowles reached down to the body nearest the door and lifted the sheet. Porter looked at the head, then quickly glanced away. "Okay," he said. "That's him."

Bowles dropped the sheet back in place. "They're kind of a mess right now. Been dead several days."

"Anybody from the coroner's office been out?"

"Not yet. We're waiting on them right now."

"Anything in the house?"

"Not really. But there is a footprint." Bowles stepped back inside the garage and pointed to the floor. Porter moved closer for a look. Bowles knelt beside the print. "Think your lab can get a match on the tread pattern?"

Porter took a cell phone from his pocket. "I'll get somebody out here to help."

CHAPTER 106
FORT MEADE, MARYLAND

FROM THE BENCH on the National Mall, Esther walked to her car on the parking deck. News of the attempt on Wiseman's life made her angry. The thought that someone in the United States government might be involved made her furious. She was determined to find out what happened.

An hour later, she arrived at Fort Meade. Though her name was not on the visitors list she cajoled her way past the guard and was admitted to the base. From the main gate, she drove to the building on Cooper Road, parked in a space near the sidewalk, and went inside. A guard met her in the lobby.

"I need to see Roy Dawson." Her voice was stern but not combative.

"I'm sorry, but Mr. Dawson is not available. Perhaps you would like to make an appointment?"

"No. I don't want an appointment. I want to see Mr. Dawson." She took a business card from her pocket and handed it to him. "Give him this. I'm sure he'll see me."

The guard glanced at the card, then turned away and disappeared down the hall. A few minutes later, he returned with Roy Dawson.

"Ms. Rosenberg, I understand you wanted to see me."

"We need to talk. Which way is your office?"

"I'm afraid I—"

"I'm afraid you'll have to interrupt your schedule."

"Ms. Rosenberg, I find this—"

"Someone took a shot at Anthony Wiseman. An agent protecting him was killed. We need to talk."

"What does that have to do with me?"

"I'll tell you about it in your office."

Dawson waved off the guard, then turned back to Esther. "Perhaps I could make some time." He gestured toward the hallway. "Right this way." He led her down the hall to his office and ushered her inside, then closed the door. They stood in the center of the room.

"I'm sorry for Mr. Wiseman's trouble, but I fail to see what that has to do with me or this facility."

"I'd like to see his records."

Dawson was taken aback. "His records? All of them?"

"Yes."

"That would be impossible. Not even a court order can get them. You know that. What's the problem?"

"Mr. Wiseman was wounded. He required treatment at a hospital. The doctor treating him found an RFID chip implanted in his shoulder." She jabbed the air with her finger for emphasis. "One of your RFID chips."

"Ridiculous." Dawson folded his arms across his chest. "We don't implant detainees."

"Someone did."

"Not here."

"Then show me his medical file. Surely you have a medical file."

"I'd show it to you if he had one, but he doesn't have a medical file," Dawson explained. "Other than the examination when he arrived, he received no medical treatment here."

"He was treated by a dentist."

Dawson had a puzzled frown. "Really?"

"I want to see the file."

"If there is a record of dental care, it would be at the office where the treatment occurred."

"Find it." Esther took a seat. "I'll wait."

"I don't have time ..." Dawson put his hands on his hips. "You come here without an appointment, asking for—"

"Mr. Dawson, I have the rest of the day to wait. I want to see the file."

Dawson jerked open the door and disappeared up the hall. Twenty minutes later he returned carrying a manila file folder. "This is all they have."

"They still use hard files?"

"They do in that office. Everyone else has converted to electronic files."

"Let's have a look. What does it say?"

Dawson took a seat beside her and opened the file. Esther looked over his shoulder at the first page. Dawson glanced in her direction. "See anything suspicious on that page?"

"No," Esther shook her head.

He turned the page. They read it together. After a moment, he looked over at her. "Anything there?"

"No."

When they'd looked through all the pages in the file, Dawson closed it and laid it on his lap. "As I said, Ms. Rosenberg, we accorded Mr. Wiseman the same respect we would have given any other American citizen."

"Except that you wouldn't charge him with anything."

"That was not our call. We house them and care for them. We don't investigate and prosecute." He stood. "Now, is there anything else?"

"Who was the dentist?"

Dawson opened the file and glanced inside. "Dan Miller."

"I'd like to see him, please."

"Ms. Rosenberg, this is a military base. We have rules and procedures. You can't just—"

Esther stood and faced him. "What are you hiding?"

"Nothing."

"Then let me talk to him."

Dawson sighed. "Oh, all right. Come this way."

They walked down the hall to the elevator and rode to the basement. When the elevator doors opened they made their way to the transportation corridor. A tram picked them up and whisked them to a stop marked by the number 5. Esther followed Dawson from the tram through a doorway to another elevator. From there, they rode up four floors and emerged on a hallway in a medical ward. Dawson showed his ID badge to the receptionist.

"We'd like to see Dr. Miller."

"He's in back."

Dawson led the way through a dental ward to an office in the far corner of the building. Miller was seated at his desk. He looked up when they entered.

"Roy, back so soon?"

Dawson gestured over his shoulder. "This is Ms. Rosenberg. She represents Anthony Wiseman."

Miller looked in her direction. "Something wrong with Mr. Wiseman?"

"You saw him for a problem with a tooth."

"Extracted it, as I recall."

"Anything else?"

"I don't think so."

"He was treated at a hospital in Israel yesterday. They found a chip implanted in his shoulder."

"A chip?"

"RFID," Dawson added.

Miller frowned. "You think I did that?"

"I think it happened while he was detained here." Esther looked him in the eye. You're the only one who's treated him."

"I didn't implant him with a chip. I don't know how to do that."

"Did you sedate him when you extracted the tooth?"

"Yes. I believe we did." He gestured to Dawson for the file. "Let's have a look." Dawson handed him the file. He opened it on the desktop and leafed through the pages. "Right here," he said, pointing. "We sedated him."

"Who else was in the room?"

"No one." Miller's eyes darted away. "Just my assistant."

"Are you sure?"

"Two guards brought him up."

"Who else?"

"There was a guy with him." Miller sighed. "I don't know him and I've never seen him before. Said his name was Saylor or Naylor or something like that. I don't remember."

Esther had a knowing look. "Was it Taylor? Steve Taylor?"

Miller's face brightened. "Yeah. That's it."

"And you allowed him in the room while you were treating Wiseman?"

Miller shrugged. "The guards seemed to know him. We have people in and out of here all the time. I assumed he was supposed to be there."

Esther shook her head in disgust. "I can't believe what you people do." She turned away and started back toward the elevator.

Back at the building on Cooper Road, Esther and Dawson parted company in the lobby. A guard opened the door for her as she stepped outside. The cool, crisp air was a welcome relief. She took a deep breath and let it fill her lungs as she walked toward the car.

In the car, she retraced her path back to the main gate and out to the freeway. When she was well south of the base, she picked up the phone and called Brody to tell him what she'd learned.

CHAPTER 107
LOS ANGELES, CALIFORNIA

WILSHIRE BOULEVARD TEMPLE occupied a city block between Hobart and Harvard boulevards. The facility included four buildings and two parking lots, one alongside the temple facing Wilshire and a second in back facing Sixth Street. The entrance to the lot in back was patrolled by a guard. The one on Wilshire was unmanned.

Posing as parking attendants, police took over the lot on Sixth Street. Others were stationed atop a sports bar at the corner of Harvard Boulevard and at a used car lot on Hobart. Then, under the guise of servicing the temple's security system, FBI agents obtained access to eight cameras located around the property. A live feed from those cameras appeared on screens in an incident command post located on the third floor of a bank building across the street from the temple. Jason Hanks, the FBI's incident commander, monitored events from that post.

On Friday morning, a gray Honda Accord came down Wilshire Boulevard. A patrolman spotted the car as it passed through the intersection at Wilton Place. An analyst monitoring the same view from the NEST command center saw it, too, and relayed the information to Hanks. He picked up a radio and keyed the microphone to alert agents on the ground. "We got another one coming. Keep your eyes open. Gray Honda Accord."

"That's the fifth one we've seen today," someone replied.

"Popular color."

"Good car."

"Cut the chatter," Hanks intervened. "This one's still coming."

At Western Avenue, a traffic camera mounted near the streetlight caught a picture of the car as it moved through the intersection. A camera pointed in the opposite direction followed it as the car continued traveling east. It slowed as it passed in front of the temple, then moved to the turn lane.

"This might be him," Hanks radioed. "He's making a left onto Harvard."

As he watched on the monitor, the car turned onto Harvard, then made a left into the parking lot beside the temple. It came to a stop in a space near the center of the lot. A moment later, the driver's door opened and a young man stepped out wearing blue jeans, a hooded sweatshirt, and baseball cap. He pushed the door closed behind him and checked to make certain it was locked, then walked out to Harvard Boulevard and up to the corner. A red car was waiting for him there. He got in on the passenger side and the car moved away.

A voice came from the radio. "You want us to follow the red car?"

"Follow it," Hanks replied. "But do not apprehend them. And don't let them see you."

"Roger."

"Where are you now?"

"Sixth Street. Continuing west."

"Keep me posted on your location."

"Roger."

When the red car was gone, Hanks picked up his cell phone and called Sarah Brenner. She answered immediately. "Something happening?"

"Are you ready?"

"Waiting on you."

"Okay. The car's in the lot. Get the case."

Five minutes later, two yellow school buses came to a stop at the curb on the Wilshire Boulevard side of the parking lot. At the same time, a van pulling a utility trailer turned into the parking lot from the Harvard Boulevard side. The trailer held a riding lawnmower and two large containers for yard debris. It came to a stop in front of the Honda Accord and four men stepped out. The men wore green T-shirts with the logo for Evergreen Lawn Care printed in yellow on the back. The first one took a handheld dosimeter from his pocket. He pressed a button to turn it on, then walked past the Honda. He had an earpiece in his left ear. A mini microphone dangled from a thin black wire that hung across his chest. "I'm getting some gamma rays," he noted as he reached the far side of the car.

A second man from the crew slid beneath the car and located a drain hole from the trunk. He took a cable from his pocket and stretched it out to its full length, then attached a tiny camera to one end. Working carefully, he pushed the camera through the drain hole and threaded the cable after it.

The rear door of the van opened and Shawn Drummond stepped out with a laptop computer. He walked to the trunk of the Honda and attached the cable from the camera to the USB port on the computer, then raised the computer screen in place. Images from inside the trunk appeared. "Push it to the right," he directed. The man lying beneath the car manipulated the cable. Images on the computer screen were blurred, then the aluminum case appeared.

Drummond pressed the node on his mini microphone and spoke to Brenner. "Okay. It's here." He leaned down to the man beneath the car. "Bring it back and go to the left. We need to check the other side."

After checking all four sides of the case, Drummond disconnected the cable from the computer. "We're clear."

The man slid from beneath the car. "Are you sure?"

"As sure as we can be."

Drummond took an auto jiggler lock pick from his pocket and unlocked the trunk. The men standing nearby shrank back. Drummond grinned. "If you're within a mile of this thing when it goes off, turning a shoulder toward it won't make much difference."

They stared past him at the trunk. One of them pointed. "Just get it over with."

Drummond raised the trunk lid and leaned over the case. "Looks good from here." He took a second cable from his pocket. "Now, let's see if it's armed."

The man with the dosimeter came near the car. "I'm getting some heavy readings here." He looked at Drummond. "Work faster." He turned to the others. "Back up past the truck. Act like you're cleaning the flower beds. You need to avoid as much of this as you can." The men dispersed and looked busy.

Drummond connected one end of the cable to the laptop and attached a sensor to the other. He held the sensor against the lid of the case and glanced down at the screen of the laptop. Four blue bars appeared on the screen. Beneath each bar was a number. He pressed his microphone once more. "It's armed."

"Did you get the code?"

"Yeah." He set the sensor aside and turned to the man with the dosimeter. "Help me lift this out of here. Gotta get it out so we can disarm it."

They each took an end of the case and lifted it from the trunk, then set it on the pavement near the back of the car. Drummond searched along the back of the case and located four large rivets on the side opposite the handle. He counted to the third one from the left and twisted it aside, revealing a tiny hole in the shell of the case. With the hole exposed, he took a paper clip from his pocket and bent it straight, then slid it inside as far as it would go.

The man beside him spoke up. "What does that do?"

"Disarms the lock so we can open it, I hope."

Beneath the handle was a small keypad with four buttons.

Drummond pressed them in the sequence indicated by the numbers that had appeared earlier on the computer screen, then he reached for the latches. "This is where we find out if we're right." He flipped the latches and raised the lid on the case.

A panel on the left side held a keypad and small screen. An indicator light beside the screen glowed red. One of the men leaned closer. "Is it still armed?"

"Yes."

"When is it set to go off?"

"It's not timed," Drummond answered. "It's detonated by a cell phone."

"How do you know?"

"I get paid to know things."

He took a small screwdriver from his pocket and pried off a plastic cover behind the screen. Beneath it was a tangle of red, blue, white, and black wires. He attached one end of a USB cable to the laptop. The other end of the cable divided into two wires with gator clips on each end. He carefully placed the clips on red and white wires inside the case. Then he pressed a button on the laptop keyboard. A screen appeared with a text box in the center. Moments later, five numbers appeared in the box.

Drummond entered the numbers on the keypad inside the case. The device beeped, then the red light turned green.

"Okay," Drummond sighed. "That about does it for now." He disconnected the wires from the laptop and closed the screen. "If you gentlemen will put that case in the van, we can be on our way."

Two men appeared at the trunk. They closed the case and carried it to the van. As they closed the van doors, a car turned into the lot and came to a stop a few yards away. Drummond and the man with the dosimeter got in back. The rest of the crew climbed in the van. When they were inside, the van started forward across the parking lot toward the temple, turned right at the end of the row, and came back down a second row of parked cars. It exited the lot at Harvard Boulevard, turned right, and disappeared in traffic.

Hanks' cell phone rang. The call was from Sarah Brenner.

"Okay. We're done."

"Good," Hanks replied. He switched off the phone and picked up the radio. "Get the car."

CHAPTER 108
PORTLAND, OREGON

AFTER THEY WERE ARRESTED at the club, Nikolai Elson and Brad Ramsey were taken to the Multnomah County jail, where they were fingerprinted and processed. On Friday morning, Ramsey was transferred to a facility in neighboring Washington County. Shortly after he arrived there, Donnie Brown took him from the jail on a federal subpoena. Ramsey was placed in handcuffs and led to an unmarked car.

With Ramsey seated in back, Brown drove the car toward the airport. When they reached Columbia Boulevard, he pulled over to the side of the road and brought the car to a stop. "Let me see those cuffs."

Ramsey turned to one side and brought his arms around as far as possible. Brown reached over the seat and unlocked them. The cuffs fell to the floor. Ramsey handed them to Brown and settled back onto the seat. "Are you sure they won't know what happened?"

"They'll never find out."

"I hope not."

Brown steered the car onto Airport Drive and drove around to a hangar at the far end of the runway, beyond the commercial terminal. A Gulfstream jet was parked there. The steps were down and the door open. Brown brought the car alongside the plane and stopped at the foot of the steps. Ramsey got out. Brown came around from the opposite side of the car.

"Where would you like to go?"

"Anywhere, as long as no one knows where I am."

"What about this," Brown suggested. "What if the pilot takes off. Then, after you're in the air, you tell him where to take you. That way, no one here will know where you're going."

"Okay," Ramsey grinned. "That'd be great. But what do I do for money?"

"There's a satchel in the plane. It has what you need to get started again."

"All right." Ramsey started toward the steps, then paused and looked back. He stood there a moment, scanning the horizon.

Brown grinned. "Missing Portland already?"

"Just want to remember it."

"You'll find plenty of places just as good."

"Maybe," Ramsey nodded. "Maybe I will." He tossed Brown a wave and started up the steps.

CHAPTER 109
MIAMI, FLORIDA

DRESSED IN PLAINCLOTHES, Craig Carnley, a sergeant in a U.S. Marine special missions unit, walked through the parking lot at Temple Beth Shalom. He carried a small dosimeter. Overhead, the bright Florida sun beat down on him and even though it was fall, sweat trickled down his back.

Deployed at NEST's request to assist the FBI, he had followed the same routine every hour that day and the day before, moving methodically up and down and between the rows of cars, always with the same result. Then, as he came around the bumper of a pickup truck, the dosimeter beeped. The sound of it startled him. He stopped and moved back along the bumper. This time, the dosimeter was quiet. He pressed a button to check the battery strength and found it at full power. A flick of another button tested the unit's calibration. Everything seemed to be working correctly.

When he was unable to duplicate the reading, Carnley stepped past the bumper and moved down the side of the truck, passing between it and a car parked in the next space. Once more, the dosimeter beeped. He continued toward a Chevrolet van parked a few feet away, but nothing happened. Then he backed up and moved alongside a late-model BMW sedan. Colored bars on the dosimeter screen spiked all the way to the top. An alarm beeped rapidly, then began a constant squeal. He looked through the window of the car and found the interior was empty.

Carnley backed away from the car, took a cell phone from his pocket, and pressed a button to make a call. A voice answered on the first ring. "Find something?"

"It's here."

"Stay put. We're on the way."

Five minutes later, a delivery truck turned into the parking lot and came to a stop behind the BMW, shielding it from the street. Someone opened the side door of the truck and a team of technicians climbed out.

"It's in the trunk." Carnley gestured with his thumb toward the car. "I checked the interior."

George Spotswood and John Watts lifted a black case from the truck and set it on the ground near the back of the car. The case held a laptop computer and an assortment of tools. Spotswood took out a battery-powered drill. He placed his finger on the edge of the trunk lid a little to the left of the lock and glanced over at Watts. "Right here?"

"Yeah," Watts nodded. "Make sure it's big enough for the cable."

Spotswood tightened a drill bit in place on the drill motor and pressed the trigger. In a matter of seconds, the drill bored a hole through the trunk lid.

Watts took out the laptop and set it on the pavement. He found a cable in the toolbox and attached one end of it to the USB port on the laptop. He attached a small camera on the other end and threaded it through the hole in the trunk. Images from the trunk appeared on the screen. Spotswood took the cable. Watts sat on the pavement and watched the screen.

"Okay," he said. "The case is in there. Move the cable to the left."

Spotswood twisted it in that direction. Watts studied the images on the screen. "Looks good on this side. Turn it to the right."

"Make sure you check the back side."

"You just move the cable. We'll check all the way around it."

Spotswood manipulated the cable around the edge of the case and across the back. Watts nodded. "That's good. I don't see anything."

Spotswood glanced at him. "You sure? We don't want a mistake."

"I'm sure." Watts disconnected the cable from the computer and stood. "It's good."

Spotswood turned to the rest of the unit. He gestured to a man standing by the truck. "Get it open."

Mark Newton stepped up with a crowbar, slid the end of it underneath the trunk lid, and pulled on the bar. The lid popped open. Everyone stared down at the aluminum case.

"Okay." Spotswood pointed. "Let's get it out." He took hold of one end. Newton grabbed the other. They lifted it from the trunk and set it on the ground.

Watts felt along the back edge of the case and found the rivets that held it together. He counted down to the third one and twisted it out of the way, revealing a tiny hole. He inserted a wire and pressed it as far inside the hole as it would go.

"I hope that works," Spotswood chuckled.

"Me, too," Watts replied. He turned the case around and lifted the handle out of the way. Beneath it was a keypad with four buttons. Watts pressed them in order, then reached for the latches.

"Wait!" Spotswood shouted. "How do you know the correct sequence to press those buttons?"

"They broke the code already." Watts grabbed the latches again. "Cover your head."

"Why?"

"In case it blows," Watts laughed.

"You're sick," Spotswood chuckled.

Watts flipped the latches and lifted the lid. "Sorry, George. No fireworks today."

"Good." Spotswood breathed a sigh of relief. "We live to fight another day."

Watts went to work disarming the bomb. When he was finished, he closed the case and gestured to Spotswood. "It's all yours."

Spotswood took the case to the truck, set it in a lead-lined container, and closed the lid. Watts and Newton brought the black toolbox. The others climbed in after them and closed the door. Moments later, the truck started forward.

As the delivery truck drove away from the parking lot, a tow truck entered. It backed up to the BMW, hooked to the car, and towed it from the lot.

CHAPTER 110
NEW YORK CITY

AGENT BART MCNEIL sat on a bench in the midst of a clump of trees across Ocean Parkway from The Jewish Center of Brighton Beach. He'd been there since Thursday afternoon, huddled in the shadows, watching. Now, in the Friday morning rush, cars sped up and down the Parkway. They came and went from the parking lanes on either side, but nothing looked suspicious.

A block up the street to the left, another agent sat inside a van, watching the Center from a different angle. To the right, two more occupied an apartment overlooking the Center and a surrounding three-block area.

On his hip, McNeil carried a radio that was wired to a tiny earphone pressed into his ear. A microphone was hidden in the cuff of the sleeve of his jacket. He pressed a button on the microphone. "Anybody see anything?"

"Nothing."

"Nothing from up here, either. I'm thinking this thing is a bust."

McNeil wanted to agree with them, but the threat was serious. They needed to let things play out. "We have a little time left. It's not noon yet. I'll get somebody down there to relieve you in a little while."

Just then, a car came to a stop in front of the Center. A young man climbed out and locked the door. He glanced around as if checking for something, then walked up to the corner. A car came alongside him and stopped. He opened the door and jumped inside. Then the car sped away.

"Hold on," McNeil said. "I think I may have something."

Mc Neil ended the call and rose from the bench. A traffic light was half a block away in either direction. McNeil glanced to the right. There was no time to walk to the corner. Instead, he threaded his way through traffic and ran to the opposite side of the street. Car horns blared as drivers braked to avoid hitting him.

A blue Audi sat directly in front of the steps at the Center. McNeil approached it as if he intended to walk past it. As he drew near, he slowed his pace and took a handheld dosimeter from his pocket. He switched it on and glanced at the screen. Bars on the screen registered normal. The machine was silent.

Farther up the block, he doubled back and passed the car again on the opposite side. Still, the dosimeter indicated nothing. A voice came through the earphone.

"What was it?"

"Nothing on the dosimeter," he replied.

"Maybe it's nothing."

"Maybe, but that kid was acting really suspicious."

An agent in the apartment chimed in, "You want a team?"

McNeil took a deep breath. "Yeah," he said finally. "Send a team."

Ten minutes later, a van pulled up beside the Audi. Two technicians stepped out. A quick survey of the car's interior showed nothing. They moved to the back and used a jiggler to open the trunk. Inside, they found a spare tire and jack, but nothing else.

CHAPTER 111
CHICAGO

AT PETE RIOS' REQUEST, agents from the Chicago FBI office located Vitali Safronov Friday afternoon at his grandson's birthday party. They took him into custody without incident and brought him to the office downtown. With his attorney present, they made little progress in finding out about the cases. Then Bob Gordon arrived from the U.S. Attorney's office.

"Okay," Gordon said finally. "I can give you use immunity."

"What does that mean?"

"It means," Gordon explained, "whatever you say can't be used against you."

Joe Esposito, Safronov's attorney, explained it to him in greater detail. "Talli, he's not telling you they won't prosecute you. He's saying they won't use what you say to prosecute you. But they can still develop information against you from other sources and use that information to prosecute you for anything you discuss that might be a crime."

Safronov had a confused frown. "Is that good?"

Esposito looked at Gordon. "Give us blanket immunity for the matters we discuss, or my client has nothing further to say."

"I can't do that."

Esposito stood. "Then we will be leaving now."

"I haven't released him."

"You have no probable cause to hold my client for anything."

"I can detain him for as long as I want."

"By what authority?"

"The Patriot Act. This is a national emergency."

"You better check your Act one more time."

"I need to talk to him," Gordon insisted.

"Then give him immunity and he'll talk."

Gordon threw up his hands in frustration and stalked from the room. He returned a few minutes later and slid a piece of paper across the table. "There," he said flatly. "Immunity."

Esposito read the document and gestured with a pen to Safronov. "Sign it."

"What is it?"

"An immunity agreement."

"Blanket immunity," Gordon added.

Safronov signed the document and slid the paper to the middle of the table. Gordon pushed it toward Esposito. "You sign it, too." He pointed to a signature line at the bottom of the page. "Here."

Esposito signed it and shoved it to Gordon. "We'll talk as soon as you sign."

Gordon took a pen from his pocket and signed the document, then looked up at Safronov. "We know you obtained a case that was delivered to you by or at the behest of Yuri Ivanovsky. The case came from a Russian general, Demetrius Nilus. It contains a bomb believed to be nuclear in nature. Where is the case?"

"I do not know."

"Mr. Safronov, we have granted you immunity. That means you can talk or you can go to jail until you do. You have no choice now."

"I am perfectly willing to talk to you," Safronov insisted, "but I do not know where the case is."

"You had it?"

"Yes."

"What did you do with it?"

"They told me I was to place it in an automobile and send the automobile to New York City."

"Where in New York?"

"They gave me no particular location."

"No synagogue?"

"No." Safronov shook his head.

"Community center?"

"No. I am telling you, they gave me nothing." While he talked, Safronov nervously twisted a ring on his left hand.

"What was supposed to happen to it in New York?"

"I was supposed to see that the car was parked in a safe place and that was it."

"Safe place? What did that mean?"

"A place where it would not be towed."

"Drive it to New York, park it someplace, and walk away?"

"Yes."

"Were you given a particular time to do this?"

"The car was supposed to arrive in New York City by Friday afternoon."

"Why Friday?"

"Because on Saturday it will blow up."

"You realize that if this case contains a nuclear bomb, millions will die."

"Yes," Safronov nodded defiantly. "That was the point. Millions of Jews will die."

Gordon looked perplexed. "This bomb will kill millions of innocent men, women, and children."

"That is true. But Jews are so intermingled in New York City, there is no one particular location that is better than any other. Besides," he said with an imperious tone, "everyone accepts them there, so they bring their own result upon themselves."

"What kind of car did you use?"

"A Mercedes."

"What color?"

"Black."

"Illinois license plates?"

"Michigan."

"Who is it registered to?"

"A dealership in Detroit."

"Is it stolen?"

"No."

"What is the name of the dealership?"

"Dearborn Mercedes Benz."

"You own the dealership?"

"No."

"Who owns it?"

"My cousin, Branislov Khon."

Gordon pointed to Safronov's finger. "You keep twisting that ring. May I see it?"

Safronov laid his hand flat on the tabletop. The ring on his left hand was made of gold with a Maltese cross inlaid across the top in red onyx.

CHAPTER 112

NEW YORK CITY

LATE THAT AFTERNOON, Matt Castellano glanced across the front seat of the patrol car at his partner, Jimmy O'Malley. "Catch any of the game last night?"

Jimmy shook his head. "Nah, too boring."

"Boring? Whadd'ya mean boring? It was the Giants and the Eagles."

"Not interested."

"You're kidding me. You live here all your life and you ain't interested in the Giants and the Eagles?"

"I got two little girls. I'd rather spend time with them."

"Yeah? What did you do?"

"We went to the park."

"At night?"

"Nah. In the afternoon."

"So, what did you do last night?"

"I was with them."

"Doing what?"

Jimmy looked embarrassed. "We had a tea party, all right?"

"A tea party?"

"Yeah. A tea party." Jimmy pointed to the left. "Turn here. There's a parking garage on Fifty-fifth."

"City's got a million parking garages." Matt brought the patrol car to a stop in the intersection and waited for traffic. "We ain't never gonna check them all." When the street was clear, he turned left.

"We don't gotta check them all. Just the ones on our beat."

"Why this one?"

"Central Synagogue's just down the block." Jimmy gestured to the left. "Here's the entrance. Don't miss it."

"Oh, it's underground."

"Yeah, it's underground. Don't you ever come down this street?"

"Nah," Matt shook his head. "I usually patrol with George. He doesn't like this street."

"Why not?"

"He's not too excited about Jews."

"He ought to get over that."

"Yeah. Well. George ought to get over a lot of things." Matt brought the car to a stop at the tollbooth and glanced up at the clerk. "We're gonna cruise your deck."

"Be careful," she smiled. "They got a lot of construction down there."

"Sure thing." Matt pressed the gas pedal. The car started forward. "Yeah right, lady. Lot of construction." He glanced in Jimmy's direction. "They gotta lot of things in here, but construction ain't one of them."

"Okay." Jimmy took a spotlight from the floor by his foot. "Drive slow. You check your side. We're looking for a black Mercedes with Michigan plates."

"You look for all that. I'm just looking at the plates."

"They could have changed them."

"I don't think they're that smart."

"How do you know?"

"I know things about people."

"You don't even know who we're dealing with."

"Neither do you, Einstein. For all you know they could'a painted the car green by now."

They rode through the first level of the parking garage in silence. When they had checked all the rows, Matt turned the car to the right and started down to the next level. "This is one wild goose chase."

"Goose chase? You ever chase a goose?"

"You got me there," Matt chuckled. "I've chased a lot of things, but never a goose."

"Yeah, well…Hold up."

Matt stopped the car. "You got something?"

"Black Mercedes." Jimmy pointed out the window to the right.

Matt leaned around him. "Yeah. Black. But it's got New Jersey plates. And that old guy's coming to get in it."

Jimmy jerked around. "What old guy?"

"That one right there," Matt pointed.

Jimmy looked up to see an elderly man walking toward them. He made his way to the Mercedes and opened the door. Matt reached across the seat and whacked Jimmy on the shoulder. "Pay attention, wise guy. We got work to do here."

"Yeah, yeah, yeah." Jimmy gestured toward the windshield. "Let's go. And keep it slow." He shined the light out the window of the car. "You about blew me out of the car back there."

"I don't know what you got that light for. Just tells everybody we're looking for something. Ain't that dark down here. They got lights."

"I can't see that good." Jimmy pointed the light toward the next car. "Besides, we might see something else. Tells people to—" The car jerked to a stop. Jimmy flew forward. "Hey," he shouted and put out his hand to catch himself against the dash. "What are you doing?"

Matt pointed out the window to the left. "Look at this."

Jimmy leaned around him. "Hey, that's a black Mercedes."

"And it's got a Michigan plate."

"We better call somebody."

"You call them." Matt put the car in park and opened the door. "I'm gonna check it out."

CHAPTER 113
WASHINGTON, D.C.

IT WAS LATE FRIDAY EVENING when Esther returned to her townhouse in Georgetown. She parked at the curb and stepped out to the sidewalk. In her mind she wondered whether the bombs had been found, what the morning would bring, and what it would be like if the worst actually happened.

As she started toward the front door, Brody came from the shadows. His sudden appearance startled her but she quickly recovered. "You know, you can call on the phone like a normal person. Or come by in plain sight. They can see and hear every word you say anyway."

Brody ignored her sarcasm. "They found Steve Taylor."

Esther had a puzzled frown. "You had to look for him? I could have taken you to his house. His phone number isn't unlisted. A simple Google search would give you the address."

Brody was unfazed by her attitude. "He was floating in the Potomac. They say he fell overboard while trying to load his boat."

"You don't seem convinced."

"He had been hit in the head."

"Could have happened when he fell."

"He was hit in the back of the head, but he was floating facedown."

"Isn't that the way every dead body floats?"

"Maybe. But this guy had water in his lungs."

"Which means?"

"Which means he fell face-first into the water before he died. He died from drowning. Not the whack to the back of the head." Brody's eyes darted from side to side. He lowered his voice even more. "We got Jiroft, too."

Esther's face lit up. "Where was he?"

"At a cabin in North Carolina."

She looked surprised. "He made it that far?"

"Yes."

"How'd he get across the border?"

"How?" Brody scoffed. "They still have places you could drive a convoy across and no one would notice."

"What about the suitcases?"

"They located three of them. Wilshire Temple in L.A., Beth Shalom in Miami. Central Synagogue in Manhattan." Brody grinned. "You got two out of three."

Esther nodded. "Who thought of Central?"

"No one. Two cops on patrol found it."

"Good. At least they were doing their job. What about the fourth?"

"They are looking for it now."

She folded her arms cross her chest. "I wanted to tell Rios, but there was no way to tell him without telling Thompson. Oren said I shouldn't—"

"It's okay." Brody cut her off. "These things don't always work out the way we plan." He stepped back. "I just wanted you to know we got three of them, and Jiroft." He looked around once more. "I gotta go. I'll be in touch." He started up the sidewalk and disappeared in the shadows. Esther watched until he was out of sight, then took the keys from her purse to unlock the door.

News that the cases had been found left her both exhilarated and relieved and the two sensations washed over her like waves, leaving her excited one moment and unbelievably grateful the next. At the same time, the enormity of what happened was overwhelming. Nuclear bombs. In America. Targeted against Jews. By people determined to wipe them from the earth...and she had helped keep that from happening.

Instead of opening the door, she dropped the key into her purse and took a seat on the top step. The night air was cold against her skin and her nose tingled as she breathed. It felt good and fresh and clean and she took a deep breath, filling her lungs until it seemed they would burst.

Above her, the stars looked unusually bright and vivid against the night sky. She stared up at them and let her mind surrender to the enormity of the universe and its unending nature. By the count of rabbis and scholars, the stars and planets had existed for thousands of years, and she had the privilege of living one more day. Two weeks ago, that day would have been a small thing, just one more day measured against the eternity of time. Now it was the most wonderful gift she'd ever received.

If only Paul were here to see this ...

Paul—he was still sitting at the synagogue. She jumped to her feet and hurried toward the car.

* * *

From the townhouse, Esther drove to Starbucks on M Street and purchased two cups of coffee. With the cups sitting safely on the seat in a cardboard carrier, she drove up M Street and made the block around the White House. The lights were bright and clear against the refined Georgian mansion.

Although she'd been born in the U.S., for most of her professional career she had thought of herself as Jewish first, an Israeli second, and only third as an American. Now, for the first time in a long time, she had a sense of pride at knowing she had done something to preserve the republic that had provided her the life she'd come to love.

She continued on to the corner of Sixth and I streets and found Bryson's SUV parked near the I Street entrance to the synagogue. He was sitting behind the steering wheel reading the newspaper as she brought the car to a stop in a space across the street. She took the coffee from the seat, threw open the door, and started toward the SUV.

"I see you're still alive," she grinned.

"Alive and well," he smiled.

She handed him a cup of coffee, then climbed in on the passenger side and kissed him. "Anything interesting happen?"

"Well, a few hours ago a man came by and told me he was Santa Claus."

"What was he doing down here?"

"He didn't get that far before a police car came by."

"They arrested him?"

"No. But apparently they didn't want to take any chances."

She looked across the seat at him. "You know they aren't coming here with a suitcase bomb."

"Yeah," he nodded. "I didn't think so."

"When did you figure that out?"

"About the time Thompson got out of the car the other day."

"What?" She hit him playfully on the shoulder. "You thought that all along? Why did you come down here?"

"Because it seemed important to you."

Her eyes softened. "You sat down here all last night because of that?"

"Yes." He took a sip of coffee, then looked her in the eye. "I'm gonna be there for you, Esther. I don't have all the answers about our situation. But whatever you're doing, I want to be a part of it. Whether it's flying off to Israel or sitting in a car on I Street all night."

Tears filled her eyes. She leaned toward him. Bryson pulled her closer and kissed her. She rested her head against his shoulder and sighed. "They found three of the cases."

"Were they where you said they'd be?"

"Not in New York."

"Where was that one?"

"Central Synagogue. In Manhattan."

"Two out of three. That's pretty good. They were actually nuclear bombs?"

"Yeah," she sighed.

"Hard to believe someone would do that." He choked back tears. "Hard to believe we actually did something about it."

They sat in silence a moment, then Paul glanced at her. "But there were four cases."

"Yeah."

"They didn't find the fourth one?"

"They're looking for it now."

"Do they know where it is?"

"Brody didn't say, but I think they have a pretty good idea."

He took another sip of coffee. "So, we don't have to sit here?"

"No."

"Then why are we?"

"Just enjoying a few minutes with nothing to do but talk. Trying to make sense out of an incredible two weeks."

Bryson started the engine. "We can do that at your place." He set the coffee cup in a holder on the console and started the engine. Esther sat up straight. "I need to get my car."

"Okay. But let me—"

A green Range Rover appeared at the corner of Sixth Street, then it slowed and made the turn onto I Street. Bryson caught a glimpse of the driver as the car passed beneath a streetlight. His eyes opened wide. "That's Doyle right there," he exclaimed.

"Doyle?" Esther looked puzzled. "What are you talking about?"

"That's him." Bryson pointed. "Right there. In that Range Rover." Esther craned her neck to see. Bryson watched through the side mirror.

The Range Rover moved slowly down I Street. Brake lights came on. In the middle of the block, it turned right into a parking lot and came to a stop in a space near the back.

"This is weird." Bryson reached for the door handle.

"Wait." Esther grabbed his arm. "I don't think you should."

"I'm just gonna see what he's doing. Maybe we can help."

"We should let it go."

"Why?" He shoved open the door.

"Oren told me—" Esther stopped in mid-sentence. By then, Bryson was out of the SUV.

He closed the door behind him and started toward the opposite side of the street. Before he was halfway across, Thompson came from the parking lot on foot. He glanced around, checking the street in both directions, then started up the sidewalk toward Sixth Street.

"Hey, Doyle," Bryson called.

Thompson stopped dead in his tracks—eyes open wide, a startled look on his face. Bryson continued toward him. As he came near, Thompson slipped his hand in the pocket of his jacket. "Paul. Didn't expect to see you here."

"What are you doing?"

"You know. Just working." He looked around warily. "I gotta go."

"What's wrong?"

"Nothing. Nothing at all." Thompson started up the street.

Bryson walked after him. "You look worried. Do you need some help?"

"I gotta go, Paul." Thompson quickened his steps. "It's been real." Then suddenly he broke into a run.

Bryson stood there a moment, startled and confused by what he'd seen. Then a sense of realization hit him. The fourth case was there. It was in the Range Rover.

From the corner of his eye Bryson saw Esther standing near the front fender of the SUV. He shouted to her, "Call Brody. The fourth one is here!" Then he took off up the street after Thompson.

CHAPTER 114
WASHINGTON, D.C.

BY THE TIME BRYSON REACHED Sixth Street, Thompson was already on the opposite corner. In spite of the distance between them, Bryson charged after him at a full sprint.

A little way up the next block, Thompson suddenly veered left into a small park at the intersection with Massachusetts Avenue. Bryson raced after him, cutting into the park at the corner and reducing the angle. He pumped his arms in time with his legs, determined to find out who Thompson really was and why he ran. As they neared the opposite side of the park, Bryson was only ten yards behind.

Thompson reached the sidewalk first and charged into the street. As he did, he glanced over his shoulder to check for Bryson. Just then, a taxicab turned the corner. Tires screeched as the driver applied the brakes and swerved to the right. He did his best to avoid a collision but the front fender banged into Thompson's hip. The force of the collision sent Thompson to the ground. He hit the pavement on his left side but bounced up and hobbled toward the opposite side of the street. Bryson darted around the taxi and ran to catch up with Thompson.

Three apartment buildings occupied the block across the street. An alley separated them. Thompson limped up the block and turned into the alley by the center building. It was dark and narrow but Bryson ran after him anyway. As he did, he realized he'd made a mistake.

A hundred yards from the street, the alley came to an abrupt end against the back wall of a building that faced the next street. There was a dumpster in the corner to the right and trash cans in the corner on the left. In between was a service entrance to the next building. A single light bulb burned above the door. Bryson grabbed the doorknob and gave it a twist but found the door was locked. He squinted against the glare and looked around, searching for Thompson.

"Doyle," he called out. "What are you doing?" There was no answer. "Doyle. I know you're in here somewhere. Come out and let's talk. What's going on?"

There was a rustling noise near the dumpster. Bryson wheeled around to see Thompson emerge from the shadows. In his hand he held an automatic pistol.

"You should have left it alone," Thompson said flatly.

"What are you talking about?"

"You got three of them. You should have let the fourth one go."

"Why?" Bryson threw his arms wide apart in a bewildered gesture. "Why are you doing this?"

"Why?" Thompson had an angry frown. "You ask me why? You, of all people, know the things they asked me to do. Murders...kidnappings...and not just killing someone or blowing something up or making them disappear. No, they wanted it done in the grossest manner possible. They had me cheat and steal and lie, and all the while they were doing the same thing to me." He had a pained look on his face. "They stole my heart. They stole my soul. They stole my life." His voice was loud and he emphasized each phrase in a dramatic fashion. "And after I did everything they asked, they sat me at a desk and told me I hadn't done enough."

"Doyle," Bryson said, trying to act as calm as possible, "everyone in government feels that way at least some of the time. But they don't try to blow up synagogues with nuclear bombs."

"Well, those people aren't one of us," he said defiantly.

"One of us?" Bryson had a questioning look. "What are you talking about?"

"The Knights of Malta," Thompson answered proudly.

Bryson felt deflated by the revelation. "No," he said in disbelief. "Not you."

"Yes," Thompson nodded.

"Why?"

"It gives me purpose. I may not get paid for what I do, but at least I do it for a cause and a kingdom that has no end."

"And along the way, you do a favor for Yursky by eliminating his competition."

"Yursky was an added benefit."

"Next you're going to tell me he's a member of the Order, too."

Thompson's lips turned up in an ironic smile. "You're as smart as everyone says, aren't you?"

"Look." Bryson stepped closer. "You can't do this, Doyle."

"Yes, I can." Thompson raised the pistol and pointed it at Bryson. "I can. And I will."

"I'm your friend."

"Maybe once you were." Thompson shook his head. "But not anymore. Now you're just a traitor."

"A traitor? How have I betrayed anything?"

"By taking up with that Jew woman," Thompson snarled. "You've become one of them."

Anger swept over Bryson at the sound of those words. "Don't talk about her like that."

"I'll talk about her any way I want," Thompson sneered. "And when I'm through with you, I'll take care of her." He smiled. "Any way I please."

In an instant, the anger Bryson felt before turned to rage. Without taking time to think, he charged forward, his muscles fueled by the rage he felt inside. Startled by the sudden movement, Thompson jerked his finger against the trigger. The pistol fired but the shot went wide to the left. Before he could shoot again, Bryson was on him.

With the full weight of his body behind him, Bryson slammed his forearm against Thompson's chest. The jolt knocked the pistol from Thompson's hand and sent it tumbling to the ground. Thompson staggered backward and fell against the dumpster. He pushed away from it and swung at Bryson's head. His fist landed squarely against Bryson's jaw.

Bryson's knees buckled, but he recovered in time to block a second punch and countered with a swing of his own that sent his fist crashing into Thompson's nose. Blood spurted across his face but the pain only angered Thompson all the more.

Thompson found a two-by-four scrap and wielded the broken piece like a club, swinging it from side to side. One swing missed Bryson's head by inches. He felt the wind from it as it sliced through the air. The next swing caught him full on the shoulder. The force of it jarred his neck and numbed his arm. He staggered backward and raised his free hand to cover his face. A third swing from Thompson caught Bryson on the side, just below the ribs, and dropped him to his knees. Thompson drew back the board one more time and swung it toward Bryson's head. At the last second, Bryson rolled his shoulder up and tucked his chin. The board struck a glancing blow to the back of his head. Bryson slumped forward and fell facedown on the pavement.

Just barely conscious, Bryson could hear the sound of Thompson's heavy breathing as he hovered over him. Then the board slipped from Thompson's fingers and bounced on the ground. "What does it matter," Thompson grumbled. "If you aren't dead now, you will be in a few minutes." He took a deep breath. "This whole place will be gone. And good riddance."

Bryson heard the sound of footsteps as Thompson turned away and started toward the street. After a moment, he struggled to his feet and started after him, but by the time he could stand, Thompson was nowhere to be seen. Then, from somewhere in the distance, came the wail of approaching sirens. Blue lights reflected off the buildings at the far side of the park. "Esther," he whispered. "She reached Brody."

Thoughts of her flooded his mind—the sound of her voice, the smile on her face, the way it felt when she kissed him. He had to find her. Had to get to her. Had to make sure she was safe.

During the chase and the fight in the alley, he had been oblivious to the physical strain and the energy he expended. Powered by anger, rage, and adrenalin, his muscles responded with all the force demanded by the situation he faced. Now his legs felt like lead. Muscles in his thighs quivered and his hands trembled. His head throbbed with pain and he felt drained and exhausted. The street seemed miles away.

Then a police officer appeared in the alley, pistol in one hand, flashlight in the other. "Hands where I can see them," he shouted.

Bryson staggered to a halt and raised his hands meekly above his shoulders. He felt his body sway from side to side. His legs shook violently, and then everything went black.

CHAPTER 115
WASHINGTON, D.C.

TWO BLOCKS AWAY, Philippe Jobert sat quietly in the front seat of his Acura sedan. From the parking lot on Fifth Street he had a clear view to the right, all the way to the corner at I Street. He'd been staring out the window at that corner for the past thirty minutes—much longer than he had planned.

Directly across the street from Jobert was a nondescript Pontiac, parked in an unmetered space outside the Fifth Street Hardware store. Beyond the car, the glow of a streetlight illuminated the darkened windows of the store, giving them a mirrored effect. In the reflection he could see the passenger side of the car. No one had been in or out of it since he arrived.

As he sat there waiting, he recounted the events of the past hour. Using a description forwarded to his cell phone, he had located the green Range Rover with little difficulty. He followed it to the turn at Sixth Street, then continued to the corner one block farther. When he reached the corner at Fifth and I streets, the Range Rover was just passing the synagogue, one block to his left. He waited until the Range Rover's brake lights came on, then he proceeded across I Street, parked the Acura at the rendezvous point, and waited. Nothing had impeded his schedule. He had made no mistakes. Still, the Pontiac was untouched. No one had arrived to take it.

Jobert checked his watch. He had expected to be home by now. Isabelle would be asleep. He had hoped to return before she went to bed with at least time for a kiss. He glanced down the street once more and sighed. "What could be keeping him?"

Then he saw something, a motion, a movement in the shadows along the sidewalk. He sat up straight and craned his neck to see around the headrest on the passenger seat. And there Thompson was, limping slightly, but walking at a steady pace. Jobert followed him as he crossed to the opposite side of the street, stepped over the curb, and continued toward the Pontiac.

He took his cell phone from his pocket and checked the photograph that arrived with the message. "It is him all right," Jobert whispered. "Doyle Thompson." He closed the phone. *And with this I shall be finished with my arrangements for the year. Perhaps we can have Christmas in peace.* He smiled at the thought of it. *No more late-night…appointments.*

Thompson reached the car. The alarm system chirped as he pressed a remote for the lock. He stumbled against the side of the car, then jerked open the door and flopped behind the steering wheel. Jobert watched as Thompson swung his legs inside, placed a key in the ignition, and pulled the door shut.

The engine turned over once, then made a clicking noise. In the shadows from the streetlight Jobert saw Thompson strike the top of the steering wheel with his hand in frustration. Again the engine turned over once and made a clicking noise.

Jobert eased open the door of the Acura and stepped out. Moving effortlessly, he crossed the street and approached the Pontiac from the rear. He came to the driver's door and rapped on the window with his knuckle.

Thompson looked startled. He pressed a button on the armrest to lower the window. When nothing happened, he jerked on the door handle and pushed open the door a little way. Jobert smiled at him. "You are having trouble with your car." He spoke with a French accent. "And this is not such a good neighborhood."

"It won't start," Thompson snapped impatiently.

"Perhaps you should have thought of this before taking on such a project."

"What?" Thompson frowned, then jerked on the door to close it.

Jobert caught it with his left hand and held it open. "The Order sends its regards." As the words slipped from his lips, he pulled an automatic pistol from his pocket. In one quick motion, he placed the silenced muzzle of the pistol against Thompson's head and squeezed the trigger. With only the slightest noise, the bullet exploded through Thompson's skull. His body went limp and crumpled over the steering wheel. Jobert pushed the door open wider. He leaned inside the car and placed the muzzle against Thompson's head, just above his ear, then squeezed the trigger once more. Thompson's body fell over to the right. His head flopped onto the passenger seat.

Satisfied that Thompson was dead, Jobert closed the car door and turned away. With practiced ease, he took a handkerchief from his pocket and wiped the pistol clean. He tucked it inside the waistband of his trousers, pulled his jacket over it, and walked back across the street. As he reached the sidewalk on the opposite side, he glanced at his watch. *Too late for Isabelle, but perhaps there is still time for an evening drink.*

CHAPTER 116
WASHINGTON, D.C.

SOMETIME LATER, BRYSON became aware of a bright light shining in his eyes. Slowly, his eyes came into focus and he saw a man dressed in blue scrubs standing over him. He held a penlight in his hand and flicked it from side to side. The light irritated Bryson's eyes and he turned his head in an effort to avoid it.

"Mr. Bryson, my name is Drew Powell. I'm a physician at Washington Memorial. How are you feeling?"

"Sick," Bryson replied weakly.

"Feel like you're gonna throw up?"

"Yeah. Maybe."

"Let me know before you do." Powell checked Bryson's eyes once more, then backed away. "They said you were in a fight. Did you get hit?"

"No," Bryson replied, then quickly corrected himself. "Yes. I got hit in the jaw."

"By what?"

"Doyle Thompson's fist." Bryson rubbed his chin. "It hurts a little and the back of my neck aches. Where's Esther?"

"I'm right here." Esther stepped to his side and took his hand.

He looked over at her. "Did they find Doyle?"

"Yes."

Powell stepped up again. "Mr. Bryson, I think we'll keep you overnight. The punch to the jaw, aching neck muscles, and nausea are consistent with symptoms of a concussion. I think we'd better hold you for observation." His face was emotionless. "I'll have them get you a room. A nurse will be in here shortly to talk to you. Just lie there and rest."

When he was gone, Esther leaned close to Bryson and kissed him on the cheek. "They found the bomb in the Range Rover," she said quietly.

"Good," Bryson whispered. "It's over?"

She smiled. "It's over."

"This spy stuff is a little dangerous."

"It's a lot dangerous. Too dangerous."

"What do you mean?"

"I told Brody I'm done."

"Done?"

"I lost the first love of my life to this business. I'm not losing the second."

"What are you going to do?"

"I thought I'd take you up on that offer."

"Which offer was that?"

"The one about the porch swing, the beautiful Texas sky, and coffee in the morning."

He grinned and clutched his stomach. "Don't mention coffee right now or I will throw up."

She smiled at him. "You were very brave."

"I didn't feel brave."

"What did you feel?"

"Mad. Angry...Scared." His eyes narrowed. "Doyle was a member of the Order of Malta."

"I know. They found the ring on his finger."

"These people are everywhere. We would never be safe on the porch in Texas."

"We won't be safe in Georgetown, either."

He gave her a knowing look. "Unless we fight."

"We'll see," she whispered. "But you still have to bring me coffee in the morning."

"Okay," he groaned. "But not now." He clutched his stomach. "I'm gonna be sick."

EPILOGUE
STEGNA, RHODES

IN A COTTAGE ON A CLIFF high above the village, Ignacio Spoleto stood near the window and stared down at the beach. His eyes traced the thin ribbon of shoreline all the way to the marina at the cut in the mountains. It was a beautiful scene, with the sun rising over the Mediterranean and the morning dawning bright and fresh.

Carmine Russo appeared at his side, a cup of coffee in hand. Spoleto turned to him with a smile. "Such a wonderful new day."

"Yes, Your Grace." Russo handed him the coffee. "Wonderful indeed."

Spoleto took the cup and sipped from it. "This is good." He gestured with the cup and took another sip. "It is still Friday evening in America?"

"Yes."

"Have we heard from him?"

"Just now, as I was making the coffee."

"And what does he say?"

Russo took a cell phone from his pocket and pressed a button. A message appeared on the screen. "Package delivered," he read triumphantly. "Contents accepted. Final payment due."

"We have arranged the payment?"

"It is being transferred to his account as we speak."

"Good." Spoleto took another sip of coffee. "We should return to the castle now." Spoleto handed Russo the coffee cup. "We have been given a mission by the Council. It remains incomplete and must be fulfilled."

"What mission?"

"To annihilate the Elders of Zion, of course." Spoleto patted Russo on the shoulder. "And for that we need good men. Our first task shall be to find them."

"Don't we need a plan?"

"We have the plan." Spoleto turned to face him. "Busca's plan was not a bad one, he just chose the wrong people to execute it. We shall not make that same mistake again. We shall succeed where others have failed. Many have tried, but few have succeeded. Lenin and Hitler tried, but they did not succeed. Even the radical Muslims have tried but they have allowed their attention to be diverted by their hatred of the "Great Satan"—America. We shall succeed in wiping out the "Little Satan"—Israel. We have the talent and the commitment to the cause."

"The cause," Russo mumbled.

"The Jews must die and killing them is our calling ... our vow." He turned away and started across the room. "Come, my friend. There is much work to be done."

ACKNOWLEDGEMENTS

My sincere gratitude goes to the Shalem Center in Jerusalem for their assistance with this project, and a very special thank you to Dr. Amachai Magen, who was enormously helpful. Special appreciation goes to my brilliant partner, Joe Hilley, to my executive assistant, Lanelle Shaw-Young, and to Arlen Young for his proof-reading skills.

A book project of this magnitude demands a grueling schedule. For her patience, compassion, encouragement, and sacrifice, I am eternally indebted to my beloved wife, Carolyn.

AUTHOR'S NOTE

THE FIRST QUESTION an author is often asked is: What prompted you to write this book?

Before answering that question, let me pose three more important questions and their answers:

- *What is the real reason for the ongoing conflict in the Middle East between the Jewish and Muslim populations?*

- *What is the root of that reason?*

- *What is the source of that root?*

Q: *What is the real reason for the ongoing conflict in the Middle East between the Jewish and Muslim populations?*

A: It is important to establish that the conflict in the Middle East has never been about a Palestinian state. It's not about the division of Jerusalem, checkpoints, fences, land or borders. The issue is Israel's right to exist as a nation.

The refusal of the Arab world to accept Israel as a nation is at the heart of the conflict that has raged since May 14, 1948. Until this is acknowledged as the sole barrier to meaningful dialogue, there will never be peace, and in fact the very phrase "peace in the Middle East" becomes an oxymoron.

It is impossible for Israel to negotiate with an entity that refuses to acknowledge the Jewish state's very right to exist. This critical point of contention is ignored by those calling for Israel to capitulate and surrender her defensible borders. Many believe this refusal is nothing more than an honest misunderstanding or raw stubbornness. It is rather a total ignorance of the facts as they apply to the mindset of those urging Israel to give in to her detractors.

The Arab refusal to acknowledge Israel's right to exist as a nation, while at the same time posing as a true partner in seeking the emergence of a peaceful Palestinian state, is, perhaps, the greatest, longest running, and most widely accepted hoax ever perpetrated on a gullible world. The refusal to see this incongruity is remarkable.

Anti-Israeli sentiment has in fact become the new anti-Semitism. It makes Israel the new "collective Jew", and then assaults the individual Jew as an extension of the state.

Q: *What is the root of that reason?*

A: The real reason for the present Middle East conflict has an even more sinister and deeply established root....one that is consistently ignored by the world in spite of the overwhelming and repetitive proof of its existence. This root, expressed in history again and again, is played out everyday around the world. Blind, well-meaning people refuse to believe in its existence today for the same reason they refused to believe in the existence of the ovens and cattle cars of another day: Because it shocks their rational sensibilities. The real root is not merely Israel's right to exist as a *state,* but the right of the Jewish *people* to exist at all.

Peaceful co-existence has never been the goal, nor has the concept of Jews living dispersed in other lands without a country been an option. The real goal has been the very extermination of the Jewish race. This is why

Palestinian children are taught to hate and kill Jews from their first breath and why the Islamic world throws parties in the streets every time Jewish blood is shed. It is why in radical Islamic theology the successful maiming and murdering of Jews represents the highest aspiration many Palestinian mothers have for their children.

Does the world really believe that if the nation of Israel ceased to exist tomorrow, and all the Jews left Israel, and all territorial claims were abandoned by Israel forever, the joy over the shedding of Jewish blood would cease? History screams the answer: NO!

The Grand Mufti and Moslem Brotherhood were complicit in proposing and implementing the Final Solution when there was no Jewish state. The pogroms of Russia were not in response to some argument over deserted land on the East coast of the Mediterranean. The rockets raining down on Jewish homes today from Hezbollah in Lebanon and Hamas in Gaza are not about the soil upon which these homes are built.

The root cause of the Middle East conflict is the refusal to acknowledge the right of the Jewish state to exist, and the right of the Jewish *people* to exist. One is predicated on the other as surely as the dawn is predicated on the turning of the earth.

With this as the ultimate issue, what form will negotiations with Israel's enemies take?

Q: *What is the source of that root?*

A: What is the source of this Jewish hatred? What is the reason for this obvious and sinister racism? The answer to that question is also the answer of why I wrote "*The Protocols.*"

The Protocols of the Learned Elders of Zion originated in France as a diatribe against the French government. It was taken to Russia and plagiarized in pre-revolutionary Russia as one more historical attempt to divert blame from those in power and cast it on the Jewish population. This may be obscure to most of the Gentile population, but every Jew in the world should be aware of its existence. They should be aware of the role it has played and continues to play in the rise and continuation of anti-Jewish sentiment and the hatred of the Jewish people around the world.

First published in Russia in 1903, *The Protocols of the Learned Elders of Zion* was translated into multiple languages, and disseminated internationally in the early part of the twentieth century. Henry Ford funded the printing of 500,000 copies which were distributed throughout the United States in the 1920s.

Adolf Hitler was a major proponent. It was studied, as if factual, in German classrooms after the Nazis came to power in 1933, despite having been exposed as fraudulent years before. In at least one scholar's opinion, the *Protocols of the Learned Elders of Zion* was Hitler's primary justification for initiating the Holocaust — his "warrant for genocide."

The book purports to document the minutes of a late 19th-century meeting of Jewish leaders discussing their goal of global Jewish control by subverting the morals of Gentiles, and by controlling the press and the world's economies. It is still widely available today, often offered as a genuine document, on the Internet and in print, in numerous languages.

Despite being proven a hoax as early as 1921, a large number of Arab and Muslim regimes and leaders have endorsed the protocols as authentic, including Presidents Gamal Abdel Nasser and Anwar Sadat of Egypt, one of the President Arifs of Iraq, King Faisal of Saudi Arabia, and Colonel Muammar al-Gaddafi of Libya. More recent endorsements have been made by the Grand Mufti of Jerusalem, Sheikh Ekrima Sa'id Sabri, and the education ministry of Saudi Arabia.

The 1988 charter of Hamas, a Palestinian Islamist group, states that *The Protocols of the Elders of Zion* embodies the plan of the Zionists:

> "Today it is Palestine and tomorrow it may be another country or other countries. For Zionist scheming has no end, and after Palestine they will covet expansion from the Nile to the Euphrates. Only when they have completed digesting the area on which they will have laid their hand, they will look forward

*to more expansion, etc. Their scheme has been laid out in the
Protocols of the Elders of Zion, and their present [conduct] is
the best proof of what is said there. Leaving the circle of conflict
with Israel is a major act of treason and it will bring curses on its
perpetrators. 'Who so on that day turns his back to them, unless
maneuvering for battle or intent to join a company, he truly has
incurred wrath from Allah, and his habitation will be hell, a
hapless journey's end.'"*

Former US President Jimmy Carter, wrote a book entitled: *We Can
Have Peace in the Holy Land: A Plan that Will Work.* Carter's solution is
straightforward; Israel should embrace the Quartet's so-called peace plan.
This plan is backed by a group known simply as "The Elders". Carter is one
of three appointed as "Elders" to the Middle East. How could he ask the
Jewish people to embrace a group known as The Elders?

Mr. Carter's plan is to allow the Quartet to solve the Middle East
problem. He calls for "peace-loving organizations" such as Hezbollah and
Hamas and states like Iran and Syria to be involved in the negotiating
process in order to have peace in the Holy Land.

Carter refers to Jews again and again as "radicals," another word
for terrorists. He called Menachem Begin a "radical" and then went on to
describe him as the "most notorious terrorist in the region." Of course, he
said the British said that, not him. He describes Benjamin Netanyahu as a
"key political associate and naysayer" who was strongly opposed to Israel
relinquishing control over the Sinai.

It appears that Jimmy Carter is revising history. The Benjamin
Netanyahu I know was attending college during the Camp David meetings.
In fact, when I recommended him to Begin for a government job, the prime
minister did not even know who Benjamin was. I have no idea how Carter
was so aware of Benjamin Netanyahu's political ideology; at that time,
Benjamin was selling furniture.

The former president writes that Begin agreed to divide Jerusalem. I
found that to be astonishing—especially since Mr. Begin had given me a copy

of the letter he wrote to Jimmy Carter on September 17, 1978. He wrote:

*"Dear Mr. President....On the basis of this law, the government of
Israel decreed in July 1967 that Jerusalem is one city indivisible,
the capital of the State of Israel."*

According to Begin, Jimmy Carter informed him that the U.S.
government did not recognize Jerusalem as Israel's capital. Begin told me he
responded, "Excuse me sir, but the State of Israel does not recognize your
non-recognition."

The former president writes that Prime Minister Menachem Begin
agreed to a freeze on building Jewish settlements. Begin told me he had not
agreed to a total freeze; he only agreed not to build new settlements for three
months, during the negotiations. Carter gives the impression that he and
Begin were close friends by saying that Begin and Sadat visited him in Plains
to reaffirm the personal commitments each had made to the other.

I found that quite humorous; Mr. Begin told me he had refused to
meet with Jimmy Carter when the president traveled to Jerusalem. At that
time, he was no longer Prime Minister but was outraged that Carter had
misrepresented events that had taken place during their meetings.

Carter viewed Yasser Arafat as a Middle East George Washington. He pens,

*"We pursued the concept of non-violent resistance of Hamas
leaders and gave them documentation and video presentations
on the successful experiences of Mahatma Gandhi, Dr. Martin
Luther King, Jr., and others."*

Menachem Begin told me of a meeting with Carter during which he
gave the president a list of cities in the United States with Bible names,
i.e., Shiloh, Hebron and Bethel. He asked Carter, "Could you imagine the
governor of Pennsylvania would proclaim that anyone could live in the city
of Bethlehem, Pennsylvania, except Jews?" President Carter agreed that such
a man, if he did such a thing, would be guilty of racism. Begin replied that he
was governor of the state in which the original Bethlehem, and the original

Jericho, and the original Shiloh were located. He asked me, "Did Carter expect me to say that everybody could live in those cities except Jews?"

Why is the peace process so complicated? The Jews have suffered through forty-one years of non-stop attempts. To the Muslim world the answer is simple, Jews are Zionists—and Zionists are devils and must die.

TO SUMMARIZE:

What is the real reason for the ongoing conflict in the Middle East between the Jewish and Muslim populations?

The refusal of the Muslim world to accept Israel's right to exist as a nation.

What is the root of the problem?

The refusal of the Muslim world to accept the right of the Jewish people to exist at all.

What is the source of that root?

A fraudulent, anti-Semitic text purporting to describe a Jewish plan for achieving global domination, written in 1903, proven a hoax in 1921, but promoted around the world to this day by the enemies of Israel and the Jewish people as factual.

So we come back to the original question. Why did I write this book "The Protocols"?

FOR THREE REASONS:

1.   It was written in order to expose the lie of *The Protocols of the Learned Elders of Zion* and to reveal the extent to which this lie has led to the ongoing hatred of the Jewish people and the state of Israel by her racist enemies.

2. It was written in fiction form in order to reach beyond an audience of scholars, academics and political pundits to the common man. Most are unaware of the extent to which even their own opinions about modern Israel and the Jewish people have been subtly influenced by the anti-Semitic slurs which ultimately flow from this hate literature.

3. It was written as part of my ongoing, forty-year, non-stop battle, in the United States and around the world, to fight with "the pen rather than the sword" both for the protection of the Jewish people and the guarantee of the right of the state of Israel to exist, within safe and secure borders, free from harassment, persecution, and war.

As a Christian Zionist, a *New York Times* best selling author, and an untiring and relentless friend of the nation of Israel I offer *The Protocols* as one more arrow in the quiver to slay the lies of anti-Semitism and expose the true motivations of her enemies.